D0485213

THE WINTER RIDDLE

SAM HOOKER

BLACK SPOT BOOKS

This Book is sold subject to the condition that it shall not, by way of trade or otherwise, be lent, re-sold, duplicated, hired out, or otherwise circulated without the publisher's prior written consent in any form of binding or cover other than that in which it is published and without similar condition including this condition being imposed on the subsequent purchaser.

ISBN Print: 978-1-7324007-0-2

ISBN Ebook: 978-1-7324007-1-9

Cover design by Najla Qamber

Cover Illustration by Dragan Paunovic

Edited by Melissa Ringsted

Interior design layout by Rebecca Poole

Black Spot Books

All rights reserved.

This is a work of fiction. All characters and events portrayed in this novel are fictitious and are products of the author's imagination and any resemblance to actual events, or locales or persons, living or dead are entirely coincidental.

For Shelly. If each heart sings a single note, yours is the perfect harmony to mine. May we bask in our song from now until forever.

ACKNOWLEDGEMENTS

I don't know many authors who've gotten a second chance at their first novel. I am beyond grateful to each and every one of the immensely talented people who have applied their crafts to this book. They are the difference between a good manuscript and a book worth publishing.

This book would be an utter mess without the brilliant staff at Black Spot Books. Melissa Ringsted, Najla Qamber, and Rebecca Poole did phenomenal work on the editing, cover, and layout respectively. Lindy Ryan, publisher and trusted friend, has set our course and navigated us through the torrential waters of marketing, printing, distribution, and more with great success.

To my mother-in-law, Dee Dee, for her endless support, and for watching Jack so I could get some work done. She's babysitting as I write this, in fact.

To my parents, David and Ann, for seeing to it that I contracted some sort of literary madness at a young age.

To my beautiful and charming wife, Shelly. Had she not thrice winked at me, we would not be where we are today.

And, last but not least, to Jack. Naps are for suckers, am I right, son number one?

PREFACE

I've always been fascinated by the North Pole. I wanted to live there when I was a kid so I could be Santa's neighbor. That desire never changed, but I've been soundly outvoted by my wife and son who prefer the climate of southern California for some reason.

The working title for this book was *Santa vs. the Frost Giants*. I'd always thought that there was more to old Saint Nick, and every Yuletide season I'd indulge in flights of fantasy. Where was he from? Could he have been so jolly if he'd never known sorrow?

I decided that this story was going to be the one. The first novel that I would see through to the end. Sure, the dozen or so novels lying unfinished in my drawer had each been the one in their day, but this time I meant it. Sure, I'd meant it before, but … oh, shut up.

Try as I might, I just couldn't make a main character of Santa *and* maintain his mystery. I have too much awe and admiration for the old man to lay him bare, so I searched the story for a character who could weather the scrutiny. Volgha was clearly the best choice, but a little bit too close to home. I'd based her loosely on myself, and I felt a particular connection with her. Spilling her secrets was essentially the same as spilling my own.

That was the realization that clinched it. The thing that makes a story worth telling is truth. The author's truth. If this was going to be the one, the first novel I finished and one of which I could be proud, it had to be her. It had to be Volgha.

And so, because we hurt the ones we love, I've dragged Volgha out of her comfort zone and forced her to deal with every nightmarish situation that could befall an introvert for a few hundred pages. For your amusement. Enjoy!

ONE

MOST SOUTHERNERS ALIVE TODAY HAVE NEVER HEARD OF THE Kingdom of Aurora, especially if one permits the people of that kingdom to define the term "southerner." Given that Aurora was built almost exactly atop the North Pole, they use the term to mean "everyone not from the Kingdom of Aurora." They also extend it to any native Aurorian who won't shut up about how cold it is. Use of the term in this context is understood to be pejorative.

It shall be accepted as fact that the royal family ruled over Aurora from Castle Borealis since time immemorial, given that no credible evidence to the contrary exists. From the parapets of the castle's impossibly tall and permafrosted towers, one could gaze out over the little villages and fiefdoms nestled into the snowy pine forests, stretching off into the horizon.

Likewise, anyone standing in one of the aforementioned villages and fiefdoms could look up at the impossibly tall towers of Castle Borealis, and think ... well, whatever they wanted.

"Those towers are impossibly tall," an average Aurorian subject might think.

"The people who run that place are absolutely nuts," another might think, though he'd do best to leave that thought locked inside his head. If it escaped within range of the wrong ears, the royal family might have the aforementioned head removed and examined, just to be sure that no further heresies lay within it.

"I can't see it right now because it's too dark." While stating obvious truths has never made anyone popular or rich, it would be accurate for several of what we know as "months" out of every year.

At the North Pole, one day and night take place over the course of one year. The sun rises in late March, kicking off the spring. It continues moving upward until the summer solstice, and then starts working its way downward until it sets in early November, ringing in the long dark night of winter.

It should be noted that while there is a summer season, it is generally only included for the sake of tradition. The "summer" part of the year is only slightly less snowy than the other seasons, and anyone seen wearing a bikini is forced to undergo a full psychiatric evaluation.

Other than perpetual snow and the passage of a single day per year, the subjects of the Kingdom of Aurora had everything in common with the subjects of southern kingdoms, especially if the monarchs of those kingdoms happened to be stark raving lunatics.

All of the Aurorian monarchs throughout the history of the kingdom have called themselves the White King or Queen, generally in step with the standard definitions of gender, but there were exceptions. Monarchs get to do what they want.

The title came about because the first of their line was said to rule over everything that had snow on it. The first White Queen had been a great warrior and military strategist. Back in those days, the land was just silly with foreign powers who were all too happy to go to war with Aurora; but one by one they fell, until only the Vikings of Midgard might have taken up arms and marched on Aurora, but they never did. For reasons known only to the leaders of the two great powers, there was a lasting peace between them that hadn't been broken in hundreds of years.

In those centuries of peace, the need for the White Kings and Queens of Aurora to be great warriors waned, and they became more and more decadent, though "decadent" in this case is simply a polite way of saying that they went entirely mad. Of course, they had money, and rich people become eccentric in lieu of going mad. In the case of the White Kings and Queens of Aurora, the vastness of their wealth qualified them to identify as *delightfully* eccentric, which took the edge off of labels that might have been more accurate, such as sadist, tyrant, or despot.

At best, they might have smiled upon being referred to as libertines, then quietly had the referrer dragged off to the lower dungeons. People needed to be dragged down there from time to time anyway, according to the Aurorian monarchs. Very effective tool for keeping everyone on their toes—literally, for those having been dragged and subsequently chained to a wall, and figuratively for any bystanders on the verge of getting the wrong idea about their social standing.

Not so very long ago, the White King and Queen were a particularly ridiculous pair of libertines named Roderick and Beatrice. They spent most of their time drinking, gossip-mongering at court, and having people dragged off to the lower dungeons for gossiping either too well or too poorly. Back in those days, the art of being just good enough at gossiping was one of the most popular programs at the universities where nobles and aristocrats sent their children.

Between rounds of gossip, King Roderick and Queen Beatrice occasionally remembered that they had two daughters: the Princesses Alexia and Volgha. Alexia was the kind of girl who was hard to forget, though anyone who met her would certainly want to, as quickly as possible, and at any expense. She was well-versed in the art of screaming bloody murder upon not getting whatever she wanted from her parents, and she'd never had a mild reaction to anything in her life—much like the average teenager, only she'd managed it practically from birth.

Volgha was very different. Different from her sister, but also the sort of person who was referred to as "different" by people who were too polite—or afraid—to call her weird. She would have done well in a gaggle of teenagers who wore lots of eyeliner and took strolls through graveyards and said things like "woe is me" a lot, only she found that sort of teenager to be utterly ridiculous. At least she shared their complete lack of self-awareness.

While Alexia only communicated at the top of her lungs, Volgha was a mumbler and a glarer. She was the only member of the royal family who didn't care for the adoration of other people; in fact, she preferred to be left alone entirely.

There was one person whose company she didn't mind, and that was Osgrey. He was the court wizard, or at least that was the office that he held. Osgrey was actually a druid, not that it mattered to the ridiculous White King and Queen. He could have been nothing more than a moderately skilled juggler, and they'd have been impressed. Or not, depending on their mood, but Osgrey was consistently able to refrain from being dragged off to the dungeons. That skill alone qualified as magic in the minds of most people who knew the king and queen.

Osgrey worked with the royal gardener to keep the castle's winter garden teeming with vibrant colors. Strange and wonderful flowers, berries, foliage and trees grew together in great clumps and rows, weaving a wonderland of delights undreamed of in all the world. It was Volgha's favorite place in the castle. She'd spend hours there, finding little alcoves in which to lurk, or begging Osgrey to tell her the stories of all of the plants—where they came from, which ones could kill you, or which ones made the best potions.

He talked to trees. It seemed as though they talked back to him, but Volgha could never hear what they were saying. He grew colorful fungi on the brim of his pointy hat, and he was friends with a snow lion named Sigmund. Sigmund was all white, except for his piercing blue eyes. Volgha wasn't exactly afraid of Sigmund, but she worked hard at presenting herself as being poor for digestion whenever he was around.

Osgrey encouraged Volgha's love for all things natural and supernatural. She'd spend hours leafing through the Witches' Grimoire in the impossibly tall wizard's tower. He'd promised to teach her how to summon a familiar, an animal companion that could help her with some of the more powerful spells, as soon as she was old enough. Volgha was enraptured with the idea, and spent a lot of time learning about animals, figuring out which ones would make the best companions.

Both Volgha and Alexia grew up—as girls are wont to do—to become highly opinionated women. They were other things besides opinionated as well, but most of the adjectives that could have been applied to Alexia are very impolite.

Alexia was the apple of their parents' eyes, a spitting image of their mother as well as an impressive spitter. They'd always thought that Volgha would come around, join them in debauchery and gossip, but she never did. She fell in love with the mysteries of nature and learned all that she could from Osgrey.

That wasn't to say that Volgha didn't love her parents. She loved them very much, and cried when their mother passed away. Queen Beatrice expired of excess during a masquerade ball, in the course of scientifically proving how much wine was too much. Volgha cried, though she didn't cry as much as Alexia, who looked on that sort of thing as a competition. Alexia had stamina, and she played to win.

It wasn't long after their mother's death that their father succumbed to the same scientific experiment that claimed their mother, and all eyes turned to Alexia and Volgha to see which of them would take up the White Crown of Aurora. Volgha cried again, though Alexia gave mourning a miss and launched herself whole-heartedly into pestering Lord Chamberlain, the late king and queen's most trusted advisor, to read the royal will.

As expected, the crown passed to Alexia. She was the older daughter, and she had her parents' temperament. King Roderick had often implored Volgha to have a few bottles of wine and relax, but she'd been obstinate. He and Queen Beatrice acted as though their feelings were hurt, insisting in a very pouty and churlish way that she loved dusty old books and not them. It was this sort of talk that had made Volgha very skilled at rolling her eyes as a teenager.

After Alexia had taken the throne, things started to change. Anyone who'd ever slighted her—including many people whom she'd never met, but looked similar to people who'd slighted her … well, not slighted *per se*, but certainly hadn't been first to wish her a happy birthday—wound up in the dungeons. One of them had been the royal gardener, who'd been given no warning that the new Her Majesty required a hedge maze in the shape of her favorite pony, but was punished for failing to provide one all the same. Ignorance is no excuse, according to Her Majesty.

Volgha was angry that the royal gardens were left to wither with the lack of care. That anger aided her in moving right along to fury when Alexia tried to imprison Osgrey, though he escaped and fled the castle. He'd left without saying good-bye to Volgha, and while she'd understood that he didn't have a choice, it made her very sad. She hoped to find him again someday.

The post of court wizard was given to an old necromancer by the name of Ghasterly. He smelled like death, always wore black, and snarled from beneath his long, black beard as he glared at Volgha. His first act as court wizard was to forbid Volgha from ever entering the wizard's tower again.

It's hard to tell whether he did it just to be mean, or simply because that's the way necromancers are. Magic, to them, is a powerful secret to be hoarded as jealously as possible from everyone. Druids and witches held a very different view: that magic is a powerful secret to be hoarded as jealously as possible, with the strict exception of the one or two people you really like. Druids and witches tended to be introverts.

How dare he ban her from the tower? Volgha was a member of the royal family! But Ghasterly had convinced Alexia that it was for her own safety, and wouldn't Her Majesty prefer it if her sister lightened up? Forgot all about this magic business, put on a fancy dress, and drank until everyone else had passed out but the two of them, and then passed out just before Her Majesty did, making Her Majesty the winner?

Fortunately for Volgha, Ghasterly never changed the enchantments that kept people out of the tower, and so she was able to sneak in one last time and steal the Witches' Grimoire and a few other books, namely the ones having to do with the Witching Way. She doubted he'd even notice that they were gone. All the same, she kept them hidden at the bottom of her underwear drawer. He'd have a lot of explaining to do if he'd been caught looking for them there.

As time went on, life at the castle grew more and more intolerable for Volgha. Ghasterly convinced Alexia that Volgha wanted the crown for herself, and she insisted that Volgha formally renounce her royal status to secure her rule. Volgha had never cared about ruling the kingdom, though nothing she said could convince Alexia. She ultimately relented and renounced her title, taking as a consolation prize the title of "Winter Witch." It didn't really mean anything, but according to the Grimoire, witches rely quite heavily on mystery and intimidation. A name like "Volgha, the Winter Witch" would carry a lot more weight if it were backed by the crown, and was frankly much better suited to her than "Princess Volgha, a Witch." With nothing remaining to tie her to the castle, she left quietly one evening, under cover of darkness at the winter solstice.

Osgrey had once told Volgha about a little grove in the valley, where the spirits of the forest spoke to him. She roamed the land and cast scrying spells until she found Sigmund grooming himself under a gnarled old oak tree. There was something familiar about the tree, and it didn't take her long to figure out what it was: the tree was Osgrey.

She'd found references in one of her books to druids turning themselves into trees near the ends of their lives, but they'd said nothing about the trees ever turning back into lovable old druids. She'd assumed they forgot how to do magic, their brains having turned to wood and all.

Though she was disappointed that Osgrey was gone, she was glad to have found the grove. Osgrey had a little cottage there, and she moved into it. She befriended some of the local fauna, including Sigmund, who seemed keen on sticking around. She started learning how to speak with the spirits of the grove—or rather *to* them, as they rarely spoke back—and would have been perfectly content to live out the rest of her days there, in peace and quiet.

Unfortunately, since her sister was no longer worried that Volgha would challenge her for the throne, she summoned Volgha up to the castle all the time. Ignoring her just meant that she'd ask louder and more frequently; and on one occasion in particular, it would turn out to be far more trouble than she'd imagined.

TWO

VOLGHA HAD MET LOKI BEFORE. MORE THAN ONCE. HE NEVER seemed to remember her, but that wasn't why she despised him. She despised him because for all of his power and charm and wit, he was a fool. He was a fool, and he never resisted an opportunity to plague her with his foolishness.

"Kneel before your queen, peasant!" His falsetto was piercing. Volgha was surprised that the mostly-empty wine bottles strewn around the room didn't all shatter.

"Wearing my sister's dress doesn't make you the queen, Loki."

"How dare you!" The word "dare" was drawn out and warbling, in the latest fashion of old money aristocrats who were prone to losing monocles when sufficiently outraged. "You shall address me as Your Majesty, lest you lose your head on the choppy thingy, in my mercy. Now kneel!"

"I am kneeling," said Volgha. "Your goon here has seen to that."

One did not impersonate the sister of a witch, have said sister's guard force her to her knees, and expect to *not* have all of the milk in one's presence instantly curdle for the next year or so. That spell would require rockwort and toadstool. She already had rockwort. She must remember to gather some toadstool.

"Right," said Loki, "but not humbly enough."

"Where is my sister?"

"How should I know, peasant? I've been busy queening over my queendom all afternoon! I've better things to do than look after your sister, whoever she is."

A muffled tittering drifted from behind one of the ornate sofas. Volgha recognized it at once. At least her sister had not befallen some horrible fate, and was merely complicit in her protracted annoyance.

"Call off the goon, will you?" Volgha was being held in her kneeling position by a mail-and-leather-clad guard. Not too roughly, but he wouldn't let her rise. Itchy warts for him, then. She'd have to remember thistle. Earthbloom and thistle.

"So you can further affront My Majesty? Do you think that I was queened only yesterday?"

"That's not a verb," said Volgha, who appeared more bored than vexed, proving that appearances can be deceiving. She was quite vexed, and it's never a good idea to vex a witch.

She was going to have to follow through on these hexes, not that that was how she wanted to spend her time. Witches generally disliked the whole hexing game, but it had to be done. Vex one witch without repercussions, and the whole system of respectful fear just sort of falls apart. "A hex for a vex," as the old saying goes. Volgha didn't consider herself a fierce traditionalist, but some customs simply shouldn't be breached.

"Your *face* isn't a verb!" countered Loki. The farce was spiraling rapidly. A wedding cake in a hailstorm had a better chance of keeping it together.

The tittering from behind the sofa was nearly uncontrollable now. Volgha could picture her sister, red-faced and writhing, most likely dressed in whatever ridiculous get-up Loki normally occupied; or rather *usually* occupied, for there was certainly nothing normal about him. Alexia undoubtedly thought the pair of them very clever.

"Look," said Volgha, "you're neither the queen nor my sister, both of whom are—I mean *is*—behind that sofa, giggling like a fox in a wine barrel. I'm not buying into this garbage game the two of you are playing. I don't appreciate being dragged here like this, and I will wither this goon to a husk in just a moment if you don't—"

The tittering finally rolled itself into full-bellied laughter, as the White Queen emerged, as predicted, in Loki's doublet and breeches.

"We got you!" she wheezed, breathless with laughter.

"No," grumbled Volgha, "you didn't."

"You should see the look on your face! The one that isn't a verb!" She and Loki were both in stitches, rolling on the ground, fully impressed with themselves.

Volgha tried to stand, but the guard's grip on her shoulder remained firm. She turned to him and summoned her most harrowing look.

"Withered to a husk," she said through clenched teeth. The guard pulled his hand away. Volgha rose to her feet. She didn't want to wither him to a husk, so she was glad that he relented. She didn't even have a firm idea of what withering a person to a husk would entail, but it sounded dreadful. He was smart to avoid making her figure it out.

She stood there, arms crossed, waiting for the royal nitwit and her idiot friend to finish their ridiculous self-amusement. She was aware that it might take a long time, but knew that any attempt on her part to speed the process along would do just the opposite. Far better to simply suffer it in silence.

Volgha was hungry. She only realized it when her sister started eating a sausage she'd found in Loki's pocket, which he no doubt only kept there for the obvious pun. Volgha never actually wished for any harm to befall her sister, though she indulged in the wistful hope that Her Majesty might choke on the sausage long enough to stop her laughing. She'd never seen a person eat while laughing that hard, but the White Queen was no average buffoon.

Volgha had to hand it to her sister ... she was ridiculous, but it was the sort of practiced ridiculousness that might have won gold at the Olympics, had it but been a sport.

The guard was fidgeting while Volgha watched what must have been the most vulgar display of laughter in history. The two of them had stripped down and traded clothes back, cackling all the while. Since Her Majesty had never dressed herself, her ladies-in-waiting were summoned and made quick work of all the lacing and buckles while she writhed and giggled and guffawed.

"Beg your pardon, ma'am," said the guard, "but I wanted to apologize for the whole holding-your-witchness-down-on-the-floor thing. I was just following orders, you see. I'd never want to offend you or anything, but you know how Her Majesty can be when she's being clever."

Volgha studied the man's face. It was smiling, if you could call it that. The lips were curled up at the edges, but rather than friendly, it was deeply unsettling. Pork sandwiches were not as greasy. Still, it appeared sincere.

The White Queen snorted. She'd fallen over the back of her armchair, and her dress had gone up over her head. There were a startling number of petticoats, enough to constitute a quorum if anything came up for a vote.

"I understand," Volgha said.

"So maybe we can avoid the whole 'husk' thing?"

"What is your name?"

"Reginald, ma'am," he replied. "The boys all call me Reg."

"I suppose I could overlook it this time, Reginald," said Volgha. "In exchange for a favor."

"Of course," said the guard, looking eager. "Whose head would you like knocked in?"

"What? No," exclaimed Volgha. "Well, probably not. I haven't decided yet. Until I do, just remember: you're in debt to the Winter Witch, and there's no escaping that."

Reg thanked her profusely. The laughter rolled into what must have been its fifth encore.

The queen ultimately laughed herself into a stupor, which turned into a nap. Loki did the same. Volgha called for supper to be sent in, and dined well on courses of cheeses, soup, fish, pheasant, bread pudding, and finally a nice glass of port with little chocolates. It was usually considered unseemly for a witch to dine with such decadence, but in this case, it could be considered the price paid for her inconvenience.

The hour rolled into evening, and Her Majesty's servants came in to gently carry her off to her rooms. Lord Chamberlain, once trusted advisor to their parents and now to the current White Queen, had Volgha's room readied for her. As she drifted off to sleep in the big feather bed, she was unsure of what had become of Loki—most likely left to sleep where he lay, under the chaise. She hoped to catch her sister early the next morning, before a fascination with some newly discovered means of mimicking flatulence kept her from getting to the point of her summons.

THE WHITE QUEEN AND LOKI WERE TWO FECULENT PEAS IN A SCHEMing and ludicrous pod. Her Majesty always had a mad gleam in her eye when she talked about Loki. To be fair, she nearly always had a mad gleam in her eye, but it put on a florid air of bloodthirst when he came up, like a pair of sharpened stiletto heels for special occasions. Nervous smiles tended to bloom on the faces of those who saw that gleam, followed by hasty retreats involving things that needed doing elsewhere.

The two of them had a strange relationship. Not quite a friendship, as they were often at each other's throats; not a courtship, as they were never romantic; and certainly not a partnership, as those tended to involve paperwork and taxes, and they wouldn't have been able to get on with their hijinks until they'd sorted out who was senior partner.

Whatever the two of them were to each other, they were a plague upon Volgha. The most recent symptom of said plague was screaming bloody murder upon waking to find the pair of them sitting at the foot of her bed.

There were obvious benefits to a big feather bed, none of which offset this new and deplorable downside. She got straight to the business of longing for the little straw mattress in her cottage, the one that had no room for a pair of idiots at the foot. They burst into laughter.

"Will you two stop amusing yourselves long enough to tell me what you want?" She had not woken sufficiently to deal with this level of annoyance. To be fair, she'd need the time from that moment until the sun had set and risen again for that degree of wakefulness.

"You should tell her," said Loki.

"It's your idea, you should tell her!"

"That's why *you* should tell her. It's such a good idea, I'll sound like I'm bragging."

"One of you should tell me while I still have a shred of patience."

"Fine," said the White Queen, turning to Volgha. "You see, dear sister, Loki does a spot-on impression of me. So we thought that we should dress him up as me, and—"

"No, no," interrupted Loki. "We did that one, tell her about the other thing."

"There's not another thing, I'm sure I'd know about it."

Volgha got up and started getting dressed.

"Where are you going?" The queen looked genuinely perplexed.

"Home, probably. I've got things to attend to, and you can't even remember why you summoned me, so I'm leaving."

"No!" Loki leapt from the bed, rolled, and came up to a kneeling position at her feet. He took her hands in his, looked up at her sweetly, and produced a high-pitched fart that seemed to ask a question. Volgha was mildly amused, but not nearly enough to crack so much as a smirk. If word got out that witches' ire could be appeased by flatulence-based humor, Volgha would find a formidable enemy in the joke shop sector.

"Then out with it! I'm utterly out of patience with the pair of you!"

Loki's shoulders slumped a bit. Clearly, he'd wanted to dance around the purpose a while. He stood up, straightened his doublet, and started pacing around the room. Her Majesty had become fascinated with an enormous saber that had been hanging on the wall, and Loki ducked easily under her wild swings.

"I don't know if you're aware," he began, "but I'm a bit of a prankster. I've played pranks on nearly everyone worth pranking. Gods and kings, philosophers and servants, rich and poor have all fallen prey to my japes. There's only one foe whom I have yet to confound, and I need your help to attempt it."

"Some other god?" Volgha asked.

"Close. A god, yes, but none other than me!"

"You're going to play a prank on yourself?"

"Probably. In a manner of speaking."

"Go on."

"I'm not sure yet how it will unfold. In fact, I can't even begin to decide on the game until you've played the part that your majestic sister has implied that you can."

Volgha said nothing. She had him talking now, and thought an interruption might slow him down. Then this would take longer.

"I will devise a riddle, and I will solve it ... and I will need two of me."

"You want me to make you a twin?"

"No," shouted the queen, wildly swinging her saber around. "He wants you to cut him in half!"

"Cut you in half," repeated Volgha, wanting to be sure that she'd heard correctly.

"More like dividing my mind."

"Are you sure you have the wits to spare?"

"Thanks for joining the party, love." Loki grinned at the gibe.

"You have that creature, Ghasterly," said Volgha to her sister. "Why don't you make him do your dirty work? You saw fit to replace Osgrey with him, is he not up to the task?"

"I want you to do it!" Her saber slashed clumsily through the air, as well as a painting of a stodgy-looking noble wearing a garish quantity of gold. "We never do anything together anymore." Her lower lip was out. The royal pout. "Don't you like doing sister things?"

"No, and neither do you."

"Fine," said the queen with an eye roll and a sigh. "Ghasterly said it's dangerous to fool with that sort of power. He's no fun."

"For once, he and I agree," said Volgha. She turned to Loki. "And you, you think being astrally bisected is a good idea?"

"Why not? I am a god, after all. What better way to prove I'm cleverer than all of the other gods in Asgard than to solve a riddle devised by the greatest trickster of all time?"

"Well, *half* the greatest trickster."

"We'll let the bards work out the details in their ballads. Can it be done?"

Despite her misgivings about getting herself involved with a scheme that had anything to do with her sister, Volgha had to admit that the proposition was intriguing. Gods were always toying with the hearts and minds of mortal folk, she could use this opportunity to chalk one up for the other side.

"I suppose it's possible," she said. "But I'd need to use the wizard's tower."

GHASTERLY WAS A ROTTEN OLD CURMUDGEON WHO GRUMBLED UNder his rotten breath in the presence of anyone who was younger than he was, and that included roughly everybody. He was especially cantankerous toward Volgha over the stolen books—oh yes, he'd noticed—and doubly so when ordered to give her access to anything in his stores that she needed to accomplish her task. He'd banned Volgha from the tower long ago, and seethed at her insistence that she had to work from within it to brew a potion for Loki.

"You think you're clever, I suspect." Ghasterly wasn't doing any work, as far as Volgha could tell, unless lurking and leering counted as work. It may have. No one really knows what necromancers get up to.

"At least I try to be clever," she said, not taking her eyes off the herbs she was grinding. "Why was it that you couldn't do this?"

"Not couldn't," said Ghasterly, "wouldn't! There are horrors that this sort of magic might unleash. No responsible wizard would get mixed up in this business, and no witch with half a brain would either!"

"What about a necromancer with half a brain? I'm sure you could find half a brain in one of your musty old corpses that you could use."

"Mock me all you like," said Ghasterly with a smile that would be useful for scaring children into brushing their teeth. "You'll regret this soon enough."

"Could you refuse to do your job elsewhere? I'm trying to do magic over here."

AFTER SEVERAL AFTERNOONS OF READING THROUGH WHAT SHE STILL thought of as Osgrey's books, sniping with Ghasterly, getting the cauldron bubbling just right, stirring it counter-clockwise, and waiting for the proper alignment of stars (which was more for dramatic effect than anything else—a witch can't be seen finishing her work at any old time), she'd finally done it. She'd devised a potion that would permit Loki to try and outsmart himself.

After her usual fashion, Her Majesty was on the veranda, surrounded by courtiers, most of whom who were all but punching each other in the face to win a moment of her affection. The rest were *actually* punching each other in the face. Watching all of this was one of Her Majesty's favorite pastimes, and one of the few occasions during which she managed to keep her voice inside her indomitable lungs for more than a minute at a time.

Mealtimes were a particular problem in this regard, due to the copious amounts of food that would spew forth from her inconsiderate gob. Only the greatest sycophants among her courtiers would sit next to her at the dining table, and they had to have different outfits standing by for afterward.

Her Majesty's eyes were already as wide as saucers for the drama unfolding before her. Sir Vilkus Cockscomb was dressing down Lord Lester Eventide over a courtly walk which, as he put it, "would only ever be used by a mendicant with poor training in the Gentlemanly Art of Grooming One's Nether Truss."

Needless to say, Lord Lester had taken offense and was nearly coming to a point worth making, when Her Majesty saw Volgha standing there and squealed with delight.

"You wouldn't be here if it weren't ready, would you?" Her Majesty asked.

"Maybe I just missed your company," said Volgha in an impressive monotone.

"Out!" the White Queen bellowed. "Get out, you ninnies, or I'll execute you all! Secret business! Affairs of state! Run, you curs!"

A fight broke out briefly to be the first through the doors, but no interesting injuries resulted. Most of the courtiers had seen enough executions carried out in the name of Her Majesty's quick temper to know that she didn't joke about that sort of thing.

"Where is it? What must we do?"

"Have Loki meet us in the cellar."

"Chamberlain!"

He appeared from behind a large pillar in an instant. He'd always been very good at making quick appearances.

"No need to shout, Your Majesty," he said in an exceedingly pleasant tone. "Shall we go to the cellars, then?"

Volgha couldn't remember the last time she'd walked through the castle with her sister. She only started thinking about it because Her Majesty kept starting to wander off in the wrong direction. Lord Chamberlain had a very soothing manner, and always managed to find a way to steer Her Majesty in the proper direction without indicating that she hadn't done it properly on her own. He was very good at his job.

Past balustrades and balconies, and down spiral stairs they wandered, in seemingly contradictory directions, until they came at last to a wooden door with banded iron fittings. A brutish guard had to put his shoulder to the thing to push it open.

There had once been a number of courtiers who had discovered the way to the wine cellar, and had taken liberties with Her Majesty's booze in her absence. Any courtier worth their place in the fawning line would know that one of the White Queen's least favorite things in the world was a party to which she had not been invited. Those former courtiers were now presumably adding to the ambiance of the dungeons. Any interior decorator worth his salt will tell you that a dungeon without an emaciated prisoner chained to a wall is just a stony underground room. Practically worthless.

A stony underground room full of Her Majesty's booze, on the other hand, had quite a lot of worth indeed. This was where Volgha, Chamberlain, and Her Majesty had ultimately arrived, to find Loki sampling from a cask of whiskey via a convenient bucket. He'd apparently been waiting for a while.

"Good ladies," he said, spilling just a sip of whiskey as he bowed. It apparently amused him, for he tittered and tipped the bucket so another sip splashed out. He tittered again.

"Stop that," said the queen with a scowl. "You're wasting good booze."

"You've got more." Loki nearly fell over as he made a sweeping gesture toward the innumerable stacks of casks, shelves of bottles, and rows of barrels stretching into the torchlit distance behind him.

"Yes, but it may need to last. What if we're besieged? I'd be worried sick that we'd dry up!"

"There's never been a siege so long." He sipped again and belched.

"Forget it," exclaimed the queen. "With a bit of help from my sister, I've done it! It's time for our little prank!"

"Have you indeed?" Loki's eyes lit up. He set the bucket down gingerly, then on second thought picked it up and indulged in three more swallows of very good whiskey, set it down gingerly again, then sent it flying as he tripped over it. He found his footing and hurried to embrace Her Majesty as though their waltz had just started to play. He spun her thrice, gathered her up amorously, and said in a husky tone, "How does it work? Tell me how it works."

Her Majesty blushed and started giggling uncontrollably.

"Perhaps Her Majesty's sister would explain," said Chamberlain, "so that Her Majesty might assess her sister's understanding of the plan?"

Chamberlain blinked very subtly at Volgha, which she took to mean 'forgive me for having insinuated that you are anything short of the mastermind in this undertaking, but Her Majesty does not do well with being embarrassed, and there is no way to know how many heads would have rolled in the wake of her grievance. Please accept my silent but unwavering gratitude.'

"Right," said Volgha, "I'll do my best then." A lesser woman might have blushed in the face of Chamberlain's comely grin, but witches didn't blush. Volgha was fairly certain the Grimoire expressly forbade it.

She explained, with frequent interruption, that she'd brewed a three-sip potion.

Upon taking the first sip, Loki's mind would be divided into two parts: one half would remain in his distracted globe where it belonged, and the other would wait in a barrel of wine for the mischief to be undertaken.

Then, once Loki had devised and carried out whatever tomfoolery he wished, he would return to the cellar and take the second sip. The two halves of his mind would exchange places, and he'd be off to sort out the puzzle.

Once he'd solved it or given up, he'd take the third sip, and his mind would be restored to whatever semblance of normality it was capable of aping.

"Marvelous," Loki exclaimed, his rapt expression like that of a murderous child at story time, momentarily distracted from considering which of his nannies would make the best hostage.

"Yes," said the queen. "I'd have been more eloquent, but that's the long-and-short of it."

"One thing, though … could my other half wait inside this cask of extraordinary whiskey instead?" Loki inquired.

"Better not," replied Volgha. "The strength of the whiskey—"

The queen cut her off. "Of course you can."

Volgha bristled at her sister's constant need to be the favorite.

"I wouldn't if I were you. The difference in the contents—"

"Splendid!" Loki snatched the potion out of Volgha's hand and uncorked it. "Off we go then!"

He took the first sip, grimaced, swooned a bit, and started to fall. Chamberlain was standing in a perfect position to catch the bottle as it dropped from Loki's hand and let the prankster himself collapse unhindered to the cold stone floor.

Loki writhed a bit, before a flash of green light leapt from him and passed up the spigot in the cask of whiskey. It worked! Volgha had been confident that it would, and was now very pleased with herself. She was a bit concerned about the whiskey cask, but Loki was a god after all. She was sure he'd be fine. Well, not *sure*, but she could safely say she had no concern for his well-being.

"So," began the queen, "feel any different?"

"A bit," replied Loki. "Was I this handsome when we first came down here?"

Volgha shrugged. "If that's your idea of handsome, then yes."

"No need to hide your feelings, love." Loki winked.

"I've never hidden my feelings for you," said Volgha. "My body simply lacks sufficient bile to express them."

"Cheeky," said Loki. "So now I have to think of a prank. These things take time. I'll return ... eventually." And with that, he walked into a convenient shadow and was gone.

The remaining three of them stood there silently for half a moment. Now that Volgha no longer had the intricacies of the work itself to occupy her mind, she began to consider the implications of what she'd done. Had she really just split the soul of a god in half? Was that the sort of thing in which she should have involved herself so lightly?

"What's for lunch?" The questions worrying Her Majesty, while wildly aloof in a very remarkable way, were actually more timely and actionable than anything running through Volgha's mind.

They adjourned from the cellar to the banquet hall, where Her Majesty demanded a dozen very specific cuts of meat, and then filled up on bread.

THREE

IT'S FOR LOKI'S LITTLE PRANK." VOLGHA CONTINUED LEAFING through a book in which she had no interest. It was very old—so old, in fact, that she was unable to read it or even discern what language it was written in. Nonetheless, it was infuriating Ghasterly to no end to have her in the tower, and she was enjoying the exercise.

"You've been through every book on this shelf," said Ghasterly, through clenched teeth. "You're not fooling me, girl. You're trying my patience."

"It's not my fault you couldn't do the spell," said Volgha.

"Wouldn't!"

"It makes no difference. Her Majesty had to call on me to do the work that was above your head. But don't worry, it's not as though it makes you any less a man."

It was almost too easy. She didn't understand why he insisted on lurking right behind her and being insulted. There were dark corners aplenty in the tower for lurking, since Ghasterly only lit a few black candles here and there. If that wasn't enough lurking ground, the countryside was practically littered with old cemeteries. Didn't necromancers lurk in cemeteries? She felt as though she'd read that somewhere.

Her vision dimmed a bit, and the words on the page started to go fuzzy. Volgha yawned. How long had she been at this? If she'd been at home, she'd have made herself a cup of tea by now and taken a little break. However, she wasn't at home, thanks to this ridiculous little enterprise, and tormenting Ghasterly was the most interesting way to pass the time.

Oh well, she thought, *he's had enough for one afternoon.* There were rules around teasing, and Ghasterly was either too old to know them or too stubborn to care. If he'd only done his part and stormed off, it would have been over ages ago.

Closing the book, she went to put it back on the shelf. Her vision was still blurry, and she felt very tired. Far more tired than she'd felt a moment ago. The book slipped from her hand, and she turned to see a blurry Ghasterly gesturing in her direction, a gnarled and blurry wand in his left hand.

"What're you doing?" she asked.

"You've got some natural resistance," Ghasterly hissed. "Why don't you just give in, and have a nice little nap?"

Volgha reached for her basket, but it wasn't there. Ghasterly must have moved it while she was busy infuriating him, a bit of fun which seemed ill-advised in hindsight. She said a swear word. As her vision started to dim, she remembered the little pouch of salt that she kept on her belt. A very versatile element, salt. Very useful for witchery. It just might buy her enough time to cast a counter spell.

She could feel the blissful hush of sleep tugging at her, beckoning her downward. She fought it, fumbling for her salt with numb, clumsy hands as her mind reached for the words to block the heavy veil that Ghasterly was pulling over her.

"That's right," said Ghasterly, as if speaking to her through a murky pond. "*Mumble mumble* sleep, so I can *mumble* you apart, *mumble mumble.*"

There was no snow. There was mist over the ground among the black, leafless trunks of the trees, and a sickly green light washed over everything. No wind, no birds, no sound aside from the rustling of her footsteps.

"I've got to get home," said Volgha aloud. Her words were dull and thick, not reverberating in the air as spoken words tend to do; rather they simply hung there, entirely disinterested in exploring the bleakness of their surroundings.

"You *are* home." It was Ghasterly. She knew it, but she couldn't see him. Unlike her voice, his boomed and crept up her spine. The acidulous sweeps in his baritone filled her with a sense of mocking hopelessness.

"Where are you, coward?" Her shout had the same bleak, flat tone as before. It was small and doleful. Was she even speaking aloud?

"I am where you are," the dreadful voice of Ghasterly replied. "Would you like to wake up now?"

Volgha said nothing. Despite the rising sense of dread, she was determined not to give him the satisfaction.

"So proud," remarked Ghasterly, "so willful! Whatever shall I do with you?"

His voice seemed real to her, in a way that her own did not. It was a sickly, rotten gnashing that invaded her ears. The tinny pops and clicks in his consonants sounded like the squelching of boots coming unstuck from the mud. If halitosis were an audible experience, this would have been it.

"Is this the best you can do, coward?" Volgha's voice trembled, but she went on talking anyway. "Have you ever been in a fair fight, or must you rely on treachery to win?"

"There is no treachery when dealing with enemies," said Ghasterly. "Or did you think that we were friends? I could be your friend, if that's what you wanted."

"Never!"

"Tsk tsk tsk," clucked Ghasterly, slowly, patiently, each wet movement of his putrid tongue sending a bolt of fear through Volgha. "Manners, little bird. Why not ask nicely? We can be sweet to each other, can't we?"

"Just stop this. I want to go home." This wasn't right. Everything was dim and fleeting. Volgha had trouble keeping her thoughts together. Just when she felt she'd figured out what was going on, a chill would creep through and her mind would go blank. Only a sense of foreboding remained.

She wished she hadn't been so foolish as to provoke Ghasterly's anger. She wanted a way out. She started walking through the trees, the eerie lack of air, noise, anything but the shuffling of her boots unnerving her past the point of reason.

"Fine," she said, her voice beginning to quaver. "Please let me out of here."

"Sweetly," sang Ghasterly, in a sickly, sing song way.

"Please." Volgha quickened her pace as she stumbled through the strange forest. The trees seemed as though they were coming closer together. She turned around, but they looked even more tightly grouped back the way she'd come.

"Do better," barked Ghasterly, anger apparent in his voice. The sickly green light was dimming. The forest was growing darker. There was barely room to stand among the tall black tree trunks, which were glistening with feculent slime.

"I'm sorry!" Tears welled up in her eyes, and her throat tightened. "I'm sorry that I teased you, I—"

"It's too late for that!" The green light browned its way to a malicious red. Orange flashed through the mist above, and thunder rumbled menacingly in the distance.

"Please," Volgha warbled meekly, "have mercy!"

"Why should I? No one goes up against a necromancer and lives to tell about it! I should leave you here to starve and choke and rot among the leaves in this dead place."

"No!" Panic overwhelmed her. "Let me live, please! I'll do anything, just release me from this place!"

"Admit that I have bested you."

"Yes! You have bested me."

"Your paltry tricks do not compare to my power. What do you know of true magic?"

"Nothing! I cannot match you! Please, I'll never so much as look upon the door to your tower again as long as I live, just let me go!"

"Swear it. Swear never to look upon the tower again."

"I swear it!"

She tasted dirt.

No one wakes up all at once. It's not allowed. It's a gradual process of reintegrating one's consciousness with the waking world, usually about thirty minutes before one's consciousness would have preferred. A noise, a feeling of something brushing against the skin, or just dimly becoming aware that one is dreaming will get things started, and then the rest of the senses start powering on.

For Volgha, this time started with the gritty, bitter taste of dirt. Cold came next, cold and wet. She was lying in the cold, wet dirt. She sat up.

She had been lying, and was now sitting, in the wheel-worn tracks in front of the castle where carriages arrived. She was soaked, freezing, and covered in dirt. The guards on either side of the door were making a very pointed display of staring straight ahead. If there were one particular direction that definitely did *not* have a bedraggled witch in it, they were looking in that one. It was the sort of direction where one could find the complete lack of awkwardness that the presence of a bedraggled witch might possess in abundance.

One of the guards cleared his throat and opened the door in a way that acknowledged the complete absence of bedraggled witches in the area, while insisting that the sooner that any such non-existent persons got moving in that direction, the sooner everyone could start forgetting what they'd not seen in the first place.

It was all that Volgha could do to move in the direction that had been non-judgmentally insinuated by no one in particular. She stumbled through the castle in a daze, eventually finding herself soaking in a copper tub full of hot soapy water, and though the warmth relieved her aching muscles and clammy flesh, her heart felt like a curdled lump in her chest.

She'd been foolish. Ghasterly had bested her. He'd struck when she hadn't been looking, and used some sort of vile wand magic to play on her fears. It was a despicable tactic, but one that had been wildly successful.

She'd begged for her life. She'd cried, she'd sniveled, and she'd admitted defeat. She could go to her sister, cry and tattle, but then what? Alexia was just as likely to laugh as she was to punish Ghasterly, and in any case, wasn't that just further admission that she couldn't best him?

The worst part was the oath. The fact that Volgha had been coerced by an evil spell didn't matter—she'd sworn never to look upon the tower again, and a witch was nothing without her word. She'd have to defeat Ghasterly to unbind the oath. She'd always thought that she could beat him in a fair fight, but who expects a necromancer to fight fairly?

She wanted to swear revenge, but in that moment, she honestly didn't think she was capable of claiming it.

She surrendered to her defeat. Rising from the tub, she dried herself off, slipped into a clean, plain black robe, and got into her bed. She wasn't sure how long it had been since she had slept properly, or how long she might have lain there in the mud, or if she was even tired now. But lying there, warm in the sheets, she curled up and let the tears roll from her eyes, and wept herself to sleep.

FOUR

THE PASSAGE OF TIME IS DIFFICULT TO MARK IN THE NORTH POLE, given the year-long day. It's doubly difficult figuring out how long one has slept, so most of the people who live there simply don't bother trying.

So it was that Volgha awoke because she no longer felt like sleeping. Her cheeks stung of salt, and her face felt puffy.

The memory of her defeat at Ghasterly's hands returned, albeit unbidden. She pushed it aside, vowing to think on it more once she had the strength. Though she was still unnerved by the experience, she didn't seem to have any tears for it at the moment, and that was something.

Getting out of bed, she looked around for her basket, which had all of her herbs and components in it. She tried to remember where she'd left it, and then it came to her—it was in the tower.

She said a swear word, and her heart sank. She started thinking through its contents. She could replace most of what was in it, but it would take a very long time.

Above all else, she loved that basket. It was the first thing that she'd made in her cottage that had really, entirely been her own. Her clothes had been made by the castle's seamstresses, her boots by a cobbler in the village—the basket, though, was all her work. She'd found the long grasses in the woods around the grove, picked them, dried them, and woven them together.

She had to admit that it wasn't a very good basket—it was the first thing she'd tried to make, after all—but it held things, and wasn't that the entire point of a basket? She'd have to get it back, even if only to replace it. Better to say, "I want to make a better basket," than, "A mean old necromancer stole my basket, and I'm afraid to get it back."

Later. She kept a few things in her wardrobe which would do for now. After grinding a few dried herbs, she mixed them with a bit of ash from the fireplace, and wiggled her fingers over them as she mumbled an incantation.

Removing her long cloak from the wardrobe, she fastened it around her neck and drew the hood up over her head. She mumbled another incantation, threw the powdered mixture of herbs and ash up in the air, and took a step to stand beneath the cloud as it fell. She took in a breath and whispered a "*hushhhhhh*" as the mixture further obscured her.

It was an interesting feeling, being Dim. She felt as though she could hide behind the very air in the room. Sure, there was no one else in the room with her, but if there had been, they wouldn't see her.

That's not to say that they *couldn't* see her—she'd have to be invisible for that. Being Dim was a lot like being invisible, in that she could walk around in a room unnoticed; however, unlike invisibility, being Dim didn't allow the light to pass through her. It was more like a mind game. So long as she didn't make eye contact with anyone or say, "hello, I'm over here," anyone nearby would simply find themselves disinclined to notice her.

It was a very useful spell, and far less taxing than invisibility. She didn't really need the cloak for it, she just found that it kept her in the right frame of mind. She crept out of her room and headed for the kitchens.

It wasn't difficult, but she had to tiptoe and avoid making sudden movements. It was like hide-and-seek, but she was the best player in the world, and no one else was aware that they were supposed to be playing.

The kitchens presented a challenge. They were a constant whirlwind of activity, as the frequent, lavish meals required a lot of preparation. Volgha managed to duck her way past cooks and their assistants, tucking half a loaf of bread, a couple of sausages, a wedge of cheese, and an apple into the folds of her cloak. She even purloined a nice bottle of wine on her way out, then made her way up to the belfry.

It was the second tallest tower in the castle, which made very little sense. It was so tall that the bell couldn't be heard from anywhere in the castle. Her ancestors had been far more concerned with grandeur than practicality, and this sort of thing was the result.

Volgha liked the belfry. Lack of overt mysticism aside, she actually liked it more than the wizard's tower. No one ever went up the belfry stairs, even though the view of the surrounding kingdom was nothing short of majestic. It was a treasure hidden in plain sight, not unlike herself in her Dimness, according to a moment of self-indulgent vanity (for which she duly chided herself).

Aside from the view, the belfry was her secret way in and out of the castle. Her broom was there, leaning against the frost-covered wall, where she'd left it when she'd arrived. Her sister's capriciousness had once prevented her from leaving through the front gates for most of the spring, which Volgha found intolerable. Plus, appearing inexplicably added to a witch's sense of mystery.

As she ate her pilfered feast, she thought about home. Her little cottage in the grove on the valley floor was an ideal place for brooding. Volgha was good at brooding, and she had quite a bit to mumble angrily under her breath about.

It was hard to brood in a castle. One could easily manage waxing philosophical, to be sure, but brooding? Hardly. Brooding was a stern and stoic undertaking, very difficult to manage when one had a pastry chef available at all hours.

The cottage was an ideal spot for a good brood, not to mention sulks, ruminations, or even the occasional languish. It was almost as though Osgrey had designed it specifically for the purpose.

Osgrey. If there could ever be a proper time for her mentor to turn himself into a tree, Volgha couldn't imagine when that might be; however, she was certain that he'd done it too soon. Couldn't he at least have waited until he'd seen her through summoning her familiar? It was perhaps the most important spell a witch would cast in her life, and now she'd have to figure it out on her own.

She missed the old man. If anyone could have spared an encouraging word to brighten her spirits, it would have been him. She usually didn't go in for that sort of thing, preferring solitude. There's quite a bit of hermitry in witchery, and there probably was in druidry as well.

Volgha shook her head. She'd hit her limit of feeling sorry for herself. Once she'd seen Loki's madness to its end, she'd have her revenge on Ghasterly, and then she'd manage the familiar business on her own.

Revenge. Nothing quite like it for keeping you warm.

Rising, Volgha took one last look around. It seemed warmer than it usually was, despite the frost that still clung to the cold stone. The sun was setting slowly, casting gold and crimson hues across the landscape, and long shadows as well.

Defeated, she thought, *but only for now*. The food and the sleep had done her good, and the security of the Dimness emboldened her. She headed down the stairwell, resolving to have a quiet lurk around the castle, in lieu of a proper brood.

Loki was back, and Volgha was still Dim. The two nitwits giggled in their tubs, both trying to speak but apparently failing for the uncontrollable laughter over some joke that Volgha had arrived too late to hear. It probably wouldn't have amused her anyway. It may have even been at her expense.

"Have you got any ducks?" Loki managed to ask, with a straight face, several minutes after Volgha had seated herself on a little stool in the corner. She felt compelled to observe them for a while, not wanting to waste the opportunity to witness uninhibited madness.

"Not a one," replied the queen. "Why do you ask?"

"Because we're being watched by a silly, silly goose!" Loki looked at Volgha and laughed at his own cleverness. Dimness was no use against the gods, then. Good to know.

"There's no goose in here!" The queen started laughing anyway.

"He's talking about me," said Volgha.

The queen yelped and sank herself quickly amongst her bubbles, sloshing a great deal of water out onto the stone floor. Loki tittered. Resurfacing, the queen wiped the soap from her face, and pointed an accusing finger toward her sister.

"How long have you been there?" Her eyes were full of that delighted rage that she was so prone to spew. Beheadings often followed.

"Just for a moment," said Volgha, with an utter dearth of the cowering and quaking that her sister undoubtedly would have preferred. "Long enough to witness a really spectacular display of lunacy. Honestly, do you two ever stop giggling long enough to feed yourselves?"

"Jealous?" the queen asked, wearing nothing but a grin that was all teeth.

"Not a bit."

"Well, you should be," said Loki. "We're a riot, and you're boring."

"Then I guess I'll take my potion and go home."

"No!" the nitwits shouted in unison, leaping from their tubs and rushing toward her. Caught completely unaware, Volgha's instincts took over, and suddenly she was running through the castle, being chased by a pair of soapy, naked ninnies. Past servants and guards they ran, careening into trays of food, laundry carts, and a host of other hapless obstacles that could have been avoided, if only the servants would stop freezing in their tracks and shutting their eyes when they saw Her Majesty in her state of undress.

Volgha started breathing heavily from the exertion of a flat-out run, and that returned her to her senses. People ran from witches, not the other way around!

She thought a simple glamour should bring the chase to a close. She whispered a mouthful of consonants, stopped, and turned around.

"Enough!" Flames erupted from her eyes and mouth. Shadowy tendrils licked out from underneath her dress, writhing threateningly around her. Her voice was a booming echo, a chorus of terrible monsters bellowing from out of a nightmare, from which all who heard sincerely wished to wake.

Alexia and the servants within earshot fell into various cowering poses. Only Loki was grinning like an idiot, clapping his hands to applaud Volgha's effort, but suffering from no tormented visions.

She allowed the glamour to fade. The servants scrambled away in every direction, and it was just the three of them in the hallway.

Her Majesty said a bunch of swear words and then yelled for Chamberlain. Lord Chamberlain was standing by with a pair of bathrobes, one of which he flung toward Loki, freeing his hands to hold the other one open for the queen. He managed not to peek as he got Her Majesty appropriately trussed, which was an impressive feat, given that she was less than cooperative. It was unclear whether she was struggling solely because she was drunk; she may have felt that Chamberlain needed a challenge.

"Is this what passes for witchery now?" asked Loki. "Spooky parlor tricks and sneaking into the baths of incredibly attractive people?"

"No," said Volgha, "what passes for witchery is nothing short of splitting the mind of a god in half. Do keep in mind that you need my witchery to reunite the halves of your cleft globe before you presume to jibe with your betters, fool."

That was satisfying. Volgha really enjoyed watching the smugness drain from his face as she spoke, leaving behind a sulking frown.

"That's no way to speak to my friend," said the queen. "Apologize at once, or you'll not be welcome here!"

Volgha shrugged. "Fine," she said, then turned and sauntered away. It wasn't often that her sister needed something from her, and the power was delicious. She wondered how far she'd get before one of them realized that—

"Wait!" The queen had run to stand in front of her, blocking her exit. "Just this once, I will forgive your impudence out of hand. But only on the condition that you fulfill your part of the bargain. What say you?"

"That's too generous Your Majesty," Volgha replied with a smile. "I couldn't possibly accept such an extravagance." She stepped around her sister and continued along the hallway.

The queen ran around to block her path again. "Fine," she said through clenched teeth and a frown. She took a breath and straightened her posture, so that she looked very regal. "I'm ... sorr ..." The first word was well-projected and firm. The second was barely audible.

"What was that?" Volgha's fists rested on her hips.

"I said I'm sor-*rur*."

"Sor-rur?"

"Chamberlain!" Her Majesty stomped off to stand beside Loki. Lord Chamberlain stepped in front of Volgha, bowed, and cleared his throat.

"Her Majesty bids you kind regards and wishes to obviate any misunderstanding on your part that might have been misconstrued as having intended offense. Her Majesty bids you remain in the care and comfort of Castle Borealis, and invites you to proceed with the riddle conceived by Mister Loki forthwith."

"Fine." Volgha's eyes rolled hard enough to curl her eyelashes. She gave Chamberlain a begrudged curtsy because that's what you did for a proper gentleman of the court. He returned the gesture with an equivalent bow.

"There, was that so hard?" Her Majesty's unfailing air of dignity was entirely unaware that her mop of wet hair was committing some sort of interpretive dance across her face, or else it didn't care.

"To the wine cellar then." Volgha strode off with a walk that was as fast as possible while still conveying indignation. As she fully expected, the two nitwits followed her, giggling and whispering to one another all the way. Honestly, it was like Loki was the vapid little sister that Her Majesty had always wanted.

There it was. The whiskey barrel with half a Loki in it, glowing faintly in the gloom of the cellar. Chamberlain lit a torch on the wall.

"Here we are then." Volgha produced the potion from within the folds of her cloak. A good witch's cloak was full of pockets. Strikingly useful, pockets, and the occasional opportunity to produce something from them with a flourish was a real treat. Nothing says "I'm not to be underestimated" like casually flourishing potions and the like.

"Another sip," she said, handing the potion to Loki. "Not all of it, leave enough for the last one."

Loki winked and nodded. He raised the glass bottle in salute to everyone, then briefly lowered it and scowled at Chamberlain. He uncorked it, took the second sip, recorked it, and fell to the floor. Chamberlain caught the bottle as he'd done the last time. Two lights, one from Loki and the other from the cask of whiskey, shot from their hosts and traded places. A faint smell of burnt hair lingered in the air for just a moment, and everything was still.

The queen knelt by Loki's head and brought her hands up to her cheeks, framing her broad and manic smile. She was a child at her own birthday party, waiting with a slender thread of patience for her toy to open itself.

"How long should it take?" she asked, not taking her eyes off Loki, or sparing the effort to blink.

"Not long," said Volgha.

She wasn't wrong. After a moment, Loki began to stir. He sort of flopped around on the floor a bit, like a fish in an old man's boat. Then he vomited and flopped around in that for a moment. Then he sat up, belched, and stared at each of them in turn. It was clear that he didn't recognize any of them, based on the confused faces he was making. What was unclear was whether he could actually focus on any of their faces. He was very bleary, as though he'd skipped sleeping several times in order to continue drinking.

"Is that normal?" The queen's manic smile had sunk into an uneasy sneer.

"Nothing about Loki is normal," answered Volgha. "Plus, I told him to go with the wine."

"Uff," said the queen. "Know-it-all." She grabbed Loki's face between her palms and tried to get him to focus on her face.

"That's done then," said Volgha. "I'll be leaving presently. Give him the last sip whenever he wants it."

"Oh, but you must stay!" The queen's insistence was somewhere between hospitality and a prison sentence. "We can't have you leaving, not with such an important game afoot!"

"Very well," Volgha replied, thinking of her broom in the belfry. Slipping away later would be easier than arguing now.

"I'll have the maids turn down your bed," said Chamberlain with a bow.

"Do something with Loki first," instructed the queen. Chamberlain hadn't even straightened from his bow yet. The impregnable expression on his face showed the slightest hint of chagrin, leading Volgha to wonder if Chamberlain's patience for her sister had limits after all.

"Very well, Your Majesty," he said. "And what would you have me do?"

"Just send him on his way. He's no fun like this. Maybe after he sobers up and solves his stupid riddle, he'll be fun again."

"Very well." Chamberlain called for a guard and pointed at the arguably conscious Loki. "Keep an eye on him for a moment." He turned and walked toward the door.

Once Chamberlain had gotten her cleaned up, Her Majesty had only enough energy remaining to eat eight of her nine supper courses before she fell asleep with a bottle of brandy in her royal fist. As Chamberlain was gathering her up to take her to her bedroom, Volgha thanked him for his accommodations and went off to her room.

She napped for an hour or so, then Dimmed herself again and slinked off to the belfry. The air at high altitude was still warm, which was odd. As she made for home in a smooth stream of air, she tried to calculate how much time remained until the winter darkness was upon them.

FIVE

THE FLIGHT HOME WAS ALWAYS MUCH EASIER THAN THE FLIGHT to the castle. It felt that way, at least. She always managed to find a nice tailwind, as if the castle itself was the source of the wind. And why not? It has to come from somewhere.

On this particular trip, the current that she followed led over Santa's Village. She'd flown over it a few times before, and had always meant to visit as soon as she could come up with a pretense. Pretenses were essential things. How would it look for a witch to simply be curious about something that wasn't her business? Nosy, that's how. Witches don't like nosy people, so they have to set an example.

But despite her best intentions, Volgha *was* curious, and justifiably so. The whole place was a constant light show that needed seizure warnings all over it. She assumed he was some sort of alchemist, what with the frequent explosions. A well-funded alchemist, at that. She'd flown low enough on one occasion to see that the village was almost entirely populated by elves, most of whom appeared to be engaged in scientific work. Was this Santa character their employer?

She wondered that again as she flew over the village, watching the elves scurry about. She'd not met many elves and didn't have a good sense of how intimidated they'd need to be.

IT ISN'T GOOD ENOUGH FOR A WITCH TO SIMPLY WEAR A POINTY HAT and meddle with dark forces beyond mortal comprehension. People, dullards that they are, have expectations. They expect those who meddle with dark forces beyond mortal comprehension to have other qualities as well. In people's minds, witches should be mysterious. They should be dark—hence all the wearing black—powerful, and frankly a bit scary.

A friendly witch would confuse most people. Confused people tend to be angry people, and angry people band together with pitchforks and torches. Thus, a smart witch will approach strangers with an abrasive and intimidating demeanor.

There is a great deal of magic in witchery, to be sure; however, a lot of the routine stuff is managed through intimidation. Anyone not well-versed in the art of witchery might be surprised at how many things witches accomplish without any magic at all.

Take flying on brooms, for instance. To the casual observer, it doesn't seem possible without magic. It's certainly out of the ordinary, but there is nothing magical about it. Flying on brooms is accomplished through sheer intimidation. It makes perfect sense once the facts have been made clear.

Broom shafts are made from branches. Their natural state is to be up in the air, attached to a tree. Octomedes' Third Law of Doing Work clearly states that "a thing set to a purpose not of its own volition will resist that purpose whenever possible." Simply put, branches don't want to spend time on floors, and they certainly have no interest in cleaning them.

This works out for witches. Instead of sweeping floors, they'd rather see the brooms follow the natural inclinations of the branches from which they were made, and rise up into the air. The first witches tried gently coaxing them up, and that was why they failed. If a simple "please do what comes naturally instead of moving dirt around" would do the trick, witches' spell books would include chapters on etiquette. However, brooms, like people, have expectations. Polite requests are met with confused silence. This assertion can be tested by anyone, by politely asking a broom to do the sweeping on its own.

On the other hand, when a witch insinuates to a broom that she'll reduce it to splinters if it stays on the ground for another instant, it rises up without hesitation. It didn't want to be on the ground anyway, so a witch's threat is just the push it needs.

Unfortunately, this assertion can only be tested by witches. Brooms are wily enough to recognize that regular folks are just as lazy as they are, and couldn't be bothered to go and buy a new broom, to say nothing of the sweaty work of obliterating one.

In order to intimidate successfully, a witch has to be what everyone *expects* a witch to be. This is why they wear the pointy hats. There's nothing particularly helpful or magical about them, they're basically just badges. You see a woman wearing all black, you could think anything from 'she must be in mourning' to 'she probably listens to depressing music and spends a lot of money on eyeliner.' Add the hat, and there's no mistaking that she can answer a vex with a hex; unless, of course, she's simply bought the hat because it goes so well with her eyeliner. In any case, it's safer to avoid vexing black-clad women in pointy hats.

While it's rumored that witches can control people's minds via magic, that's patently false. Of course, none of them will admit that. If questioned on the matter, a witch would likely chide the ninny who asked and threaten to show them the hard way.

OVER SNOW-COVERED HILLS AND DALES VOLGHA FLEW, UNTIL SHE finally reached the valley. She flew down into the pine-covered bottom, finally spying the grove in the autumn twilight. Though the higher air currents were warmer than usual, they were still bitterly cold, and she felt frozen solid. It was the North Pole, after all.

She touched down gently, barely disturbing the fresh powder that had fallen in front of her cottage. The snow wouldn't have minded, but it was a part of nature, and the Witching Way had taught her to respect nature. She took that to mean that she should disturb it as little as possible. How was she to know that the spirits of the forest weren't agonizingly specific in their arrangement of snowfall, and likely to be very put out if some oblivious pair of boots went crashing through their work with abandon?

She didn't. She couldn't. The spirits of the forest—and the ones in her grove in particular—were temperamental, and it wouldn't be a good idea to go around vexing them, disturbing their snow and such. That was a sure-fire way to guarantee that every woodland creature in the grove went out of its way to relieve itself on her porch until sun-up.

Volgha had an agreement with the spirits. At least, she felt that she did. The conversations that she'd had with them to date were less substantial than she'd have liked, mostly on par with small talk about the weather. Not that discussions about the weather weren't important, especially to the spirits of nature.

There was a line of demarcation that started at her front porch. She did her very best to maintain the serenity of the grove on the other side of it, and kept most of her affairs in the immediate vicinity of the cottage. As she walked up the steps, she used her broom to clear off the snow—much to the broom's chagrin—and pushed the front door open.

It was dark inside. She used a piece of flint against her little knife to spark a candle alight. She could have magicked a flame onto its wick quite easily, but she was neither pressed for time nor trying to impress anyone. Flint and steel would do nicely.

As the tiny light stretched itself thinly into the corners of the room, she saw that everything was just as she'd left it. Dried herbs hanging from the ceiling, seeds and other ingredients lining the little shelves in bottles, the Grimoire open on the stand to a spell that would gently persuade chipmunks to favor the nuts recently fallen from the trees, and away from the ones she'd recently planted.

The log in the fireplace was half-burnt from the last time it had been lit. She coaxed a flame from it with the flint and added a pair of new logs to thaw the frozen stew in the little cauldron that hung there in the hearth.

It was a proper stew, one that she'd inherited from Osgrey. There was no recipe. Recipes are for soups and casseroles, which are occasionally confused with stews. No, this very cauldron of stew had been hanging in the hearth when she'd first moved into the place, and she'd had no idea whether Osgrey had started it, or possibly his own mentor before him.

No one knows how stews get started. It's a mystery for philosophers to puzzle out, and they usually do so over a bowl of stew, to which they've made no contribution. Philosophy doesn't pay very well, generally just enough to cover leather elbow patches. Those who inherit a proper stew just start adding meat, vegetables, and leftovers from other meals, and thus set themselves about maintaining it.

Eating a proper stew is dining on history. Depending on the particular confluence of the pot, the story it tells can be triumphant, tumultuous, or even a bit bloody in the case of rare beef.

Volgha had inherited a rather dull pot of history and elevated it with some nettle, earthbloom, and a bit of black pepper. Now she was slicing an onion into it, and trying to avoid thinking about where it had acquired a faint aroma of strong cheese. It hadn't been there before, and she hadn't added any.

Best not to think too hard about stew. Volgha trusted that her stew knew what it was doing, and it had never treated her poorly.

Once the onion was in, she hung her blankets from the hooks under the mantle. They blocked some of the heat from entering the room, but they'd be colder than a joke about puppies with cancer if she didn't warm them up before bed.

She sat in her chair while the stew and the blankets soaked in the warmth of the fire. In the stillness, her mind had nothing to do but bully her into reliving everything that transpired at the castle. Reconciling it all was about as simple as herding kittens, though significantly less adorable.

What was Ghasterly's problem, anyway? The two of them had always been at odds, and it had always been his fault. It wasn't that she wanted to be friends with a dusty old skeleton who had religious objections to hygiene, but he didn't seem to like *anybody*. That couldn't be good for the kingdom, him being the court wizard and all.

She was severely vexed by their last encounter, but she was having trouble calculating revenge. It was an awful state of affairs, given her hatred of the sneering old worm sack and her love of revenge.

She knew why. As much as she hated to admit it, even quietly to herself, she was afraid of him.

Taking a deep breath, she pondered the Witching Way. What did it have to say about fear? Fear isn't rational, it's a fantasy. Being a witch meant living entirely in the light of truth and reason, with the exception of telling as many lies as she wanted.

But those lies were for other people. She needed to be truthful with herself, no matter how inconvenient.

She rose from her chair, went to her bedside table, and picked up the little silver mirror she kept there. It had been her grandmother's, or possibly her grandmother's ferret's (they were constantly stealing it from each other, so it was hard to tell). She studied herself in its tarnished surface, locking eyes with her reflection and pursing her lips severely.

"I am afraid of Ghasterly," she said aloud. There. That was the ugly truth.

"I am afraid of Ghasterly. I am afraid of Ghasterly."

Admitting a fear is the first step in overcoming it, and telling the truth aloud three times means its truth is no longer open to debate. Volgha knew this because it was written thrice in the Grimoire.

Anyway, it was just a little bit of fear. Keep in mind she'd split a god in half, thank you very much. A *god*. It would have been impressive enough to divide the mind of a person, but a god? Ghasterly couldn't claim to have done that! He didn't even try, the coward!

Then again, if she were totally honest with herself, she understood why Ghasterly had refused to do it. She actually felt a bit foolish now, cutting gods in half all will-nilly. She'd feel childish, only she hated to imagine the child who could manage that sort of thing. Beware the monstrous toddler who goes around bisecting deities.

Feeling foolish was the downside of total honesty with one's self. Small wonder that regular folk avoid it.

Volgha's mind was running in circles. The only thing that could make it stop was sleep. Fretting over that which she couldn't control this close to bedtime was a recipe for bad dreams, worse than the naked in school one.

Her feelings of foolishness had robbed her of her appetite, so she said good evening to the stew without sampling it. She whisked her blankets from their hooks, twirled as she leapt for the bed, and was tightly cocooned in warmth and softness and security. Within seconds, she was snoring at the top of her lungs, as though her life depended on it.

It was dark as pitch in the cottage when she awoke. The fire had gone out, so at least a few hours had passed. That was good.

Nothing soothes the nerves like a good sleep, and sleeping at the castle was about as soothing as a sugar-overdosed toddler playing the drums.

It had been a dreamless sleep, which was rare for witches. When you spend a good deal of time traipsing across the void into the shadow realms, things tend to seek you out in dreams and engage you in bizarre, unintelligible conversations. That was the whole point of witchery, of course. Living in the light of truth and reason shouldn't have to be boring.

She opened the shutters a crack. It was grey outside—no surprises there—and it was snowing a bit, to her further lack of surprise. There were a lot of things that would need her attention, first of which would be her late autumn herb garden. She pulled on her boots, reached for her basket, and said a swear word as she realized yet again that it was lost to her.

Oh well, she thought. Crying over spilled milk, in Volgha's experience, was the province of royalty. She grabbed an old basket that she'd taken when she'd first left the castle and walked out into the grove.

She marched through the trees with a determined expression, signaling to everyone who wasn't there that she was still a witch, and not to be trifled with.

Trifle with a witch, and you'll be sorry you did. Then, as though some fool had been paying attention and decided to call her bluff, she saw a heap of twisted metal that had dropped onto her garden to the tune of one severe trifling.

The thing had elfish written all over it. Even if it hadn't been literally covered in elfish script, she'd seen enough elfish craftsmanship in her day to recognize it now. Santa's Village was the only place nearby where one might find elves, a fact that Santa would choke upon soon enough.

Santa's Village was always giving off some sort of minor nuisance that she could overlook. The occasional thunderous boom, the erstwhile blinding flashes in the sky, and the rare fluctuation in the Northern Lights were all easy enough to forgive and forget, but the wreckage of some infernal machine gone clog dancing over her herb garden was just the sort of thing to land an insolent neighbor at the top of the revenge list.

Oh, yes! The spirits were simply philanthropic with cause for revenge of late. There must have been a surplus. It was shaping up to be a very busy winter.

Adding insult to injury, Santa probably had no idea that his detritus had inconvenienced anyone. If she did nothing about it, he'd most likely go on with his life as if nothing had happened. Not a chance! Walking away from this would require legs! Functional ones, with knees intact!

Volgha stood there, fuming. She wasn't very handy in dealing with people. Plants, yes. Animals, to be sure. The occasional Viking was fine, as long as they were full of mead and beef and you toasted Valhalla with them once or twice. However, your standard, run-of-the-mill person came with all sorts of things. Feelings, needs, complications. It was disgusting, really.

She swore revenge and stomped back to the cottage, where her spirits were lifted somewhat at the sight of Sigmund, the snow lion. Volgha liked having him around. She never saw bears in the grove, and while she had no solid proof that Sigmund was keeping them away, she had no solid proof that he wasn't either.

He sat on her porch next to a magnificent stag, or rather, the earthly remains of that which was once a stag. Although the Witching Way prevented her from killing a creature from the wilderness, Sigmund had no similar compunctions, and occasionally murdered her up some fresh meat. She was grateful, although she was aware that a cat bringing her a fresh kill meant that he thought her a lousy hunter.

Well, he wasn't wrong.

Volgha looked over the offering and scratched the top of Sigmund's head in thanks. Irrespective of the spirit in which it was given, good meat was good meat. It was turning into a busy afternoon, between the new cause for revenge and the deer that needed dressing; but her cauldron would benefit from the venison, and she was running dangerously low on ground antler without her basket. Supposing she needed to draw down the moon, and she hadn't enough antler to balance out the cobwebs? She'd look a right fool, it goes without saying.

The spell she intended to cast later would have to wait for the clouds to part, so she passed the time by carving the stag into its useful parts, gathering firewood, preparing tallow for candles, and a dozen other mundane tasks that, for anyone else, might join together for an entirely humdrum collection of chores.

So much of witchery was bound up in this sort of thing. Between chores and revenge, witches had precious little time for magic. At times like these, there was little to differentiate them from hermits (intending no offense to those practicing hermitry, of course). This was all fine and dandy for Volgha. She was curious, but she wasn't a sensationalist. She was curious on a very practical level, not one that would get her into trouble, like Pandora or Prometheus who, like her sister, were nitwits by trade.

She was trying to work out some maths around the wards that obviously hadn't done much to protect her garden when a certain stillness crept into the air. She saw the light from the setting sun between the parted clouds, and a smile crept across her face. It was time to do some real magic.

The logs in her bonfire circle had nearly burned away, but the flames were still hot. She piled on a few more logs, and within moments the flames were leaping for the sky with an earnest fury. It was a princely sort of fire, one that the spirits of the grove were sure to appreciate. She didn't yet know what secrets the spirits would reveal to her, but any little whisper could be valuable beyond measure if she knew how to apply it.

Sometimes it was just gossip. The spirits of the forest were like anybody else, really. They wanted to tell you the secrets that they knew, but without being too obvious about it; hence all of the ceremony. They needed to have it wooed out of them a bit.

Other times it was griping. "You've planted where our gnomes like to dance," or, "Do you really have to put so many pine needles on the bonfire? They smoke terribly, you know."

On rare occasions, she'd learn something truly useful that would make all of the rubbish worth the bother. As she chanted over the fire and cast ground herbs into it, the veil lifted for her and showed her that this would be one of said rare occasions.

"Osgrey?"

"No, I'm Osgrey."

She'd only seen his silhouette at first—that was how things looked beyond the veil, very shadowy and murky—but she'd known it was him. She would have recognized him anywhere, murky shadows or not.

"It is you!" She ran to embrace him, but he dispersed in a puff of smoke.

"Careful!" said Osgrey, his cloud of smoke coalescing again a few feet away. "It's not easy being visible. I can barely remember what I looked like as it is!"

"Sorry," Volgha couldn't help the grin that spread across her face, "I'm just so happy to see you!"

"I'm happy to see you, too," replied Osgrey, with a smile that didn't quite look right. He'd had a very warm and bright smile as a person. Volgha imagined that trees probably didn't do smiles, so he'd probably forgotten how.

"It's a good fire," said Osgrey, "very princely. You did know that there is royalty among fires, didn't you?"

Volgha nodded. "I did. You taught me a long time ago."

"Did I?" Osgrey looked off into the distance for a moment, as if trying to remember. Then he shrugged. "Well, it's good that you know. What's new in the world?"

"Nothing much," said Volgha. "Alexia is still the queen, and that vile Ghasterly is her court wizard."

"Court wizard," Osgrey exclaimed. "I thought I was the court wizard. Is that not right?"

"You were, until my parents passed away. Now you're a tree."

"A tree ... oh yes! I'd forgotten."

The two of them stood in silence for a moment, gazing into the fire, watching the regal flames dance. Volgha hadn't talked to Osgrey in so long, she didn't know where to begin. He'd been her teacher, more father to her than her father had been. She wanted to ease into it, but, "Why did you turn into a tree?" fell out of her mouth with all the grace of a wet laundry pile.

"It's what druids do when it's time to retire."

"I'm sorry," said Volgha. "I didn't mean—"

"It's all right," Osgrey replied. "You're a little girl, and little girls have more curiosity than couth. You're famous for it, in fact."

"I was a little girl a long time ago."

Osgrey looked at her, squinting. "Oh yes," he said. "You're a woman now. When did that happen?"

"Gradually ... " She smiled at him. "I've taken up in your cottage. I say hello to you every evening."

"Of course you do," said Osgrey. "You'll have learned manners, being an adult and all. How do you spend so much time in the grove? Aren't you busy running the kingdom?"

She suppressed a grin. Trees have horrible memories, it would seem.

"No, that's Alexia. She's the queen. I'm just a witch now, I don't run the kingdom."

Osgrey's expression turned even paler. A ghost who'd seen a ghost.

"That can't be right," hepuzzled. "No, that can't be right."

"Yes, she's the queen."

"Oh fine," Osgrey gave a dismissive wave, "she can wear the crown, but royals don't run the show. I mean, not *really*." He winked and tapped the side of his nose conspiratorially, causing a tiny wisp of smoke to curl from his face.

"Of course she does," replied Volgha. "I know she's not the wisest person ever to sit a throne, but she's no more ridiculous than my parents were."

"Right, but I was running things back then, and you're running them now. *Properly* running them, I mean."

"What? What do you mean?"

"Royals may make the laws, but they don't run the bigger picture." Osgrey leaned in very close, his eyes wide and urgent. "There's a balance that must be maintained!"

Volgha knew about maintaining balances. Witches and druids all knew about living in harmony with nature and such, but she didn't think that was what Osgrey was talking about.

"What are you saying?"

"You must return to the castle," said Osgrey. "The kingdom needs a Warden."

"A Warden? What's that?"

"The king is the land, and the land is the king. But when he is not … do you understand?"

"No." Volgha began panicking as she realized that the clouds were starting to close up. "Quickly, what's all this about?"

Osgrey's eyes shot up to the darkening sky. "Darkness falls."

The spell was ending. Volgha felt the veil closing before her.

"I'll find you again!" she said.

"Set things right!" Osgrey's words echoed as he turned dark, and then he was gone.

If she'd been given a choice of things to have piled upon her, warm blankets would have been high on the list. New oaths of revenge and cryptic mandates from druids-cum-trees were still better than beehives, but it still counted as proof that what one wants is rarely what one gets.

Best to focus on the bright side. That's what an optimist would say, though that sort of haphazard cheer might land them in dangerous territory, with pessimistic witches. They've been known to hex people for less.

One piece of good news lurched into her mind from the gloom, despite her deepest desire to remain as angry as possible. Osgrey was alive! Well, sort of. He was *there* anyway, in the grove. If she could talk to him once, she could do it again. He'd seemed confused, like he'd forgotten how to talk to the living. Would that happen to her as well someday? Witches didn't turn into trees, but she'd heard stories of old ones who'd gone all warty and cackling, spending the rest of their lives stirring cauldrons full of glowing ichor atop windy crags. Not the worst way to go, she supposed, but neither was it her idea of a good time.

She needed to find out more about this Warden business. What was a Warden, and why couldn't her sister do it? She was the queen after all. Then again, if Osgrey had been this "Warden" while her parents were on the throne, perhaps Wardens had to be serious people, or know something about magic. Alexia would be disqualified on both counts. Volgha would have to dig into the Grimoire to learn more.

One last thing to do before bed. She still had a charge of magical energy within her and she knew just what to do with it. Smoothing her wild black hair back from her face, she looked skyward and loosed a howl that would send a shepherd into fits. It was a throaty, wolfen *aroo*, impossibly loud, and it carried up and over the ridge that framed the snowy valley.

She stumbled back to her cottage, thoroughly exhausted, rather annoyed, and ready for a long, rejuvenating sleep.

Moments later, miles away, the ears of the wolves slumbering around the forge in Santa's smithy perked up, and they were running in an instant.

SIX

VOLGHA FLEW ON HER BROOMSTICK, MUMBLING SWEAR WORDS as she watched the wolves drag the metal wreckage toward Santa's Village. They were repaying a favor, Volgha having misdirected some hunters from them a couple of summers earlier.

Volgha didn't like calling in favors. Those in her debt knew where they stood with her. Their heads didn't fill with funny ideas about being peers or friends. However, in this case, she didn't have any other means to move the wretched inconvenience across miles of rough terrain.

There was no road connecting her grove to Santa's Village, or to anywhere else for that matter. The absence of roads leading to the grove was Volgha's way of relaying to any would-be visitors exactly how welcome they'd be made.

She wished she could just ignore the entire thing. Economically, she was taking a loss. She was down one winter garden, her time and effort, and one favor from the wolves, for which she'd gain a single favor from Santa. She thought of asking for two favors, but that's just bad witchery. Witches aren't supposed to be greedy.

She'd also be upholding the Witching Way by showing this Santa character that vexing a witch—intentional or not—would not go unanswered. That was worth a great deal to witches everywhere.

The high timber walls around Santa's Village were covered in permafrost, which served to reinforce them as well as help them blend in with the surrounding countryside. However, it was doubtful that the camouflage was considered very important, given the constant noise of the place and occasional explosions or gouts of flame shooting up into the autumn gloom, like a war zone that had decided to retire somewhere snowy.

What had appeared from a distance to be a pair of great coal lamps standing on opposite sides of the main gate turned out to be something altogether less ordinary. Atop the wooden pedestals, which were banded with iron and twice Volgha's height, stood what appeared to be diminutive winged persons made entirely of brilliant golden light. The lamps were capped with great glass domes and no frost had gathered on them. Perhaps they were newly installed and hadn't had the opportunity to frost over yet.

The wolves dragged the twisted wreckage in front of the gate and started howling. That was unexpected. Volgha stood there, in the light of the golden lamps, realizing that she'd not decided exactly how she was going to reprimand this inconsiderate lout. She wanted to do her witchy duty, of course, but her natural distaste for people was rearing its introverted head.

The next unexpected thing to happen was the gate opening, just wide enough for the wolves to start moving through single file, which they did. Someone had just opened the gate to let a bunch of howling wolves come into the village. Non-standard behavior for villagers, to say the least.

The gate closed behind them, and Volgha was alone. Gritting her teeth, she suppressed the urge to simply rise up into the sky and have done with the whole thing. How would that look? She had to avoid giving him the idea that she was the sort of neighbor who always had cups of sugar to lend.

"Hello?"

The voice had come from within the walls. A wide-and-short portal opened in the gate, and there was a pair of eyes on the other side of it, looking at her.

"Hello," said Volgha, her mind suddenly going entirely blank.

"I want to speak to Santa," she said. "He lives here." She stood there silently, though she was mentally shouting the same swear word over and over, chastising herself for not having said something cooler.

"Who shall I tell him is calling?"

"Volgha, the Winter Witch," she replied. "And be quick, I do not appreciate being made to wait!"

That was more like it. It was the sort of "listen here, you" talk that made people act without thinking too much about it.

The tiny portal slammed shut. There was some excited chatter on the other side of the gate, which had the general air of several people scrambling to avoid being turned into undesirable things. That was a pleasant sound to Volgha, one she didn't feel she heard often enough.

After a few more seconds the gate swung slowly inward, and there stood a very short man in a woolen cloak and a pointy green hat. *Not a man*, she corrected herself, *an elf*. That was further cause to assume that Santa was the only non-elf living in the village; otherwise, guarding an enormous gate would be an odd duty for someone so small.

"Welcome to Santa's Village," he said with a smile and a flourish. "Won't you come in?"

Volgha walked in as quickly as she could without seeming rushed. Using one's gait to convey a sense of foreboding could have a particularly intimidating effect, though that wasn't something she'd learned from the Witching Way. It was something her parents had done.

"Right," she said. "Where can I find Santa?"

"Just stay on this road," answered the elf. "It ends at Santa's house. You can't miss it."

"Deal with that, won't you?" Volgha waved a hand over her shoulder, vaguely indicating the pile of wreckage. She didn't wait for an answer, but started walking toward Santa's house.

Volgha had flown over several villages on her broom before, but the only one she'd ever walked through was Innisdown, which stood about a mile from the gates of Castle Borealis. Innisdown had an inn, a smithy, cobbled roads, and all of the other things that proper villages were supposed to have—according to Volgha, who'd only ever been to Innisdown.

Santa's Village had some of the things she'd expected. It had a smithy and cobbled roads, as well as a bunch of buildings that she probably wasn't going to be able to identify without knocking on doors and acting like a policeman, asking questions like, "What's all this then?" Innisdown had those, too; both nondescript buildings and policemen.

But the smithy was much larger than the one in Innisdown—larger than the one in Castle Borealis, for that matter—and full of elves, hard at work making very hot pieces of metal bend into different shapes. It was also full of wolves, namely the ones who'd helped her deliver the wreckage. Why were they lying around in the smithy? The obvious answer was to warm up, as smithies tend to have heat to spare. However, the crux of this particular question was less *why* and more *how*. How did they come to have leisure privileges at Santa's smithy?

She'd expected a pub, but she didn't see one. What kind of village didn't have a pub? Beyond serving as a convenient social venue, pubs filled an essential role in village life, being the place from which people dragged their spouses home, nagging them all the while for having drunk too much. There was no way that the village was simply making do without one. She must have overlooked it.

The cobbled streets were exceptionally clean. The cobbles themselves were ground flat, which must have been expensive, and the streets were brightly lit by more of the strange lamps, like the ones she'd seen outside the gates.

There was something troubling about the fact that Santa's Village had a gate. Gates do not exist independently of walls, and walls around villages were meant to keep people out. None of the other villages—or rather, *the* other village—she'd seen had walls, which begged the question: is Santa expecting—or worse, *likely*—to be invaded?

If invasion is likely, then the wall is a good idea, but Volgha should be suspicious. If invasion is unlikely, then the wall is pointless, Santa is paranoid, and Volgha should be suspicious. Paranoid people make the worst sort of neighbors, always peering through the blinds at you.

Suspicion, then. Certainly the best weapon against paranoia, and far simpler than trying to work out who might be trying to invade.

Just as she was pondering that, Santa's house shrugged. It was more of a lurch, really. A massive, violent lurch, sending snow flying over everything nearby. When the powder settled, the house appeared to be covered in holly.

Houses don't shrug, Volgha thought, *or lurch for that matter.* The policy of suspicion decidedly applied to the house, then. She continued warily toward the door.

It was closed. That made sense, since it was cold out. But be that as it may, it always took Volgha a moment to remember what she was supposed to do with closed doors. She grew up in a royal family, and doors were never barred to her. After leaving the castle, the only door she had to cope with was the one to her cottage, and she went through it as she pleased.

She knew that knocking was the custom, no problem there. Just a quick rap to let someone inside know that someone outside had business within. The thing that she'd never sorted out was the inflection. By knocking faster, or harder, or in certain patterns, was one's knock interpreted as more or less confident? More or less important, urgent, or sincere? How long should one wait before knocking again, if there was no response?

She didn't mind coming off as brusque, she just wanted to avoid timidity. She settled on five firm knocks, half a second apart. It sounded almost ominous in her head.

One ... two ... three ...

The door opened, and Volgha's fourth knock charged inward, becoming a punch that sailed over the head of the elf who'd opened the door. He flinched. Volgha glared down her nose at him, adopting her best I-meant-to-do-that demeanor.

"Er, hello," said the elf. "Can I help you?"

"I'm here to speak with Santa," Volgha replied. "This is Santa's house." She cringed. "Is it not?" she added in haste, so as not to seem like the sort of person who offered up obvious facts when she was nervous.

"It is." The elf gave her a sidelong look. "Please come in. My name is Sergio, and you are?"

"Volgha, the Winter Witch."

"Pleased to make your acquaintance. May I take your, er, broom?"

"Certainly not." *Nice try,* she thought. He'd have to be a lot cleverer if he wanted to disarm her.

"As you wish," he said. "Right this way."

Sergio led her into a sitting room, to an overstuffed armchair in front of a blazing hearth. After pouring her a glass of wine that smelled like honey, he extended the glass to her, saying, "Please make yourself comfortable. Santa will be with you shortly."

She made no move to take the glass from him, and did her best not to let on that it was possibly the most exquisite chair in which she'd ever had the pleasure to sit. It was the sort of chair that you'd just about have to cover in nails to make it anything short of luxurious. Sergio gave a nervous shrug, set the glass on the end table beside her, and left the room at a quick step.

Stupid, wretched chair. The wine looked irritatingly delicious as well. The condensation on the glass told her that it had been served cold. On purpose! They'd managed to keep this room so warm that an ice-cold glass of wine actually sounded refreshing! As indignant as she was, she had to hand it to Santa: he was a shrewd negotiator.

The chill had completely faded from her bones after a moment. The entire situation was beyond decadent. It was tempting, and that was the worst part. Witches weren't the sort of people to be caught indulging in comfort. Dabble in indulgence, and very soon her little cottage—which had been more than sufficient up to that point— would start to seem too small. Not cozy, *small.* Not the sort of place she was used to, where chilled honey wine danced provocatively in her glass as she succumbed to the wiles of overstuffed chairs.

She wasn't having it! Was that his game then? Trying to butter her up, or showing off his extravagance to make her feel small? Envious? He had another thing coming if he thought—

She heard two faint thumps, like a pair of boots coming to rest. Her hackles raised, and her hackles were never wrong. Santa was standing behind her, in the other doorway that led into the room.

She suppressed a grin. If he weren't nervous, he'd have strode into the room without hesitation. That's what her father did when he wanted to put people on edge. Time to take the upper hand, while he was still summoning his courage.

"Come in," she said without turning around. It was her room now, and he was her guest. She'd not be plied with creature comforts. It was time for him to answer to the witch he'd vexed.

She remained seated when he came stiffly into her view, smiled, and extended a hand. She returned neither gesture, but merely stared at him coolly.

He was bigger than she'd expected. Tall, yes, but not excessively. He was trim and broad-shouldered, not young but certainly not old enough for his hair and beard to have gone completely white, not that it stopped them.

"I am Volgha," she said, "the Winter Witch."

"Santa," he replied, letting his hand drop to his side. "Santa Klaus."

"Yes, I know. I'm usually able to ignore that, yet here we are."

Santa sat in an armchair identical to hers, facing her. He seemed genuinely uncomfortable in the overstuffed abomination. This was going well.

"Here we are," he repeated. "The elves have told me that the wolves came with you, and they brought the wing."

"That's right," said Volgha. She hadn't thought about it, but now that he said so, it rather did resemble a wing. One that had been severely damaged in a long fall, but a wing nonetheless.

"I'd like to thank you for returning it to me. I'd thought it lost and was just about to make another. Even in its current state, repairing it will be easier than replacing it."

"That's fantastic," said Volgha, indulging in a bout of sarcasm that she typically reserved for her sister.

"Uh, yes," said Santa. "Like I said, very nice of you to return it to me. I hope it wasn't too much trouble."

"Oh, no," said Volgha, her eyes wide and her head lolling about as she spread the sarcasm about even thicker. "No trouble at all! In fact, I should thank you for carelessly letting you garbage tumble down into my grove!"

Sighing, Santa fidgeted with the long braids in his beard. "I've inconvenienced you. I'm very sorry about that, it was not my intention. May I ask—"

"Not your intention?" Frigid sarcasm yielded the stage to open hostility. "What was your intention, exactly, in flinging your debris about my forest?"

"It was an accident, I assure you. I had no intention—"

"I'm not interested in your intentions. I'm interested in your actions. I'm interested in why that monstrosity befouled my garden, why I was made to deal with it, and what you have to say for yourself!"

"I'm sorry," said Santa.

"What was that?"

"I'm sorry," he said again. "I had no idea that I'd so carelessly intruded upon you like this, and I offer you a full and unreserved apology."

She hadn't expected that. An apology, yes, but it entirely lacked panic. People who'd vexed her generally blubbered and tried to explain how she'd gotten it all wrong, and it was really kind of funny if you really thought about it. Oh, the laughs they'd share about it later!

But not this time. Not Santa. He wasn't begging or blubbering. He wasn't even trying to talk his way out of it, or blame it on one of his elves. He was taking it on the chin, and simply, sincerely, apologizing.

What was his game? Telling her what she wanted to hear, so he could placate her and earn forgiveness the easy way? He'd obviously never vexed a witch before.

"Keep your apology," she spat. "We have no friendship to mend. You owe me much more than a few kind words, Klaus."

"Of course," said Santa.

Finally a little urgency! A trembling chicken, come to roost in a coop of fear!

"How can I make it up to you?"

"I haven't made up my mind." All part of the dance. She'd intimidated people over this sort of thing before, and she was good at it. This was proper witchery in action.

"Take your time," said Santa. "Can I offer you some supper, some more wine?"

"Oh, that's rich. No such offer from you in all the years we've been neighbors, but now—since you find yourself under the scrutiny of an angry witch—now you decide to play the generous host?"

"You have me at an advantage. I didn't know that I had any neighbors."

"That's because I'm an exceedingly good neighbor. The kind from whom you've never heard a peep."

Santa nodded. "A better neighbor than I am, to be sure."

"Is that supposed to make me think better of you? A little grovel to undo an insult, is that what passes for deference with you?"

"I only meant that—"

"I'll not tell you again that I'm not interested in your intentions!"

Volgha was standing. She didn't remember rising from the chair, but she found herself looming over Santa in a very witchy pose, which most people found intimidating. Santa, it seemed, could not be counted among most people in this regard.

There was no urgency on his face, no fear. He gazed up at her with unnerving patience, like a wolf who'd stuffed himself on pilfered sheep, trying to decide if it was going to eat the tiny bunny who had just traipsed into his yawning maw. She'd sought his fear and found his teeth by mistake.

Intimidation is a battle of wills, so she couldn't back down. She stood there looming over him, willing him to blink. He didn't. She eventually managed to sit back down in her lavish monstrosity of a chair and lock eyes with him in silence.

The fire crackled in the hearth, the only movement in the room for several minutes. Santa looked away first, turning his eyes to the fire. She had the upper hand again, but only because he gave it to her. The nerve! As though she weren't capable of taking it back by force! This was going on her list of grievances.

Doing business like this was intolerable. She should have been back on her broom by now. Having reached a stalemate, there was nothing to do but blurt, "A favor."

"A favor?"

"Yes," replied Volgha. "I trade in favors, and now you owe me one. A big one. You wrecked my garden, and yet I returned your property to you with not so much as a minor hex on it."

Santa stared at the fire for a moment. He grimaced and sighed. Then he nodded.

"Very well," he said in a satisfying you-drive-a-hard-bargain sort of way. "On two conditions."

The fool was trying to negotiate! That counted as a vex in and of itself! She was strongly considering going right past favors and getting on with the hexes, but that was not the Witching Way. Witches don't walk away from favors, especially not from capable persons of means.

"You're on thin ice," she warned him. "Tell me your conditions, and I'll decide what arrangements can be made."

"I won't kill anyone. I'm firm on that, no more killing for me."

"No more?"

Santa's jaw flexed. It was apparent he hadn't meant to give that away. His expression became a warning, a beast bristling in its cage, daring her to come closer and trust the bars that held him.

"Fine," said Volgha, "no killing. I'm sure I'll have plenty of murder-free uses for you."

"And your second condition?"

"As long as I hold up my end of the bargain, no hexes or magic that harms me or anyone under my protection."

There it was! That was proper fear! Volgha didn't bother suppressing a grin at that one.

"Do you think me vengeful?"

"Frankly, yes," he said. "You have every right to be angry with me, and this is just the sort of situation in which vengeance tends to arise. The only thing about you that I can trust is that you're angry, and until that changes, I need your word."

Shrewd, wasn't he? Nice to hold sway over such a capable operator. This favor was costly, but turning out to be well worth it.

"Very well Mister Klaus," she said. "No obligations to murder anyone, and your village needn't worry about my vengeance."

"And I will fulfill whatever favor you ask as quickly and thoroughly as possible."

"We'll see if you're as good as your word."

"Yes," said Santa, "you shall. I don't suppose you're ready to claim it now, are you?"

"No," said Volgha. "When I am, I will find you."

"I look forward to setting things right. Just one more thing, if you'll humor me."

Volgha was near the end of her patience. "Yes?"

"There's a boar roasting in my kitchen ..." Santa smiled. "Won't you stay for dinner?"

THE BOAR WAS DELICIOUS. NOW THAT THE WHOLE FAVOR BUSINESS was settled, Volgha tried to relax a bit. It wasn't the sort of thing she usually went in for, but Santa was an amiable sort of fellow, or was at least sufficiently worried that she'd use witchery against him that he kept on his best behavior.

True, she'd promised not to place any hexes on him, but there was no real trust between them. That was normal for witches, of course, but why shouldn't *he* trust *her*? After all, the fire hex that she was keeping on the tip of her tongue was just a standard precaution. The fact that she'd standardized that on the way over shouldn't be read into too deeply.

No matter. She'd soon be on her way back to her cottage to enjoy what little measure of peace and quiet would be afforded her, until Alexia called her back for Loki's third sip. Of course, if that took too long, some other distraction would dangle in front of her like a sparkly bauble that simply screamed "don't forget about Volgha! She needs a good annoying, and it's not like anyone else will rise to the occasion!"

They ate in silence. Volgha thought that it was a perfectly lovely silence, which was a shame. Perfectly lovely silences never last, so the best option available to her was to break it on her own terms.

"Tell me about the lamps," she said.

"I'm sorry?"

"The lamps all around the village," she repeated. "What are the little winged lights?"

"Oh," said Santa, "those are faerie shadows."

Volgha's ears perked up. The Grimoire was infuriatingly silent on the subject of faeries, and she was keen to pick up whatever tidbits she could.

"They don't look like any shadows I've ever seen," remarked Volgha, as casually as possible. "Where are the faeries?"

"Probably asleep in the crooks of some great pine trees."

"Without their shadows?"

"Without *those* shadows. They have two apiece," explained Santa. "One for when the sun is up, and another for when it's set."

"And they let you use them when they don't need them?"

"Sort of. I'm keeping them safe until they need them again. I tried keeping them in a box, but they didn't like it."

"Why would the faeries care what you do with their shadows? They're not using them."

"No, the *shadows* didn't like it. They prefer to have a view. The faeries didn't seem to have an opinion one way or the other."

"I suppose you hold the dark shadows for them the other half of the year?"

Santa nodded. "The dark ones prefer the box. I think they sleep the whole time."

"Awfully nice of you to facilitate all of that."

"Nicer of them, really," he said. "They could just go hang them behind the moon like they used to do. The elves had to negotiate with them for a long time to seal the deal."

Volgha nodded. They finished eating through another lovely silence. As an elf was clearing the dishes, the house shuddered briefly, as though it had been rocked by a very efficient earthquake. No one reacted.

"What was that?" Volgha exclaimed.

"What was what?" asked Santa.

"I don't know, that's why I asked. Was it an earthquake or something?"

"Ah," said Santa with a grin, "that would be the jumping holly!"

"Jumping holly?"

"Really clever botany, if I do say so myself. And a bit of magic, but what isn't these days?"

"The house sort of lurched," said Volgha, "just as I arrived. All of the snow flew off it."

"That would be the holly," Santa replied. "It insulates the house from the outside. More importantly, it keeps the snow from sticking. Permafrosted walls always make a house colder."

"Very inventive," Volgha conceded, but not in an excited way. If she got too chummy too soon, she couldn't count on his trepidation.

"It's evening by our reckoning," he said to Volgha. "Would you like to take a rest before you head back?"

It was then that Volgha realized how tired she was. A big meal and a neighborly chastisement could really take it out of you.

"That would be nice," she said. "But don't think that counts as your favor."

"Of course," said Santa. "Consider it a further apology. I really am sorry, you know."

"So it would appear," she said. He seemed sincere, but he could still be up to something.

"Sergio will show you to a room," said Santa. "Feel free to stay as long as you'd like."

SEVEN

SANTA'S EVENING LINED UP FAIRLY CLOSELY WITH VOLGHA'S OWN. Like southerners, the folk who lived at the North Pole get tired about every sixteen hours, and need about eight hours' sleep to "even" things out—hence the term evening.

They don't all do it at the same time, however. That would require the sort of large-scale coordination that meant governing bodies and multilateral agreements, and those meant asking people to pay taxes, which was a subject best avoided. "Poking the sleeping bear" would be both an apt metaphor and, taken literally, a better idea.

Volgha was pleasantly surprised by the little room to which Sergio had led her. She'd originally thought Santa's house to be needlessly extravagant, but that extravagance turned out to be high-quality practicality. Witches appreciate practicality.

Her little room was far less lavish than the ones in Castle Borealis—not that she minded that in the slightest—but in the few minutes it took for her to drift off to sleep, she noticed that every feature of the room appeared to have been very intentionally crafted, down to the smallest detail.

She investigated it further when she woke. The mattress seemed to be filled with a mixture of straw and wool, woven in a pattern that offered a dense yet soft cushion. It stayed warm where she lay on it, and though there was only one blanket, it was more than enough to keep her toasty through her slumber. A fine woolen weave. Almost worth calling in her favor for one.

Almost.

It didn't end there. The carved wooden bed frame fit the mattress perfectly, and seemed to be joined entirely by clever cuts in the ends of the boards. She couldn't find a single nail. The floorboards were as smooth as glass, no risk of splinters there. There were pegs for her clothes, shelves for her things (had she brought any), and even a water basin that could summon water by simply twisting a pair of knobs. She could even adjust the temperature. Hot water! Without hearth or kettle!

She was sure that there was some sort of trick. There must have been an elf sitting silently above her in the ceiling, pouring water from a kettle when he saw that the knob had been twisted; still, it was fine treatment, and she appreciated the ruse. She decided to stay for a few more evenings, to learn a bit more about her neighbor.

The one thing about the room that made her a bit uncomfortable was the round thing on the wall. It was a polished wooden disc with a needle on it. One end of the needle was attached to the center of the wooden circle, with the other end moving around its edge very slowly, on a course that led it in a lap around the circle.

Sergio explained that they had discs just like it all over the village. It helped them to know where the village's evening officially began and ended. It kept them all operating on the same "skedgille," as he'd called it. She'd found the concept worrisome. Why was it that they needed to all be working at the same time? She'd hate it if she had to wait for all of the other witches to be around for her to do rituals and hexes and such. People should sleep when they were ready to sleep, that's how she saw it.

The concept did come in handy, as it meant she got to wander around the village when no one else was around. Sure, she'd been told that she was welcome to poke around anywhere she liked, but people tended to be on their best behavior when they knew there was a witch watching. Unseen, she could catch them acting naturally.

Santa was hiding something. It's a well-known fact that everyone is hiding something. To find out what, people needed catching unawares. Even if it was something completely uninteresting to her, finding out what it was would tell Volgha more about him than the combined weight of all the words that would ever stumble from his gob.

Most of the buildings in the village were dedicated to Santa's work. Some of his experiments were very large, so there were large barns that served to house them. She still hadn't managed to find the pub, but there was a long house where all of the elves seemed to live. Perhaps they did their drinking there, so their spouses wouldn't have far to drag them. That was considerate, but didn't irate spouses prefer to berate while walking through the streets? They did in Innisdown, anyway.

The most peculiar building was at the end of a cobbled street and across a steel-and-wood bridge over a large gully full of rocks. She thought it peculiar that only burly-looking elves ever seemed to go to it.

About half of the elves in the village appeared to be stockier than the other half, and while they were just as polite, they seemed a bit more … intense. They were more watchful, more intently focused on whatever was in front of them at any given moment.

Volgha spent a couple of evenings exploring the rest of the village, talking with the elves as well as the horses, none of whom voiced any serious complaints about their white-bearded boss. She only watched the building across the gully from afar, though, sensing that there was something sacrosanct about it.

It was the only building that had guards. They worked in shifts, relieving each other regularly. They were always there, always the bigger elves, armed with simple staffs. They held them like they knew how to use them.

Even the "guards" at the main gate didn't have staffs. They were more like hosts, there to offer hospitality to anyone who came knocking—or dropping off detritus, as the case may be.

Guards! Walls with gates in them! All of this was proof that Santa was hiding something, not that she needed further proof. She was starting to like him despite her best efforts, but she couldn't trust him until she figured out his shameful secret.

One evening, she walked by one of the great barns and saw a great wood-and-steel monstrosity. It resembled a penguin standing on the back of a bear and was damaged on one side. On the other side, it had a great metal wing that was covered in elfish script—just like the one that had lain waste to her garden.

She wandered in for a closer look. There was a hole very near what would have been the shoulders of the bear, inside which there was a seat that was roughly elf-sized. The seat was surrounded by levers.

"It looked better before," said a small voice from very nearby. Volgha craned her neck to look under the remaining wing and saw an elf sitting on a little stool. He was waving a stick at a bucket of rags and a block of wax, and the rags were polishing the machine of their own accord. It would undoubtedly have taken the elf a very long time without the stick.

"You're a wizard," Volgha mused aloud.

"Not really," said the elf. "I mean, the concept is a part of the Wizarding Way, but it's mostly just Applied Thinkery."

Volgha had heard of Thinkery before. It differed from standard, run-of-the-mill thinking in that one's mind is fairly useless for the purpose; if anything, being aware that you're doing it is a hindrance.

Volgha imagined that Applied Thinkery must be roughly the same, except you could make the rags do the work without your hands getting involved at all.

"What does all the writing on the wing say?" asked Volgha.

"This Side Up," answered Krespo, looking over at it. "Flaps To Rear, Ice May Form, Stand Clear During Flapping, that sort of thing."

"Ah," said Volgha, only slightly disappointed that there was no deeper mystery there. "The other wing landed in my garden, you know."

The elf froze, and his eyes went wide. The rags stopped their polishing and fell to the floor. His mouth hung open and his jaw quivered, as though he were trying to remember how to speak.

"Yes?" Volgha was irritated. She didn't often go in for idle chit-chat, and when she did, she wanted it to be pleasant. If she'd wanted his fear, she could have had it.

"I-I-I'm—" The elf abruptly shut his mouth, stood up, and took off his stocking cap. He held it in his hands in front of him, looking down as he turned it in his fists.

"I'm sorry," he groaned, the words surfing forth on a wave of blubbering.

"For what?"

"For your g-g-garden!"

"Yes," said Volgha. "Well, Santa and I have come to terms on that score, so there's no need to—"

"It was all my fault!" The elf burst into tears.

"*Your* fault?"

"Yes, ma'am. I was driving the flying machine. I'm so sorry!"

"You were driving it?"

"Yes, ma'am, I'm afraid so! I didn't want to be, but I was. I panicked, and the thing nearly fell off the cliff into the valley with me strapped into it!"

"Why were you driving it, if you didn't want to?"

"My name was on the form. It doesn't matter." The elf took a deep breath, trying to stop sobbing. "I made a complete mess of the entire thing! If Santa hadn't rescued me, the whole *thing* probably would have ended up in your garden, and me along with it!"

Volgha looked at him for a moment, and then at the wing that was still attached to the flying machine. It was an enormous contraption, and though a single wing was enormous on its own, it was only a small piece of the machine.

She considered what might have happened had Santa not intervened in the accident. It could have been a lot worse.

Then she considered what would have happened had Santa kept his affairs entirely upon the ground, where they belonged. Honestly, did he think that the sciences had any business putting things in the sky?

At least this blubbering coward seemed to have been bullied into his part in it. Intimidation was the key to flying, unless you happened to be a bird.

"Please don't hurt me!" Water was flowing freely from his face, and he was bawling with abandon. He had none of the silent stoicism of the big burly elves. Why hadn't one of them been chosen to be the driver?

"I'm not going to hurt you," said Volgha, "I'm not allowed, per my terms with Santa."

The elf exhaled sharply a few times, a wheezing sort of maneuver, possibly intended to control the physical act of fear. Witches were good at working with fear, but his was so palpable that it was hardly any fun at all.

"But you did cause me a deal of inconvenience," said Volgha. "Tell me your name."

"K-Krespo," he said.

"Do you know who I am, Krespo?"

"Of course ma'am. You're the Winter Witch."

Volgha's lips drew into a thin smile. She wasn't vain *per se*, but it was nice that her name had gotten around.

"That's right. You've inconvenienced a witch. You know what that means, don't you?"

"It means that I'm in a lot of trouble?"

"Right again."

Krespo whimpered. "Oh, I hate being in trouble! Is there anything I can do to make it up to you? Once I'm done polishing the machine here, of course."

"Of course. I can't think of anything I could possibly want from you right now, but you seem like an honest sort of fellow. Honest fellows are good to have around."

"Thank you, ma'am."

"We'll just say that you owe me a favor then," said Volgha. "I'll call on you when the time is right. Agreed?"

"Of course, ma'am! I'd be happy to!"

"Very well then Krespo. You and I have come to terms. So long as you fulfill your debt when I call on you, I have no quarrel with you."

"Oh, thank you, ma'am! I'll keep my promise, I promise!"

"I'm sure you will," said Volgha. "Until then, I need you to tell me something. A little token of good faith."

"Yes, ma'am?"

"That building at the end of the lane, the one with the guards. What is it?"

"That? Oh, that's the armory."

"Santa has an armory?"

"Yes," Krespo replied. "Well, he and the Faesolde do."

"Faesolde?"

"Elfish warriors," said Krespo. "Well, they used to be, anyway. A bunch of them live here in the village."

"I see," said Volgha. "And what's in the armory?"

Krespo shrugged. "I'm not sure, to tell the truth. I never go in there. Some stuff from the war, I know that much."

"What war?"

"The one between us and the goblins. It was a long time ago."

"And you're not allowed in?"

"Oh, I'm allowed," said Krespo. "Everyone's allowed, but only Santa and the Faesolde ever go in. The rest of us just sort of ... don't."

"I see," said Volgha. "So I wouldn't get in trouble if I went in?"

"I wouldn't think so, but I'm not sure. I've never seen anyone who wasn't Santa or Faesolde try."

Volgha cocked her head to the side and considered Krespo for a moment. Unlike everyone else she'd ever met, he didn't seem to be hiding anything. It was as though he'd been absent the day that guile was being handed out.

Nonsense. *Everyone* was hiding something, even this little devil. His apparent sincerity earned him an extra measure of suspicion.

"Thank you, Krespo. You've been very helpful."

"My pleasure!" Krespo smiled and gave a little bow.

LATER THAT EVENING, AFTER THE FORGE HAD GONE COLD AND MOST of the elves had retired to their longhouse, Volgha made her way to the armory. As she crossed the bridge, she kept an eye on the two guards flanking the door, each standing under a faerie lamp. They didn't move, just stood there, staring straight ahead. She mused that staring straight ahead must be prescribed in some sort of universal guarding manual, which all guards seemed to have read.

She took slow, purposeful steps down the path from the bridge. She could have simply gone Dim, but that would have failed when she opened the door. She needed to find out what Santa was hiding, and there was a good chance it was in there.

"Hello," she said to the guards, as she approached. They didn't react.

"I am Volgha, the Winter Witch." She stood up as straight as possible. "I'm a guest of Santa's, and was given leave to wander where I please. I think I'll go into the armory now."

Asking for permission might have cleared up any ambiguity, but what if they'd said no? Then she couldn't say, "I didn't know I couldn't do that." Not as good as a "yes," but it gave her some wiggle room.

They gave no response. Short of a crack on the skull from one of their heavy sticks, it didn't look as though anything was going to prevent her entering.

"Okay then," she said. "In I go."

She slowly made for the door, repeatedly glancing at the guards for any indication that they were going to object. They didn't move. She placed her hand on one of the big iron handles. Still nothing. She pulled the handle and the door flew open, surprising her at how well-balanced the enormous thing was. A hallmark of Santa's intentional craftsmanship.

Still nothing. She walked inside.

She was alone in what appeared to be the single room of the armory. A simple rectangular room, just silly with armor and weapons. The long walls were lined with elf-sized suits, each with different deadly implements mounted next to it. Swords, axes, spears, daggers, and more. All of them gleamed, from constant polishing or elfish charms, she couldn't be sure which.

At the far end of the armory, there was a single suit of armor and a massive rack of weapons. They were all human-sized, made of dull red steel, some pieces with gold or silver trim that had tarnished with age. The weapons had dark wooden hafts, and the pointed helmet had a painted white tip. They had to be Santa's, no question.

Just then a burly Faesolde elf came in behind her. She turned, and their eyes met for a moment. He seemed caught off guard to find her there. But he said nothing, just walked silently over to one of the elfish suits of armor, and sat in front of it, back straight, with his arms and legs crossed. He just sat there, as still as a stone, staring at the suit.

The armory was steeped in a forceful sort of silence that was more than just the absence of people talking. It was the sort of silence that would defend itself. Volgha's hackles went up, certain that they sensed the stares of a dozen armed librarians, patiently longing for a reason to hush her with extreme prejudice. She tried to breathe as little as possible.

"No more killing for me," Santa had said. The nicks and dents in his swords and armor left her with little doubt that he'd seen enough bloodshed to last a lifetime. She didn't know if this grim place was the thing that Santa was hiding, but he'd certainly never brought it up.

She sat on a little bench just beside the door, the only spot in the armory where she didn't feel as though she was intruding upon the lone Faesolde's vigil. She stared at Santa's armor, her mind working to incorporate all of this into what she knew about him.

For ages he'd been the noisy neighbor she was happy to ignore. Then he'd been the inconsiderate lout who'd ruined her garden. Then he'd been a gracious host, and now he was a warrior.

Former warrior, anyway. He had bothered neither to glamour his armor nor to polish it. It stood there, scarred, scuffed, and battered, with all of its patches and repairs. It was a memory of a different time, one that he hadn't talked about, but obviously one that he didn't want to forget.

Pasts are often complicated that way, she thought.

The faerie lamps in the corners cast a serene glow around the sparse room. It was a calm-before-the-storm sort of feeling. Volgha felt very much at peace, though the hairs on the back of her neck simply would not stand down.

Her reverie was broken by the sound of howling. She made her way out of the armory, the sound growing as she opened the door. She hurried through the door and closed it as quickly as she could, not wanting to disturb the room's other occupant any more than she'd done already.

As she crossed the bridge, she could see that the wolves had left the forge. They were milling around on the road, howling, sniffing each other, doing all of the standard wolfish things that they might be doing at any given moment, but in a more agitated way.

Santa was walking toward them as well, his big boots crunching over the fresh snow. He wore a stocking cap and had furs layered over what appeared to be a dressing gown. He'd obviously been sleeping.

"What's happening?" Santa approached a group of elves who were watching the commotion and talking excitedly with one another.

"We're not sure, Santa," answered one of the elves. He was wearing a stocking cap as well, and bundled in his cloak. "They just started howling."

Santa turned to look at Volgha as she approached. "Does this mean anything to you?"

"I'm afraid not," Volgha said. "They seem agitated."

"That much is clear." Santa stroked his beard, as if thinking. "Nothing else is amiss?"

"Nothing as far as we can tell," said the elf.

Leave it to a bunch of wolves to wait until everyone is asleep to start howling for no apparent reason. Who else was going to do it? Volgha supposed they were merely fulfilling some whim of a bored and capricious universe. Volgha was all too familiar with the whims of the bored and capricious.

The moon was behind the clouds, so that wasn't it. Volgha knew that the wolves had a special kinship with the moon, and would howl at her when she was full. She'd never heard an explanation for this, and that was fine. Explaining things robs them of their mystery, and witches appreciate mystery.

"They're not letting up," Santa said after a while. He shifted from foot to foot, breathing great puffs of steam into the cold air.

"Do you have any dried rockwort?" Volgha asked.

"Probably," Santa nodded, "in the apothecary."

"Bring me some," said Volgha. "And a brass bowl, and a flint and steel. I'll ask them."

"Go," Santa instructed one of the elves who'd been close enough to hear the list. "I don't suppose that counts as your favor?"

"And I don't suppose it earns me another one."

"Right."

The elf returned with the items Volgha had requested. She took them and walked closer to the wolves, who didn't appear to notice. They were very busy doing wolf things, namely howling and sniffing each other's nethers.

Kneeling on the snow, Volgha got to work. She used a handful of snow to cleanse the bowl and then crumbled the rockwort into it.

She whispered a few words of magic. Had anyone been close enough to hear, they'd have sounded like a sackful of consonants crashing through a thicket. She struck the flint three times over it, and a small flame rose up.

She drew in a breath and made a high-pitched whining noise

from the back of her throat like one might hear from a dog showing remorse over a besmirched region of carpet. One of the wolves trotted over and sat very close to her, their noses nearly touching.

Volgha made a gesture over the bowl that looked like it required a couple of broken fingers to achieve, and the little flame turned from yellow-orange to a deep shade of red. She whispered another bunch of consonants to the wolf, who gave a few syllables of bark-and-whine in response.

The red flame disappeared in a puff of smoke. Smiling at the wolf, Volgha scratched the top of her head. She smiled and panted, then got back to wolf business.

Volgha stood, crossed her arms, and frowned at the wolves.

"What is it?" Santa asked.

"An answer," replied Volgha.

"An answer? To what?"

"That's what I'm trying to figure out."

"What did the wolf say?"

"She said 'an answer.' Or something very similar to that. Wolfish isn't exactly a language like the one we use. It translates poorly."

"An answer," said Santa again, hoping perhaps that repeating it would add clarity.

The two of them stood there, watching the wolves and clutching their cloaks about themselves against the chill. Neither of them said anything for several minutes, during which time the wolves continued delivering whatever answer they'd started before.

Santa's face lifted abruptly, his eyes bright with realization. He looked at Volgha, appeared to decide that whatever he was thinking would take too long to explain, and turned toward the wolves again. Spreading his feet wide, he took in a huge breath, and shouted a great "HAOOOOOO!" in a deep and scratchy baritone.

For just a brief moment, all of the wolves stopped howling and turned to look at Santa with a sort of scowl. Unbeknownst to Santa, he'd just yelled a swear word in wolfish that would have him relegated to the back of the pack if an alpha had heard him.

The sound of Santa's howl echoed off into the distance, and a brief silence followed it. Then, faintly, they heard a response from somewhere beyond the walls. It sounded like another pack of wolves. The wolves heard it as well and resumed their howling.

"What was that you said to them?" Volgha had never heard that particular swear word howled before.

"Just making a fool of myself, probably." Santa smirked. "I wanted to distract them so we could hear what they were answering."

Volgha smiled. "Well played."

"Thanks. Sounds like they've got some cousins in the area, and they're saying hello."

"I don't think so."

"Didn't you hear the howling?"

"I did," said Volgha, "but that wasn't wolves."

"It sounded like wolves to me. What else could it have been?"

"I'm not sure, but it definitely wasn't wolves. Wolfish may translate poorly, but it always means something. That was gibberish. Wolves don't waste time with gibberish."

The wolves kept howling. More elves emerged from the long house, bleary-eyed from sleep and bundled in their cloaks. The wind moved the grey clouds slowly along the ever-darkening sky. No one spoke.

Volgha scanned the horizon, but nothing appeared out of the ordinary. She strained to hear the howling in the distance over the howling of the wolves, but it was no use. They could obviously still hear it and were persistent in offering answers, so she could only assume that it hadn't let up yet.

"Prepare the sleigh!" Santa turned and strode off in the direction of the house. Volgha followed.

"Where are you going?" Volgha's legs were not as long as Santa's, so she jogged to keep up.

"I'll figure it out once I'm beyond earshot of the wolves. I need to find out where that noise is coming from."

"No time like the present then," said Volgha.

"Indeed. Feel free to stay as long as you like." Apparently, Santa liked to work alone. Or possibly with his elves, but Volgha got the distinct impression that she wasn't invited.

"Thanks," she said, "but I'd better be on my way. Things at home need my attention."

Santa nodded. "Safe travels." He didn't look at her. He was focused on the task at hand. She walked a few paces behind him back to the house, where he went his own way, and she went back to her little guest room. She was already dressed, so she gathered the few things she'd left in the room, then threatened her broom severely and was on her way home.

EIGHT

N O SURPRISES AWAITED VOLGHA UPON HER RETURN TO THE COT-
tage. That was good. She took great pains to ensure that the
cottage was no more and no less than exactly what she wanted it to
be, so it stood to reason that there could be no such thing as a pleasant surprise.

Even on the rare occasions that they were pleasant, surprises
tended to be needy. They couldn't wait. She'd have to drop whatever it was that she was doing and say, "oh thank you, isn't that just
lovely!" Otherwise, she'd seem ungrateful; and even if she was, her
gratitude was her own business, as was her seeming.

Volgha preferred surprises that came with sufficient notice to decide whether she'd prepare to receive it, or possibly pretend that she
wasn't at home.

She wasn't tired, even though she felt as though she should be.
Her mind had the events of the last several evenings running on an
endless loop, and she knew she'd be useless until she'd had a proper
rest in her own bed. She lit a fire in the hearth, added some venison
and potato to the stew, and boiled some snow down to make tea. A
nice cup of rockwort tea would convince her mind that it was tired.

Among rockwort's many uses was a sort of forgetful, tingly
feeling that it produced when the tea was made just right. Not the
swimmy-headed, giggly feeling like with earthbloom, which tended
to make every idea sound like a good one, especially when it came to
writing poetry about former sweethearts and then sending it to them.
Rockwort had no poetic side effects.

As the cauldron and the kettle got down to business over the fire, she started leafing through the Grimoire, looking for any mention of a Warden. The few that she found were cryptic, off-hand references along the lines of "look ye to the Warden before ye pass," or "seek ye the Warden's approval," or "bring ye the Warden some of those nice cheeses he likes." The last one was circumspect, having been scrawled in the margin.

Osgrey had said that the kingdom needs a Warden, and that she should go back to the castle. She already had a job, thank you very much. Why should she take on extra work, especially if it meant having to solve problems all the time? Did the Wardenship come with assistants?

The Grimoire wasn't answering any of her questions. All it told her was that the land needed a Warden because the Warden was important. That sort of circular logic was very popular among politicians, but witches refused to think of anything as useful until it could be put to use.

It seemed that the role was vacant at the moment, so there was a job not getting done. Furthermore, it sounded like a high-profile sort of job, the kind that Volgha was keen to avoid. She'd thought renouncing her crown and moving to a cottage in the woods meant she'd given stressful work a miss. She'd hoped that, anyway.

She needed more answers from Osgrey. She needed to know more about this Warden business, namely how she might go about getting someone else to do it.

The water boiled and Volgha steeped the rockwort. It had a smoky smell, slightly pungent. She spooned a bowl of stew out of the cauldron which, coincidentally, smelled smoky and pungent as well. She read on.

There were a few other passages that mentioned the Warden, but she must have read them wrong. They seemed to refer to an animal, not a person.

The tea was strong, and it went to work right away. It wasn't long before she was having trouble keeping her eyes open. The pages of the Grimoire stopped making sense, not that they were easy to follow to begin with. Unlike wizards, who were known to eschew sleep for weeks at a time, witches knew that no good could come from meddling with otherworldly forces while drowsy. One careless mistake and a glance into the wrong mirror could reveal the shambling terrors held back from devouring our world by the flimsiest of tethers. A single glimpse of them could make one forget how to do anything more than scream themselves to sleep—or so Volgha had heard.

Time for bed, then. She'd neglected to warm the blankets, but she was tired enough that she didn't care. She could have fallen asleep in a snowdrift. It was a good thing, because that was exactly where she woke up.

What happened? She didn't remember having left her bed, though she must have done so. Had her sleeping self decided to break with the tradition of not freezing to death? That was the sort of thing she really wanted her sleeping self to clear with her first.

As her thoughts lumbered clumsily into her head from wherever they'd been while she was dreaming, one thing was clear: she'd somehow managed not to freeze to death. There was something warm behind her. She turned around, and there was Sigmund, the snow lion.

She wondered how long they'd lain there, nestled together at the foot of the tree that had once been Osgrey. She undoubtedly owed her life to Sigmund for sharing his body heat. Osgrey had once told her that Sigmund had never once been indoors, not even in the middle of winter's long night. He was immune to the cold somehow and had casually shared that immunity with her, like a southern beachgoer with an extra towel.

"Thank you," she said to him, through lips that were loathe to move. He gave her a slow blink, which in cat might mean anything from "you're welcome" to "if you wanted to drag a bit of string along the floor, I'd be much obliged."

Even with Sigmund's aid, she was nearly half dead; but that meant that she was still mostly alive, which was cause for celebration. The party consisted of lurching slowly toward the cottage. The *h'ordeuvres* were troublesome numbness and the threat of frostbite.

She only fell about a dozen times on the way to the cottage, which was an admirable performance for a woman who couldn't feel her legs. Fortune further smiled upon her when she was able to move a couple of fingers well enough to work the door latch. It only took a few minutes to get the door open and fall onto the rough-hewn floorboards. Yes, things were definitely starting to go her way.

Her cold-wrought delirium seemed to have converted her into an incurable optimist, which would feel wonderful for as long as it lasted.

She didn't have enough feeling in her hands to work a flint and steel, much less build a decent fire. There was half a log sitting in the hearth, which would be good enough for starters. She waved her hand over it and mumbled an incantation.

Everything that's capable of burning can do so because it has a little bit of fire sleeping within it. There's a lot of fire sleeping in tallow and lamp oil, a good bit in dry logs, and even just a tiny bit in water. If a witch needed to get a fire going quickly, her best bet was to look into the thing and awaken its inner fire. It's a difficult thing to explain, but it's sort of like the way one can stare at a person just right and make them notice.

Whoever had created the fire-summoning spell must have thought through this scenario. It was an unusual incantation, but very conducive to recitation through numb lips.

The log began to smoke and crackle. A little flame started to take root in the half of a log, and Volgha breathed a shivering sigh of relief. She was still painfully cold, but she was going to be all right.

She stumbled to the bed and pulled a blanket from it, then wrapped it around herself and returned to the tiny fire. It grew in size and brightness, consuming the log and soothing Volgha's shivering. After a while she regained enough feeling in her arms to add a couple of fresh logs to the fire, and before long she couldn't see her breath on the air anymore.

She sat quietly by the hearth for a long while, shivering so expertly one would think she'd taken lessons. By the time she'd managed to make herself a cup of tea and take a sip, she felt more or less herself again.

Well, not less. *More* herself, actually. Or, rather, more *than* herself. She couldn't quite put her finger on it, but there was some piece of her that hadn't been there before.

What's going on with the stew?

Volgha's head whipped around frantically but saw nothing and no one. She looked back at the fire, at the cauldron of stew that was steaming over it. It had the same smoky, pungent smell it'd had before her sleepwalking episode. That had occurred to her just before someone most certainly *had* asked about it, she just couldn't figure out who.

Shadows danced across the walls, courtesy of the flames in the hearth. Volgha heard her heart beating in her ears. She *was* alone, wasn't she?

"Hello?" she asked aloud, feeling only slightly ridiculous. It seemed her cold-induced optimism was wearing off.

It used to smell different, said the voice from every direction at once. It sounded familiar.

"Osgrey?"

What?

"It is you, isn't it? Where are you?"

Well, of course it's me, and I'm right here! There's no need to shout.

"I can't see you."

I'd imagine not! The windows are shut, and my tree is outside.

A chill washed over Volgha. Not the sort of chill you get from having slept in the snow for who-knows-how-long, but rather the another-tenant-has-signed-a-lease-in-my-brain variety.

"Wait," she said. "What? How did this happen?"

Well, I imagine you've been putting the wrong herbs in it.

"Not the stew. *You!* How did you get in my head?"

You should remember, you were there.

"Well, I don't! I was asleep!"

That's no excuse, said Osgrey. *I do some of my best work in my sleep. Consciousness muddles the faculties. Have you ever tried Thinkery?*

"Will you please just explain what happened?"

Oh, all right.

And with that, a memory poured into her mind just as the fire's warmth had poured the feeling back into her limbs. It was like a memory of her own, except she could see herself in it. She watched herself stride from the cottage, through the snow, and stop in front of Osgrey's tree, or rather, Osgrey.

Sigmund was there. He had a sort of growling conversation with the sleepwalking Volgha, who mostly nodded and gave the occasional grunt. Then he stood by and watched her place her palms on the tree and begin chanting. It wasn't any spell that she recognized, but her sleeping self seemed to know what she was doing.

Suddenly, an inky puff of smoke erupted from the tree, and the sleepwalking witch breathed it in. She collapsed on the ground, and everything went black.

Do you remember now?

"Yes," said Volgha, her brow creased in confusion. "No," she amended. "The memory is in my mind, but it isn't mine."

Think of it as ours. Neither yours nor mine, but a combination of the two.

"You're really in my head then."

For now.

"For how long?"

Osgrey shrugged, though Volgha wasn't sure how she knew that.

As long as it takes. I thought you'd be more pleased.

"I'm glad we get to talk, but this isn't the sort of thing I usually go in for."

Typical youth. When I was your age, I'd have loved to have a wizened elder set up shop in my noggin!

"Maybe druids and witches differ on that score," said Volgha. "What did you mean by 'as long as it takes?' As long as what takes?"

Sigmund and I can't be the Warden anymore. You have to do it.

"So you're both the Warden? How does that work?"

For now, suffice it to say that it does *work,* said Osgrey. *The more important question is how does the land work without one?*

"All right, how does the land work without a Warden?"

Suffice it to say that it does not.

Volgha had never been a fan of sufficing to say things, considering it a crafty way of saying, "I can't be bothered to explain it properly." Witches only ask important questions. The audacity of this cerebral interloper, evading important questions! And with all of her experience intimidating bits of trees!

Ah, ah, ah, tutted Osgrey, *you must learn to be patient. You can't intimidate all of your problems away.*

"Please," Volgha pleaded, pacing around the cottage, "can you stop speaking in riddles long enough to tell me something—anything—about the Warden? What does the Warden do, apart from being a druid and his familiar?"

Hmmm, what? Oh, right. Sorry. Give me a moment. Trees don't think as quickly as old men, you know. Have some of that stew, will you? It's hard to think over your hunger.

Osgrey was right, Volgha was starving. She spooned herself a bowl of stew and started eating.

To each their own, I suppose. I never had a taste for cragflower.

"It's my stew now," said Volgha, "no one asked you. Now tell me about the Warden."

Fine. All right, the Warden, let's see ... oh, yes! The Warden is a sort of emissary, you see. It helps if you think of the spirits of winter as a sovereign nation, and you send emissaries to sovereign nations. Only they're not a sovereign nation. Not really.

"Okay," said Volgha. "You said that you and Sigmund were both the Warden, so the Warden is a half-man, half-lion emissary to the non-sovereign, non-nation of the spirits of winter?"

Well yes, in a manner of speaking. However, if you look at it another way, that's not true at all.

"And what way is that?"

A far more accurate one.

"Then why did you explain it that way?"

The truth is a moving target, said Osgrey. *In order to hit it, we must dance around it until we can predict its path. Then we strike.*

"Go on then." Volgha gave a wave of her hand. "Maybe I'll get the gist of it if you just keep talking."

Here's hoping, said Osgrey. *The peace between the spirits and the people is like a gift. So long as it is given freely and gladly, the peace remains.*

"So the Warden brings gifts to pacify the spirits?"

No, not as such. Please don't interrupt.

"Sorry."

It's like a gift, only it's not. The people have needs, too, and the spirits are more than happy to provide, so long as there is respect. Not that the spirits need the people to show respect to them directly, of course. It's sort of ... symbolic.

The explanation wound its way through another bowl of stew, several cups of tea, and eventually one of the most uncomfortable trips Volgha had ever made to answer the call of nature.

Oh, that's it! The call of nature! Not that nature actually calls on the Warden, you understand.

"Not at all," said Volgha, "but I'm starting to notice a pattern."

Why yes, it seems that you are! But it's indistinct. Try putting it into words.

"Well," said Volgha, the beginning of a thought starting to coalesce—but that couldn't be right, could it?

Oh, just blurt it out. At worst, you'll eliminate one wrong answer.

"It's the thought that counts?"

Volgha could feel Osgrey's mind playing with the idea, but couldn't exactly read his thoughts.

That's not bad, he said after a while. *A bit oversimplified, but you've got the heart of it. Oh, you've got the makings of a Warden after all!*

"Thanks," said Volgha, "but no thanks. I'm sure we can find someone better qualified who would—"

Nonsense, said Osgrey. *You're the one, I've known since the first time I saw you. Don't be nervous.*

"I'm not nervous," Volgha replied. "I just don't want to do it."

You don't have to want to. It's your duty. Duty and wanting rarely go together.

"How is it my duty? I didn't enlist or anything!"

Your familiar should have explained all of this to you.

"I haven't got a familiar."

Haven't got one? Why not?

"You were going to help me with that before you turned into a tree."

Osgrey went silent, except for a pang of regret that Volgha felt from him. He hadn't wanted to become a tree, she realized.

"Becoming a tree," Volgha began, "it was your duty?"

Something like that, said Osgrey. *Spilled milk now, not worth crying over. In any case, you're going to need a familiar if you're going to be the Warden, so we'll need to sort that out.*

Despite all of the cold, the fatigue, and the headache involved in making room for a druid in her own mind, Volgha's heart leapt in elation. Osgrey was going to help her call her familiar after all! For just a moment, she was a five-year-old girl whose father had brought her new pony to a tea party.

Could you please stop that squealing? Osgrey shouted.

"Sorry," said Volgha, unable to suppress a smile, but doing her best to calm the little girl down.

Never mind. Open the Grimoire to the spells about woodland etiquette, will you? We'll get started there.

There were several chapters in the Grimoire that dealt with familiars. There were spells for attracting just about any sort of animal one could think of, as well as several she couldn't. Some of them had been written by southern witches, who had seen a number of creatures that couldn't survive the harsh winters at the North Pole.

There was, for example, several varieties of legless creatures called "snakes," which had poisonous teeth and were fond of biting people. An unfortunate combination. The only poisonous creatures she'd ever seen were spiders, who, unlike snakes, had more legs than they knew what to do with.

Then there were "butterflies." Their wings made them look a lot like faeries, but according to the Grimoire they were about as magical as tree bark, trees who were formerly druids notwithstanding.

She'd always thought that this enormous creature called an "elephant" would make an interesting choice for a familiar, but aside from their dislike of the cold, they ate more than she could reasonably provide.

Regardless of what sort of animal answered her call, it would be able to help her with the particularly difficult business of speaking with animals. She'd always thought how useful it would be to carry on deeper conversations than her basic wolfish fluency permitted.

Past the glottal intricacies of speaking with walruses, there were many spells in the Grimoire that required a familiar's assistance. Plus, she'd always have a friend around.

Right. There was that. *Always* having a friend around. She supposed that she could send it away on little errands, or that she could have some luck and partner up with something like a cat. Cats are fiercely independent, and she could relate. Unfortunately, Sigmund was already bound to Osgrey, and those bonds are like noses: most people only get one.

What if she ended up summoning a wolf? She cringed at the thought. She loved wolves, but wolves are pack animals. Pack animals like to be around their pack most, if not *all* of the time, and she'd be its pack.

She'd once spent a winter in a cave with a wolf cub that had lost his pack. His name was Errol, and he never stopped yipping incoherently about things he'd smelled or naps he planned to take when he was older. By some miracle, she'd always managed to refrain from yelling, "Why not take a few of those naps now?" with a dozen or so swear words mixed in. While it would have been momentarily gratifying, it wouldn't have been worth the eternity of crying that would have inevitably followed. When the sun rose and she reunited Errol with his pack, she was purposely vague in telling him where the cottage was, in case he felt like popping by.

She read over the spell to conjure a familiar. It turned out that one didn't really get a choice in the beast that answered the call. It would be something in the vicinity, and its spirit would bond with hers instantly. There were a lot of wolves near the grove, so she started thinking of other places to cast the spell.

Familiars did, of course, become more intelligent as a result of the process. They shared in the wisdom of the witch to whom they'd bonded. They also lived a lot longer, often as long as the witch him- or herself. It's practically a marriage, a thought that made Volgha's nose crinkle.

A lot of witches ended up with birds. Birds are a lot like cats, despite their natural rivalries. They hate being cooped or caged, and spend lots of time away from their flocks building nests, digging worms, or looming over carcasses, all the things that birds like to do. Volgha rather liked birds and thought that she certainly wouldn't mind having one of those around.

And then it came to her all of a sudden, the way that inspiration likes to do. Why not go somewhere where only birds can go?

The belfry! The wizard's tower would be better, though a certain necromancer who would remain nameless had put a damper on that.

You mean Ghasterly, don't you?

"What part of 'would remain nameless' did you not understand?"

All of it. He's already got a name. Ghasterly.

Volgha very nearly engaged in an explanation of idioms, but knew that she'd have more success explaining the concept to … well, to a tree. It was a silly line of inquiry, and the Witching Way did not agree with silliness.

The belfry would be fine. It was very tall, and besides, there were no wolves near the castle. Her sister had hunters kill any wolves who wandered into her forests. Volgha had consequently spent a great deal of time setting up wards that would wave off any wolves who came near. The wards were like magic warning signs that suggested the rabbits who lived there were poisonous. It sounds ridiculous, but wolves are notoriously gullible.

She had most of the herbs on hand already, as it was fairly common stuff: earthbloom, frostberry, gravelmoss, and a few others. The real problem was the pearls. The North Pole didn't have oysters. They were coveted treasures in the North Pole, and those who had them usually hid them away. The only person likely to have any would be Her Majesty.

She said a swear word. If only she'd had this idea at the outset of Loki's stupid riddle, she could have gotten some pearls in return! It was too late now. Since they were children, she and her sister had always insisted on upfront terms with one another, and it was really the only thing that kept them from each other's throats. Volgha couldn't even collect favors from her sister because Her Majesty's lawyers would insist on suing Volgha into absolving the crown of the debt. The crown didn't like to have debts, which was horrible news for witches.

In any case, since she didn't get it in writing up front, the whole

Loki business was just a nice thing she'd done for her sister. It was a disgusting state of affairs, but there it was.

No matter. The White Queen was always asking Volgha for something. If she simply waited long enough, the opportunity would present itself again.

That would be it, then. She'd work on acquiring the rest of the things she needed, and her sister would probably ask for something in the meantime. She'd seen a clump of gravelmoss near the edge of the grove about a month ago and was fairly certain it would still be there. She'd go and get it after a good evening sleep.

She was so tired that it was a perfect time to start darning a pair of wool socks. She could barely keep her eyes open so she wouldn't have to work on it for long, and she could tell herself that she'd tried. As a rule, witches don't lie to themselves, but darning socks was so boring! She *would* need to get it done eventually, as fully intact socks at the North Pole was essential to survival. Well, survival of a full complement of toes, anyway.

The sun was well on its way to setting for the winter, and the winter at the North Pole was very, very cold. It was the sort of cold that didn't want to leave until the sun started to rise at Imbolc, the first observance of spring in the Witching Way. Something as careless as a hole in the toe of an otherwise perfectly cozy sock was basically an invitation for frostbite, and this would *not* be the winter that she lost a toe.

Volgha usually hibernated her way through the brutal cold of the North Pole winter. The time between sleep and wakefulness blended together, and she was often unsure which was which. It was a time of year that witches lived for, aside from the relentless cold. The veil that separates this world from that of the spirits is remarkably easy to traverse when you're half asleep and half starved.

Or you're just having fever dreams, said Osgrey.

"Quiet, you."

The trick was to keep track of the passage of time so that she could determine the precise moment of the winter solstice, marked in the Witching Way by the festival of Yule. It was the exact middle of the long winter's night, and the point at which one could practically reach a hand through the veil with no preparation at all, and give a dear departed relative a good smack for something they'd gotten away with by expiring before justice had been served—if she were interested in that sort of thing.

She got a few stitches in, and as predicted, started nodding off. Satisfied with the progress she'd made, she set the sock aside and got into bed.

NINE

S HE SPENT SEVERAL EVENINGS AT HOME, WHICH WAS A NICE CHANGE of pace. Despite circumstances entirely within her control, she had to spend most of her waking hours *not* darning socks. It would have taken her no time at all if she'd simply sat down and done the work, but then she'd have been entirely lacking sources of angst and existential struggle.

A witch needed angst, especially in the North Pole. Otherwise, all she had to focus on were the very real problems of freezing to death, starvation, cottage fever, or in light of recent events, the fate of everyone who lived in the North Pole, according to the druid living in Volgha's head.

Angst was easier. *It's the socks,* she allowed herself to think. *Everything else would be easy if it weren't for the socks.*

You know that isn't true, said Osgrey.

"Don't tell me what I know," she quipped back at him.

But I know what you know, said Osgrey. *We're sharing thoughts, remember? I know as well as you do that it's not just the socks.*

They'd had this conversation more than a few times. She'd sit down, stare at a sock for a minute, mumble about it under her breath, and eventually pick up the needle and thread. A couple of stitches in, she'd remember a bunch of herbs that really needed bundling or a holly bush whose trimming was far too essential to put off for another minute. She'd feign annoyance in setting the sock aside and rushing off to manage the distraction.

She'd also spent quite a bit of time going through the Grimoire, reading tea leaves, counting the clouds hanging near the moon, and even scrying into some very deep corners of the spirit world via her bonfire. That had provided some very helpful insight as to how one might host an Airing of Grievances with one's ancestors, which was sure to come in handy someday, given her family tree.

Oh well, nothing to be done about the socks then. She thought of calling in her favor from Krespo. Would a lifetime of sock-darning be that tall an order for someone skilled in Applied Thinkery?

She had almost everything she needed to summon her familiar, with the singular exception of the blasted pearls. She considered asking for Santa's help with that, and wished that she could dismiss the idea out of hand. She was about as fond of cashing in favors as grannies were of paying full retail, but she was out of options. She couldn't go south and buy pearls because she didn't deal in money. She had neither the time nor the patience for the sort of work that yielded coin.

Osgrey didn't see the problem with cashing in Santa's favor, but then why would he? What do druids know about favors?

I'm doing you a favor right now!

"Oh no, you're not!" Volgha waggled a finger at the ceiling of the cottage with remarkable veracity. No one, not even a witch's mentor, decided what did and did not constitute a favor on her behalf.

I'm training you up to be the Warden. It's an important job!

"I still haven't decided that I want to be the Warden," said Volgha, "and calling it a job doesn't help. I presume that this 'job' doesn't pay anything, does it?"

Only the satisfaction of knowing—

"So no, then."

Only if you find no value in assuring—

"I don't."

The feeling of someone else's irritability from within her own head was unsettling, but not as unsettling as her own.

It was still warm above the clouds, Volgha mused as she headed for Santa's Village. Osgrey noticed it, too. Could he perceive temperature if he only had access to her mind? She resolved not to think about it too deeply. She couldn't imagine any useful answers resulting from further inquiry.

Since she had a truce with Santa—favors notwithstanding—she flew over the gates and landed inside the village. One of those big wooden circles with the needle on it was mounted above the entrance to the forge. It indicated that it was near the end of the skedgille. Santa was probably just sitting down for supper. A fortunate time to have arrived.

Once a witch has donned the pointy hat, there are two distinct smiles that she quickly becomes accustomed to seeing: the panicked 'please don't turn me into something without bones' sort that's equal parts fear and politeness, and the oafish 'nice hat' sort, that's entirely devoid of self-preservational fear.

The elves that she passed were still giving her more of the former, which was good. Truces with witches should be brokered individually, not as a class action.

She reached the door to Santa's house, and nearly opened it out of a habit she must have formed while she was his guest. Consider the ramifications! There was a very real possibility that he might find occasion to call upon her home someday. If she barged in on him now, would turnabout be fair play?

Her blood went cold at the thought. What if he didn't call ahead at all? What if he showed up unannounced, and she said something completely stupid when he knocked, like, "Who is it?" before a more rational, logical part of her thought to say something like, "Sorry, you've just missed her," … or better still, nothing at all?

She panicked. She spun around, fully intent on flying back over the gate and knocking on the little portal in the front gate and doing the whole thing properly. Unfortunately, Santa was standing right there.

"Volgha," he said with a smile that was at least half genuinely glad to see her, "to what do I owe the pleasure?"

Pleasure? The nerve! When did people stop dreading visits from witches? She needed to get this under control.

"Nothing!" she blurted. "What? Don't get any ideas!"

"Sorry," said Santa, his eyes wide and focused intently upon the ground.

The tension between them sought frantically for a knife with which to cut itself. Even Osgrey seemed fidgety.

"I was just about to have supper," said Santa, breaking the silence. "Would you care to join me?"

"Only if I'm invited," she replied, feeling certain that she'd spend half the evening picking that response apart instead of sleeping.

"Please." Santa opened the door and ushered her in.

Sergio took her cloak, and she even relinquished her broom this time. She didn't really need it if things got ugly, and she thought perhaps Santa could do with a false sense of security.

Santa offered Volgha a glass of honey wine in the study while the table was being set, which she accepted.

Don't drink too much, warned Osgrey.

"Mind your own business," Volgha snapped.

"What?" asked Santa.

"I've never had wine cold before," she told him, enjoying the crisp sweetness of it.

"I hadn't either, until we got the insulation right." Santa gestured toward the walls. "We rigged up a system that runs hot water through copper pipes. It helps the jumping holly keep the permafrost from collecting, and it stays nice and toasty in here. No need to keep your wine warm when you don't even need to wear fur."

It was a humble boast, but Volgha let it drift past without comment. He'd done some amazing work with the house. She was impressed.

That's how it starts, said Osgrey. *First, you're admiring the walls, and then you're an indoor person with clothing for different occasions.*

"Keep it down in there," Volgha hissed.

"I'm sorry?"

"What have you been doing lately?" she asked, changing the subject.

"Working in the forge, mostly. Some of the fittings for the flying machine's wings sheared a little bit too easily, so I'm remaking them from steel instead of brass."

"Interesting," she said, letting the word trail off into a gloom of mistrust and suspicion.

Santa leaned forward conspiratorially. "I'll fly it somewhere else."

"That would be wise."

"Oh," Santa suddenly stood up, "and then there's the hill." He walked over to a small desk in the corner of the room, opened one of the drawers, and brought out a roll of paper. He unrolled it and Volgha saw a charcoal sketch of a hilltop, bearing what appeared to be a series of giant eggs sitting on pedestals. The eggs looked like they'd been pinched in the middle until there was a hole going through them.

"These were the 'wolves' that our friends were answering," Santa explained. "The wind howls when it passes through them. They were probably covered in frost for ages, but they're not anymore. It's pretty high up, and it's warm up there."

"I've noticed," said Volgha. "Warmer the higher you go. But what are they?"

I've seen those before, said Osgrey, *but I can't remember where.*

"No idea," said Santa. "They're old, that's for sure. Really old. We put some wooden boxes over them for now, to prevent the howling. It was getting hard to sleep around here."

"Fascinating," Volgha mused. "I'd love to see them sometime. Maybe I can do a bit of scrying to determine what they are, and who built them."

"Wolf decoys, maybe?" Santa suggested. "Perhaps people who lived in the hills a long time ago figured out that they could get the wolves to leave them alone if they thought there was already a pack up there."

"That's possible."

They sat quietly for a moment, sipping cold honey wine and staring at the crackling logs in the hearth.

Now's as good a time as any, said Osgrey.

"Let me handle this," whispered Volgha.

Santa looked at her expectantly.

"I need a favor," Volgha said. "You asked 'to what do I owe the pleasure,' and that's the answer. I've come to collect my favor."

Smiling, Santa nodded. "Happy to be free of my debt. What will it be?"

"I'm planning to cast a very important spell," Volgha explained, "and one of the components is out of my reach. You will help me procure it."

"And what is it that you need?"

"Pearls," said Volgha. "A dozen of them."

Santa stroked his beard. "That's a tall order. I don't have any, and that's not something that the elves can hammer out in the shop."

"I know," said Volgha. "Fortunately, I know where we can find some … but you have to swear never to breathe a word of what I'm about to tell you to anyone."

"My lips are sealed."

"Good." Volgha loved keeping secrets, and telling them meant they weren't hers anymore. They were no longer secrets, for that matter. They were just little-known facts. Those were all right, but not as good as secrets.

I already know it, if that makes it easier to say.

"My sister has some pearls," said Volgha, ignoring Osgrey.

"Oh …" Santa paused. "Sorry, but that's not much of a secret."

"There's more," she said, still working out how best to say it.

When in doubt, blurt it out!

"My sister is the White Queen."

Respect for your elders, that's new.

Volgha momentarily cleared her mind of everything except a particularly ominous peal of thunder. She hoped Osgrey was capable of gleaning a warning from the subtext.

"No kidding?"

"I'm afraid not."

"So that makes you …"

"The Winter Witch."

"To be sure," said Santa, "but if the queen is your sister, that makes you … what, a princess?"

"By birth," Volgha replied with a sigh, "but I've renounced it."

"Really? Why?"

"Because I like being left alone," Volgha snapped.

Well said, Osgrey concurred. *That's good hermitry there.*

Santa nodded, apparently understanding that further inquiry would be fruitless. Introverts are particularly adept at shutting down subsequent "whys." They're most likely to answer with, "I knew that talking to you was a bad idea," but only using swear words to say it.

"And Her Majesty won't give them to you?" asked Santa.

"She'll ask a thousand questions, and she'll want a thousand things in return. She's an intolerable debutante. It would be far easier to steal them."

"Easier to steal treasure from a queen than to have a conversation," said Santa. "We live in interesting times."

"Indeed we do. Are you up for it?"

"I owe a witch a favor. Does it matter if I'm ready?"

"No, I was just being polite. Can you dress like a noble?"

TEN

"TELL ME EVERYTHING," SAID THE WHITE QUEEN. HER FACE WAS inches from Volgha's, her manic expression so taught that Volgha could hear the blood pumping through the giant vein in her forehead.

"Very old money," said Volgha.

One of the things that their parents had tried to instill in them was an appreciation for the age of a person's wealth. New money was vulgar. The faces stamped on it belonged to people who were *still alive* in some cases! Who could say whether those people would even be remembered in a hundred years? The White Queen would sooner die than spend unfashionable money.

Of course, Her Majesty's treasury was actively coining money with her face on it, but that was different. That was for the common people to spend. *Her* money was old, and every face on it belonged to someone who was both renowned for something and long since dead.

"Fabulous," the queen exclaimed. "And how did you meet him?"

"Er, in the Innisdown market. He was trying to buy—"

"The whole market?" The queen was fanning herself, despite the chill in the room.

"Um … yes. Why not?"

"He sounds like quite the entrepreneur!"

"That much is true," said Volgha, glad to finally inject a bit of truth into the story. The best lies were always rooted in the truth, and this was the only bit of the story thus far that had so much as touched the ground.

"And he's coming here?"

"Well, he was talking about his collection of money piles, so naturally I started going on and on about how big and old *your* money piles are, and he said that you sounded like a very beautiful and intelligent person that he simply had to meet."

She really is your parents' child, remarked Osgrey. *I often wondered how you managed to escape the madness.*

"Splendid!" The queen's fingers were drumming against each other just below her chin. That move meant that a scheme was imminent.

"Chamberlain!"

"Yes, Your Majesty?" He'd been standing just behind her, as usual.

"Plan a reception for this Baron Klaus of North Uptonshire."

"North Uptonshire, Your Majesty?" Chamberlain's eyebrow was raised. "Are we familiar with such a place?"

The Queen's face tightened into a rare moment of thoughtfulness. Her eyes went all squinty and started moving toward the ceiling. It was obvious that the exertion didn't agree with her.

"It's southern," Volgha blurted. Both the queen and Chamberlain turned slowly to look at her, noses wrinkled in distaste. "But still far enough to the north to be credible," she said, wishing that she'd come up with a different sort of lie.

"*How* far north?" inquired Chamberlain.

"Well, they don't wear short pants or anything," said Volgha. "And we all know that people *too* far south don't respect old money enough to maintain piles of it."

"That's true," said the queen. "And borders shift all the time, don't they? Just because North Uptonshire isn't an Aurorian province today, doesn't mean it can't be one tomorrow?"

"Very true." Volgha was relieved that she'd managed to move the conversation back on track.

"Well, that's settled then," said the Queen. "We'll have a reception for the Baron of North Uptonshire as befits his piles!"

"At once, Your Majesty. And how much fanfare and pomp will the baron require?"

"Trumpets," answered the White Queen. "But no doves."

"Very good, Your Majesty. The usual amount."

"Maybe just a few doves," Volgha suggested. Distracting her sister with trivial details would keep her from thinking about important things that might foil her plan.

The queen appeared to think about it for a moment. "Yes, of course. Old money expects doves, doesn't it? But we still want to seem aloof."

"Your Majesty's most standoffish doves, then." Lord Chamberlain's face was unreadable.

Did he just make a joke? Osgrey seemed surprised. *I don't think I've ever heard him joke before.*

"Marvelous!" exclaimed the queen, who stood abruptly and started walking from the room. Lord Chamberlain hurried to follow her because that was his job. Volgha did as well because her sister might throw a tantrum otherwise.

"When will he arrive?" The queen stopped briefly in her brisk walk down the hall to sneer at a vase on a pillar. She pushed it over and smiled as it shattered before continuing on.

"He's already on his way," answered Volgha. "I don't believe he'll make it for supper, so he'll rest at the inn's most posh suite before he comes to the castle."

"A brunch reception then, Your Majesty?"

"Obviously." The queen rolled her eyes. Then, apparently having had a thought, she spun around to face them with a wide-eyed smile.

"Where is Loki?" she practically screamed. "Is he here?"

"I'm afraid not, Your Majesty," said Lord Chamberlain. "He's not been seen since we dropped him in Innisdown, following his second sip of the potion."

"Aww," muttered the queen, sulking and kicking a puppy that wasn't there.

"But we can have jugglers." Chamberlain drew the last word out in a sing-song way.

"Flaming jugglers!" The queen's face was instantly manic again.

"Very good," said Chamberlain.

She means jugglers with flaming pins, doesn't she?

"Who knows?" said Volgha.

"I do!" said the queen. "Come, Volgha, we'll need to sort out our gowns and hairstyles for the brunch!"

Volgha had seen this coming but had to suppress the urge to retch nonetheless. She hated playing dress-up with Alexia, partially due to the general silliness of the exercise, but mostly due to the tantrums that would inevitably erupt when her sister thought that Volgha looked better in a dress than she did, failed to compliment her accessories frequently enough, or dared to wear a different shoe size.

Just think about the pearls, she thought.

That's the spirit, said Osgrey.

The jugglers were not on fire, to Osgrey's relief, and to the relief of the jugglers as well, no doubt. Chamberlain assured Her Majesty that they would juggle some flaming things later, after the baron had arrived. Her Majesty seemed placated and proceeded to spend all of her time fussing with Volgha's gown.

"I look ridiculous," Volgha murmured.

I wish I could argue, said Osgrey. Volgha could hear him smiling.

"Oh, shut up."

Following the tantrum that largely consumed the entire wardrobe planning fiasco, Her Majesty had settled on a flamboyant white-and-gold gown for herself, and a ridiculous green-and-pink one for Volgha. It was Volgha's fault for looking too good in everything, of course. This was simply the equalizing solution. While Her Majesty's coiffure created a truly regal plinth for her crown, Volgha's head looked like a tousled family of weasels who'd been cursed with ringlets.

She'd considered astral projection, thinking that literally escaping her body would be a suitable coping mechanism for this particular brand of humiliation; however, being in her body was the one vantage from which she couldn't see herself. Plus, Osgrey had insisted that she not leave him alone in there.

The standard courtiers and sycophants were all in attendance, most notably the Viscount of North Downyhedge, who'd had so much to drink just standing in line to enter the castle that he'd fallen asleep, and was pressed into service as Her Majesty's footstool.

The court musicians had yet to make it through an entire song without Her Majesty commanding them to stop and play something else. Just as she was in the middle of ordering them to play, "The one that goes dum-dee-dum-DEE-dum-dum," the really long trumpets in the gallery went up to toot the arrival of their special guest.

The enormous doors at the end of the hall opened and in strode Santa, wearing an outfit that overshadowed Volgha's for insanity.

Before she'd left Santa's Village to come to the castle, she'd had a long discussion with Krespo about what all of the most fashionable hangers-on at court were wearing, so that he could stitch up something for Santa. Osgrey had tried to point out that Volgha didn't pay attention to fashion, but was dismissed as lacking authority on the subject himself. She could see now that he may have been onto something.

It was a bright red suit with extremely tight breeches and a coat with long tails. It was trimmed in white fur. That much might have passed for respectable, but Volgha cringed when she realized that she'd provided too much detail, especially pertaining to what the *ladies* of the court were wearing. As a result, it had great poofs at the shoulders, a tightly-laced corset, insatiable high heels, and a matching handbag. The cumulative effect certainly turned heads, whatever else could be said about it.

Whether Santa was wearing too much rouge or was simply mortified was impossible to tell.

"Baron Klaus," announced Lord Chamberlain, "of North Uptonshire."

The musicians took up the prearranged fanfare. The lackadaisical doves were released and promptly flew to the nearest places to perch and look bored. Santa walked slowly, awkwardly down the long, red carpet while trying to ignore how closely he matched it. He was followed by Krespo, who was dressed in an equally ghastly green velvet waistcoat and matching skirt. Krespo had less trouble walking in the heels.

The courtiers gawked in silence. *They'll certainly have plenty to say to one another later*, Volgha thought, though they were undoubtedly waiting—with baited breath—to see how Her Majesty would react before displaying any opinion of their own.

Volgha didn't move. In addition to the shock of Santa's ridiculous appearance, she was frozen with fear at the possibility that the jig was up. The whole caper was on the verge of going horribly, horribly wrong, and she was going to have to run to the belfry in a dress that was wider than she was tall.

Does he really look more ridiculous than everyone else here? asked Osgrey. *I've never understood fashion.*

Santa stopped in front of the high table and wobbled on his

heels. The fate of their entire venture teetered on that scrumptious come-hither footwear. Fortunately, Santa remained afoot.

"Your Majesty," said Santa, who then removed his wide-brimmed hat, crouch low with one toe pointed forward, and delivered the most furiously formal bow that Volgha had ever seen.

That was saying something. She'd been a princess once.

It was magnificent, the sort of maneuver that doctors advised against performing without a significant amount of stretching beforehand. Volgha looked to her sister, who appeared to be just as impressed as she was. It was helpful that the queen lacked the capacity to hide her emotions, the will to do so, or both.

"Baron Klaus," said the queen, "won't you come and sit between my sister and me?"

Santa nodded. Volgha muttered a swear word under her breath and moved over a seat. She'd hoped to keep herself between them, the better to maintain the ruse. She didn't know if Santa was as good an actor as he was a bad neighbor.

Making his way up onto the dais was a challenge. Santa's ensemble included a cane of polished ebony, to which he clung for dear life. His eyes burned with hatred for the bizarre and unnatural footwear.

Those shoes have to be a cruel joke, said Osgrey, *obviously invented by someone who'd never personally had to wear them.*

Volgha hated high heels as well, and actually found them easier to walk in after a few glasses of wine. Or at least she minded falling down less.

He finally found his seat, though Krespo was left standing by without one. He caught Volgha's eyes with a panicked glance, and she jerked her head toward a line of valets standing behind the high table. He scurried with remarkable speed, given the height of his heels.

"It's such a ... *unique* pleasure to meet you," said the queen, her eyes constantly scanning his ensemble. "And how do you find our castle?"

"Easily," replied Santa. "It's enormous."

The queen laughed, and then Volgha, and then everyone sitting next to them, and so on in concentric rings until the laughter reached the dregs of the aristocracy at the tables near the walls.

"You make quite an entrance," the queen remarked. "This season, everyone here is doing the Turning Goose or the Capitulating Yeti. What do you call that move with the toe?"

"Oh that," said Santa. "Very new, that bow. It's called the ... Plausible ... Hello?"

"Interesting," said the queen. "And that's popular in North Uptonshire, which is where, exactly?"

"South of here," said Santa.

"Yes," said the queen, still staring at Santa's outfit with a mixture of confusion and curiosity.

"But not *too* far south," added Volgha.

"Of course not," Santa hastened to reply. "Not so far south that the day falls out of step with the year." His sneer at the thought was rather convincing.

"Of course," said the queen. "Now tell me about your ensemble."

"He designed it himself," said Volgha. "He told me that he designs all of his own clothing."

The queen's eyes widened. "Really?"

Santa gave a one-shouldered shrug, which looked very awkward given the poofs on his shirt. "Why not? That sounds like something I'd do. Er, when I'm not counting my money, of course."

The queen laughed again, sending another concentric wave toward the walls.

Nice touch, said Osgrey.

"How unique!" said the queen. "A noble who designs his own clothes! Tell me, is that typical in North Uptonshire?"

"Oh yes," said Santa. "Obviously, we have a different sort of fashion there. It's almost as if someone who had no idea what they were talking about tried to explain royal fashion to us, and we got it embarrassingly wrong!"

The room erupted again into concentric laughter. Volgha glared at the back of Santa's head.

I told you so, said Osgrey.

"Like you know any better," hissed Volgha.

I know what I don't know, Osgrey replied. *At least I'm tree enough to admit it.*

Dozens of white-gloved waiters descended on the room, filling the tables with silver-domed trays that brimmed with fragrant meats, adorned with oddly-arranged vegetables that were obviously not for eating. Their food was locked in a battle with modern art.

Half of the assembled nobility left the food alone entirely, either due to fad diets or utter confusion regarding whether they were meant to eat it or simply discuss it with the gallery owner over a glass of chardonnay. Santa, on the other hand, had knocked the strange vegetables aside without hesitation and was waving at a wine bearer while he chewed a hunk of beef.

The queen's face was slowly growing more manic as she watched Santa break with nearly every fashionable custom of the court, shifting the bulk of his utensils away from his plate in favor of the dinner fork and steak knife.

"Sensational," growled the queen, who then grabbed her silverware by the handful and threw it onto the floor. In a fierce display of one-upmanship, she grabbed the steak from her plate with both hands and started gnawing on it.

Predictably, like lemmings over a cliff, the assembled bootlickers followed suit. The sounds of clattering silverware and monstrous gnawing drifted into the kitchens, setting the stage for the future nightmares of everyone who heard. The entirety of the court had devolved into the children's table, casting etiquette aside because that, apparently, was the fashionable thing to do in North Uptonshire.

Volgha was impressed. She'd never seen the point to all of those forks anyway, and cast her own aside. She managed to relax for a moment and enjoy her meal. Santa had, against all odds, managed to win enough of the White Queen's favor to not land them in the dungeon. One step closer to the pearls.

By the time after-brunch cocktails were served, everyone had three courses of culinary marvel festooning the front of their attire.

"Tell me, Baron," began the queen, gesturing at him with a wine glass so forcefully that it splashed all over him, "is this how all meals are held in your hall?"

"Not exactly," said Santa.

"Oh?"

Volgha elbowed him in the ribs. "Only the special occasions, right, Baron?"

"Oh, right," he replied. "Special occasions only."

"Delightful," said the queen. "I'd love to visit North Uptonshire someday soon, to see more of this outrageous fashion! Are your designs very popular?"

"Oh yeah," said Santa, "all of the locals love my stuff. No one can afford it, though, so there's not much to see."

"Really?" The queen cast her glass aside in excitement. Predictably, the sound of breaking glass then sounded throughout the room, and all of the wine bearers found themselves in the grip of a collective existential crisis.

"Yeah," answered Santa "That's why I'm usually the only one wearing my designs. Well, me and my valet, that is."

"I must have them!" The queen stood up onto her chair. "Exclusive designs! Cost is no object! A dozen for me first, obviously, and then one for my sister. No more of those awful black rags for her!"

"Hey!" Volgha started to take offense but decided there were more important hills upon which she might die. Her sister was distracted, and that was the best thing that could have happened.

"And then Lord Chamberlain, then my wig powderers, and the butler. You'll need to meet them individually for measurements, I presume? Then there are the banister polishers, the ice sculptors, and Tickler, of course."

I'm glad I'm no longer at court, said Osgrey. *He doesn't decorate trees, does he?*

Volgha smirked.

"A meeting with Tickler will require some special planning, Your Majesty," said Chamberlain. "Shall I call for him?"

"Obviously." The queen rolled her eyes. "But for now, I simply must have this hunk of man to myself for a while!" She was clutching at Santa amorously, in an unexpected turn of events.

"Your Majesty," Santa was leaning away from her advances as adamantly as possible, "I'm not sure that we should—"

"Of course we should! Why, is there a Baroness Klaus?"

"Well, no—"

"Yes!" Volgha's blurt might have been timed more poorly, but at present, she couldn't see how.

"Want him for yourself, eh?" The queen glared at Volgha, and sneered. It was her look that preceded tirades and public executions.

"No," said Volgha. "Maybe. What?" She looked around, desperately searching for a distraction. Where were the levers that released the doves?

"Well you can't have him, I saw him first!" The queen was trying to crawl into Santa's lap, though the sheer enormity of her dress was a sufficient impediment.

"No you didn't," said Volgha, reflexively slipping into the standard sisterly mode of debate. "I told you about him! I invited him here!"

"Well, he's far too noble to slum with you in your little hut. He's a fashion designer, for crying out loud!"

"My cottage is lovely!"

"I'm the queen here!"

Volgha called Alexia a swear word. Unfortunately, it was one she knew.

"Guards!" Half a dozen mail-and-leather-clad guards rushed to the high table. "My sister had forgotten her place. Take her to the dungeons!"

"Stop!" Volgha used the same glamour she'd used to stop Loki and the queen from chasing her through the hallways all soapy and naked, the one with the fiery eyes and shadowy tentacles. The guards—sensibly—hesitated.

"Fine," said Volgha, "you win. But I'm not going to any dungeons. I'm going to my room, and I'm taking the baron's valet with me."

"Really?" said Krespo with a worried look.

"Really?" said the queen with an incredulous look.

"Really?" said Santa with a fearful look.

"Yes," said Volgha. "Really."

Quickly then, urged Osgrey.

The queen didn't contradict her, so Volgha used the momentary pause to leave the high table of her own volition. She snapped her fingers for Krespo to follow her, which he did with haste, his high heels clip-clopping a staccato retreat across the stone floor. She gave a quick glance back at Santa who, for the first time since she'd met him, looked very much the rabbit, and not a bit the wolf.

ELEVEN

I DON'T KNOW WHAT YOU HAVE IN MIND," SAID KRESPO AS THEY hurried down the hall, "but you should know that I don't have a lot of experience with women."

"What? No!" Volgha looked at Krespo with disbelief. "I need you to help me get my sister's pearls."

"Oh." Krespo sighed with relief. "I thought you meant to—"

"Please don't finish that thought. Where did you get that idea?"

"I thought everyone got that idea!"

He's right, you know.

"Never mind," muttered Volgha.

"But what about Santa?" asked Krespo. "We have to go back for him!"

"Santa can handle himself." Of course, it wasn't *himself* that required Santa's handling. Things hadn't gone according to plan, not that she'd had much of a plan beyond getting in the door. She knew that Santa could pass for nobility, and he was smart enough to distract his sister for a while. She was making up the rest as she went along.

"Why did Santa bring you, anyway?" asked Volgha. "I assumed he'd bring some muscle, one of those Faesolde guys."

"Thanks a lot." Krespo seemed offended. "I don't imagine he anticipated having to fight his way out of here. He brought me because I made the outfits."

"On your own?"

"Yes, and he needs help getting in and out of them."

"That makes sense. So you're a tailor?"

"Among other things," said Krespo.

They continued their walk down the empty hallway, the percussive barrage of their high heels inventing heavy metal as they went.

"Were you trained as a tailor then?"

"Not exactly," replied Krespo. "I learned the basics in the course of my schooling, and filled in the gaps with some Applied Thinkery."

"So you used magic to put his outfits together?"

"As far as Thinkery is a bit like magic," said Krespo. "It's certainly a lot faster than doing it by hand. I can throw together a complete outfit in a matter of hours."

"Oh, that's good to hear," said Lord Chamberlain, as he stepped out from a doorway just ahead of them.

"Lord Chamberlain," said Volgha. "How did you—"

"I took my leave while you and Her Majesty were engaged in dispute. I needed to arrange a meeting between Tickler and the baron, and as luck would have it, he's available now!"

Volgha knew very little about Her Majesty's Tickler. No one really knew anything about him, and it was kept that way for a very good reason.

The White Queen, like all of her recent ancestors, was a renowned libertine. She was famous for seeking out pointless diversions, often to the point of neglecting dire affairs of state. Lord Chamberlain personally handled much of the business of running the kingdom and was very good about keeping that fact under wraps.

One of the least publicized extents of Lord Chamberlain's power was the fact that he was, by royal decree, the legitimate ruler of the kingdom while Her Majesty was engaged in diversion in the royal ticklarium. The queen often threatened the lives of anyone within earshot while she was being tickled. It was half the fun, really.

Unfortunately, when she gleefully screamed, "Off with his head!" the order would be carried out by the nearest guard without hesitation. She couldn't—or wouldn't—restrain herself, and they had lost several Ticklers before they arrived at the current solution.

The way Volgha understood it, no one but the Tickler himself knows his identity. He only appears when summoned by the big gong in the ticklarium to perform his appointed duty. During this time, all of the White Queen's power is transferred to Lord Chamberlain, who oversees the diversion. While the queen is shouting orders to her guards to perform acts of murder, torture, or other incivility, Chamberlain politely but firmly countermands said orders.

Throughout the rest of the castle, the work proceeds in earnest. In addition to the general feeling of safety from unwarranted threats, all of the queen's subjects are grateful for the opportunity to get their work done in an uninterrupted fashion. At any other time, they may have been called off to play the part of pony, footstool, or human cannonball in one of Her Majesty's diversions or another. But participating in a bit of fun, required or not, was no excuse for not having finished making the tea, hanging up the washing, waxing the catapult, or any of the other tasks necessary to keep the castle running at optimum efficiency. Work was left unfinished at a servant's peril.

Thus it was a positively gleeful half hour or so for the servants, until Chamberlain brought the diversion to a close. The mysterious masked Tickler—who was naturally the target of most of Her Majesty's threats—would be given a moment to collect his implements and sprint for the door before power reverted to Her Majesty.

Tickler's identity was kept so secret because, according to Her Majesty, he was the most wicked and naughty little knave in her employ, and she would not rest until his head was on a pike, at which point a new Tickler would need to be appointed at once, curse his wicked hide. She'd once gone so far as to demand that Lord Chamberlain divulge Tickler's identity, after what she considered to be a particularly brutish session. To avoid perjuring himself, he'd reluctantly done so.

After that, it was Her Majesty's turn at reluctance. On pain of never being tickled again, she signed the royal decree that rested power with Chamberlain in future sessions, as it was the only way a new Tickler could be hired. Since then, not even Chamberlain has known who wears the mask.

"I can also light a candle in the ticklarium," said Lord Chamberlain, "which will compel Tickler to meet me there if I need anything from him outside the queen's diversions. I was just going to do so when I happened to find him in there, double-checking Her Majesty's restraints."

"Smart lad," said Volgha.

Chamberlain nodded his agreement. "And a fortuitous coincidence. He has time for his measurements now, although the baron is ... well, *engaged* at the moment. But if his assistant here can do it, we'll seize the opportunity!"

"Oh," said Krespo.

"A fine idea," said Volgha through clenched teeth.

Chamberlain stepped in closer to Volgha, to speak with her in a hushed tone. "Don't worry, it will only take a moment, and then you and the baron's assistant can tiptoe off to your little tryst."

"Um, right." Volgha's cheeks turned bright red. "That's why we were sneaking around, definitely."

"Oh I'm not judging," whispered Chamberlain with a smile and a wink. "I think we should all get to do what makes us happy every once in a while, don't you?"

"Well said." Volgha smiled, yearning to crawl under a rock and die of embarrassment.

Old pervert, said Osgrey. *I always thought there was something odd about him.*

Chamberlain directed her to a bench nearby. "Feel free to wait here.

"Right this way, young sir," said Chamberlain, unaware that elves live for hundreds of years. Krespo was most likely far older than Chamberlain's great-great-grandfather would have been.

"Er, right. Thank you." Krespo gave Volgha a worried look as he was led into the ticklarium. Chamberlain closed the doors behind him, nodded to Volgha, and sauntered off down the hallway to solve the next in a string of crises that were his life's work.

He'll be fine, said Osgrey.

"How do you know?"

Tickler's not dangerous. If it's still the fellow from the livery, he's probably in more danger from the elf than the other way around.

"I thought no one knew who the Tickler was!"

Largely true, replied Osgrey, *but knowing the unknown is my job, remember? Or rather, it was my job. It'll be yours soon.*

Volgha had forgotten about the Warden business in all of the deception. Just the stress of stealing the pearls was gnawing her stomach with worry. She tried to clear her mind and focus on worrying about Krespo. One debacle at a time, that was all she asked.

Though it felt like an eternity, it had probably only been a matter of minutes before Krespo emerged from the ticklarium with a handful of notes.

"Hey!" Volgha jumped up when she saw him. "Did everything go all right? Was he suspicious?"

"Well, he was wearing a mask," said Krespo. "That's a little bit suspicious in its own right."

"Suspicious of *you.*"

"Oh. No, it went fine. I got the measurements I need, and there's a very nice bolt of wool back at the workshop that will—"

"Forget about that," said Volgha. "We've got to get to my sister's pearls!"

Krespo put his hands on his hips and narrowed his eyes.

"We can go and get the pearls," he said, "but don't tell me to forget about the measurements or the wool when I'm doing you a favor!"

"No you aren't!" She pointed a very stern finger in Krespo's face. "You owe me a favor, and I'll tell you what it will be. You don't get to decide!"

"Fine," said Krespo, "we'll just get the pearls and go. Then the next time you come to visit your sister, she'll say, 'Where are those fancy new outfits I ordered from that well-dressed Baron?' What will you say? 'Oh, sorry, I made him up to steal some jewelry from you, isn't that awfully funny?'"

He has a point, you know.

They were right. Yet another thing standing in line for her to worry about later. Santa was actually going to have to come through with the clothing order!

"You may be right," Volgha acquiesced.

"I *am* right," said Krespo.

"Can we please discuss the terms later? We're losing our window of opportunity!"

"So long as you promise me that between the pearls and the clothes, once all of this is said and done, my favor to you will be paid."

"Fine," said Volgha. "I get the pearls, my sister gets her clothes, and we're square."

"Right," said Krespo. "Now, where are we going?"

They didn't speak as they walked through hallways, up stairways, and through the royal solarium. The guards posted at the hallway that led to the queen's apartments stopped her, not recognizing her under the ringlets and silks and makeup. She'd had to resort to a little glamour to convince them that she was the queen's sister. It was the first time she'd ever had to cast a glamour to make herself look more like herself. The guards let them pass so that Volgha could return the queen's dress.

Once down the hallway, past the sitting room, the bedroom, and into the wardrobe, they had to work fast. Volgha really did intend to return the awful dress, and her own was somewhere in there. Her Majesty's laundry staff wouldn't have been foolish enough to do anything with it.

The wardrobe was enormous. It had many rooms, each with six walls, arranged like a honeycomb if you could look at it from the top down. Each room represented a different section, but nothing so mundane as "evening wear" or "formal wear"—it was much more nuanced.

Volgha headed straight for the Last Year's Travesties room, and sure enough, there on a peg was her dress and hat. She shuffled out of the pink and green war crime she'd had to endure since brunch, glad to be rid of it. Her own went on easily enough, but the hat was going to have to work its way past a horde of ringlets, and they didn't have that kind of time.

There's more clothing in one of these rooms than I owned in my entire life! exclaimed Osgrey.

"Where are the pearls?" Krespo asked.

"No idea," said Volgha. "Better start looking."

After an exhaustive search of Informal Mourning, Krespo had moved on to Spring Severe, then Wartime Casual, and was now tossing drawers in Experimental Plaids. Volgha had decided to start at the other end, making her way from Competition Gardening to Medium Fancy Tea Party, and had just started digging through Seaside Picnics: Beef Entree, when she heard a *whump*, followed by footsteps.

"Quick!" she hissed at Krespo. "Hide!" She dove for the back of the nearest closet and hoped that Krespo had heard her. Getting caught digging through Her Majesty's wardrobe would not go well for either one of them.

"H-Hello?" The voice was entirely lacking in baritone, as though it had come from a child. An older child, though, one who hadn't been called "adorable" in quite some time. One well on the way to becoming a youth and developing an interest in loitering near garbage cans. Volgha didn't move. She hoped that if they were both quiet for a moment, whoever it was would—

"Um, yes?" It was Krespo. Volgha thought a swear word very vehemently, though she gave it no voice. The little fool had signed his own fate, and it wouldn't be long before the guards had them both.

"Tickler," said Krespo's voice, "is that you?"

"None other," replied the voice of the junior miscreant, with a bit of panache. "Isn't the queen's sister with you?"

Not a word, Volgha thought. *Just say you're alone, you halfwit little—*

"How did you know?"

Volgha made a mental note to give Krespo nightmares for a month, then stepped from the closet. Krespo and Tickler were in Merciless Undergarments, two rooms over. Tickler was short and lean, dressed all in black, and wearing a grinning mask with an absurdly long nose.

"I'm here," she said. "And what does the queen's Tickler think he's doing in my sister's wardrobe?" Intimidation was a convenient blunt instrument when the complete truth is not on one's side. Time to smash her way out.

"Following you," said Tickler, his hands on his hips. "The better question is how do you two know each other, and why are you looking for the queen's pearls?"

"She said she'd loan them to me," said Volgha.

"Pull the other one," said Tickler. "She'd have had Chamberlain send a servant to fetch them, not leave it to her sister and a nobleman's tailor."

"I'm a witch, you know."

"I hope you're a better witch than a liar."

"Do you really want to find out?"

"Volgha, Tickler, please!" Krespo wasn't actually bold enough to step between them, and had in fact been backing away during their exchange. He'd shouted all the way from Holiday Footwear, the next room over. They stopped and turned to look at him, and he walked back over as quickly as he could.

"Mister Tickler," he said, "we really need to get our hands on those pearls, and I'm not keen on getting into the family rivalry behind it. Surely, there must be something we can do to earn your, er, discretion on this?"

Tickler's gaze turned away from Krespo after a moment and landed on Volgha. The mask was smiling, but the head to which it was strapped was melting sheepishly into the shoulders beneath.

"There is, actually," said Tickler. "I'm in a bit of a bind, and you could probably get me out of it."

"What sort of a bind?" asked Volgha.

Tickler fidgeted, proof positive to Volgha that everyone was hiding something. He stared at the floor, shuffled one foot around, and mumbled something.

"Sorry," Krespo cocked his head to the side, "what was that?"

Tickler exhaled loudly. "I need to get rid of a body."

I don't think this is the fellow from the livery, said Osgrey.

Krespo's eyes went wide, and he started backing away again.

"You what?" Volgha exclaimed. "Who did you kill?"

"No one! I mean, he had a name, but I don't know what it was. And I didn't kill him!"

"Start talking," said Volgha, her arms folded.

"He was Tickler until a couple of evenings ago," said Tickler. "He was an old man. I was supposed to train under him for a while, and then take over so he could retire. But he died the first time I was going to observe him in secret, and I had to start right away!"

"That's bad luck," said Volgha. "Where is the old man now?"

Tickler's head tilted from side to side a few times, and he made a little groaning sound.

"Oh, out with it," said Volgha. "We're running out of time here, we can't afford to be bashful!"

"Fine," said Tickler. "There are some old tunnels in the walls. He's in the one very near the ticklarium."

"There are tunnels in the walls?"

"No one knows about them," said Tickler. "Only me."

"I didn't know about them," said Volgha. "I explored the castle endlessly when I was a child, I'm surprised I never found them."

I knew about them, said Osgrey. *It was my job to—*

"Not now!" snapped Volgha.

"I thought you were running out of time," said Tickler, hands on his hips.

"Fine," said Volgha. "You help us find those pearls, and we'll sort out your old man."

"Deal."

"I don't suppose you might know where to look?"

Tickler brought a gloved finger up to tap his mask's dimpled chin. "She wore them several evenings ago. With a green brocaded ball gown and a tiara full of rubies."

"That'll be Forest-Toned Binge Drinking," said Krespo, "or possibly Leisure Arguments."

He was right on the second count. There they were, in a drawer under the ruby tiara. A string of a dozen pearls.

"Great work!" Volgha stuffed them into the folds of her dress. "Now let's get out of here before we're found out."

"Shouldn't we tidy up?" Krespo waved his arm, indicating the massive mess they'd left in their wake.

"No time," said Volgha. "Anyway, she'll just think she did it herself. She's a tornado in here. How did you get in here, Tickler?"

"Secret passage," he answered. "Behind the coats in Outlandish Snobbery."

"We should go out past the guards," said Krespo. "They'll think something's going on if we don't."

"Meet me by the portrait of Saint Perplexia in the servants' stairwell in an hour," said Tickler. "We can handle the body then."

"A deal's a deal," said Volgha.

They parted ways, and Krespo started fidgeting once they made it past the guards.

"What's wrong?" asked Volgha.

"It's Santa," he replied. "Do you think he's been with the queen this whole time?"

"Oh," said Volgha, her blood curdling at the thought. "Probably."

"Any idea where they are?"

"We'd better find out," said Volgha. "My sister tends to be ... incorrigible."

TWELVE

VOLGHA TOOK THE SQUEALS COMING FROM DOWN THE HALL AS A bad sign. They were definitely her sister's, and she never squealed like that for wholesome or savory reasons.

She hadn't thought that any harm would come to Santa in the performance of this favor. Severe inconvenience, yes. Agonizing conversation, gratuitous binge drinking, even some ferocious heavy petting—she'd been intentionally vague in describing her sister's temperament, but there would be no way she could have foreseen them ending up in the Hall of Armaments.

It was a bloody history of the realm. Most of the weapons in there were antiques, though under no circumstances did that mean that they weren't dangerous. On the contrary, the steel in that hall was still capable of wreaking the sort of carnage that it had done over the centuries, thereby securing their family's position as indisputable rulers in perpetuity.

If that weren't bad enough, the White Queen was fascinated by it. All of it. Every scrap of steel, every bloody mural. Volgha remembered that since they were children, nothing else about history interested her a bit. Only her family's legacy of carnage.

The only thing that gave Volgha any hope as she and Krespo stood at the entrance to the Hall was the memory of Santa's armory. Whatever else he'd become since his old days, Santa was a warrior. He knew how to handle himself. She just hoped that whatever was happening, he'd seen it coming.

"We have to go down there," said Krespo, his voice quavering. "Don't we?"

"No," Volgha replied. "I'll go alone."

You mean we'll *go alone,* said Osgrey. *Thanks for asking my opinion.*

Krespo heaved a sigh of relief. Volgha had to hand it to the little fellow, he possessed a few shreds of bravery. He was simply loathe to employ them.

"Then what shall I do?"

Volgha pointed to a doorway leading off the main hall.

"Through there, about a hundred paces to the left—maybe two hundred for you—and you'll find the servants' stairwell. The portrait of Saint Perplexia is at the bottom. Keep out of sight until it's time to meet Tickler."

"And you?"

"I'll be there," answered Volgha. "With Santa."

"Best of luck." Krespo ran over to a huge planter, and then behind a big tapestry on the wall. He was obviously trying to stay hidden, but unlike tailoring or Thinkery, he had no talent for it. Volgha hoped that he'd be smart enough to avoid surrendering himself to any guards who walked within earshot.

At least he'd abandoned the high heels.

"I'm going Dim," said Volgha.

Good idea, said Osgrey. *I'll keep quiet. I've no idea if inner monologue with wise old mentors might break it.*

"Right," replied Volgha. "That would be best."

She quickly worked through the incantation and started silently creeping down into the Hall of Armaments. She heard the twang of a crossbow, the thud of metal hitting stone, and a peal of her sister's mad cackling. At least she hadn't heard Santa screaming. If he wasn't already dead, he just might have escaped.

"Oh, Baaaron," the queen sang. "Come out, come out, wherever you aaare!"

Volgha was careful to walk silently across the floor. Being Dim just meant that people were extremely unlikely to look at you, but loud noises were a sure way to break the enchantment. As she came around the corner and into the room where her sister was lurking, she was astonished at the state of the place. Suits of armor had toppled over, swords lay strewn about the room, and the charred wreckage of the foyer looked as though Her Majesty had fired a cannon at some point. Volgha smelled gunpowder. It must have happened while she and Krespo were in the queen's wardrobe. Volgha felt fairly certain that she would have heard a cannon going off indoors, yet clearly she had not.

She resolved not to ponder it further. It was a big castle with lots of thick stone walls, and she had bigger problems.

"This will all be so much easier if you just surrender." The queen rounded to her left, yelled, "Ha!" and fired her crossbow. The bolt collided with a large mirror, shattering it. Frowning, the queen traded crossbows with one of the two big guards who was following her. The guard started reloading the empty one.

"I liked that mirror," she said. "You'll pay for that, Baron!"

Volgha slowly, carefully made her way around the room, looking for Santa. He was either better at hiding than she was at seeking, or he was elsewhere.

After a few minutes of searching and a few more pieces of history ruined by crossbow bolts, Volgha gave up and crept back out into the hall. She hurried to an alcove not far off and fished a few things out of her pockets: some salt, a brass coin, and a bone sewing needle.

She made a circle on the floor with the salt, put the coin in the center, and lay the needle across it. A quick incantation and a few bent-finger gestures later, the needle spun around a few times and pointed back to where she'd just seen her sister.

Volgha gently picked up the coin, and the needle stayed true in the direction it indicated. Quietly and Dimly, she crept back into the room. The queen had moved on to the next room of the gallery, and the needle indicated that Volgha should follow. This room had a great stone circle in the center of it, about three feet tall and fifty feet around. Suits of armor stood all around the circle, and an ornate catapult stood behind them in the center of it. The catapult was almost entirely festooned with filigreed gold and looked to be capable of hurling boulders weighing several thousand pounds.

Volgha had seen the catapult before, of course. It had been in her family for generations. It had been a gift to her great-great-great-great grandfather, Alonso, who had apparently used it for flinging all manner of things over the castle walls. Enemies, friends, livestock, expired produce—he held court outdoors so he could watch things being flung for his amusement.

The last time it was officially used was during Alonso's funeral. His boat was set alight in the Viking tradition, then flung in the general direction of Valhalla. His heir was told that he made it, but that wasn't the first time that lies were employed to shield the dainty feelings of royalty from unpleasant truths.

The needle was pointing directly at it. The queen was stalking her way around the circle, firing bolts through a few very old suits of armor. Every time she found one to be empty, she'd say, "Oopsie," giggle, and swap crossbows with a guard.

Volgha slipped between two suits of armor at the needle's urging, and there he was. Santa was wearing nothing but the tight red pants from his brunch outfit and was covered from head to toe in what appeared to be soot. His big white beard was completely black with it. He was standing nearly perfectly still in the spot of darkness created by the catapult's upright supports.

Volgha pocketed the coin and needle and crept closer to Santa while keeping an eye on her sister. She resisted the natural urge to get really close to Santa and shout, "Boo!" given her sister's apparently murderous frame of mind. Instead, she waited until the queen had moved on to the next room, then stood directly in front of Santa and waved a hand in front of his face, ending her Dim spell.

Santa jumped a little, then scowled. "Where have you been?" he asked, in a barely audible whisper.

"Getting the pearls," said Volgha. "Come on."

They crept carefully out of the room, moving as quickly as they dared, but not making a sound. Once they were out in the hallway, they started dodging from alcove to alcove.

"How did this happen?" asked Volgha.

If I know your sister, said Osgrey, *this outcome was as likely as any other. Are you just making conversation?*

"She's a lunatic," said Santa, because sometimes the obvious does need to be stated. "One minute she's trying to ensnare me with her wiles, the next she's literally trying to ensnare me! With snares! And then there were crossbows."

"Did she fire a cannon at you?"

"I thought that would have gotten your attention a lot sooner."

"The walls around my sister's wardrobe must be exceptionally thick."

They darted between the alcoves until they were close to the door that led to the servants' hall. Volgha pointed to the big tapestry where Krespo had hidden earlier, then raised her hands with the palms facing him. Santa nodded and crept away, slipping soundlessly behind the tapestry.

Volgha hurried quietly through the door. It had been a long time, but she was fairly sure that she could remember how to get to the laundry from there. Two right turns, then straight to the end, then a left—no, that's the kitchen. She said a swear word and retraced her steps. It must have been two lefts, then a right and down to the end—no, that's the cannery. Perhaps it had been longer than she'd thought.

"Osgrey!" she shouted in a whisper. "Which way to the laundry?"

How should I know? Dangerous occupation, washing clothes. Affects the scent, animals don't recognize you.

Volgha said a swear word. "Never mind, I'll find it myself."

After a few more wrong turns, she wound up in a bedding closet. It would have to do. She grabbed a couple of big woolen blankets and made her way back to the door. She opened it a crack and whistled for Santa, who came rushing over.

"About time," said Santa once the door was shut behind him.

"I don't know the place as well as I once did." Volgha shoved the blankets into his hands.

"Thanks," he grumbled. He knotted the corners of the two blankets together, making himself a sort of extra-large cape. Still covered in soot, he looked like a chimney sweep moonlighting as a crime fighter.

"One more thing we have to do," said Volgha. She started jogging down the corridor toward the stairwell.

"I thought we were just here for the pearls!" Santa jogged along behind her.

"Complications arose," said Volgha. "This one should be easy."

They found the stairs, wound their way down, and reunited with Krespo.

"What happened to your clothes?" There was more reproach than concern in Krespo's tone.

Before Santa could reply, the portrait of Saint Perplexia opened, as if on hinges, and revealed the entrance to a little hallway. Tickler's mask emerged from within.

"Good," he said. "You're here."

"Who's this?" asked Santa.

"This is the queen's Tickler," answered Krespo. "He helped us find the pearls, and now we have to help him move a body."

"Move a body?"

"It's a long story," said Tickler.

"Give me the short version."

"He was an old man, and his heart gave out at an inopportune moment."

"You didn't kill him?"

"No!"

Santa eyed Tickler for a moment, the sort of stare that parents employ on children feigning ignorance regarding a broken cookie jar. Tickler must have passed scrutiny, as Santa shrugged and nodded. They made their way into the tunnel.

Volgha was surprised that it existed. As a child, she'd read books about secret passages in old castles, and had searched in earnest to find one. This one seemed very haphazard and poorly constructed, almost as though it were naturally occurring within the otherwise expertly architected walls.

Past a few twists and turns, having banged heads and elbows in the darkness and responded with liberal swearing, they eventually came to the temporary resting place of an old man wrapped in a linen sheet. He'd been a small man, about the size of Tickler.

"That's him," said Tickler, presumably to assuage any doubt that there might be other bodies lingering nearby, and that this was just one they'd happened upon by chance.

"How did he get here?" asked Santa.

"He was the former Tickler," said Tickler. The new one, that is.

Santa looked at Tickler. His eyes narrowed.

"It's not like that! I was going to take over once he retired. His heart just gave out before we could make it official."

"No one but the Tickler knows who's behind the mask," Volgha told him. "It's like a state secret. I'll explain later when we're not mid-performance in several crimes."

"All right. Where are we taking him?" Santa asked.

"Out through the dungeons," said Tickler. "There's a patch of trees at the base of one of the ramparts that will make a decent burial plot for him."

Santa nodded, picked up the former Tickler gently, and put him over his shoulder.

"Follow me," said Tickler.

Tickler led them through more secret passages, past a hidden door, down a few more hallways, and finally out into the grey and snowy yards on the side of the castle. He grabbed a pick and shovel along the way, which they used to dig out a grave. Once they'd gotten him buried, Krespo took off his hat.

"Would anyone like to say a few words?"

Tickler reached up, hesitantly, and took off his mask. That is to say, *she* took off *her* mask.

"You're a girl!" exclaimed Volgha.

"So are you! My name's Matilda." Tickler looked to be about thirteen years old.

"I thought you were supposed to keep your identity a secret," said Santa.

"We're all wrapped up in each other's secrets now," said Matilda. "Call this a token of good faith."

"Thanks," said Volgha. "Your secret is safe with us."

"I feel better," said Matilda, "knowing that somebody else knows. Knowing that there will be someone who can put a name on my grave when I go."

"You won't have to worry about that for a long time," said Santa.

"I hope you're right. In any case, though I don't know his name, I'd like to thank the old man for his years of service. He said he'd been Tickler for a long time, and he helped us all live in peace. Now it's my turn."

THIRTEEN

O N THE BRIGHT SIDE, SAID OSGREY, *SANTA WILL BE OFF THE HOOK for the tailoring.*

Volgha felt awful. It was one thing for her sister to have thrust unwanted advances upon Santa, but hunting him? She was mostly aghast, but also insatiably curious as to how a bit of light romance had evolved into the Most Dangerous Game. Perhaps, after several years and twice as many liters of wine, Santa would retell the tale.

Between the fashion fiasco, the hunt, and the corpse disposal, Santa had no good will left in him. He scowled like a moody teenager and kept mumbling swear words under his breath.

"Let's get you home," said Volgha. "I have one more thing to do here, but I can sneak you into the stables first, and—"

"No." Santa started lumbering off, away from the castle. Did he mean to walk home? He was nearly naked under his grimy blanket cape.

"Where's he going?" asked Matilda, who'd put her Tickler mask back on.

"Don't worry about us." Krespo started to jog after him. "Santa's always prepared. We'll be in touch!"

Krespo waved. Volgha and Matilda waved back. Santa continued storming off.

"I'd better get to bed," said Matilda. "Thanks for your help, you really did me a great service."

"No problem," said Volgha. "We helped each other."

Matilda nodded. "Where will you go?"

"The belfry, then far away from here."

"I can get you close. It's on my way."

They made their way through the hidden tunnels until they were back in the servants' hall. Matilda opened a secret door that was cleverly disguised as a normal door, but one that had been locked for as long as anyone could remember, and everyone had given up on locating the key.

"Thanks again."

"See you."

The door shut, and Volgha was alone. She took a deep breath and savored the silence. People were great in small doses, but they never seemed to run out of things to talk about.

Indeed, said Osgrey. *Alone at last!*

Fun while it lasted, then. Having Osgrey aboard like a geriatric hitchhiker had nearly put her off the idea of pairing up permanently with a familiar, but that would be different. Animals, magical or otherwise, are not people. Whereas people have a tendency to muck up silence with their presence, animals are able to just sort of become a part of it.

Down the hall and up the stone steps. Her broom and cloak were right there where she'd left them, along with the rest of her ingredients. The moon was shining brightly through the clouds, and she heard an eagle calling in the distance. It was a lovely time for a summoning, barring the unnatural warmth. No matter, she'd look into that in due time.

Any questions about the spell? asked Osgrey.

"No, I think I've got it."

Very good. I believe I'll have a nap while you're at it. Good luck!

"Thanks."

She started by tipping her hat to the wind, which obliged her by dying down a bit. She was glad that the wind responded to courtesy, as her circle of ashes wouldn't fare very well otherwise. Drawing the circle took quite a while, what with all of the little sigils she had to mark around the outer edge. Then she started burning a mixture of moonstalk and chillwillow in a brass bowl with a little bit of sulfur.

Volgha called on the inner fire in the moonstalk, and it set the mixture in the bowl roiling with smoke. She spoke a few words of magic and the winds came back with renewed vigor, in a pattern that sent her little column of smoke spiraling up into the air. Once the top of the column had risen out of sight, she crushed a couple of the pearls with the pommel of her little knife and sprinkled the dust into the bowl. It shot up the column of smoke, causing it to sparkle in the moonlight.

Volgha whispered another incantation. Nothing happened. The column of smoke was still there, but it was starting to dwindle. Not wanting to lose the fire, she crushed two more pearls and sprinkled the dust into the bowl. The column sparkled even more brightly, and she repeated her incantation.

Then she heard a call. *The* call, she was sure of it. It wasn't the eagle who'd called before, but it certainly wasn't a wolf, and that was a relief. It was the unmistakable caw of a crow! Definitely that, but it had a certain rumbling underneath it. A hot, searing rumble which lingered on the air ever so briefly.

Then she saw it. The silhouette of wings beating toward her, in front of the moon. She watched it approach, and she didn't have to wonder if the spell had worked. She felt him. She felt the rush of the wind as though it were on her own face, felt the lithe, powerful muscles in his wings working to stay on the current. She spread her arms in greeting and felt a smile spread across her face.

With a great final flap to slow himself, he touched down on the stony ledge. He stood there in the moonlight, staring at her while she stared at him. There was something ... peculiar about him. She'd thought it was just a trick of the pale light at first, but after a moment, she realized that it was not.

Red crow, she thought. *You're a red crow!* Her eyes grew wide as she took in the sight of him.

Oh, that's good, cawed an unfamiliar thought in her mind. The thought wasn't hers, but it came from within her. It wasn't the same as Osgrey speaking in her thoughts, more like the shapes of words and the shades of their meaning. She detected the shape of sarcasm as well.

"Hello," she said aloud.

Yeah, hi, cawed the crow, using her mind as its voice. *Is that really the best you could do?*

"What do you mean?"

Redcrow, cawed the crow. *A bit on the nose, isn't it? What do they call you, Big Haired Witch?*

"I'm Volgha, and for the record, my hair doesn't usually look like this."

Too bad, cawed Redcrow, *I could have nested in that. Looks all tangly and cozy.*

"You're just a bit surly, aren't you?"

Well, I would be, wouldn't I? Summoned and given a name like "Redcrow." How would you feel if you'd been named "Pasty Human?"

"I didn't mean that it should have been your name, I just—"

Oh, that's perfect, cawed Redcrow. *Did you even read the post-summoning spell, or are you just making it up as you go along?*

"*Post*-summoning spell?"

Right, never mind. The first thing you do is tell me my name, and it's not something you get to think about. It's set now. Is this where *you live?*

"Of course not," said Volgha. "This is a belfry!"

Oh, brilliant. You're supposed to do the spell from home so I can *anchor to it.*

"I didn't know," said Volgha, suddenly feeling very sheepish. "I was worried I'd end up with a wolf if I did it from home."

Oh, that's just capital! Wolves! So I'll be woken by howling at *odd hours, assuming I'm able to find my way home. This is just coming up roses for me, "me" being a red crow named Redcrow.*

"That's enough," said Volgha, relying on the classically taciturn inflection of a witch who is inches from being vexed enough to do something about it. "We've had a bit of a stumble, but we're together now, and that's what counts."

If you say so, cawed Redcrow. *Just get me home, so I have a* *chance of learning where it is before all I can remember is this belfry.*

Volgha opened her mouth to say something, but nothing came out so she shut it again. How was it that Redcrow—who she'd assumed would already have a name, though now that seemed like an obvious oversight—knew more about this than she did? She wasn't a formally trained witch, but there was no university for that sort of thing. Was there a university for potential familiars? What would be the mascot?

No matter. They were off to a rocky start, but things would turn out smoothly in the end. Time to get home, then. The two of them took to the warm sky together. Bathed in crimson and violet sunset, they found a high current and followed it to Volgha's grove in the valley.

A THICK MIST SHROUDED THE GROVE. IT WAS VERY COLD, AS IS CUStomary in the North Pole, but not in the usual way. It was usually a very dry cold, but the mist made it very humid. Stranger still were the frozen puddles in the snow. Water didn't usually collect outside in its liquid state. It was too cold. It was still too cold for a puddle to remain a proper puddle for very long, but the collection of little depressions all around her house with the frozen discs in them could hardly be anything else.

Had it ... *rained*? She was fairly certain she was saying the word correctly. She'd heard it once as a child, when a southerner had visited the castle and told her about drops of water falling from the sky. Like snow, only warmer.

This is intolerable, cawed Redcrow. *How do you live here? Why would you want to inflict this horrible dampness on others, namely me?*

"Knock it off," said Volgha. "It's not usually like this. Why is it all wet?"

Oh, good, cawed Redcrow, *it's usually a dry hovel.*

"It's not a hovel!"

If you say so. It's got all the telltale signs of being a hovel from where I'm sitting.

"It's not flashy, if that's what you mean. Where were you nesting that was so posh?"

Atop the tall tower. The one that's taller than your belfry.

"The wizard's tower," said Volgha. "That might explain why you're red. All of the magic leaking out of that place can have side effects."

My color requires an explanation now? Is that the sort of casual racism that passes for normal with you? And what side effects does all of this wet have on your hovel?

"Stop calling it a hovel! It's your home, too, you know."

Well, that's just perfect.

In the south, they say that the rain lets a homeowner know where the roof has a leak. In Volgha's cottage, the rain was far too kind in its thorough summary. Just as the puddles had frozen outside, there were little splashes of ice covering everything she owned, and tiny icicles hanging from dozens of spots on the ceiling.

Volgha's heart sank. All that she wanted was to close her eyes for a bit and recuperate. She knew that as soon as she lit a fire, the ice in the cottage would all melt, leaving everything miserably wet.

Warm enough to melt, but still cold enough for frostbite. What a perfect storm of discomfort you live in.

"Something's warming the air," said Volgha. "It's never been wet like this."

Likely story. I'll leave you to it.

Redcrow fluttered off to a shelf and perched between two books, in what may have been the one dry spot in the entire house. If he was scoffing at her, he at least had the courtesy not to think it aloud.

She beat the little shards of ice off her top blanket, then used her broom to knock most of the icicles from the ceiling, and swept as much ice as she could from the furniture. That would keep the damp from sinking in too deeply when she lit the fire.

The wet wood was slow to start, so she waved her hand over the hearth and mumbled an incantation. She found the fire sleeping inside the log at the bottom, and slowly coaxed it out. Just a bit. She didn't want it to burn too quickly, but she was cold, tired, and fed up with the lip she was getting from her new familiar, who had no lips. Getting warm was the one thing that was within her power to fix right now.

She hung her blankets and put the kettle on for a cup of tea.

There was a clump of herbs on the table that had once been dried, but was now reconstituted. She dropped them into the big cauldron of stew and gave it a stir.

Redcrow cawed a swear word. *What is that stench? I think it's singed my nostrils!*

"That's a proper stew," said Volgha. "If you don't like it, you can go find your own supper. And you shouldn't use words like that. Where did you learn it, anyway?"

I've got your vocabulary now, cawed Redcrow smugly. *No one to blame but yourself.*

She had to admit that she was making a fairly poor first impression, though the warm and the wet were hardly her fault. Oh, what did she care if Redcrow had a foul mouth? She was the only one who could hear him, as far as she could tell. Besides, it was every other word for her on particularly difficult occasions. Might as well get used to it.

That's pragmatic of you.

"Are you going to listen to my thoughts all the time?"

Probably not all *the time,* cawed Redcrow, *but you can hardly blame me. You're a loud thinker.*

"Am I?"

Has no one ever told you? That's surprising. You'd think your inner monologue had one of those ... oh, what do you call them ... the big horns that shepherds blow atop mountains.

"I can never remember what they're called."

I know.

She sipped her tea and ate a bowl of stew, much to Redcrow's chagrin. She liked that stew, and she didn't care what Redcrow thought. It had history. Character. Those weren't flavors that you could just whip together in a pot, they were the result of ... well, not planning, but persistence at the very least. And history. It was a proper stew with a lineage all its own.

She let her mind wander as she ate. She'd been through a lot lately, and she needed to try and make sense of it all.

If you're going to keep shouting, cawed Redcrow, *you may as well do it sensibly. What's the whole story with this Loki fellow?*

"A friend of my sister's," answered Volgha.

As she was telling him the tale of Loki's riddle, she had a sudden realization. The rising heat levels started during the time between the two sips of the potion that Loki had taken. The two have to be connected, but how?

So the dampness is your fault!

"Don't be ridiculous," snapped Volgha. "I may have been obliquely involved, but if there's fault here, it's Loki's!"

Touchy, touchy, cawed Redcrow. *You could be right, though. It's warm all over, and that sort of magic is beyond your capacity.*

Volgha took umbrage with that, its accuracy notwithstanding. This new means of sharing thoughts was going to take some adjustment. Normally, one would speak the thoughts they wanted other people to hear as they liked. Redcrow, it seemed, had unfettered access to the archives of her thought, and could peruse them at his leisure.

It's weird for both of us. And at least I know when I'm shouting.

"I'm sorry!" Volgha threw up her hands. "I don't know how to think any more quietly or I would!"

All right, look, I'll help you, cawed Redcrow. *I can tell you're tired, just get into bed, and I'll give you something to practice on.*

Volgha stoked the fire, then wrapped herself up in her blankets and curled up in bed. Redcrow opted to remain in his dry spot on the shelf. After a moment of settling in, both of them were still and quiet.

The straw mattress was damp in a few spots, but Volgha managed to mostly avoid them.

All right, cawed Redcrow. *Now relax, and think about a tree.*

Volgha closed her eyes, and the first tree that came to mind was the one that had formerly been Osgrey.

No, no, no! You're thinking way too loudly, mostly about the old man! He's really a tree now?

"Yes," said Volgha. "That's part of the Druiding Way."

Wait, there's more to it than that. It's like I can hear him.

"Oh right," said Volgha. "He's ... well, he's—"

He's in here, isn't he? Inside your mind?

"Well, yes."

But it wasn't your idea?

"Well, no. Not exactly."

Redcrow said a swear word from the back of Volgha's mind. She'd nearly forgotten about that one. It had been ages since she'd used it.

It's not right, he cawed, *setting up in someone else's mind without their permission! Where is this knave, I'll deal with him!*

"Leave it," said Volgha. "It's odd circumstances, but so is everything else nowadays. We'll sort it out in due time."

All right. For now. But I'll need to speak with this Sigmund character, at the very least.

"That can be arranged," said Volgha. "Let's get back to business for now."

Very well, cawed Redcrow. *Okay, just think of a different tree. Preferably one that's always been a tree, and not one with whom you've had a conversation.*

She pictured a pine tree, covered in snow, standing tall and silent in the forest.

Right, good. Now think about the tree's shadow, but leave the tree out of it.

It was difficult to picture the shadow of a tree without the tree, but she sort of crossed her mind's eyes and faked it.

Err, okay. Close enough. Now think about the ground under the shadow, but leave the shadow out.

Snowy ground, undisturbed powder.

Now you're getting it, cawed Redcrow. She could vaguely tell the difference, and it seemed as though he was thinking more quietly, too. He guided her through thinking about the rocks under the snow, the dirt under that, the roots of the tree under the dirt, and so on, until they slipped into a state between consciousness and something rather like consciousness, only different.

She might have mistaken it for a dream, but for a certain acute stillness that was far too thick to have been born from a dream. They'd slipped beyond the veil, if only by inches, like a child hiding behind the curtains. With a crow on her shoulder.

The sky was a cloudless hush, and everything in it was different. The heavens were lousy with stars, and none of them were right. The moon was brighter than it should be; larger, too. The snow danced around them in serene little cyclones, propelled without wind or sound.

Volgha heard only the sound of her breathing. Then Redcrow gave a disapproving groan.

"What is it?" she whispered.

There you go, cawed Redcrow with an encouraging lilt. *You're not shouting! Well done, you.*

"Thanks," said Volgha, "but you made a noise. What was it for?"

Oh, you'll see.

The little cyclones seemed curious. They gyred lazily about, bending as though staring up at Volgha. They were standing in a little clump of trees, and she kept catching movement in the branches out of the corners of her eyes.

"Who's there?" she asked aloud. The question repeated onto itself, like an echo whose reverberations each took up different voices. Echoes aren't supposed to do that.

Some of the voices mispronounced the words. Echoes aren't supposed to do that either.

I hope this doesn't take too long, cawed Redcrow. *I won't sleep right for ages if they keep us here all evening.*

"If *who* keeps us here? If *what* takes too long?"

"Volgha! How did the summoning go?" Osgrey was standing there as he had before, all smoky and ethereal.

"Osgrey!" said Volgha, her voice doing the strange echoing thing again.

Osgrey? Oh, so this is the interloper!

"Not now," said Volgha. "Wait, you're *here*. You're not in my head. Or are you? Where are we?"

"We're in the Winter Court," said Osgrey. "I must admit, I didn't think you'd find it so soon. Your mind has never seemed quiet enough to notice the path."

Told you, cawed Redcrow.

"Know-it-all," said Volgha.

Know-more-than-you, anyway.

"Ha! Very witty, your friend," said Osgrey.

"You can hear him?"

"Of course," said Osgrey. "It's our spirits that enter the Winter Court, not our bodies. I'm still in your head, so to speak, or rather I will be again, when you move back across the veil from here."

Volgha nodded. "What's the Winter Court, then?"

"It's where the true governance of the land is done," explained Osgrey. "It's where the Warden engages with the spirits of winter."

Wait, cawed Redcrow, *I thought I recognized you! I thought you were still the Warden, but you're now a tree who goes jumping into the minds of sleepwalking witches! Where is the new Warden? I've got to tell him about this!*

"There's no new Warden yet," said Osgrey. "That's the business we're here to sort out, now that you've been summoned."

"Business?" asked Volgha.

"I had hoped to have more time to prepare you," said Osgrey, "but we'll muddle through. Are you ready?"

"How could I be? I'd no idea I was supposed to prepare for anything!"

Redcrow cawed a swear word. *You were doing so well! I know you're flustered, but please stop shouting!*

Volgha was about to give Redcrow a stern lecture when Osgrey held up a hand. He appeared to be listening to the little cyclones, which Volgha could not hear. After a moment, he nodded solemnly and turned back to her.

"As my last act as Warden, I'm to charge you with a sacred quest."

"Oh right," said Volgha, throwing up her hands. "Because I don't already have enough to do!"

"The spirits bid you return balance to the North," said Osgrey. "Restore the peace between the land and the people, and my mantle shall pass to you."

Warden? You? I mean us! Wow, I didn't see that coming.

"But I don't want to be the Warden!"

What? You're joking!

"You must," said Osgrey. "It has been decided. There can be no other way."

Why wouldn't you want to be the Warden? Don't you know the power that comes along with it?

"I don't care," said Volgha. "All I want is to be left alone, to do witchery in peace. If I'd wanted to be in charge of anything, I'd have fought my sister for the crown of Aurora!"

"I know," said Osgrey. "I wanted the same thing before the duty passed to me. It's not fair, but very little in life is. It's your destiny, I'm afraid. The land needs you, needs your strength. The fate of the entire North is coming to rest upon your shoulders."

I knew I was destined for greatness, cawed Redcrow. *The Warden's familiar! I'll see some proper respect now, that's for sure!*

"I have to think about this," said Volgha. "What's this balance, anyway? How would I restore it?"

"Sort out this warm air for one," replied Osgrey. "Then the spirits need to be given assurance that the people intend to have peace with the land. That assurance is maintained by the Warden. It's the bulk of the job, really."

"What peace? How can the spirits be assured?"

"Right," said Osgrey. "How shall I explain it? It's complex, but not exactly complicated, if you know what I mean."

"I do," said Volgha, who didn't.

"Think of the seasons as the land's parents. They only want what's best for their little tyke, so they're constantly looking it over for things that are worrisome. Scrapes and cuts that need bandaging, that sort of thing."

Volgha nodded.

"People are unpredictable," Osgrey continued, "especially given that the seasons don't really perceive the passage of time. In their eyes—they don't actually have eyes, mind you—people are inventing fire one minute and burning castles with it the next. Not that people *invented* fire, so much as discovered how to make it.

"The Warden is like the family doctor. Whenever something happens to the land that worries the seasons, they look to doctors for explanations. They'll want to know if his tides are coming in as expected for a boy his age, or if they should be concerned that his mammals aren't evolving as expected. That sort of thing."

"And I'm supposed to tell them that the tides are normal? Based on what, my vast experience in evaluating tides of other lands?"

"Oh no," said Osgrey. "The Warden is like a special doctor that deals with the land's people. A very trusted specialist. When the people are just milling about, tending sheep and gossiping in taverns, the seasons don't take much notice. However, when they do something that gives the seasons cause for concern, they look to the Warden to tell them whether it's something serious."

"So I tell them whether the people are doing something that will harm the land?"

"That's the long and short of it," said Osgrey. "Most of the time, they're worried over nothing."

"And the other times?"

"They get rid of the problem."

"Oh," said Volgha.

"It's best to talk to them often," said Osgrey. "If they aren't reassured about something they think might be wrong, they may just take action to be on the safe side."

"That's frightening," Volgha remarked. "Who's been talking to them since you left?"

"I have," answered Osgrey. "Lately, I've been telling them not to worry about this warm air business, but they're less inclined to listen to me now that I'm a tree. They really need to hear it from a person."

"I'm not sure it isn't something to be worried about."

"Then find out," said Osgrey, "and reverse it, if you can."

"And what then?"

"And then you'll be the Warden," said Osgrey.

Excellent, cawed Redcrow, a bit too eagerly for Volgha's taste.

"I'll sort out the warm air," said Volgha, "but I don't want to be the Warden."

Yes, she does! Don't ruin this for us!

"It's your destiny," said Osgrey. "Sleep now, things will conclude as they must."

AND SLEEP THEY DID. VOLGHA WASN'T SURE FOR HOW LONG, BUT SHE didn't have an opportunity to mull it over because she was violently awoken by a ball of green flame erupting at the foot of the bed.

"Hey! I think it's working!"

Redcrow flapped and cawed. No words that Volgha could tell, more like some instinctual part of him that was just swearing in crow.

Had her sister been a part of the dream? Volgha could have sworn that it had just been her and Redcrow, but in her bleary state, she could hear Alexia's voice so clearly.

Unfortunately, as the seconds passed, she found herself careening toward a dreadful realization: the green ball of flame *was* her sister.

"What? How the— What the—"

"Surprise!" The White Queen's face, approximately five feet tall and wreathed in green flames, beamed at her with wide-mouthed glee. Her unblinking eyes were roughly the size of dinner plates, so cruelly portioned with lunacy as to coax Volgha's flesh to crawling.

Does this happen often? cawed Redcrow. *If so, you'll need to build a wing onto the hovel for me, and don't even think about making a pun of that.*

Somewhere between bleary-eyed and awash with dread, Volgha

stood on her bed in an impromptu defensive posture, hair tangled in a reflection of her horror, attempting to grasp the sheer insanity that was unfolding before her. Had her time in the Winter Court left her with hallucinations?

No, said Osgrey, who was inside her head once again. *I can see it, too.*

"How did you ... what? Why?" None of the swear words that she knew seemed adequate for the madness that was unfolding, so she just cringed there, dumbstruck.

"Oh, it's just a little something I had Ghasterly cook up," said the White Queen. "I'm tired of sending letters to you, it takes forever for you to respond."

"That cretin made you into a ball of fire? In my house?"

Our *house,* cawed Redcrow. *You really need to run this sort of thing past me, if I'm expected to live here.*

"In a manner of speaking," replied the queen, her boundless glee unwavering. "I've had him open up a portal in one of the spare rooms of the castle, so I can come in here and talk to you whenever I want! Isn't it sensational?"

"You mean to say that you can appear in front of me like this anytime you want?"

"No, silly." She rolled her eyes dismissively. "You'll only be able to see it when you're standing next to yours."

"Mine," she said, not quite understanding. Then it hit her. "This thing is permanent?"

"Yes!"

What?

"A huge ball of green flame, permanently installed in the middle of my house!"

"Yes!"

No!

"How in the world am I supposed to get any sleep?" She was shouting now, but Redcrow said nothing. Even he must have felt it justifiable, given the circumstances.

"Just go to one of the other rooms of your house," said the queen, the dinner plate-sized eyes rolling emphatically.

"I live in a cottage! It's one room!"

"Well, perhaps this is the motivation you need to spruce it up. Honestly, do you think I built this lovely castle by staying in a one-room shack?"

"It's not a shack! And you didn't build your castle, it's a thousand years old!"

"Sticks and stones," said Her Majesty. "That sort of talk isn't making your shack any bigger, you know. By the way, you haven't seen Loki, have you?"

"What? No, I haven't seen that idiot!"

The queen smirked an "oh well" sort of face. "No one has, just thought I'd check. Well, I must be off!" Her face disappeared before Volgha had a chance to unleash a torrent of slander, but the great ball of green flame remained.

It was entirely insubstantial. She could pass her hand right through it, and it generated no heat. At the moment, Volgha lacked the optimism to see the good in it not burning the cottage down.

Oh, come on, cawed Redcrow. *You're a witch, can't you do anything about this?*

"This is wand magic," Volgha answered. "Wizarding stuff. If it can overpower the wards I have on this place, it's too powerful for me."

"You're learning," said a greasy baritone from the portal. Ghasterly's seething visage came into the fiery wreath, snarling with delight at Volgha's frustration.

Ghasterly! Osgrey exclaimed.

"You!" shouted Volgha, her lips curled, baring her teeth in a fury.

"Me," said Ghasterly. "Foolish girl, let this be a further lesson to you. I'll be watching." He started laughing. It was guttural and cruel, the sort of thing that necromancers probably spend countless hours practicing in front of a mirror to achieve. He stepped away from the portal then, his face and that awful laugh fading away, but staying with her just the same.

That's the old geezer from the tower, cawed Redcrow. *He's bad news. I don't need a glowing portal to know that much.*

Right you are, said Osgrey. *We'll need to deal with him.*

Tired though she was, there was no way she could bear to stay in the cottage for another minute. She wrapped herself in her cloak, grabbed her hat, broom, and basket, and strode out into the snow.

Her plans of experimenting with a late-season garden evaporated in a wisp of sworn revenge. Her sister, raging carnival of annoyance that she'd always been, had really gone a circus too far. Whether she or Ghasterly had been the ringmaster behind this little plot didn't matter. They were both going to pay.

Volgha visited the castle as often as she could stomach, but nothing was ever enough for Her Majesty, the White Queen. She wouldn't be satisfied until Volgha had abandoned the Witching Way altogether, painted her face like a clown of the court, and dedicated the rest of her life to gaudy baubles and vapid dinner conversation.

This could not stand. She wouldn't let it. You didn't vex a witch and skip the consequences. That's just not the way it worked.

Now you're talking, cawed Redcrow. *This is the sort of revenge I'd heard witches had in their hearts! What's it going to be, then?*

"I don't know yet," said Volgha. "I just want to sleep, I can't think straight!"

Had her sister said that no one has seen Loki? That was a problem, especially if her guess was right and he had something to do with all of the warming. Midgard was as good a place as any to look for him. He was one of the Vikings' gods, after all.

She used her blankets to cover the shutters, in order to block any of the light from that ghoulish monstrosity escaping through the cracks and disturbing the spirits of winter any further.

Then, with nothing else to be done but run, she threw her leg over her broom and paused.

It wasn't like Alexia had respected Volgha's privacy in the past, but she'd always been able to get away from her here. But now Her Majesty, the White Queen, had invaded her sanctuary in such a vile and thoughtless manner that leniency was simply out of the question.

Yeah, she'll feel our wrath all right! And what about the necromancer?

"He'll never see another sunrise." Volgha normally felt that that sort of dramatic response was over the top, but her blood was boiling. Redcrow was right—she *did* have revenge in her heart.

But heart full of revenge or no, she was still dead tired. Luckily, Midgard wasn't far, especially if one was able to travel by broom. She'd go there, get some sleep, sort this whole Loki thing out, and then have her revenge on Ghasterly and the White Queen.

FOURTEEN

EVEN IN THE DARKNESS OF THE LATE AUTUMN TWILIGHT, MID-gard was easy to find from a very long way off. Yggdrasil, the Great World Tree, radiated a pale green energy. It positively thrummed on all of the spiritual wavelengths. The Vikings believed that the tree was the world itself, no concern being paid that they could walk away from it and still be on the world. Very conceptual thinkers, the Vikings.

She'd heard before that Vikings were fond of witches, but she wasn't about to test that theory by flying down and landing right next to Yggdrasil while she was too tired for quick getaways. She opted instead to land on the outskirts of the town at the base of the tree and walk into it to find an inn. More effort, but less conspicuous.

All of the buildings were very sturdy, made of stone and thick, rough-hewn lumber. The roofs were covered with permafrost, like just about everything else in the North Pole. She walked past men in great horned helmets carrying massive axes and swords. The older ones had big beards in a variety of colors: red, blonde, brown, black, and the oldest ones were grey or white. The white-bearded ones reminded her of Santa, including the long braided bits.

Poor Santa. Nothing could have prepared him for his harrowing tryst with the queen. He was upset with Volgha over that, and she could certainly see why. Just one more flaming disaster that had somehow become her fire to fight.

Some of the streets were cobbled, others just icy earth. Bonfires burned in great stone rings, many surrounded by Vikings telling stories, laughing, and drinking from horns. It seemed a pleasant and happy life. Volgha would have traded it for being born royalty.

Don't cling to thoughts like that, said Osgrey. *Had you been born a Viking, where would you be now?*

Volgha didn't answer. She was too tired to stop errant thoughts from popping into her head, much less defend them.

She had heard that Viking women were warriors like the men, and she was pleased to see that this was true. Many women, with swords on their hips and shields on their backs, drank and joked with the men, patrolled the streets with the watch, or slept in pools of their own sick near the fires, having overestimated their limits as well as any man.

There was a lot of commotion around a big inn near the center of town, which—according to its sign—was called The Leaping Stag. It was stuffed with revelers, no doubt due to the skill of the minstrel playing the lute inside. As tired as she was, she'd loved to have stepped in and listened to the sublime music for a while. Unfortunately, the throngs of onlookers outside were packed too tightly for her to even get close to the door.

No one actually likes being in crowds, it's merely a condition to be tolerated when everyone wants to be in the same place at the same time. Between Osgrey and Redcrow, Volgha already had all the crowd she could handle. She opted to give this one a miss.

Wandering through the town, she stayed close to the base of the mighty Yggdrasil. It would have taken her all night to walk all the way around it, but luckily there was another inn not too far away. The sign out front bore a cozy looking fireplace with a pair of hounds sleeping in front of it. Just the sort of ambiance she was seeking. She pushed against the door, and it opened.

There was no one inside, only a couple of candles burning on top of the bar.

"Hello?" called Volgha, surprising herself at how hoarse her voice had gone. The lack of sleep might give her a shot at that new career as the husky-voiced lounge singer she'd never wanted to be.

"Yes?" came a voice from the back. "Hello! Have a seat, I'll be there in a moment!"

Tell him to be quick about it, cawed Redcrow. *We Wardens wait for no man!*

"Hush," pleaded Volgha. "Can you please just be quiet for a moment?"

I don't know if this place is fit for a Warden, cawed Redcrow, *but it's certainly a step up from our old hovel.*

"These lodgings are temporary," said Volgha. "And the cottage is not a hovel."

I should say it isn't! Osgrey bristled. *I built that cottage with my own two hands, and started the stew myself!*

Well, it's certainly gone hovel in the meantime. The same can be said for your stew, by the smell of it.

Volgha took a seat at the bar while they bickered, and fought to stay awake. After a couple of minutes, an old man who looked nothing at all like a Viking emerged from the door behind the bar. He was short, had wispy white hair, and no beard at all.

"Welcome to the Old Stone Hearth," he said with a smile. "Sorry there's no supper on, you're the first visitor I've had in ... well, more evenings than you could count on both hands, I reckon!"

"That's okay, I'm not hungry. Everyone's at the huge inn down that way, I take it?"

"The Leaping Stag." The old man grimaced. "It's that minstrel. He's magnificent, I'll give him that, but he's drawn away all of my business! I don't know why he hasn't moved on, that's what his sort like to do."

"He *is* superb," said Volgha. "I heard him when I passed by in the street, but there's no room to so much as stand in there. Not the sort of place that's conducive to a good evening rest."

"Well said. You'll be wanting a room, then?"

"Please."

"It's five pennies an evening."

Volgha said a swear word. She didn't have much money, and what she had was still in the cottage. Witches deal in favors, not cash.

"I'm afraid I don't have any money," said Volgha.

The old man looked her up and down. "You're a witch, aren't you?"

"Well, yes," she answered cautiously.

"Then let's not worry about the money," he said with a smile. "I've got a couple of things that could use a witch's attention, and I'd be happy to give you a room in exchange for services."

That was lucky, cawed Redcrow. *I've heard villagers like to burn witches.*

"And where would you have heard that?" inquired Volgha, turning brusquely to stare at Redcrow.

In your thoughts, crazy lady who yells at birds.

She looked back to the barkeep, who had a sort of surprised expression. Their eyes met, and he suddenly found something in the rafters above the bar that demanded his rapt attention.

"What sort of services?" Volgha was tired, but not so tired that she was going to give the old man a blank chit. She'd negotiate terms before she agreed to any favors.

"Nothing that would be too difficult for you, I imagine. Grinding some herbs, examining a few of my animals out back, and maybe a potion to relieve my gout? Is that something that witchery can do?"

"Yes," replied Volgha, "all of that sounds reasonable."

Druidry could manage it as well, said Osgrey. *If only I were corporeal at the moment, I could—*

"Well you're *not* corporeal, are you?" Volgha was looking up at the ceiling since Osgrey had no face in which her finger could wag. "So since you can't help, why not quietly let me handle it?"

"Er, all right." The old man reached under the bar and produced a little iron key. "Up the stairs, first door on the right. If you need anything, my name is Hans."

"Thank you, Hans. I am Volgha, the Winter Witch."

"Oh," his eyes widened, "I didn't know that there was a witch representing the entire season."

"There are witches for all kinds of things," said Volgha. "Winter is mine."

"Impressive," said Hans. "Sleep well, Volgha, the Winter Witch."

"Good evening."

She had barely shut the door behind her and collapsed into bed before sleep overpowered her, like the smell of milk left out long enough to go fuzzy and start having opinions.

THERE WAS A MOMENT WHEN SHE AWOKE THAT WAS PERFECTLY STILL. She took in a deep breath and let it out. The curtains over the window were parted very slightly, and there was a long ray of crimson sunset painted across the ceiling. She stared at it for a moment, just appreciating the stillness before her mind was flooded with thoughts of everything she needed to address: the horrid portal that her sister had Ghasterly open in her cottage, all the business with Loki, the Warden business—

Do you mind?

Volgha could sense Redcrow's annoyance.

"Do I mind what?" she asked.

You were doing all right there for a moment. That part where you were just staring at the ceiling barely woke me up at all.

"And then my thoughts were too loud, I take it."

He's right you know, said Osgrey. *The Warden must have a quiet mind to attend to her duties.*

"That's just the sort of thing that you should tell the new Warden, whenever you find someone who's interested."

She's interested, said Redcrow. *Would you at least think about it? Don't ruin my big shot for me!*

"It's my decision, not yours."

It's not your decision, said Osgrey, *it's your destiny.*

"I don't believe in destiny!"

Please stop shouting!

"I'm trying, but you two won't give me a moment's peace! I just woke up! Can't I just have a moment to collect my thoughts?"

You share your thinking grounds now, cawed Redcrow. *If you want quiet, you have to be quiet for me as well. And for Osgrey, too, I suppose.*

Volgha sighed. He was right. She knew she'd adjust, just as she'd adjusted to the cottage after growing up in the castle. She just didn't know how to think any more quietly.

You're much louder when you're worried, cawed Redcrow, *and louder still when you're angry. Maybe try to avoid those.*

"Easier said than done," Volgha muttered. "Let's work on it later. For now, we need to find Loki. I'll worry less about that once it's done."

Obviously.

She'd have to help Hans at some point, if for no other reason than to keep people avowing that witches keep their word. But first, she needed to find Loki. Midgard was a big place, and her only friend here so far was an old man who kept an inn with no patrons. Asking around would take far too much effort, so it would have to be magic.

She looked at Redcrow and almost instinctively thought about him circling around the area in a tone that said "please."

Yeah, all right, cawed Redcrow. *Not bad. You're still yelling a bit, though.*

She went to the window and opened it. Redcrow leapt through and took wing.

She could still feel him, though the clarity of the sensation seemed to wane very slightly as he moved farther away.

Going into her satchel, she found salt and rockwort. She ground them together, made a circle on the rough timbers of the floor, and sat in the middle of it.

She'd cast the Seeking spell before, but now that she had Redcrow, it was far more complicated. Then again, it would also be far more powerful. She started whispering her incantations while her hands moved through the motions that accompanied the words. She felt the tug of Redcrow's mind, and the two fell into sync.

Seeking someone out in the Witching Way is very different from scanning a crowd for a familiar face, or looking through a tome for a particular spell. The field in which the Seeker seeks isn't a physical space, it's more like the personality of that space. The Seeker isn't looking around so much as delving into what it means for the space to be what it is, and finding their target is like determining the influence that they have on the space.

So Seeking for Loki in Midgard was like getting to know Midgard, then finding the source of why it was so Loki-like.

When she'd cast the Seeking spell before, it had been like combing through a field of flowers, taking each one in hand and having a sniff. Now that she had Redcrow, the two of them were like a hive of bees, splitting the work not just between the two of them, but among thousands of smaller shadows of their collective self. It was a far more efficient way to search, but the effort of coordinating all of the moving parts was exhausting.

Midgard teemed with life. People were everywhere, and with Yggdrasil so close and Asgard in its branches, the thrumming of power seemed to radiate from everywhere all at once. It was difficult to distinguish between one thing and another.

High above the rooftops, Redcrow widened his circle. The Seeking lost a bit of acuity, but the emanations from Yggdrasil's roots were less overpowering. He dove, rose, circled, and banked until he found a vantage that was far enough from the World Tree to reduce its influence, but close enough to see what they needed to see.

The Vikings were very close to their gods. Any of them would have said so if asked, but the evidence in the Seeking was overwhelming proof. Their gods had made them in their image, and had done such a good job that they were virtually indistinguishable. After a good deal of trial and error, Volgha figured out that the trick to finding gods was to look for Vikings, and to find the ones that simply seemed to be extra *Vikingy*.

She found a couple of the gods, but easily determined that they weren't Loki. The one in the Jarl's longhouse was definitely Thor. He bristled with electricity and reeked of burnt ozone. That must have been Baldur down by the docks, blessing the newest ships in their fleet.

None of the big ones seemed to be Loki. She'd started to think that maybe he wasn't in Midgard at all, or possibly outside the city in one of the farms on the outskirts, when she remembered that she was only looking for half of him. Of course! He wouldn't be as big as the other gods, but he'd still be bigger than the Vikings. So she delved deeper into the hordes of Vikings, examining each one in turn until she finally found him. Bigger than any Viking, dimmer, soaked in wine, and he had an air that made her feel equal parts impatience and loathing. It had to be him. He was at the Leaping Stag with just about everyone else.

She crossed back over, opened her eyes, stood up, and promptly fell back to the floor. Even though she'd just slept for several hours, she felt as though she'd flown the length and breadth of Midgard twice over without the benefit of a broom.

One of us did, cawed Redcrow. *Credit where credit is due.*

She was starting to lose track of where she ended and Redcrow began.

All a part of the process, said Osgrey. *You'll get the hang of Redcrow assisting in your spells, not to worry.*

She crawled back into bed, panting and covered in a sheen of sweat. The frigid breeze felt good, but she knew she'd need to close the window if she didn't want to freeze to death.

She sought for Redcrow. He was exhausted as well, and had taken roost in the branches of a snow-laden tree.

She closed the window. Together but apart, they both drifted off to sleep.

SHE AWOKE AGAIN SOME TIME LATER TO THE SOUND OF FLAPPING wings and rustling branches. Redcrow had left the tree where he'd napped, and woken her with his thoughts of breakfast. So that was what *that* was like. She hoped that they'd learn how to tune each other out a bit as time went on.

Volgha was ravenous. She wasn't sure how long she'd been asleep this time, but in any case, it had been a long while since she'd eaten anything.

She straightened herself up a bit, donned her pointy hat, and walked down into the bar to find it exactly as it had been when she'd first arrived: empty with a pair of candles flickering on the bar.

"Hans?" She sat down at the bar. After a moment, the old man's head poked through the door behind the bar, smiling.

"Hello, Volgha," he said. "How's the room, to your taste?"

"It's lovely," replied Volgha. "Could I trouble you for something to eat?"

"Of course!" he said, then disappeared back through the door.

In the dim light, Volgha could see that the bar was ancient. By the way that the wooden top of the bar had been worn smooth, she guessed that it was older even than Hans. The shelves behind the bar were lined with bottles filled with brown and amber spirits like you'd find in any bar. There didn't seem to be a speck of dust in the place, even on the bottles on the top shelf. It was apparent that Hans cared deeply about the Old Stone Hearth.

It wasn't long before she caught the scent of meat cooking, and not long after that, Hans came back into the room with a wooden plate bearing some sort of meat pie smothered in gravy. He set it down in front of Volgha, poured water from a pitcher into a wooden cup, and offered that to her as well.

"Thank you." The pie smelled a bit bland, but when one is accustomed to proper stew, everything else pales in comparison. She shoveled it in, not sparing time for such frivolities as tasting and enjoying. In no time at all, her fork clattered on the empty plate.

Slow down, said Osgrey. *You'll sprain something, wolfing your food down like that! We took our time with our food in my day, when we were lucky enough to have it.*

"You're a generous host," said Volgha. "I have time to see to part of your payment, is there one thing in particular you'd like done?"

"Er, the gout, if you don't mind." He grinned sheepishly. "The cold goes right into my joints these days, and it's been hard to get much work done."

"Very well," she said. "I have most of what I need upstairs, but I'm afraid I'm all out of cragflower. Do you have any?"

"Is dried okay? I have some dried."

"It will do."

He disappeared into the back again and returned with a wooden jar. Volgha looked into it, stood up, and nodded.

"This won't take long." She went upstairs and closed the door.

Redcrow wasn't far away now, so she opened the window and set herself about the task of measuring out her herbs.

She'd just finished grinding them when Redcrow returned. She poured the powdered mixture back into Hans' wooden jar, picked up her broom, and went back downstairs with Redcrow on her shoulder. Hans was standing behind the bar.

"Make a pot of tea from two spoonfuls," she said. "Drink a pot every evening until you run out, and it should keep you as fresh as the falling snow until the sun rises again."

"Oh, thank you," Hans smiled. "I'll make a pot right now!"

"Good," said Volgha. "I'm off to handle some business."

"Farewell!" Hans smiled and waved.

The air was brisk. She wasn't sure she'd remember the way back to the Leaping Stag until she tried to recall where it was, and then she realized that she remembered the whole of the town as though she'd flown over it herself.

You're welcome, cawed Redcrow.

It was just as full as it had been when she'd first seen it, if not fuller. It was practically infested with Vikings who were hell-bent on weaponizing their collective body odor. Her hackles mounted stilts at the thought of having to wade through the sea of people. Still, the music coming from inside sounded too delightful to pass up. She could at least have a listen while she tried to find Loki.

Oh, that's just lovely! Osgrey started to hum completely out of tune with the music, which set Volgha's teeth on edge. She didn't care, though. She simply strained to tune him out.

"Redcrow, could you clear us a path?"

Look alive, peasants! Redcrow cawed aloud. *Wardens coming through, Wardens of the North Pole!*

"Caw!" was all that anyone but Volgha heard, as Redcrow flapped low over the crowd. The Vikings in the doorway stepped aside reflexively, giving Volgha a look. She stepped past them before they had a chance to say anything about it and started weaving through the crowd.

No need to kneel before the Wardens this time, just get out of the way!

No one seemed to notice them, aside from those close enough to the flurry of red feathers to be startled aside. It was slow-going, slithering amid the enraptured throng of unwashed beasts. Volgha tried not to breathe.

She eventually made her way up to the little stage, and there he was: Loki, in significantly less grandeur than his full complement of wits would have tolerated. He looked as though he hadn't slept in days, and was being fueled by wine alone—so at least that much hadn't changed. His eyes were dark and forlorn, but his fingers danced over the strings of his lute with impeccable grace and expertise.

The little stage was surrounded by Vikings, raptly staring while he played. Truly, the music was beautiful. Haunting. Volgha felt herself being drawn in.

Not bad, cawed Redcrow, *if you're into that sort of thing.*

"It's wonderful." Volgha smiled with wonder. "Shall we listen for a while?"

Oh, let's! said Osgrey.

Redcrow's feathers shook, and he flapped his wings.

Let's not. There's something odd about this tune, don't you think? Volgha? Osgrey?

No response. Redcrow flapped and squawked. Squawking was singularly undignified behavior for a crow, but Redcrow sensed that desperate times were afoot.

Volgha willed Redcrow to be quiet, not wanting to slip out of the reverie. She just wanted to sit and listen to this glorious music for as long as she could.

The Vikings sitting around Volgha apparently wanted the same thing, and one or two of them swatted lazily at Redcrow to hush him up. He dodged and flew up into the rafters.

"Quiet," said Volgha.

Redcrow cawed a swear word. *It's an enchantment! Don't listen, you'll get trapped in it!*

It is not, said Osgrey. *I'd know if it was, believe me. It's just the sweetest music I've ever heard! I could listen to it forever.*

Volgha made no reply. She simply sat and listened, enraptured by the chords and scales that rang out from the lute. Sublime arpeggios trilled from Loki's fingers with practiced ease. They delighted her. She only wanted to hear what came next.

Redcrow had finally gone quiet. She could still feel his presence up in the rafters. He was fine. He was ... plotting something ...

Oh, but such music!

She forgot about Redcrow, let him fade into the background with the din of all of her other thoughts. The notes rose and fell in measured patterns so sublime, that—

In the name of the Warden!

In a flurry of scarlet feathers, Loki was bowled backward over his chair. The music stopped, the lute flew out of his hands, and Loki hit his head on the polished wooden boards of the stage. Redcrow ended his gallant charge by flying back up into the rafters. Volgha and all of the Vikings rubbed their eyes, shook their heads, and looked around as though they had no idea where they were.

"I'm starving," said a great red-bearded Viking next to Volgha.

"What happened to the music?" asked another Viking with a black beard. "I was listening to that!"

A few other Vikings growled and grumbled their agreement. Others yawned, the bags under their eyes as big as sausages.

What started as confusion flew past annoyance with alarming speed on its collision course with rage. In a crowded room, the worst thing that could possibly happen is for the angriest among them to start coming up with the ideas. Especially when the angriest are the ones with the big swords and axes strapped to them.

To make matters worse, there is a single catalyst that makes it very easy for anger to run the show, and at that particular moment, that was exactly what happened.

"Yeah?" shouted a blonde Viking woman who had accidentally bumped her shield into a blonde Viking man, who'd given her the old watch-it-with-that-thing. "What are you going to do about it?"

It is a well-known fact across every world culture that there are a certain number of magical spells that may be cast by any person at any time, whether they're a wizard, witch, baker, or student just out of the university who hasn't quite decided what she wants to do with her life. One such spell is an eight-word incantation, which compels a person to punch the caster in the face without hesitation. Predictably, in this instance, the magic succeeded.

"Hey!" shouted a different Viking who also had a great blonde beard. "You just punched my sist—" and was punched as well.

Vikings' affection for a good fight rivals that of adolescent girls for yawning kittens. As soon as one starts, there's no keeping them away from it. So it was that the entire room gave gleeful smiles and started punching whatever faces happened to reside within the proper distance.

Volgha ducked, weaved, and generally concentrated on being in whatever spot wasn't occupied by a fist at any given moment. She rolled under a table and did her best to stay there, until one Viking pushed another over the top of it, and the table went crashing to the side behind him.

In the rush that followed, she got the wind knocked out of her with a kick that may or may not have been intentional, and then a big armored boot planted itself squarely on her ankle. She cried out, scrambled up, and started limping her way toward the door.

She was rushing, careless. She didn't see the fist that clearly had the right-of-way in the busy traffic and darted blithely into its path. Her head spun, and before she could find her bearings, she felt herself being lifted up, flung through the air, and then colliding twice: once with the shelves full of booze behind the bar, and again with the floor behind said bar.

She used the brief respite to crawl into a corner and cast the spell to make herself Dim. *Best just to wait this one out*, she decided.

Good idea, cawed Redcrow from his perch in the rafters. It appeared as though they'd be there a while.

FIFTEEN

"THAT WAS A GOOD ONE," SAID THE BARTENDER, A BIG, BURLY VI-king with a grey beard.

"A good one?" Volgha shouted, partially from the adrenaline still coursing through her, but also because all of the roaring and shouting during the brawl had left a persistent ringing in her ears.

"Yeah." The bartender smiled. "It's nice when the whole community comes together like that. Reminds us all that we've got friends and neighbors just like us."

"It was a brawl!"

"Sure, but only punching and kicking. There may have been a bit of biting, too, but no steel came out."

"They destroyed the place!"

"Hasn't happened in a while. We were overdue. Besides, now all of the furniture makers, glass blowers, carpenters, and the like have orders to fill. The occasional row is good for the economy."

"Are you serious?"

"Aye," said the bartender. "Besides, I finally had a reason to punch Sven. Been wanting to do that for years. I think he lost a tooth! It was a fine dust-up."

Volgha stood up. Her head spun a little and her ribs hurt, but the worst was her ankle. She was fairly certain it wasn't broken, but she'd be limping for a while at the very least.

She straightened up, donned her pointy hat, and made her way over to the stage where Loki was part of an unconscious pile, which snored loudly enough to go professional.

I don't think brawling is our game. Redcrow looked down from the rafters, where he'd watched the whole show.

"I hope you're pleased with yourself," she said with a grimace.

The two of you were just going to sit down and drool along with the music, cawed Redcrow. *You should be thanking me! I broke the spell!*

I was working on a plan, Osgrey protested. *I just wanted to enjoy the music while I was doing it.*

"Be that as it may," said Volgha, "you started a fight. We could have handled it with more subtlety!"

You'd have subtly starved to death, cawed Redcrow. *You got off easy, with what? A few unanswered punches, a twisted ankle, and a little toss behind a bar?*

She hadn't thought about the punches having gone unanswered. Her bruises would mend, but some cretin—or rather, several cretins—had gotten away with knocking a witch around. Volgha knew that she had far more important things to deal with, but it galled her to think that these vexes were going to go unanswered.

Wasn't that something? asked Osgrey. *We took a mighty toss! We went flying through the air, whoosh! And then, bang! And then, thud. It must have been painful. Unlucky for you, having a body and all.*

"Thanks for reminding me." Volgha winced as she stretched, now acutely aware of which of her ribs had been involved with the aforementioned "bang" and "thud." She'd survey the damage later, preferably during a soak in a nice hot tub. For now, she set herself about the task of liberating the unconscious Loki from under a pair of snoring Vikings. She managed to wake one of them and had to settle for rolling the other one away.

"Loki," she said, trying to gently shake him awake. No response. She shook him harder.

"Loki!" She gave him a good slap. He snored.

She slapped him again and tried to suppress a grin.

You enjoyed that one, cawed Redcrow.

"He had it coming."

Another slap. Still nothing. Loki snored with a vengeance, as though he were trying his hand at lumberjacking simply by making the noise of the saw.

That doesn't seem to be doing any good, cawed Redcrow.

"So now knocking someone around is a bad idea? Mind your own business!"

"Is he all right?" asked the bartender, who was giving her a look that one might give a crazy person who got into shouting matches with birds.

"More or less," Volgha replied. "How long had he been playing?"

"A dozen evenings, at least. It was amazing, I've never seen anything like it!"

"He needs to sleep," said Volgha. "Can you have him brought up to a room?"

"Sure, but who's going to pay for it?"

"Take it out of whatever you were going to pay him."

"I wasn't going to pay him," said the bartender. "Minstrels are paid by the patrons, he knew the deal."

"Then where is the money the patrons gave him?"

The bartender shrugged. "Must have gotten swept away in the fight."

The look that Volgha gave the bartender could have curdled a block of stone.

I know that look, cawed Redcrow. *Give him the business!*

"So you mean to tell me," Volgha growled, "that this man gave you an enormous crowd for a dozen evenings, a brawl that will be the talk of the town until spring, provided a boon to the economy, played himself nearly to death, and you have the gall to ask 'who's going to pay for his room?'" She hadn't intended to turn on a glamour, but there are times when a witch's magic just sort of seeps out unexpectedly, like farts in church.

Her eyes went black. Thunder rolled through the rafters, and shadowy tendrils started to creep out from under her dress.

"Put him in a room right now," said a pair of voices, one Volgha's and the other several octaves lower, "and let him sleep until he wakes! Never mind the cost, and never ask another stupid question of a witch again!"

A streak of pale and clammy bartender whisked Loki over its shoulder and hoofed it for the stairs.

The thunder faded, the shadows dissolved, and Volgha's eyes went back to their natural color—though one of them was still black, but only in the post-brawl sense.

Oh, you've got the hang of that, said Osgrey. *That's the sort of intimidation that only comes from practiced witchery! You'll make a fine Warden, I'm sure of it!*

"I'm still not interested!"

Yes, she is! Redcrow flapped and cawed. *Look, just don't make any decisions until we've got this mess sorted out. You're not thinking clearly.*

Volgha made a dismissive noise, somewhere between a groan and a growl. She knew perfectly well that she didn't want to be the Warden of anything because she knew her own mind. It was the same mind that was far too groggy to fight about it.

She picked up her broom, which had ended up near the edge of the stage. Half of its bristles were gone, but it was otherwise serviceable.

"Let's go," she said to Redcrow. He flew onto her shoulder as she hobbled toward the door.

"It's true," said one of several Vikings standing outside the door. His beard was grey.

"What?" said Volgha.

"A witch with a blood red raven started a great brawl in the tavern!"

Crow, cawed Redcrow.

"It's not important." Volgha pointed a finger at Redcrow. "Fine, word's gotten around. What of it?"

"Heimdall sent us for you," said the Viking.

"Did he?" asked Volgha. "Or she? Sorry, I don't know who that is."

"He guards Bifrost," explained a woman holding an enormous axe, "the bridge that leads to Asgard. He said Odin wants to speak with you."

"I didn't start any brawl," said Volgha.

"That's all right," she replied. "Odin still wants to speak to you."

There were half a dozen Vikings there, armed to the teeth and intent on bringing Volgha before the chief of their gods. Volgha didn't particularly want to play along, but considered that they might have wanted to appease their god more strongly than she wanted to go lie down with her ankle in a bucket of snow.

"Fine," she muttered. "Lead on."

One of the Vikings struck the ground twice with the butt of his spear, and they all started marching toward Yggdrasil. Volgha limped along behind them. They readily outpaced her, stopping every so often so that she could catch up. She made no great effort.

"Can't you walk faster?" inquired one of the Vikings, as she caught up with them for the fourth time.

She glared at him. "No, I can't. One of you horn-helmed idiots stepped on my ankle in the brawl, and it hurts to walk on it. This is how fast I can walk."

"It's going to take you until spring to climb the ten thousand steps."

"Ten thousand steps?"

"The staircase," he said, pointing to Yggdrasil. "Asgard is at the top."

"Oh, forget it." Volgha mounted her broom and rose up into the sky, a bit less smoothly than usual for all of the missing bristles. The shouts of the Vikings below quickly faded from her ears. Redcrow flew alongside her, and within a few minutes, they were high enough to see the great golden doors that led into the halls of the gods. They were quite impressive, though enormous golden doors generally couldn't help but be. She touched down just outside the doors, and two guards crossed spears before them to block her way.

"Halt!" demanded one of the guards. "Who approaches the gates of Asgard?"

"Volgha the Winter Witch."

"Caw!" said Redcrow, which Volgha understood to mean "ahem."

"And Redcrow," she said.

"A red raven!" The guard stared with his mouth open. "Surely it's an omen!"

"It's a crow," said Volgha, having the grace to pass on the obvious pun.

He's *a crow*, cawed Redcrow reproachfully.

"It doesn't matter!" Volgha snapped. "Just be quiet!"

I'm here, too, you know.

"Not the time, Osgrey!"

"Right," said the guard, his eyes narrowed. "And why do," he waved his hand toward Volgha and Redcrow, "the lot of you wish to enter the hall of the gods?"

"I don't," said Volgha, "but this Odin fellow insisted that I do."

"Odin is not just some fellow," balked the guard. "He is the All-father! First among the gods, and Lord of all Vikings!"

Oh, how nice for him.

"That's not helping," Volgha said to Redcrow. She turned back to the guard. "Look, I've had a rough time of it, and this summons is the only thing standing between me and a well-earned nap. So if you don't mind—"

"If you were summoned, you'd have an honor guard. Where is your honor guard?"

"Walking up thousands of stairs, I presume. I made my own way." She lifted her broom slightly for emphasis. "Now I'm done talking to underlings, are you going to open the door or not?"

"I can't just open the door for everyone who claims to have been summoned by Odin. What would happen if word got out?"

"Block me if you like, only give me your name so I can give a reason why I didn't turn up when Odin Allfather summoned me."

He balked. "Well, that's not— It's just— Wait here, I'll have to check."

"I'm not that patient," said Volgha. "Just give me your name, and I'll go."

"I— Oh, fine, but I'll have to escort you in."

Volgha smirked at him. "If it's not too much trouble."

The guard opened the doors and led Volgha inside. The vaulted ceilings were impossibly tall, disappearing into shadows above that the torches ensconced on the walls could not reach. Statues, suits of armor on stands, great urns with fruit-bearing plants, and other divine spectacles lined the great hall. One plant in particular bore berries that continually changed colors. Their fragrance was mesmerizing, nearly enough to make Volgha forget how incurably grumpy she was.

They walked on past more splendor until they finally came to a great banquet, with most of the gods in attendance. Odin sat at the head of the table, his great white hair and beard slowly flowing in a breeze that wasn't really there. His left eye bore a jeweled patch, with an enormous ruby in the center.

The guard stopped at the foot of the table, struck the floor twice with the butt of his spear, and announced her in a bold voice.

"Volgha," he announced, "the Winter Witch. And her crow, er … Redcrow."

"Thank you," said Odin. "You may go."

The guard glared at Volgha for a second, then spun around on his heel and went back the way they'd come in.

"Please." Odin gestured to a seat on his left, on the other side of a man who could only have been Thor. Volgha limped over to the chair and sat. A wine bearer filled her cup with a honey-colored, fragrant liquid.

"Nectar of the gods," said Thor. "For your wounds sustained in glorious battle."

"Glorious battle!" shouted one of the other gods, standing quickly and raising his cup. It was Tyr, she assumed, from the missing hand.

"Glorious battle!" the other gods shouted in unison, standing and raising their cups and horns. They all paused and looked at her.

When in Asgard, said Osgrey, *maybe do as the Aesir gods do?*

"Glorious battle." Volgha stood, raising her cup. They all drank. Volgha couldn't help but drain her cup, it was so delicious! It was like honey and sunshine and magic all mixed together and massaged into her face by angels!

A different wine bearer refilled her cup with red wine, and she looked around for the other one—the one with the nectar.

"Wine for you now," said Odin with a smile. "The nectar of the gods is potent, and more than a little has driven mortals mad."

"Thank you." Volgha reluctantly settled for the wine. She took a sip. It was excellent as well, though it paled in comparison.

"And thank you for trekking the ten thousand steps," said Odin. "How do you find our realm?"

"It's lovely," said Volgha, avoiding the issue of the stairs. Witch's prerogative.

"Tell me a tale," Odin boomed. "Unfold for me the glorious battle that took place below."

"Glorious battle!" shouted all of the gods in unison again, on their feet with cups held aloft. Volgha jumped up as well, wondering if it would be the only compulsory phrase of the event.

"It was a massive brawl," said Volgha. "All of your Vikings seemed to enjoy it very much."

"And how were you inspired to start it?"

"Well, in truth, it was Redcrow who started it."

Sure, blame the handsome one.

Odin stood up and raised his cup. Everyone else followed suit.

"To Redcrow," he said. "Cousin to my ravens, whose fiery blood is plain on his breast. Battle bringer, blood avenger, may the songs of the bards carry your glory aloft!"

"To Redcrow!" shouted everybody, who then drained their cups and cheered. Redcrow spread his wings and cawed, posing as though someone was painting a flag of him.

A fellow could get used to this!

"I can see how he inspired the Vikings to fight," said Thor.

"Not that it takes much," said Frigga, on the other side of Odin.

"He was trying to break a spell," said Volgha.

"A spell?" Odin put his cup down and leaned in toward her. "Was there another witch there? Or a wizard?"

"It was Loki, actually."

"Loki!" Thor shouted, as though the name was a swear word. "What has that idiot done now?"

Volgha saw an opportunity. Loki's riddle had gotten out of hand, and it appeared as though he'd proven himself right in one regard: he was clever enough to outfox himself. Maybe the other gods could undo the damage before it got any worse.

"Yes," said Volgha. "Well, half of him anyway." She explained the riddle to the gods, told them about the rising temperatures, and how she'd found him in the guise of a minstrel in Midgard below. All of the gods listened to her story, paying rapt attention and barely drinking heavily at all as she spoke.

"So he's fooled himself?" asked Odin.

"It appears that way, yes."

Odin burst into laughter, as did all of the other gods.

"Serves him right!" Thor's fist pounded the table as he laughed, sending forks and knives clattering to the floor.

"Perhaps," said Volgha, "but it's still getting hotter. That can't be good, can it?"

"It's a small matter," said Odin. "Let the fool work it out when he wakes up. It's his affair, and we know better than to fall for his trickery."

"But I don't know if he *can* work it out," said Volgha. "It's been so long already, and he's only got half his mind to work with!"

"He'll do it soon enough." Thor smiled broadly. "Until he does, enjoy the warm air!"

Odin stopped laughing abruptly, and his face went pale. He sat back in his throne and took up a posture designed specifically for brooding.

"What is it?" Volgha saw the concern in Odin's face, and it mirrored the dark feeling that had been growing in her heart for a while.

"It's getting warmer ... everywhere?"

"Just in the high places, though it seems to be moving lower. The snow turned to water in my grove not long ago."

"What of Niflheim," asked Odin, "is it warmer there as well?"

Thor's expression went grim at the question. He looked to Volgha for an answer. All of the gods had grown quiet.

This doesn't bode well, said Osgrey.

"I don't know," she replied. "I've never been to Niflheim. I didn't think there was anything there."

There was a sense of urgency in Odin's brooding. His eye shifted back and forth between Frigga and Thor, both of whom shared his dour expression.

"The frost giants," said Thor.

Odin shot a pointed look in his direction, and he grew silent.

"I thought the Vikings didn't like the frost giants," said Volgha. "Didn't you banish them there, Odin?"

"That's right," he answered. "A long time ago."

"Will something happen to them if Niflheim gets too warm?"

"Possibly," said Frigga, "but what do we care?" Her eyes widened as she stared at Odin.

Strange, cawed Redcrow, *how people open their eyes wide to tell someone to keep their mouth shut.*

"Right," said Odin. "It's nothing. Let the frost giants melt, for all we care! Thoughtless beasts, the lot of them!"

The food was as good as the wine. Volgha ate her fill of pork and venison. Thor told her that they never ate beef because there was no glory in hunting a cow. Boar and deer, on the other hand, presented a challenge (insofar as hunting an animal can provide a challenge to a god).

A plate was provided for Redcrow as well, and he quickly decided that anchovies were the most sublime food he'd ever tasted. He and Volgha both enjoyed themselves immensely, though Volgha could not help but think of her sleepy little cottage in the grove, now befouled by her sister's ghastly green fire. It soured her mood, but that was just the sort of thing that made revenge sweeter in the end.

By the time she left, the pain in her ankle was entirely gone. It seemed that nectar of the gods had miraculous curative powers, and it left her feeling very light and merry. She was relentlessly giggling, though she resisted the urge when anyone was looking. It was like being drunk, only without the impaired motor skills, the urge to vomit, or—in the case of clear spirits— the repetitive shouting of, "Woo hoo!"

Past the golden doors again, she mounted her broom and took flight. The air grew cooler as she circled down toward Midgard, though the Asgardian wine kept her warm enough until she touched down at the Old Stone Hearth. Hans was nowhere to be seen, so she slipped in silently and went up the stairs to her room.

That went rather well, cawed Redcrow.

"In what sense?" asked Volgha. "We're still on our own to sort out Loki's mess."

Oh, right. I just meant the anchovies. Can we get some more?

"Hard to come by in the North," said Volgha. "Outside of Asgard anyway. But I'll see what I can do."

Volgha's head was still swimming, thanks to the nectar. She curled up in the blankets and drifted off to sleep. It may have been the most peacefully she'd ever dreamt, mostly just floating around on clouds and the like. Redcrow also slept well, blissfully unable to hear Volgha's thoughts for once.

WHEN SHE AWOKE FROM HER EVENING, THERE WERE THINGS THAT needed doing. She ground herbs for Hans and borrowed some straw so that she could repair her broom. It would fly a bit sluggishly until she could get it attuned properly, but that would have to wait. Business had started to trickle into the Old Stone Hearth, now that Loki wasn't mesmerizing a monopoly elsewhere.

She made her way back over to the Leaping Stag, where they had already done a surprisingly good job of putting things back together. There were still splintered ends on the bannisters and the bar, and a carpenter was at work replacing the doors, but the place was capable of putting booze into Vikings.

The bartender nodded to Volgha as she entered, but kept his eye contact to a minimum. One did not stare into the cold, black eyes of an angry witch and maintain a full measure of audacity. She gave him a prim smile.

"Good morning, mistress," greeted the bartender. "I trust the hour finds you well."

"Quite," said Volgha, trying not to enjoy his cowering too much. "How is our guest?"

"Still abed," replied the bartender. "Or in his room, at least. Free of charge, of course!"

Volgha nodded and walked to the stairs.

"Third door on the right!"

"Thank you," she said without stopping. She found the door and knocked on it. There was no answer. She tried the handle, and it opened easily on its iron hinges.

"Loki?"

"Who's there?"

The room was dark. Volgha opened the door, and the dim light from the hallway outlined the shape of Loki sitting on the bed. Volgha walked inside and turned her attention to the stub of candle sitting on the little table. She didn't know how much he remembered, but figured that a little bit of magic wouldn't go amiss—just for dramatic effect, of course.

She reached out with her mind, found a bit of fire residing in the tip of the wick, and coaxed it out. The candle sputtered to life. After closing the door behind her, she sat on the little chair by the table with Redcrow on her shoulder.

"How did you do that?" he asked, a haunted look in his wide eyes. "Who are you?"

"You don't remember me? Pity. I'll answer, but you go first."

"My name ..." A quizzical expression overtook his haunted one. His eyes narrowed, and his fingers traced absently about his lips. "This shouldn't be so difficult to answer."

"No," said Volgha. "You're right about that. What can you remember?"

"The lute." That much had come back to him without any consternation. He spoke more slowly after that, as though it were coming back to him in fragments.

"I walked here," he said. "From ... very far away. I had this lute, but that was all. I'm not sure how I knew the way here. What is this place?"

"Midgard."

"Should I know it?"

"Oh yes. You're close to home."

"I have a home nearby? Where? Can you take me?"

"In due time," said Volgha. "It might be dangerous if you don't know who you are. Tell me about the lute, what was that song you were playing?"

"Oh, that," said Loki. "I don't know, exactly. I started plucking the strings while I was walking, and I seemed to be pretty good. I assumed I was a minstrel, is that right?"

"In a manner of speaking. Tell me about the song."

"They let me play on the stage, and I started going through songs as they popped into my head. That one, that song ... it was bewitching, to be sure."

"Not the word I'd use, but not far from the mark."

"Sorry," said Loki, apparently just noticing the pointy hat and black ensemble. "Anyway, I really enjoyed the sound of it, and so did everyone else. I just couldn't seem to make myself stop playing it ... not until your friend here stopped me, that is."

That's right, cawed Redcrow, puffing his chest up a bit. *And I'll do it again, so don't get any ideas.*

"Easy, Redcrow," said Volgha. "Honestly, he thinks he's a warrior now!"

I'd have done the same, said Osgrey, *if I had a body!*

"Now don't you start," said Volgha.

"Who are you talking to?" asked Loki.

"To him," Volgha pointed to Redcrow, "as well as ... never mind. How are you feeling?"

"I could sleep through the winter," said Loki.

"Sleep then," said Volgha. "I'll have some food sent up for you."

"Thank you, but please, can you tell me who you are? Or who I am?"

"My name is Volgha, the Winter Witch. Yours is Loki. Ring any bells?"

"No. There's a god named Loki, am I named after him?"

"In a manner of speaking," replied Volgha. "Rest up. I'll come back for you when it's time."

"Thanks." Loki gave her a warm smile.

Volgha wished she could have frozen the image somehow, so she could show it to him after she'd restored his mind. It would gall him endlessly to see himself simpering so.

She simply nodded and left. She asked the bartender to send up some food, then made her way back to the Old Stone Hearth. She meant to have a look at Hans' animals so she could clear her debt. When she walked into the bar, she saw a trio of people eating whom she recognized immediately as Faesolde elves from Santa's Village.

One of the Faesolde in particular seemed very familiar. She'd not gotten his name, but she'd seen him in Santa's armory. His eyes met hers, and his head tilted just slightly. His gaze held a mix of familiarity and curiosity.

"I've seen you before," he said.

"In Santa's armory," she replied.

"Then you're Volgha," he said. "The witch from the valley. Santa speaks highly of you. Won't you join us?"

"Thank you." She took the fourth chair at the little table. "And you are?"

"Vaethul," he replied. "And these are my brothers, Cuidesi and Fashide."

"I'm pleased to meet all of you. What brings you to Midgard?"

"Our alliance with King Harald," explained Cuidesi. "Northmen have traditions, and we help Santa observe them."

"Santa is a Northman, then?"

"If you asked the Vikings," said Vaethul, "they'd say he was a southerner. It's all the same to us, but there are subtle differences."

"Such as?"

"Santa doesn't bend his knee to their gods," Fashide answered. "There's no enmity there, he's just not one of them. Santa doesn't agree with their ideas of glorious battle."

Volgha had to restrain herself from jumping up and toasting to glorious battle, a reflex she'd developed with alarming speed in Asgard. Fashide was right about their affinity for it, in the abstract at least.

"But I've seen the armory," said Volgha. "Santa is quite the warrior, from the looks of it."

"He was," said Vaethul. "His life was hard before he came to the North. Suffice it to say that he doesn't refer to his past as his glory days."

"Then why the grand armory? I've seen him go in several times. It doesn't seem as though he's trying to put the past behind him."

Vaethul inclined his head toward her. "There's a difference between setting the sword aside and pretending never to have picked it up. If we forget the darkness of war, then it has taught us nothing; so we carry it with us."

Best to leave it at that, said Osgrey, just as Volgha was drawing a breath to ask another question. *We delve into the mysteries of nature and the spirit. People's mysteries are theirs alone. They'll reveal what they care to.*

Volgha nodded.

"How is Santa keeping?" asked Vaethul.

Does he think Santa's with us? cawed Redcrow.

"I would imagine that you've seen him more recently than I have," she said.

"Not since before he left for Castle Borealis in his ... attire."

"We left there many evenings ago," said Volgha. "Did he never return to the village?"

Vaethul and Fashide exchanged a worried look.

"He did," said Cuidesi, "but not for long. He was in horrible shape, said he needed to lie low for a while."

"Do you know where he went?"

"Someplace called 'Howling Hill'," replied Cuidesi. "I don't know where that is, do you?"

"I can find it," said Volgha.

"We would appreciate knowing that Santa is in good health," said Fashide.

"I'll find out," said Volgha, "and send news to the village."

They talked a while longer, then the elves went off to have their audience with King Harald. Volgha fulfilled her promise to Hans, finding nothing wrong with his animals that couldn't be easily remedied. He thanked her, saying that his gout was already much improved by the tea.

After a short nap, she took to the air and headed toward Santa's Village. She'd try to Seek him out from there, which shouldn't prove too difficult now that she had Redcrow's assistance.

SIXTEEN

V OLGHA ALMOST MISSED SANTA'S SHELTER AT THE FOOT OF THE hill, but she'd seen the boxes over the howling eggs that he said he'd placed there before. It wasn't until she'd flown down very low over the surface that she noticed the tent. The top was white and blended in with the snow. It was a sort of insulated tent, well-supported by stout wooden beams. Quite comfortable on the inside, actually. A far cry from roughing it in the wilderness, as she'd expected.

"You're a hard man to find," said Volgha, unwrapping her scarf from around her face.

"When I need to be," said Santa. "Is that a red raven?"

"Crow," she replied with a smile. "He's my familiar, the reason we went to all of the trouble at the castle."

So he does your dirty work for you, cawed Redcrow. *Can I send him on an errand?*

"Hush, Redcrow," said Volgha. "He owed me a favor, that's all."

"You named him Redcrow?" Santa's eyebrow went up. "A bit obvious, isn't it?"

"Sort of a misunderstanding that stuck," said Volgha. "Anyway, thank you for playing your part. We're square on the favor."

"Almost," said Santa. "There's the matter of your crazy sister trying to murder me."

"Hello, Volgha!" Krespo waved as he ran over to where they stood. He was wearing an apron and smelled like a cooking fire.

"Did Santa tell you that we're in hiding? Is your sister going to come after us?"

"I wouldn't worry about that," said Volgha. "She does this sort of thing from time to time, but she usually forgets about it as soon as something shiny catches her eye."

"She *usually* forgets?" Santa asked.

"Well, yes." Volgha's mouth stayed open for a few more seconds, but nothing more reassuring found its way out, so she closed it.

"That's a relief," said Krespo. "We're scared to go back to the keep, in case she turns up there looking for us."

"We're not scared, Krespo," countered Santa. "We just don't want to endanger everyone there."

"Right," said Krespo, "because we're afraid of the queen."

"Stop saying that! In any case, we'll be square once you can assure me that she's not hunting me."

"I told you, you shouldn't worry about that. There are no debts between us."

"I think the pendulum's swung the other way," said Santa.

"That's not the way that favors work with witches," said Volgha.

"Maybe not," said Santa, "but being hunted wasn't part of the plan. If she *usually* forgets about these things, you can make sure she's forgotten this time, can't you? Call it a gesture of goodwill toward your neighbor?"

She frowned at that. Santa had made several gestures of goodwill since they met, and refusing this one would lose her the moral high ground. She did enjoy the moral high ground. It was an excellent vantage for looking down her nose at everyone else.

"Oh, all right," she said. "You did go through a lot, and the summoning was a great success."

Well, it worked, anyway, cawed Redcrow.

"Thank you," said Santa. "Are you hungry?"

"I am," Volgha answered.

I am, too! Does he have any anchovies?

"I don't know," said Volgha, "I'll ask. Redcrow won't shut up about anchovies. You don't have any, do you?"

"I don't," said Santa. "They're not very common in the North Pole. How does he know about them?"

"That's an interesting story," said Volgha.

Krespo laid out a spread of dried meats and hard cheeses. No anchovies, but Redcrow contented himself with some salted pork. Osgrey seemed to be asleep.

As they ate, Volgha told Santa and Krespo all about their adventures in Midgard and Asgard. Santa confessed that he'd never been to Asgard before, and was more than a little bit envious.

Volgha cocked her head to the side, as if studying him. "Vaethul and his brothers said that you used to be quite the warrior."

Santa said nothing, almost loudly enough to warrant a shushing.

"Used to be, eh?" he said after a while, if only to chase away the silence.

You've offended him, cawed Redcrow. *This is getting interesting.*

"Well," Volgha hastened to clarify, "that is to say that you no longer choose to walk that path. Not that you couldn't. If you wanted to."

Santa glanced at her and gave her a smirk. "You may have been right the first time. I never wanted to be a warrior in the first place, and it was a long time before I was able to walk away from it. In any case, it was all a long time ago. I'm done with it."

Volgha nodded, suddenly very sorry she'd brought it up.

"The snow up here is starting to melt," said Santa, grasping for a new topic of conversation. "We have to maintain trenches around the tent, like a moat."

"I'd noticed that," said Volgha. "The frost must have melted from the howling eggs shortly after it started getting warm up among the clouds."

"So it's the high places," said Krespo.

"That seems to be the case." Volgha shrugged.

"You said that Odin asked about Niflheim in particular," said Santa. "The Vikings say he banished the frost giants there ages ago. Why would he be concerned about it?"

"I don't know," replied Volgha. "He didn't seem to care if it would be too hot for the frost giants. Is there anything else there?"

"No," said Santa. "That's kind of the point. He banished the frost giants to a barren wasteland, never to return."

"That's what I thought. I've never been there because there didn't seem to be any point in going."

"Could we go there now," asked Krespo, "have a look around?"

"Not much point," said Santa. "It's a long way from here, and we wouldn't know where to begin searching through all the nothing that's there. It would be a waste of time."

"I could go," said Volgha, after a few moments of thought.

Oh come on, cawed Redcrow, *it's a long way away, it's bitter cold, and we haven't—*

"Oh, quit your moaning," said Volgha, shooting an irritated glance to Redcrow. "We don't have to go physically. I could just scry the high places, see if anything is amiss."

"There's really only one high place," said Santa. "A tall mountain at its center. Would it be difficult?"

"Not really," Volgha answered. "I'll just be able to look around, but with Redcrow's help, I'll get a better range."

So you are volunteering me. Typical.

"You complain a lot, do you know that?" said Volgha.

As would anyone in my position!

"You've been bestowed with power, and that comes with responsibility!"

Oh, that's rich, coming from Miss Doesn't-Want-To-Be-The-Warden.

"Ugh!" Volgha rolled her eyes and waved a hand dismissively. Santa and Krespo were staring, each with an eyebrow cocked.

"Right," said Santa. "Well, certainly nothing to lose by having a peek."

Santa and Krespo saw to maintaining the little moat around the shelter while Volgha walked up to the top of the hill with a blanket and her basket. She laid out the blanket, drew a circle of salt on it, and started her herbs burning in the bowl. Redcrow took flight, circling higher and higher above, and Volgha began the incantation.

There are a few universal recommendations when it comes to magic. They're not rules *per se*, but they are ignored at one's own peril.

"Don't cast spells with your mouth full" is a relatively obvious one. That's a sure way to accidentally summon a thresher demon instead of having the bed make itself. Whoever made those two incantations so similar must've had a mean streak.

"No substitutions" is another, especially when performing complicated wards. Sure, rockwort and elderfrost smell alike, but when one is trying to contain the thresher demon that one has just accidentally summoned, "good enough" usually isn't.

The one that Volgha had just overlooked was "Don't cast spells next to unknown mysterious objects." To say that what happened next was unexpected would only be true if she didn't know that she should have been more careful.

There was a great rumbling noise, and the boxes over the howling eggs started to shatter one by one. Volgha didn't dare stop the incantation, as she was already halfway past the veil separating the physical and spirit realms. She'd heard of witches who'd gotten stuck halfway like that, and she had no interest in being a cackling spinster for the rest of her days.

She felt a rush of power unlike any she'd experienced before. Something was pushing her, amplifying her innate abilities. It scared and thrilled her at the same time. She just kept pushing onward, past the veil, toward Niflheim, so close to Redcrow that she had trouble sensing the line that separated their energies.

And then she was there. It was far colder than anything she'd ever experienced, but some inner radiance kept her warm. She flapped her great red wings against the gusting winds. Her wings? No, Redcrow's wings.

Right, *her* wings. Wait ... she *was* Redcrow. What?

She looked around, bewildered but unafraid. It was her, Volgha, and it was him, Redcrow. It was as if they'd merged, which was more than a bit unsettling.

Something was amplifying her power, and that something had merged her physically with Redcrow. Well, *meta*physically anyway, as her body was actually still sitting on the hill. They'd been sharing thoughts for a while now, how was this any different?

She could still feel herself—her physical form, an anchor chanting on the hill—but she was no mere ghost of herself here. She was powerful.

The mountain wasn't hard to spot. Volgha flew toward it, but it was a long way off. The wind buffeted her wings, making it hard to steer. She seemed to know that there was a better way to do this, a way to ... *put* herself there.

She simply moved. It wasn't flying exactly, she just sort of *willed* herself toward the peak, and she was there in a flash. She came to a dead stop inches from a frost giant, who was punching a huge block of ice atop the highest peak. His eyes went wide at the sight of her. He lost his balance and went plummeting toward the ground.

Volgha gasped. She didn't really know anything about frost giants, but sending one plummeting to its untimely demise certainly wasn't her intention. She hurtled downward after him, stopping a few feet from the ground and using her wings to hover over to the crater where he'd landed.

He was lying on his back, or rather what was left of it. Frost giants are made of ice and covered in permafrost. This one was now practically shattered, more pile than giant.

"Ow," he said, stirring slowly.

"You're alive!" exclaimed Volgha, incredulous that anyone could survive a fall like that.

"Of course I'm alive," he replied. "I'm just very badly broken."

"I'm so sorry, I didn't mean to startle you like that. Is there anything I can do?"

"Don't worry about it," said the giant. "I'll freeze back together soon enough."

"Well, that's handy. Does it take long?"

"I don't know," said the giant. "Time doesn't really pass here. It's always just grey. Who are you, anyway?"

"Volgha," she said. "And you?"

"Gorsulak," he said. "Where did you come from?"

"That's a long story."

"I've got nothing but time. It's been ages since Odin banished us here. Please, don't skip any details. You have no idea how nice it is to talk to someone from the outside."

"Perhaps it's not that interesting." Probably not a good idea to tell a frost giant that you've come because your pal Odin seemed nervous about what was happening here, especially after you've just virtually shattered said frost giant. "I've just never been to Niflheim, and I thought I'd have a look."

"You're small," he said, "like a Viking. But you don't look like a Viking. They don't have wings. Or do they? It's been a long time since I saw a Viking so I may not be remembering correctly. Isn't it birds that have wings?"

"That's right," said Volgha. "Birds have wings and Vikings do not. I'm neither of those, though. I'm a witch. Well, a witch *and* a bird, at the moment. It's complicated."

"Oh ..." Gorsulak seemed interested in Volgha's story. She decided to try and keep him talking, to see if he'd volunteer some useful information.

"I've met some Vikings before, in Midgard," she said.

"Midgard. I remember Midgard. Full of Vikings, as I recall. We threw boulders at them. It was great fun."

"You don't like the Vikings?"

"It's not really a matter of like or dislike," said Gorsulak. "They charge at us with ... pole things, pointy bits on the ends. What do you call those?"

"Spears?"

Gorsulak was silent for a moment. "Maybe," he said. "Anyway, they got on the backs of these four-legged animals and charged at us with 'sneers' or whatever, and we threw boulders at them. I don't remember if we liked each other or not, it's just what we did. Those were our jobs, I think."

"And did you like your job?"

"I think so. Anyway, I was good at it. We all were. We'd meet the Vikings on the field, we'd hurl a bunch of boulders, and that was that. It must have been Odin that didn't like it. He was the one who sent us here, I think."

Gorsulak raised an arm, turned it one way and then the other, testing the joints. It seemed to be healing nicely, thanks to the bitter cold winds.

"When I saw you on the peak," began Volgha, "were you punching a big block of ice?"

"Was I?"

"That's what it looked like."

He was silent again. He tried the other arm. It seemed to be solidifying nicely as well.

"Yes, I was punching something. Thank you for reminding me, little bird. We've never been able to reach the top of the peak before because there was too much frost up there to climb it. But it's gotten hotter up there, and some of the frost has melted away. I can reach it now, which means if I can break off enough of the ice, I can free the horn."

"Horn? What horn?"

"The Horn of Frost." Gorsulak snapped his fingers, which had just firmed up. "I remember now! Odin put it there to torment us. You see, if we could blow the horn, it would unfold the bridge to Midgard. We could walk across the bridge and get out of this miserable place! Maybe we could get our old jobs back, throw boulders at Vikings again! That would be just lovely."

"Are you sure that's a good idea?" Volgha could see now what Odin was concerned about, and it concerned her as well. Frost giants hurling boulders around? How long would it be before they ran out of Vikings and turned to other targets? She didn't have to be the Warden to want to prevent that.

"Why wouldn't it be?"

"Oh, I don't know," said Volgha, scrambling for a feasible reason. "How did you figure out that it was melting up there anyway?"

"Well, I'd given up on climbing up there a long time ago. At least

I think it was a long time ago. Not sure if I mentioned it, but it's hard to tell how much time passes here. It looks the same all the time."

"You did mention it."

"I did? Oh well. Anyway, I was talking with the Giver of Secrets, and he told me about it."

"Shouldn't that be the Keeper of Secrets?"

"I thought so, too, but who am I to tell someone else how to do their job? He's just an old man that knows a bunch of stuff, and he says that secrets are dangerous. When people know about them, they're just facts, and facts aren't dangerous."

"I don't know if that's true," said Volgha.

"The Giver of Secrets says it is." Gorsulak sat up and shrugged. "Perhaps if we had some sort of Arbiter of Truth on hand, he—or she—could rule on that for us."

He stood up slowly. Even allowing for the fact that his legs had just rebuilt themselves from thousands of tiny pieces, Volgha felt that he was taking his part in the impending apocalypse a bit too casually.

"But since we have no Arbiter of Truth," Gorsulak continued, "I'll simply say that I don't want to stay here. None of us do. And since I've got nothing else to do, I'm going to break the ice away from the horn and use it to get to Midgard. It doesn't matter how long it takes. Frost giants are immortal, you know. I've got all the time in the world."

He gave his legs a few experimental stretches, then twisted his torso at the hips a few times. He seemed to be all in working order, so he stepped out of his crater and started walking to the foot of the mountain.

"Sure, that's one option," said Volgha, flitting along behind him, "but have you considered the benefits of leaving the horn alone? You could get really hurt if you fell again, you know."

"I must've fallen from up there hundreds of times before," said Gorsulak, still plodding toward the mountain. "It hurts, but I always heal. It just takes time."

"But isn't it better here? It's so cold, you must heal faster here than you would anywhere else."

"Maybe, but it's *boring*. We lived for a really long time before we came here, and even if it's a bit more dangerous out there, Niflheim is dreadfully dull. Better to have the threat of death than no reason to live, if you ask me."

"But certainly we can come up with something that can make Niflheim more livable. I could even help, if you—"

"Hey." Stopping, Gorsulak turned to face her. "It sounds like you don't want me to get the horn for some reason. Why would you want me to stay here, stuck in this boring place?"

"Well, it's just that—"

"I get it," said Gorsulak, taking a step toward her. "You're a friend of Odin's, aren't you?"

"No! I mean, I've met him, but—"

"Right, you're just a casual acquaintance of Odin's having a stroll in Niflheim, definitely not here to make sure the frost giants are staying where they belong!"

"I'm just saying, this seems like a pretty decent place for a frost giant to live!"

"So you know what's best for us? Just like Odin and his precious Vikings, you can't stand the thought of us giants doing an honest day's work. You'd rather lock us away, out of sight out of mind. Well, forget it!"

Gorsulak turned on his frosty heel and started walking away.

"Wait," said Volgha, still following along. "If you'd only let me—"

"Enough!" Gorsulak spun around and hurled a mighty fist toward her. She dodged it easily, thanks to her new-found agility. This only enraged him further, and he kept advancing and swinging as she turned and dodged.

"Please stop and listen to me," Volgha said as she flitted and dodged. "I'm far too quick, you'll never hit me."

"I will!" Gorsulak shouted between punches. "Haven't you been listening? I've got all the time in the world! It doesn't matter how long it takes, little bird. Even if neither of us ever tires, you'll eventually slip up, and I'll crush your bones!"

He was right, she realized. It might take a very long time, but infinitesimal odds always pan out over a long enough timeline; and all the while, the snow atop the peak would continue to melt. If Loki's riddle wasn't solved, Gorsulak would eventually gain the horn by simply climbing the mountain again—and he had nothing but time.

"You're right," she said. She dodged away one last time and flew up out of his reach. "I can't beat you. Not this way."

"Or any other," he spat. "Fly away, little bird. Fly home and wait for the boulders to come raining down on your little nest!"

Volgha closed her eyes and let herself slip back across the veil. She felt Redcrow's mind pulling back from her own, felt the blanket below her legs again, and opened her eyes.

The last lights of what must have been a terrific display of magical wisps died away, and she could hear the wind howling in the giant eggs. There were glowing runes on them, runes that she didn't recognize. They were fading away as well, leaving only a collection of white stone sculptures to sound across the wind.

What just happened, asked Osgrey, *and where have you been?*

"By all the spirits," exclaimed Santa, standing with Krespo a few yards away, "what was that?"

Volgha tried to stand up and promptly fell over. She'd never been so tired. She was parched and starving, though she'd eaten only minutes before she'd started the spell. She felt the long miles that she'd flown across Niflheim.

"Amplifiers," said Volgha. "They're some sort of magical amplifiers. Where is Redcrow?"

"Here!" shouted Krespo. He was lying in the snow, several feet away from Volgha. "I can't tell if he's breathing!"

"He's alive," said Volgha, "I can feel him. He just needs to rest. Bring him inside, will you?"

Krespo nodded, and gently picked up the bird. Santa helped Volgha to her feet, but she was unable to walk. Lifting her, he carried her to the shelter. He set her gently down on a bed of furs, then offered her a cup of water.

"Drink this." Santa had to help her sip it.

"I'll be all right," she said. "Just let me rest for a moment."

"What happened? What did you see?"

"I saw Niflheim," she told him. "Santa, the frost giants are coming. We're running out of time."

SEVENTEEN

K RESPO SAID A SWEAR WORD. SANTA GAVE HIM A FUNNY LOOK.
"The frost giants," said Krespo. "What does this mean? Is it the Ragnarok?"

"It's not the Ragnarok," said Santa.

How can he be sure? asked Osgrey.

"What's the Ragnarok?" asked Volgha.

"It's the end of the world, according to the Vikings," said Santa. "But this isn't the Ragnarok. Stop saying Ragnarok!"

"You've said it more than both of us," countered Krespo. Santa glared at him. Krespo looked at the ground.

"Well it's true," he mumbled.

"Whether it's the … end of the world or not," said Volgha, "it's the sort of thing that consequences are made of. We might be able to stop it, but we have to act quickly."

"But where do we even begin?" Santa was pacing back and forth in the tent. He was only able to take but two or three steps in either direction before he had to turn around, which made it large for a tent but ill-suited to pacing nonetheless. "Maybe if we knew what was causing the heat, we could do something about it."

"Well," said Volgha, "about that …"

Santa stopped. "What do you know?"

"Most of it." Volgha sighed. "It's even partially my fault, in a manner of speaking."

"That can't be true," said Krespo. "You're on our side! You're being too hard on yourself. Right, Santa?"

Santa's head tilted to one side, and he considered Volgha through a bit of a squint. "What do you know?"

"How well do you know the gods of Asgard?"

"We're not on a first name basis," replied Santa, "but I know who they are."

"Well, my sister is very good friends with Loki."

Sighing, Santa sat down, his face in his hands.

"I don't like where this is going." His words were muffled, but he clearly knew that anything having to do with Loki had the potential to end in tragedy.

"Loki wanted to challenge the most cunning foe he could find to solve the most baffling puzzle he could conceive. Naturally, he would be the most cunning foe."

"Naturally."

"So they called on me to split his mind in half. I brewed a potion. Some of my best work, actually. The first sip pulled half of his mind away so the half that remained could devise the puzzle."

You didn't! Osgrey was shocked. *Volgha, why would you get mixed up in that sort of skullduggery?*

"I didn't think it would be this bad," said Volgha. "The second sip switched them, so the other half could solve it. The third sip will make him whole again, but there's a problem."

"Of course there is," Santa muttered, face still buried in his hands.

"My sister thinks the game is just the most delightful thing ever, and she'd never hear of giving Loki the last sip until he's ready, but Loki's entirely forgotten who he is. I don't think he can solve the puzzle without his memory."

"And what was this 'riddle' of his? To make the world hotter?"

"That I don't know," said Volgha. "I just know the warming started right before he had the second sip. It can't be a coincidence."

Rising, Santa took in a deep breath, and let it out slowly. His jaws clenched so forcefully they must have had their own biceps.

"What are we going to do, Santa?" Krespo was scared. His eyes were wide, his voice cracking just above a whisper.

"We're going to get dragged into another bloody war," said Santa with a snarl, "that's what we're going to do!"

"I'm sorry," said Volgha, "if I'd had any idea—"

"You'd probably have done it anyway! You nearly got me killed for the sake of one spell," he pointed at Redcrow, "and you may have started a war with another! Do you ever consider the consequences of toying with powers beyond your control?"

"Beyond my control? I'd say I controlled them fairly well!"

"In what way do you think that this is under control? You took half the mind away from the most unstable god ever to walk the earth, and now the frost giants are returning. That's your idea of control?"

He's right, said Osgrey, *and this is exactly the sort of thing that the Warden is supposed to prevent!*

"My sister and Loki would have done this without me," said Volgha, "and it could have been far worse if her vile court wizard had done it with necromancy. You don't know him, and you don't know what my sister is capable of."

"I know all I need to know about the woman who hunted me! She's the reason I can't go home, and the end result of her lunacy is going to be war! The cost for this will be paid in lives, witch. Probably mine, from the sound of it. So don't give me excuses, just tell me how you're going to fix it!"

"I don't know!" Volgha shouted. The silence that followed made them realize how loud they'd become. She and Santa glared at each other with twisted expressions, locked in a kind of death stare.

Krespo took a page from the coward's manual and tried to make himself look as small as possible.

Volgha broke from their staring contest first. Santa was right— she'd been more concerned with how she could split the mind of a god than whether she *should*. She sat down and leaned forward, staring at the ground.

"I've made a mess of things," said Volgha. "I don't know how I'm going to undo it, but I have to try."

That's the spirit, said Osgrey.

There's a reason that no one ever says "oh look, the truth, how convenient!" She'd wheedled a favor from Santa on the pretense that his carelessness had inconvenienced her. Meanwhile, her lack of foresight in fiddling with Loki's mind was threatening to drop a war into Santa's lap.

Yes, cawed Redcrow, *that qualifies as irony.*

"Fine time for you to wake up."

Oh sure, blame the devastatingly handsome crow. Shall I point out that we weren't discussing an impending war when I was last awake?

"Where is Loki now?" asked Santa. "How do we fix him?"

Volgha looked up at Santa. His fists were clenched, his brow furrowed. He'd have been justified in yelling his lungs inside out, but he didn't. He was putting the task at hand before his own feelings, a feat which no Aurorian monarch had ever attempted in the history of the dynasty.

"He's in Midgard," Volgha answered. "We have to get him to the wine cellar in Castle Borealis, then give him the last sip of the potion."

Santa said a swear word. "I can't go back there. She may still be hunting me."

"I doubt it," said Volgha, "but I don't fault your concern. I can cast a spell to keep her from seeing you."

"It's a start," said Santa. "Wait, couldn't we just bring the potion to Loki?"

"The other half of his mind is in a whiskey barrel," explained Volgha. "We'd never get it out of the wine cellar and past the guards. Besides, my sister adores Loki. She won't harm us if he's with us."

"Perfect," grumbled Santa. "Loki, my protector."

"I can't change what I've done, but I can fix it with your help. We have to work quickly. Are you with me?"

Santa sighed and nodded.

"I'm with you, too!"

"Thank you, Krespo," said Volgha. "Now, how do we get Loki to the castle?"

EIGHTEEN

THERE HAVE BEEN SEVERAL OCCASIONS UPON WHICH WITCHES have looked into their bonfires and seen the future; however, since the future is always in motion, most don't bother. The further ahead one looks, the foggier it gets. Even if one were to see something in the distant future clearly, there's little chance that it would be useful. Probably just something like a couple reciting one of the ritual charms of bonding to each other, the most well-known being "I don't know, what do *you* want to eat?"

The general futility of the enterprise had always kept Volgha among those who didn't bother, but this time would have been a good idea. She'd probably not have opted to join Santa's sleigh ride along with Krespo and Loki. She could have made the trip by broom in a few hours, but they needed to arrive together. Even in Santa's lightest sleigh with his four strongest horses pulling it, the trip had been a spine-compacting romp spanning several evenings. Volgha was sure she'd be permanently shorter by the end of it.

They eventually arrived at the northern boundary of Innisdown, barely a mile from the castle. Volgha and Redcrow got out of the sleigh with Loki.

"Everyone knows their parts, then?" asked Volgha.

Santa nodded. "We'll leave the sleigh where we buried the old Tickler, and meet you inside by the portrait of Saint Perplexia."

"And you're sure you can remember the way through the passages?" Volgha was looking at Krespo. She'd found them very confusing before, and Santa had not been in the best frame of mind then. Being hunted tends to have that effect on people.

"I remember," said Krespo. "I'm good with directions."

He's good with directions! cawed Redcrow. *Direct him to the kitchens, I'm sure they have anchovies.*

"Anchovies later," said Volgha. "All right, that's Santa and Krespo. How about you?"

"I've done it," said Loki, forcing a toothy grin. "I've solved my own riddle by finding the thing I'd miss the least in the last place I'd think to look."

"And how did you solve it?"

"By looking there *first.*"

"And what did you find?"

"You, silly witch!"

"And where did you find me?"

"In that awful dress!" Loki's forced smile fell, and he shook his head. "That's ridiculous. It doesn't make any sense!"

"For the last time," said Volgha, "it doesn't *have* to. It's insulting to me, which will give my sister a good laugh. You laugh like crazy with her for about ten minutes—"

"That sounds like an awfully long time." Loki's short-term memory had apparently gone along with the rest of it. They'd been over this several times.

"Just trust me," pleaded Volgha. "After a few minutes, you say …"

"Oh, right. Enough dallying, frumpy little sister! Fetch me the last of the potion, so I can put my whole mind to forgetting how boring you are!"

"Good. That sounds like you."

"If that's true, I'm not sure I want the last sip. I'm a real—"

"*Caw!*"

"Just remember that, after you drink the last sip," said Volgha. "And whatever else happens, you need to undo your riddle as soon as you remember."

Loki nodded.

"Then I'll see you inside." Santa snapped the reins, and the sleigh sped away.

"All right then," said Volgha. "Let's be off."

She couldn't remember the last time she'd walked to the castle. It must have been when she was a little girl, before she'd learned enough about the Witching Way to travel by broom. Seeing the castle looming in the distance took her back. She almost expected to see her parents delivering proclamations from the battlements as she got closer, and reflexively prepared herself to jump aside, in case the catapult sent anything her way.

"Halt," shouted a voice from the drawbridge tower, "who goes there?"

"Volgha, the Winter Witch."

"Never heard of you," said the guard. "State your business."

"I'm the queen's sister, let me in."

"I'm pretty sure I'd know if the queen had a sister."

"Obviously you don't!"

Tell him I'm with you, said Osgrey. *I came through this gate all the time.*

"But you're *not* here, are you?"

"That's unlikely," said the guard. "I always work the front gate, and if the queen had a sister, she'd have come through here before now."

"I usually fly," said Volgha through clenched teeth. "I'm losing my patience with you."

"Better you your patience than me my job," said the guard. "Why didn't you fly this time?"

"She's come with me," said Loki. "I'm—"

"Is that Loki? Hello, sir, why didn't you speak up? Dark out there, I didn't recognize you. Hold on, I'll lower the drawbridge."

Ha! Redcrow gave a caw that sounded a lot like chuckling. *Not very popular, are you?*

Volgha fumed as the bridge cranked its way down. The guard had been too far away for her to be able to recognize him. She made a mental note to work out who he was after all of this was over so she could be sure that he wouldn't be running around vexing witches on a whim, one having given him the idea that there were no repercussions to follow.

"You can fly?" asked Loki.

"I'm a witch." One of the primary rules of the Witching Way stated that she should answer any questions regarding her abilities with just enough information to let people's imaginations run away with them. They tended to do so out loud, often in pubs. Half-truths and innuendos were much more satisfying when she didn't have to advertise them herself.

The drawbridge finished its descent with a thud. They walked across it, through the courtyard, and up the stairs to the big wooden doors.

Inside, the halls were unusually quiet. Not so much as the pitter-patter of servants' feet running for their very lives. Volgha held up a hand to Loki, bidding him pause so she could listen. If her sister were awake, it would be easy to hear her cackling when the rest of the castle was silent.

"Hello, Volgha," came Chamberlain's voice from around a corner. "We weren't expecting you, and with Master Loki, no less! And such an *unusual* bird!"

Who are you calling unusual?

"What brings you here this evening?" asked Chamberlain. He was flanked by a pair of guards. He usually walked alone—the easier to sneak up on people, Volgha assumed.

"Loki has solved his riddle," Volgha replied. "If my sister is busy, we can just give Loki the potion now and tell her the tale later."

Chamberlain frowned. "It will have to wait, I'm afraid. Guards!"

Then there was a blur, during which the surprisingly quick guards had knocked both Volgha and Loki over the head and shackled them. Loki was a good sport and fell unconscious. One of them had made a grab for Redcrow, but he'd dodged handily and flown off down the hallway.

"What is this?" Volgha swayed and stumbled, but kept her feet.

"A *coup d'etat*, I'm afraid." Even when seizing power, Chamberlain was unfailingly polite, violence at the hands of his thugs notwithstanding.

"How dare you!" Volgha started slipping into a fire-and-brimstone glamour, hoping that it would scare the guard into releasing her long enough to do something a bit more effective.

"Ah, ah, ah," said Chamberlain in a chiding tone, as he draped a heavy chain around her neck. It had a big rock attached to it, and she could feel the power from her glamour being sucked into it.

"A lodestone? How did you know?"

"It's my job to know," said Chamberlain. "I really do feel dreadful about this, but there's no way I can trust you to play along. To the dungeon with them, please."

"You'll pay for this!" shouted Volgha, as they were taken away.

"I've been paying for it for years," he shouted back. "It's finally time to collect!"

NINETEEN

A NOTHER CHAIN WAS WRAPPED UNDER VOLGHA'S ARMS AND locked behind her back to make sure she couldn't remove the lodestone. The guards led her and dragged Loki down a set of spiral stairs, along a torch-lit corridor, and through a slightly rusty iron gate. Their shackles were removed but not the lodestone—when they were shoved into a large cell.

"Wonderful," said a man in a filthy, long-tailed coat and powdered wig, "new players!"

There were half a dozen other prisoners in all, men and women whose rags and tatters had once been the height of fashion.

"Introductions, introductions!" shouted a squat woman whose begrimed purple hair was taller than she was. She rose from the card game she'd been playing with the men.

"Lady Inesta Sneezeworthy," she said, "at your service. And this is His Excellency, Stanley Whomsoever, Viceroy of Middle Blinkington."

"At your service," said the viceroy with a bow. His long white beard and brownish smile gave Volgha the feeling that he'd been there the longest.

I know him, said Osgrey. *Not a bad fellow, as nobles go.*

"Permit me to introduce myself," said a tall, young man who was mostly chin. "Sir Henry Stockridge Smythe, come to rescue the Viceroy and return him to Middle Blinkington."

"Oh," said Volgha. "And how is that working out?"

"There've been a few setbacks," said Sir Henry. "I'll strike when it's least expected, you can count on it!"

"Right," said Volgha. "Good luck."

"And this is my sister," said Lady Sneezeworthy. "Duchess Constance of Ibberlin-Going-Backward." Constance gave a barely visible nod, likely because anything more than that would hinder her looking down her nose at everyone else.

"Duchess," said Volgha with a nod. She knew the type: up-jumped lackwits who married well, then pretended they'd never soiled the bottoms of their shoes by walking on the ground. No doubt she could be relied upon for conversation as scintillating as the buzz of flies on a bloated carcass.

"Aren't you going to introduce me?" snarled what must have been the angriest little pig of a man ever to have lived. Generations of inbreeding were likely the cause of his little snout, permanently turned up at everyone he met. The tufts of hair growing from his ears were longer and thicker than the few he had on his head.

"If it will shut you up," snapped Lady Sneezeworthy. She smiled and turned back to Volgha. "May I present Awful Pig Man, Duke of Ibberlin-Going-Backward."

"My name is Alfred, you cur!" he shouted.

"What's it matter? You're going to insist on being called 'Duke' anyway."

"Mind your tongue," he said. "You should show some respect when addressing your betters, girl."

"Better at losing at cards," said the viceroy. Lady Sneezeworthy laughed. Duke Alfred grimaced.

"Awfully cheery for a dungeon." Volgha was only partially joking. She'd always heard that the queen's dungeons were a dreadful place. Sure, it was musty and cold, but it was bright with torchlight, there were games of cards, feather beds, and the cheese plates hardly had any rats on them at all.

"You're in the *upper* dungeons, dear." Lady Sneezeworthy placed an arm around Volgha's shoulder and started walking her around the place. "Most of us were regular fixtures in Her Majesty's court before we wound up down here for one reason or another. We're not the common rabble, you see."

"Yes," said Duke Alfred. "We're rarefied rabble, aren't we?"

"Quite," said the viceroy. The two of them were fixated on their cards.

"Not just anyone manages to be imprisoned here," Lady Sneezeworthy continued. "The truly vile criminal types are sent below, to the *lower* dungeons."

"Hey," said Sir Henry, "that's where they put me at first!"

"Until your Viceroy rescued you from them, you mean." Lord Alfred wrinkled his nose at Sir Henry.

"Quite," said Duchess Constance.

"Which brings us to the subject of you and your friend," said Lady Sneezeworthy. "You're obviously not common rabble, no matter what the cut of your dress might suggest, no offense."

"None taken," said Volgha, feeling mildly offended, but accustomed enough to japes about her simple dress from nobility to realize the futility of getting huffy about them.

"So who are you?"

"Volgha," she answered, "the Winter Witch."

"A witch!" said Duchess Constance, with the sort of feigned shock that was only ever intended to embarrass or belittle. The sweat stains on the Duchess' gown took some of the sting out of it, and Volgha's distaste for courtly intrigue did the rest.

"Not just *a* witch," said the viceroy. "You're Her Majesty's sister, are you not?"

"Sister?" said Duke Alfred, who obviously knew what the word meant, and likely only piped up for fear that he might be left out of the conversation.

"I'm afraid so," said Volgha.

"In that case," said Lady Sneezeworthy with nervous grace, "your dress is lovely!"

"Oh, *do* sit down." Duchess Constance offered Volgha the dingy overstuffed chair which, of all the chairs in the place, appeared to be the least infested with bugs who'd be keen to live in one's hair.

"So you're a princess, then?" asked Sir Henry with a courteous bow.

"Not exactly," replied Volgha. "Not anymore."

"Oh." Fluffing out her gown, Duchess Constance returned to her seat.

"Not anymore?" asked Lady Sneezeworthy.

"She renounced it, I believe," said the viceroy.

"That's right," said Volgha.

"Renounced a royal title?" Duke Alfred's brow was furrowed in confusion, and his mouth hung open. "Why would you go and do a stupid thing like that? You'd have outranked all of us combined!"

Oh, to be first among prisoners, said Osgrey. Volgha had to wonder if her liberal use of sarcasm was rubbing off on the old man.

"To appease my sister," said Volgha, "and to keep her from thinking of me as a threat."

"Smart." The viceroy gave a brief nod.

"As a boat made of snow," said Duke Alfred. "You should have challenged her, made her renounce instead!"

"I didn't want it," said Volgha. "I wanted to be left alone to follow the Witching Way."

"That's what you think," said Duke Alfred. "Girls always think they know what they want. If I'd got to you sooner, you'd have been better off."

"You mean it could have been me recoiling from your advances, instead of Duchess Constance?"

The Duke and Duchess scowled at her in equal measure. Everyone else laughed.

Well done, said Osgrey. Volgha grinned at his approval despite herself.

"And how did you displease your sister to end up in these exalted surroundings?" asked Sir Henry.

"Not my sister," Volgha replied. "Lord Chamberlain. He's staged a coup."

All eyes were upon her then, card games and other vermin-infested diversions forgotten.

"A coup?" said Duke Alfred.

"You don't say!" exclaimed Lady Sneezeworthy.

"When did this happen?" asked the viceroy.

"Not long ago," said Volgha. "Loki and I had just returned when—"

"Loki!" shouted the viceroy, his generally pleasant demeanor shifting quickly to rage. "It's his fault I'm down here! I should have recognized him, even unconscious and face-down. Sir Henry! Dispatch that knave with haste!"

"It shall be done, Your Excellency!" Sir Henry jumped to his feet and reached for the sword which had undoubtedly spent a great deal of time at his side before he ended up in the dungeons. He felt about his waist for it, then looked down to see that his hands did not deceive him. It was not, in fact, there.

"I seem to be without my sword," he said. "Would His Excellency prefer that the knave dies by beating, choking, thrashing, defenestration—"

"No one's killing Loki," said Volgha. "Not yet, anyway."

"Why not?" asked Duke Alfred.

"Because I need him alive," said Volgha. "Don't vex me on this, little man, I'm in no mood!"

Duke Alfred grimaced. His grimace had a certain practiced disdain to it. It was apparent that he'd worked at it very hard.

"It would be hard to kill him anyway," said Lady Sneezeworthy. "Isn't he a god?"

"A god?" said Duchess Constance. "Where does that title stand, somewhere around count?"

"Yes," said Volgha, "he's a god." She was omitting that he was, in fact, only half a god at present, or possibly just rounding up. "You can't kill a god, so best not to waste the effort."

The viceroy said a swear word, or at least it sounded like one. It wasn't one that Volgha had heard before, but it made Osgrey giggle. Just an old one, most likely.

"Put him over there then," instructed the viceroy, pointing and smiling wickedly. He'd indicated a green sofa, which Volgha didn't think had been green originally. It was … drippy.

"Just leave him be." Volgha glared at Sir Henry. Relenting, he went back to his seat at the card game. He must have known about the consequences of vexing witches.

"The queen's sister," said Lady Sneezeworthy. "No wonder you weren't sent to the lower dungeons."

"What's in the lower dungeons?"

"The properly horrid squalor," answered Sir Henry. "Torture implements, people hanging from walls until they die, that sort of thing."

"The upper dungeons are a privilege." Duke Alfred thrust his chin upward as he examined his cards. "It's not a palace, but it's not all bad. We get to bribe the guards to bring us things, and there's plenty of food."

"And hardly any rats," added the viceroy.

"Hardly any," Duke Alfred repeated.

"What was that about bribery?" asked Volgha.

"Oh yes," said Lady Sneezeworthy. "Provided you have something of value, you can get the guards to acquire a great number of things for you. They won't let you out, of course, or we'd have gone a long time ago."

"The viceroy relinquished a silver snuffbox to bring me up from the lower dungeons," Sir Henry told her.

"Guard!" shouted Volgha. She had to shout a few times, but eventually one of them grew to dislike hearing her shouting more than he disliked moving from his chair.

"What is it?" he said.

"Do you know a girl named Matilda, works in the kitchens?"

"Can't say as I do."

"Well, I'd be grateful if you'd ask around in the kitchens, and have her come down to speak with me."

"I suppose I could," said the guard. "What've you got?"

"Well, nothing at the moment, but—"

"Favors have prices," said the guard. "This one wouldn't cost you much, but you've got to pay. Keeping up appearances, you know."

"Lovely," said Volgha. "Look, I can pay you once I'm out of here if you could just—"

"No credit, them's the rules."

"Whose rules?"

"Rules of the people on this side of the bars, prisoner!"

"Right," said Volgha. "How silly of me. All right, do you know a guard named Reginald?"

"Oh yeah," he replied with a smile. "Everybody knows Reg, he's a legend! What's that got to do with you, prisoner?"

"I'd like to speak with him."

"You and half the other ladies in there." The guard pointed to Duchess Constance. "Not her, though, she's too stuck up."

"I'm the queen's sister," said Volgha.

"Former queen, as I understand it. We's takin' orders from King Chamberlain now."

"For now," said Volgha. "In any case, I'm not ordering you to get him, I'm asking you to."

"You haven't."

"Excuse me?"

"Asked. You just said 'I'd like to speak to him,' like your wish is my command."

Dungeon guard, as jobs go, is not as eagerly sought after as one might think. With the possible exception of those currently imprisoned in dungeons, no one thinks "Boy, I'd sure love to have a job sitting in a dank cellar, watching a bunch of unwashed people do not much of anything." Be that as it may, it's still a job that needs to be done, and it tends to be done by people who don't have a lot of other options.

The result generally empowered the people serving in this role to exercise authority over other people, which was usually their favorite part of the job. Unaccustomed as Volgha was to demurring, her ability to get people to do things for her without question was presently out of reach.

"You're right," Volgha acquiesced. "Forgive me, I never should have spoken so brashly to you. This is your dungeon after all, and you deserve respect accordingly."

"That's more like it." The guard straightened up, raising his chin.

"When you're done kissing that peasant's backside," said Duke Alfred, "the rats would enjoy the same treatment."

Volgha strode across the room with alarming speed and struck Duke Alfred across the cheek with the back of her hand.

"Apologize at once, worm!"

"Have you gone mad?" Duke Alfred's eyes went wide. Volgha struck him again.

"How dare you demean your betters, you filthy little pig man? He's no peasant! Apologize, or I will thrash you again!"

She raised her hand to strike him once more.

"I'm sorry!" he shouted.

I must admit, said Osgrey, *I may have enjoyed that as much as you did.*

Volgha nodded with satisfaction and strode quickly back over to the guard.

"I apologize for the interruption, sir," she said. "As I was saying, if it's not too much trouble, would you please ask Reginald to come and speak with me for a moment?"

VOLGHA WOKE TO THE SOUND OF CLANGING AGAINST THE BARS. REG was standing there, looking just as he had when he'd held her kneeling before Loki dressed as her sister. Matilda was with him.

"This is the girl you wanted," said Reg. "We's square now, right?"

"Yes, Reginald, your favor is paid. See that you don't vex me again."

"Keep it down over there," said Duke Alfred, not moving from his fetal position on a dusty feather bed.

"Or else what?" Volgha questioned. There was no reply. She turned back to Reg. "Thank you, Reginald."

Reg nodded, then turned and walked away.

"Lord Chamberlain is running the castle now," whispered Matilda.

"I know," Volgha replied. "He's chained a lodestone to me so that I can't do any magic, or I'd have slipped out of here by now."

"There aren't any passages down here, I can't sneak you out!"

Volgha said a swear word. "Sorry," she added. "Never mind, we'll work that out later. We've got bigger problems now, and I need your help."

"Of course, what can I do?"

"It's a long story," said Volgha. "You see, I've got Loki down here with me."

"You mean you've got half of him," said Matilda.

"You know about that?"

"You should hear your sister when she's being tickled," said Matilda. "You'd think I was torturing her for state secrets. Well, *she* seems to think so, in any case."

"Naturally." Volgha rolled her eyes. "Anyway, whatever it was that Loki did to fool himself, his other half is unable to solve it, and it's allowing the frost giants to free themselves from Niflheim. So we've got precious little time to fix things and avoid a war."

Matilda said a swear word. "Sorry," she added. "What do we do?"

"We need to get to the wine cellar, and give the last sip of the potion to Loki," explained Volgha. "Lord Chamberlain is sure to keep the potion locked away somewhere. You have to find it."

"I wouldn't know where to begin looking!"

"Santa and Krespo are waiting at Saint Perplexia," said Volgha. "And my familiar is in the castle somewhere, but the lodestone is preventing me from contacting him."

"How do I find him?"

"I don't know. His name is Redcrow, and he's a … well, he's a red crow."

"A bit on the nose, isn't it?"

"Not the time!"

"All right," said Matilda. "I'll go and get Santa and Krespo to help me, but you'll owe me one."

"What?"

"What's good for the goose ..."

"Fine."

Matilda walked away. Volgha liked the girl, though she was starting to regret teaching her about the favors game. She was clever enough, maybe she had the makings of a witch?

EVERYONE WAS MILLING ABOUT IN THE CELL WHEN VOLGHA AWOKE, including Loki. He was sitting against the bars, ably teaching a master class in moping and glumness. Volgha stood up, stretched, and walked over to him.

"How's your head?" she asked.

"Tender." Touching the lump, he winced.

"I don't suppose it jogged your memory?"

"I'm afraid not."

Volgha sighed. "That would have been lucky."

"Yeah." Loki pointed at the viceroy, who was glaring at him. "He kicked me awake this morning."

"He did what?"

"It didn't hurt or anything," said Loki. "He's exceptionally frail. He said he just wanted the satisfaction of taking out his own revenge."

"That makes sense. He said it's your fault he's in here."

"Oh," said Loki. "I'm not a nice person, am I?"

"You're a god," replied Volgha with a shrug. "Gods don't have to be nice."

I'm not sure they qualify as people either, said Osgrey.

"We don't have to be jerks either," said Loki. "Do we?"

"I imagine that gods get to do whatever they want."

Loki nodded. They sat together in silence for a while, until they heard a commotion coming down the hallway.

"Get your hands off me!" boomed a familiar voice. "Do you have any idea who I am?"

Is that Santa? asked Osgrey.

The reinforced door to the hallway slammed open, and in walked Santa—or rather, Baron Klaus of North Uptonshire—and rather than walking, he was nearly successfully fighting off three brutish guards pushing him toward the cell's gate. He was dressed in another ridiculous court ensemble. More of Krespo's work, no doubt.

In the end, they overpowered him and sent him careening headlong into the cell. He bounced up as soon as he landed and charged the gate at a full sprint. The guards had just succeeded in closing and locking it.

"You fools have signed your own death warrants!" Spit flew from Santa's mouth in great gobs. His face was red, and his eyes were a hair's breadth from opening wide enough to leap from their sockets, for a murderous rampage of their own. "Your heads will adorn pikes along the walls of North Uptonshire before the sun has set, depend on it!"

"Now there's a proper nobleman," said Duke Alfred, his smile a greasy sneer. "And such, er, unusual fashion! Is that what people are wearing at court now?"

"Yes," snipped Volgha, "you're terribly far behind. Now do shut up!"

"Volgha," said Santa loudly, "what is the queen's sister doing here?"

"Come over here, and I'll tell you," said Volgha. They walked to a far corner of the cell, standing close enough to whisper.

"What on earth are you doing?" asked Volgha.

"We need your help to get the potion," said Santa. "No one else knows what it looks like!"

"And how does it help to get yourself thrown in here?"

Santa started to answer, but Volgha put up her hand. She turned to look over her shoulder and saw that Lady Sneezeworthy, the viceroy, the duke and duchess, and Sir Henry were all lurking very nearby, obviously trying to eavesdrop. She shot them a pointed look, and they all strained to act naturally, the result of which was a collection of decidedly unnatural poses. She moved Santa farther away from them.

"Matilda told me about the lodestone." Santa dug into one of the big braids in his beard and produced a pair of slender brass picks. "I'm going to unlock it so you can magic us out of here."

"That's a start," she said, "but I can't simply 'magic us out of here'—I don't have any of my implements or ingredients!"

Santa said a swear word. Then another, and another. "Then what are we supposed to do?"

The interlopers had crept closer, still trying to listen in. Volgha and Santa continued moving around the room, creating a sort of racing circuit around the ample cell.

"Start by getting this thing off me," said Volgha. "I may be able to reach out to Redcrow, and we can take it from there." She stopped suddenly and whirled around to face their interloping cellmates.

"What?" she bellowed. "Do you really have nothing better to do than intrude on other people's conversations?"

"Well, no," said Lady Sneezeworthy. "It's been just us for so long, anything new counts as entertainment."

"And common courtesy," said Volgha, "that's just completely gone out the window?"

"Completely," replied Duchess Constance, still managing to sound entirely proper.

"Oh, fine," said Volgha. "You can at least stay out of the way."

"Not likely," said Duke Alfred, gingerly touching the growing welt she'd left on his cheek. "Not without a price."

"How would you all like to get out of here?" whispered Santa.

"Really?" whispered Sir Henry, nodding fervently.

"We don't have time for this!" hissed Volgha.

"We've got nothing *but* time," said Santa, "unless we use everything we've got at our disposal."

There were a lot of suspicious glances traded around, but they eventually gave way to nods.

"Right," said Santa. "You all go on about your business, and keep the guards' eyes off of us. Distract them if you have to."

Under cover of an argument over a game of cards, Santa managed to pick the lock behind Volgha's back and free her from the lodestone. In addition to feeling the literal weight lifted, Volgha felt her powers trickling back to where they should be. It was the pins-and-needles feeling she'd get after sleeping on her arm funny. She could feel her link to Redcrow again.

Oh, cawed Redcrow, *there you are. How do I find the kitchens?*

SEVERAL HOURS PASSED WITH VOLGHA LYING ON A FEATHER BED OF questionable cleanliness, pretending to sleep. The senior denizens of the upper dungeons grumbled swear words over cards and indulged in their standard pomp. Loki sulked in the corner, and Santa occasionally yelled swear words and death threats at the guards to keep up appearances.

Volgha was not actually sleeping, of course. She was concentrating. There weren't many spells that she could cast without her basket, and those required energy. She was gathering what she could.

Finally, as evening and the changing of the guard were drawing near, Volgha got word from Redcrow. She stood up, stretched, and gave Santa what she hoped was a subtle signal. Santa casually made his way over to her.

"I believe they've found the potion," she whispered. "They're going to meet us in the wine cellar."

Santa nodded. "Right. That only leaves us with one problem."

"Getting out of here?"

"Precisely."

"That's where we come in," said the viceroy.

"How long have you been listening?" asked Volgha.

"Long enough, witch." Duke Alfred could no more abandon his sneer than his legs, which is to say that it could be managed, but knives and blood would be involved.

"Never mind that," said Santa. "Have you got a plan?"

"Half of one," said Lady Sneezeworthy. "Sir Henry is seeing to it now."

And with that, a loud *clang* rang out against the bars near the door. They looked over to see that Sir Henry had caught the guard unawares and pulled his head hard against the iron bars. The guard was only stunned, but Sir Henry still had his grip. He quickly knocked the guard's helmet off with one hand, grabbed the front of his armor more firmly, and pulled twice more.

Bang! Bang! Thud.

"That's done then," he said with a big, oafish grin.

"Idiot," said Volgha, "the guards are due to change at any moment! Why didn't you wait?"

"Oh," he said. "That would have been better."

"Too late now," said Santa, "get his keys."

"He hasn't got any!"

"They're over there on the hook." The viceroy pointed toward the door.

A chorus of swear words erupted.

"Good thing I've still got these." Santa held up the picks he'd used on Volgha's chains. He got to work on the locked cell door. Everyone else stood behind him in a clump, fidgeting in a haughty sort of way that only the aristocracy could manage.

"What's taking so long?" Duke Alfred demanded.

"Difficult lock." Santa didn't look up. "Heavy parts."

"Someone's coming!" Duchess Constance exclaimed.

"Play along," said Volgha. A glamour was the only thing that she could manage with what she had on hand, which was nothing. Her skin turned greyish, her mouth started foaming, and she dropped to the floor and convulsed. Santa darted away from the door and rushed to her side, just as the door opened and another guard walked in.

"What happened to him?" the guard asked, jogging over to his unconscious coworker. Everyone in the cell stood stock still with their mouths slightly open, except for Volgha, who continued to convulse.

"Rats!" blurted Duchess Constance.

"What?" said the guard.

"Big ones," said Santa. "Bit the guard and our friend here. We have to help her, open the gate!"

"I can't," said the guard. "I have to call the Captain."

"There's no time," exclaimed Duke Alfred. "This is the queen's sister! Do you have any idea what will happen to you if any harm comes to her?"

"King Chamberlain is in charge now," said the guard.

"And he threw her in the *upper* dungeons," noted Lady Sneeze-worthy. "Do you want her to die on *your* watch?"

The guard said a swear word.

"Quickly!" demanded Santa.

"All right." The guard grabbed the key from the hook. "All of you, against the back wall!"

He wasn't as dumb as they'd have preferred, but they couldn't drop the ruse now that they were so close. They all backed up against the far wall. Volgha continued to convulse in the middle of the floor, desperately racking her brain for what she could do next.

Most people would agree that important decisions should be planned in advance, preferably vetted by a committee that has been informed by experts, who would then deliberate on a variety of options before committing to a course of action and seeing it through. Unfortunately, though they had a veritable committee at the ready, they had no time to deliberate.

In the absence of time, why not abandon all forethought and simply act? It would have to do. As soon as she felt the guard's hands on her shoulders, she switched her glamour to the most vile and nightmarish concoction of physical attributes that her mind could conceive on short notice. Her face rotted away, maggots swarmed everything above her shoulders, and her limbs turned into tangles of snakes. She lunged at the guard and threw him off balance, screaming with half a dozen voices all at once.

That was as far as she got. What she'd fail to account for was the guard's "fight or flight" response. As bad luck would have it, he was a fighter. Volgha took a mailed fist to the maggot pile, which conjured up a loud cracking sound and the coppery taste of blood. His other fist had her by the front of her dress, and she couldn't break free.

The guard's eyes were wide with panic, and he screamed in a

falsetto that rivalled Loki's impression of the queen. He landed two more blows and reached back for another, but before he had a chance to throw it, a rushing red blur wrenched the guard violently aside, and Volgha was sent tumbling to the ground. She let the glamour fade away and tried to will the room to stop spinning. Everything sounded far away, as though it were happening underwater.

She shook her head, sending bloody globs everywhere, and tried to pick herself up. Her vision started to focus in time to see Santa kneeling on the guard's chest, delivering three quick blows to his face. The guard slumped, unconscious. Santa stood up.

Volgha felt herself being lifted from the ground, her head still spinning. She looked up into the face of Sir Henry.

"Are you all right?" he asked.

"I think tho," replied Volgha. *That was weird*, she thought. Her tongue explored her mouth to find her front teeth missing. She said a bunch of swear words, all of which sounded ridiculous.

Sir Henry set her gently onto her feet.

"Can you walk?" asked Santa.

"Well enough," said Volgha. "We have to get to the wine thellar."

"The *wine* cellar?" said the Viceroy. "Oh no, not me. That's how we wound up here in the first place!"

"That wath you? The people who broke in and thtole my thithter'th boothe?" Volgha spat a big glob of blood, which rolled down her chin and onto her dress. It was partially concealed by all of the black she wore. A drop of dignity in a lake of throbbing pain.

That's lucky, said Osgrey. *They'll know the way!*

"Yes, that was us," replied Duke Alfred. "And we've learned our lesson. It'll be a long time before I turn up at court again. Right now, I'm going home to Ibberlin-Going-Backward just as fast as I can manage."

"Very well," said Santa, "but we're off to the wine cellar." Though he'd shown significant grace in his high heels, he'd cast them off in favor of the second guard's boots. They were good boots, from the look of them.

"I can get them out from here," said Sir Henry.

"Good luck to you," said Lady Sneezeworthy, looking for a way to hug Volgha without getting blood and spit all over herself, but settling for an awkward wave. "I am in your debt."

"And you can call on us at Ibberlin-Going-Backward if you find yourself nearby," said Duke Alfred.

"Quite." Duchess Constance was still looking down her nose, but with a hint of a smile.

The two groups struck off in separate directions, with Santa, Volgha, and Loki headed for the wine cellar.

TWENTY

THITH ONE," SAID VOLGHA, PULLING LOKI'S POTION FROM Matilda's burlap sack. They all breathed a sigh of relief together.

"We got lucky," said Matilda. "I'd found a passage that ended behind a small watercolor in Chamberlain's office."

"And I was little enough to get through it," said Krespo. "We couldn't understand what Redcrow was flapping and cawing at, so I just grabbed every bottle I could find."

Most of the other bottles that Krespo had snagged were booze, but it was no matter. They had the right one.

Thickest bunch of nitwits I've ever had to work with, cawed Redcrow.

"Be nithe," said Volgha.

I'd be nicer if I weren't so hungry!

"We'll eat later." Volgha held the potion out to Loki. "Quickly, drink it tho we can undo thith meth!"

"No," said Loki. The word had all the petulance of a child who was remaining firm that no more bites of dinner would be taken. It further demanded dessert.

"What?" said Volgha. "You mutht!"

"I can't. I don't want to be a god. By all reports, I was a real jerk and nobody liked me. I don't want to go back to that." He was holding his ground. He'd be holding his breath in protest soon.

"You have to," said Santa. "Otherwise, there will be war with the frost giants."

Loki muttered a swear word. "Well, I can't be that cause of that! Isn't there another way?"

Volgha shook her head, which caused another round of pain. "There'th not."

We don't know that for sure, said Osgrey. *There's always a chance that we could—*

"Not now!" snapped Volgha.

"What do you mean?" asked Loki. "Will there be another way later? I can wait, you know."

You didn't seem keen on messing with the minds of gods before, Osgrey, cawed Redcrow. *Curiosity getting the better of you?*

"There'th not going to be another way," said Volgha. "I'm thorry."

"But it's him! My other half! He's responsible for this," said Loki. "Maybe we could solve it without him? Or me, as it were?"

I just know what Loki is like, said Osgrey. *If I could spare him from his worse half, I would.*

"That would be nithe," said Volgha, "but now we're out of time. You have to drink it!"

"But I'll be my wretched old self again!"

"You can't run from this." Santa's voice was low and calm. "This is who you are, and you can't outrun yourself."

"But *this* is who I am now." Loki jerked his thumb toward his chest.

"And so is *that,*" said Santa, pointing to the potion in Volgha's hand. "Half of you is in that barrel, and not drinking that potion isn't going to change that. You can fight your other nature, but you can't avoid it. It's a part of you. Now drink the potion, undo what your lesser self has done, and then worry about what to do with yourself. You've been the villain, now you get to be the hero."

A single tear rolled down Loki's cheek. Volgha had no idea that she'd split his personality along with his mind, and she felt sorry for him. Still, too much was at stake to look the other way. What Loki's monstrous half had done, his gentler half would have to bear the consequences.

"Thank you," he said, "for bringing me here. For showing me the way. Perhaps I'll manage to be a better god than I was. But if not, I apologize in advance for the rest of my days."

"Apology accthepted."

Loki took the potion and drank it down. He smiled, showing Volgha one last ounce of humanity before a green bolt of light shot into him from the whiskey barrel. He dropped to the ground.

"Was that supposed to happen?" asked Matilda.

Volgha nodded. "He was thuppothed to have left half hith mind waiting in a wine barrel, but he inthithted on whithkey. It'th probably the cauthe of the amnethia."

"But it was his dominant half this time," said Santa. "Maybe he'll be all right?"

"*Ow* … It was such good whiskey! Why does it hurt so much?" Loki rolled around on the floor, like a snake trying to shed its skin.

"Loki?" Krespo seemed suspicious.

"Yes, Loki," said Loki. "Please stop shouting! *Ow*, I should do that, too."

"Ith it done then? Are you rethtored to normal? Ath normal ath you've ever been, in any cathe."

"Repeat after me," said Loki, his head in his hands. "Susurrus."

Volgha rolled her eyes. "He'th fine."

"No? How about sibilance? Specificity?"

Ha! said Osgrey.

"Quiet you," said Volgha.

Yeah, show some respect! cawed Redcrow. *That's half the Warden you're laughing at, and we don't appreciate it!*

"On your feet," said Santa through clenched teeth. He grabbed

THE WINTER RIDDLE

Loki roughly by the shirt and dragged him upright. "What did you do, cretin?"

"What?" said Loki. "Oh, you mean the riddle?" A look of realization washed over his face. He said a swear word. "I failed! *Ow!* Odds bodkins, I failed my own challenge! I'm a miserable wretch, a mediocre conman!"

Loki made a pitiful moaning sound, went limp, and slipped out of Santa's grip. He laid on the ground, moaning like a child who desperately needed a nap, but insisted he wasn't tired.

"Yes," said Santa. "You're a miserable failure. Now you've got to get up before you doom us all."

More pitiful moaning sounds.

"Loki, you have to get up," insisted Volgha. "You have to undo whatever it wath that you did."

Loki chuckled. "Wath! Ha ha! *Ow.*" He went back to moaning. It was truly pitiful to behold.

Santa's face went red with frustration. His hands balled into shaking fists. He stepped forward and gave Loki a vicious kick to the ribs. Doubling over, Loki groaned. Santa kicked him again, then picked him up and slammed him against the stone wall. He pinned the naughty god there by the throat with his forearm, their noses nearly touching.

"What did you do?" he screamed, with greater fury than Volgha had ever seen in a man. "You've doomed us all, you filthy—"

Loki lazily shoved Santa and sent him flying backward. Santa collided with a wine cask, splintering it and sending what smelled to be a delightful, full-bodied red spilling across the stone floor.

"Still a god, you know." Loki smoothed down his rumpled shirt. He stood there for a second, wavered, and sat down against the wall. He let out another pathetic moan.

I wonder if he could teach me how to shove like that, cawed Redcrow. *Might come in handy with my Warden duties.*

Volgha's not the Warden yet, said Osgrey. *Don't get ahead of yourself.*

"Oh, what does it matter? Unable to solve my own riddle, and beaten up by a mortal. What sort of god am I?"

"The kind that can fool the greatest trickster of all time," said Krespo.

Loki looked up. "How's that?"

"Think about it," said Krespo. "You managed to think of a riddle so clever that not even the cleverest god in Asgard could figure it out. Who else could do that?"

Not bad, cawed Redcrow, *even if it is utter rubbish.*

"No one," said Loki, the ridiculous gleam of self-absorption shining brightly in his eyes once again. "None of the other gods could have bested me in this, only I could! Thor couldn't rival my intellect, the half-wit. Nor Tyr, Heimdall, not even Odin himself! I'm the smartest of them all! Ha ha! *Ow.*"

"Tho tell uth," said Volgha, "what did you do?"

Loki smiled and giggled. "I moved the sun," he answered. "Just an inch! Just enough to warm things up a bit, just barely—no one would notice, no one who wasn't exceptionally clever."

"The frost giants must be exceptionally clever then." Santa rose to his feet. "You warmed the peak of Niflheim enough that one of them is very close to laying his hands on the Horn of Frost. You've brought war down upon us, Loki."

Loki burst into laughter. "What are the chances? Ha ha! Ha ha ha! *Ow.*"

"It'th no laughing matter!"

"Not if you're Odin, it's not," said Loki. "He told the Vikings that he'd gotten rid of the frost giants for good. Oh, won't his face be red?"

"You have to put the sun back where it belongs," demanded Santa.

"And if I don't?"

"We'll tell the Vikings that you brought the frost giants back."

"The embarrassment will be Odin's alone. This is just the sort of mischief that's expected of a delightful scamp such as myself!"

"Not if we tell them that you *accidentally* brought the frost giants back," said Matilda.

"What?"

"I can hear them now," said Matilda. "The Vikings will say 'dumb old Loki, can't pull off a prank without releasing the frost giants by mistake.' They'll laugh about it for years."

"It'll be worthe than that," said Volgha. "Your name will be thynonymouth with bungling. They'll thay 'oopth, I really pulled a Loki and raided the wrong village,' or 'thorry, dear, I've Loki'd the roatht, can we go out for thupper?'"

Oh come on, cawed Redcrow, *you don't actually expect this to bother—*

"No, they won't!" Loki snarled. "Ugh, fine! I'll go fix it. But only because I'm bored of this game. I've already won it anyway!"

"If you say so," said Santa.

Idiot.

"I do say so, mortal." Loki walked behind a cask of wine and disappeared.

"I hope he hurrieth," said Volgha.

"Good thinking, Krespo," said Santa, "telling him that he'd actually won."

Krespo shrugged. "Everyone likes to think of themselves as the hero of their own story. Besides, whether he solved it or not, he could have viewed either outcome as a win or a loss. If he didn't see that all along, he's not as clever as all that."

Santa laughed. "Well said. You've certainly proven your worth today, Krespo."

Krespo smiled.

You should congratulate Matilda as well, suggested Osgrey.

"Right," said Volgha. "Well done to you ath well, Matilda. That wath quick thinking."

"Glad I could pitch in," said Matilda. "Now what about the queen?"

Volgha said a swear word. It lost its veracity without her front teeth. Sibilant swear words are like that.

"We have to find her," she said.

"If she's still alive," said Santa.

Volgha's heart sank. She realized that since they'd first been thrown into the dungeon, she never once considered her sister's well-being. The two of them had never gotten along, but dislike and disregard are very different. She'd always thought that she'd have been perfectly happy if she never had to speak to her sister again, but that scenario always assumed that Alexia was alive somewhere, ruling her kingdom, drunk and braying like a donkey, eating sausages that she'd found in other people's pockets. She never wanted her sister to die—she was all the family Volgha had left.

"The withard'th tower," she said. "It hath everything I need to thcry through the cathle, I'll be able to find her in no time."

What about Ghasterly? asked Osgrey.

Volgha shuddered. "We all have to fathe our fearth thometime."

Getting to the base of the wizard's tower was easy. Getting to the top was nearly impossible unless you knew the trick to it. Fortunately for Volgha, she did—and Ghasterly had never bothered to change it, out of arrogance or laziness or both.

It was a spiral stone staircase. If you climbed it incorrectly, you could find yourself spiraling endlessly up or down until someone came and got you—or you died of starvation, which had happened on more than one occasion.

The trick was to skip every third step, unless it had a green brick on it, in which case you'd step on it and skip the one after that; unless *that* one had a green brick on it, in which case you'd need to skip the step preceding the *first* one with the green brick on it. Of course, if *that* one had a brown brick on it, you'd need to step on it with both feet and then hop over both of the ones with the green bricks. Any steps with a green brick *and* a brown brick on them should never be stepped on under any circumstances—unless, of course, it was flanked on both sides by steps with red bricks on them. In that case, any steps with green bricks should be ignored entirely. Simple.

Once they'd traversed the stairs, made it past the fake door, the other fake door, the hedge maze, and the final fake door, they took a running start at the real door—which wasn't really there—passed through it with only a modicum of motion sickness, and marveled at the wonders within.

The whole place hummed with magical energy. Bookshelves lined the circular walls of the tower, stretching as high as the eye could see. There were sitting areas, lecterns supporting very old and odd-looking volumes, some of which were leafing through their own pages leisurely, passing the time while waiting for someone who knew what they were doing to come and read them with intent.

Ghasterly was nowhere to be seen. That was good. Maybe Volgha could get in, do what needed to be done, and get out before he returned from the mausoleum he was rooting through, or whatever other detestable business he enjoyed. She knew she'd have to deal with him eventually, but without her basket or her teeth, her powers were rather limited.

What was she thinking, barging into the tower like that? Ghasterly could have been waiting for her! She'd better hurry then, and standing there gawking wasn't helping at all.

Time to move, then. Right foot first, go on. Why was nothing happening? She looked down, and saw a shadowy ichor puddling at her feet, holding her in place. Santa, Krespo, and Matilda were stuck in it as well. Krespo was crying. Volgha's blood went cold.

"Tsk, tsk, tsk," came a sickly, chiding echo from everywhere all at once. "You've broken your promise, girl. Now you'll have to be punished."

There was a stirring in the ichor beneath them. Volgha felt something crawling over her boots. She looked down and saw fingers. Pale, dead fingers.

"I don't have time for thith," said Volgha. "Jutht give me my bathket, and I'll be on my way."

Just go get it, cawed Redcrow. *What's stopping you?*

"Whothe thide are you on?" Volgha spat at Redcrow. "Do thomething, will you?"

"Talking to birds, are we?" said Ghasterly, suddenly appearing inches from Volgha's face. She cringed.

"Stop this," said Santa. "Leave us alone, or you'll regret it!"

"Big words from the frightened deer." Ghasterly strolled lazily over to Santa, but stayed carefully out of arm's reach. "Well done, running from the former queen. If I'd been hunting you, your organs would be in alphabetized jars by now."

"Release me, and we can test that theory." Santa showed no fear at all. Volgha envied that. Their last encounter had left her feeling utterly helpless against Ghasterly. She couldn't think of anything but her desire to live through this.

Why are you screaming like that?

"I'm not thcreaming, that'th Krethpo!"

"Not yet, you're not," said Ghasterly, not taking his eyes off Santa.

Volgha squirmed. The dead fingers rose from the ichor to become dead hands, clawing their way up her legs. Whether they were trying to climb up or pull her down didn't matter. She was in the midst of the only reasonable reaction, mentally screaming, *No no no no no no no no no no no ...*

Your thoughts are screaming! cawed Redcrow, as forcefully as possible. *Why don't you all just rush him, and give him the beating of his life?*

"I'd love to, but I can't move!" said Volgha.

"Wait a minute," said Matilda, her brow all furrowed.

What?

"I thaid I can't move!"

It's no good, I can't hear you over your screaming! You need to quiet your mind!

"It's not real!" said Matilda.

"Quiet, girl," said Ghasterly. Volgha watched in horror as he took Matilda's face in his hands and opened his mouth. A black serpent emerged, hissing and baring its fangs.

Krespo screamed.

"Leave her alone!" shouted Santa. He twisted his hips and pulled against the grasping corpses below him, trying to break free.

"What are you doing?" asked Matilda, squinting at Ghasterly. The serpent struck at her face, it's jaw snapping an inch from her nose. She didn't even blink.

Oh, I get it, cawed Redcrow. *Volgha, whatever you're seeing, it isn't real! If you can quiet your mind, I can show you!*

But how? How could she quiet her mind? She was being dragged into a black and hopeless void, which is exactly the sort of situation in which the mind is expected to work as hard as possible!

"Let go!" yelled Matilda, struggling against Ghasterly. She was shaking her head and grasping at his hands. "And close your mouth, your breath is rancid!"

Matilda managed to get a foot free from the grasping dead things, and planted it firmly on Ghasterly's knee. He stumbled and fell, and Matilda ran away from him.

"Curse you, child!" Ghasterly rose to his feet sneering, and started limping toward her. "I don't have to use magic to choke the life from you!"

Redcrow cawed a swear word. He leapt from the bookcase where he was perched and went after Ghasterly, flapping and clawing at his face.

Feel the fury of the Warden, cur!

When a person has never been in a physical altercation, there are several tell-tale signs that emerge during their first fight. While a seasoned brawler will put their head down and move toward their opponent, the novice will tend to lean backward, flail their arms wildly, and rely on their opponent eventually getting tired of fighting them and concede victory.

While Redcrow's anatomy left him incapable of making a martially effective fist, he'd been in a few dust-ups in his time. Ghasterly, on the other hand, obviously had not. He also seemed incapable of forming a martially effective fist, proper anatomy notwithstanding.

Unfortunately, though his flapping and clawing were able to drive Ghasterly backward, the necromancer seemed to figure out that he vastly outweighed the bird. Luckily, Redcrow had managed to put enough distance between Ghasterly and Matilda for her to get a running start at him. She leapt and collided with Ghasterly's midsection, catching him off-balance and bringing him to the floor. His head struck the cold stone roughly, and he was out cold. The ichor and the clutching dead things vanished instantly, though the force and speed of Volgha's heartbeat did not relent. Neither did Krespo's crying until he opened his eyes.

That's right, cawed Redcrow, now hopping on Ghasterly's chest, *you see what happens when you go in against the Warden?*

"It wath all an illuthion!" said Volgha, her voice quavering.

That's what I was trying to tell you, cawed Redcrow.

"Good job, Matilda," said Santa. "How did you see through the spell?"

"It just didn't seem likely," she replied, dusting herself off. "I could still feel solid ground under me, but it looked like I was standing in a bog or something. Plus, I remember from burying the old Tickler that it doesn't take long for the dead to start stinking. Dozens of rotting hands with no smell?"

"I should have thought of that." Krespo began drying tears away from his face.

You all should have, cawed Redcrow. *It was painfully obvious.*

"It wathn't directed at you," said Volgha. "Thtop acting tho thuperior."

"You were *here,* Krespo," said Santa. "That took courage."

"Courage to what?" asked Krespo, new tears welling in his eyes. "To cry myself to death?"

Santa shook his head. "Courage isn't the absence of fear, Krespo. It's gritting your teeth and charging in anyway. You're every bit as brave as the rest of us."

"I agree. Good job, Krespo. Good job, everyone." Matilda wiped her hands on her pants. "Now, what do we do with him?"

"Find me a rope," said Santa.

WHEN GHASTERLY AWOKE, HE WAS BOUND TO A CHAIR AND GAGGED. The first thing he saw was Volgha leafing through one of his books, and he started writhing and trying to shout.

"Good," Santa moved to crouch in front of him, "you're awake. You remember our last staring match, don't you? The one right before you threatened to strangle a little girl?"

"Young woman," corrected Matilda. "The young woman who took him down, for those keeping score."

"Right," said Santa, "sorry."

"Caw!" said Redcrow aloud, in a way that seemed to mean "ahem."

"Yes," said Matilda, "it was a team effort. Well done, Redcrow."

Redcrow ruffled his feathers and affected a stately pose on his perch.

"You're only alive right now because you were defeated by the young woman and the crow," Santa said to Ghasterly. "If you'd been a few inches closer to me, I'd have squashed your head to soup."

Santa put his hands on Ghasterly's shoulders. He spent a long moment just staring at him. Ghasterly seemed to know that he'd been defeated, though his sneer soldiered on unabated. He'd nurtured it for so long that it had taken on a life of its own. According to Aurorian law, he could start charging it property taxes for the use of his face.

Volgha was sitting at a desk piled high with books, scrolls, potions, ingredients, and all manner of strange and wonderful implements that defied description. She was flipping through a big red book with illuminated pages.

"Are you going to cast a spell from that book to find the queen?" asked Matilda.

"No thpellth in thith book," said Volgha. "Thith one ith jutht a directory."

The others made themselves comfortable in the overstuffed chairs and waited while Volgha found everything that she needed. She ground herbs together in a mortar, added some oils, then found a bit of fire living in the cragflower she'd mixed in, and set the concoction alight. The distillation took a long time, but once she was satisfied with the color and clarity of the potion, she waved her hand over it and mumbled a few words.

"Here goeth nothing," she said, a phrase that almost never came after "a lot of proper planning went onto this," or was followed by "that went well, I'm glad we did it." She drank the whole thing down, set the bottle on the desk, and quickly took a seat on the steps. Staring at the floor, she took a few deep breaths.

Krespo looked at Santa. "What do you suppose was in that—"

Volgha started screaming and rolling around on the floor, with her hands covering her face.

"Oh no," exclaimed Matilda, "something's gone wrong!"

"Caw!" said Redcrow. He appeared to shake his head and waited patiently on his perch.

"Give it a moment." Santa was staring at Volgha.

"Not like we have much choice." Krespo was right, of course. Short of throwing whatever magic-looking ingredients that were within reach at her, what could they do? There was no clearly labeled *Magic Extinguisher* that any of them could see.

After a moment, Volgha's screaming subsided. She sat up and ran her tongue around the inside of her mouth with her lips closed. Then her lips parted, and she bared two full rows of teeth at her comrades. Her eyes held a questioning look.

"Your teeth are fixed!" said Krespo.

"Oh, thank goodness," said Volgha.

"I thought you were worried about your sister," said Santa.

"I am," replied Volgha. "It's just that most of the incantations that I need to perform to find her are rather precise. If I get them wrong, bad things can happen."

Santa nodded. "Painful process, then?"

"All the pain of teething packed into several seconds," said Volgha. "I don't recommend it."

Volgha smiled when she saw it. It was sitting right where she left it, on the floor between two bookcases. No doubt Ghasterly hadn't thought enough of the basket to do anything with it, and that was his folly. There were quite a lot of valuable spell components in there, not to mention some powdered spices that would really stand out in the stew.

She was a bit low on a few things, though, so she rifled through Ghasterly's shelves and filled the basket with herbs, roots, powders, and the like. She gave herself a little nod, satisfied that she was fully equipped now to take on Chamberlain and put this whole thing to rest.

"Right," said Volgha, "time to find my sister. Redcrow, would you help with the Seeking, please?"

I suppose so, cawed Redcrow, *since you asked so nicely. A little humility looks good on you.*

"Thanks, I guess."

Redcrow flew out through the window and into the darkening sky with a, "Caw!" while Volgha ground salt and rockwort together. She made her circle on the floor, sat in the middle of it, closed her eyes, and began chanting and gesturing. Precise or not, it was quite sibilant.

It didn't take long to find Alexia, alive and well.

Thanks, Redcrow, she thought to him. *You can come back now. And you can stop shouting! Anyway, getting back in through that window gives me a headache. I'll just meet you in the kitchens later.*

Volgha opened her eyes.

"She's fine," Volgha told them. "She's in our parents' old tower, apparently sleeping off a massive amount of wine."

"That's good," said Krespo.

"What do we do now?" inquired Matilda.

"Chamberlain needs to answer for what he's done," said Volgha.

"For the coup?" asked Matilda. She hesitated, and then added, "Does he really?"

"What do you mean?" Volgha questioned, her brow furrowed.

"I mean no disrespect," said Matilda. "How shall I put this? Well … you know your sister."

"Of course," said Volgha.

"Well, it's been very … *peaceful* since Chamberlain took over."

Matilda showed Volgha something that she should have seen all along: she has a blind spot for her sister. All these years, she'd seen Alexia merely as a true descendant of the royal lineage—a ridiculous twit who drank too much and never took anything seriously—but in reality, she was worse than that. She really hurt people, made messes of their lives. To say the very least, she wasn't the sort of person who should be a queen.

"I see your point," said Volgha. "But did he seize power for the good of the people, or for himself?"

"Does it really matter?" asked Matilda. "Besides, all due respect, but when was the last time Aurora had a monarch who was truly benevolent?"

"Watch it. My parents were—"

"Just as bad as Her Majesty! I'm too young to know myself, but I've heard the rest of the staff talk about them. They were just as ridiculous, if maybe slightly less sadistic!"

"Fine!" Volgha threw up her hands. "My sister is a horrible queen! I even swore revenge against her myself not long ago, but Chamberlain usurped the throne and threw me in the dungeon for no crime. I can't let that stand!"

"Then we need another option," said Matilda.

"You could do it," Krespo suggested.

"What," Volgha's voice rose a few octaves, "*me* be the queen?"

"Why not?" said Krespo. "You're every bit the royal that your sister is, why shouldn't you have a turn at the throne?"

"That's not the way it works. I had to renounce any claim I had to the throne years ago to get my sister to leave me alone."

"And how's it been," asked Santa, "your sister honoring the pact and leaving you alone all these years?"

"That's beside the point," responded Volgha, who knew a weak argument when she heard one.

"Renouncements can be undone," said Matilda, "can't they?"

"Even if they could," said Volgha, "I wouldn't want it. I want to be a witch, not a queen."

"If you didn't want to be involved, you should have stayed out of it," said Santa.

"Well, it's too late for that."

"Then you're involved," said Santa. "You can't just leave an unfit ruler on the throne—either one of them—and walk away."

"I know," said Volgha, "but what you're suggesting makes it all my problem."

"I understand," said Santa. "But we may have much larger

problems very soon if Loki is too late in putting the sun to rights."

Volgha nodded. It's a horrible feeling, being unable to act in the face of too much to do.

"Matilda," said Santa, "how long has it been since Chamberlain took power?"

"Half a dozen evenings or so."

"Then your sister's not in any immediate danger. If he were going to hurt her, he'd have done it by now."

"You're probably right," said Volgha. "Let's make sure the frost giant problem is averted, and then I'm going to take on Chamberlain. By myself, if I must."

Santa nodded. "We'll do it together. After the frost giants. Can you see where they are now?"

"I'll need to scry into Niflheim," she said. "Just a quick look, it won't take long."

She reasoned that she only needed to look at the peak where she'd seen Gorsulak breaking up the ice to get to the Horn of Frost. She knew right where it was. She wouldn't even need Redcrow this time. She'd be able to get close on her own.

She swept away the circle of salt and rockwort and drew one from salt alone. Within minutes she was muttering the incantations, and effortlessly swept herself across the veil.

The last time she'd scried into Niflheim, it had been like she was actually there; this time, it was more like seeing a very vivid painting of it that moved a bit from time to time. She could see the landmarks—or rather, landmark—but it just didn't feel as real. She really missed the amplifiers on Howling Hill.

No matter. She saw the peak not far away, although it took longer to reach this time. She moved as fast as she could, but it felt like she was barely moving at all.

What are we doing in Niflheim? asked Osgrey.

"Checking in on the Horn of Frost," said Volgha. "Where have you been?"

I'm not sure. It was all black. Ghasterly must have barred me from the tower.

"You don't have to worry about him any longer. We've defeated him!"

Well done! Just don't kill him. Never kill a necromancer, no telling what shades lurk within them.

Osgrey was right. Killing a necromancer was like cutting open a big sack of snakes and spiders and lovelorn poets. It would probably be best to simply double-bag it and lock it in a closet somewhere.

Eventually, she got close enough to see the hulking form of Gorsulak, still punching away at the ice around the horn.

The winds and snow were blowing very hard, and his blows weren't breaking enormous chunks away from the horn anymore, but he was still making progress. He had plenty of room to stand there. There were only a few feet of ice around the horn now, and that was rapidly receding. Barring a miracle, it did not appear that anything would stop him from reaching the horn. Soon.

"Gorsulak!" she shouted. "Please, let's talk about this!"

It was no use. Even if he'd heard her, he wasn't listening. It appeared that Loki had already moved the sun back to where it belonged, but the ice wouldn't reform around the horn faster than Gorsulak could knock it away.

She let herself fade from Niflheim, back into her body. As the inside of the tower shimmered back into view, she saw her comrades looking at her expectantly, hopefully.

Sighing, she stood up. Santa hung his head and turned away.

"Well?" said Krespo. "Were we in time?"

"No," Volgha answered, her expression forlorn.

"How long do we have?" asked Santa.

"It's hard to say," said Volgha. "Gorsulak will have the horn any time now. I don't know how long it will take to rally the giants."

"But they're coming?" said Santa.

"Oh yes," said Volgha. "They're coming."

Santa said a swear word. "Then we have to act quickly."

"What about him?" Matilda tilted her head toward Ghasterly. Ghasterly sneered.

"How about defenestration?" Santa suggested. "Quick and easy."

"We can't kill him," said Volgha. "Bad things come from killing necromancers."

"Did a necromancer tell you that?" asked Matilda with a smirk.

"Well we can't just leave him here. Do you have any idea what he could do with that if he got free?" Krespo was pointing to what looked like a case of bent spoons that had been sharpened and given a taste for blood. Volgha didn't have the slightest idea what their use could be.

"Of course I do," said Volgha. "I know we can't leave him here, but we can't kill him."

"I don't see why not," said Santa. "He's a vile sorcerer, the type who murders children!" Santa gestured toward Matilda.

"You mean the type who *threatens* to murder *young women*," countered Matilda. "Besides, Volgha is right. Defenestration is a very *White Queen* way to get rid of a problem, and we've had enough of that sort of leadership here."

"Fine," acquiesced Santa. "What then?"

Everyone was silent for a moment.

"We could do a wizard's prison," suggested Krespo.

"A wizard's prison?" Volgha raised an eyebrow.

"Yeah," said Krespo. "His essence is stored in a bottle, and his body goes ... well, I'm not sure, but I've read about them. It's mostly Applied Thinkery, and it doesn't sound that hard."

"You're full of surprises," Santa remarked.

"Will it take long?" asked Matilda.

"I don't think so," replied Krespo, "if Volgha can do the spirit bits, I believe I can manage the rest."

Volgha nodded and grabbed the red directory book. "What do you need?"

TWENTY-ONE

BOTTLING GHASTERLY HAD BEEN SURPRISINGLY EASY. KRESPO had done most of the work via Applied Thinkery, and Volgha only needed to walk his corporeal form across the veil. His essence remained in a bottle in the wizard's tower, so his body just sort of complacently shuffled along behind her. His face did continue to sneer, though, proving his mother had been right when she'd warned him it would freeze like that.

Volgha left Ghasterly's body sitting against a rock. There it would stay forever, unless some ninny decided to uncork the bottle.

Santa had gone back to the village. He had preparations to make. On the bright side, there was no need to hide from the White Queen anymore, so he could be there without endangering anyone.

Wretched times we're living through, said Osgrey. *Not being hunted by a raving lunatic counts as a simple pleasure.*

Matilda had pleaded with Volgha to stay in the castle and help her get rid of Chamberlain.

"Ghasterly's out of the way," said Matilda. "Without his power, Chamberlain will be vulnerable. If we don't take him down quickly, he'll do whatever it takes to strengthen his hold!"

"I know," said Volgha, "and I promise that I'll return soon, but I have to do something about the frost giants. If they aren't stopped, it won't matter who's on the throne when the walls come down."

Matilda sighed. "I suppose you're right. I'll just have to ... I don't know ..."

"Get back to your regular job so you're not suspected," said

Volgha. "Come up with a plan to get the servants out of the castle if things take a turn for the worse. Can you manage that?"

"I guess." Matilda rolled her eyes when Volgha mentioned going back to work in the kitchens. "You promise you'll be back soon?"

"I swear it on my pointy hat."

VOLGHA AND REDCROW TOOK FLIGHT FOR ASGARD. SHE SIMPLY couldn't stand for the folly of the gods to be the doom of everyone else. Odin had banished the frost giants once, surely he'd be able to do it again.

As she rose up into the freezing winds, Volgha was left with no doubt that Loki had moved the sun back into place. Even her broom protested, prompting her to give it an extra threatening. It had to know that the forest was just silly with branches—did it honestly think she'd stand for a protest?

She envied Redcrow. As they flew side by side along the last remaining sliver of purple sunset, she could tell that though he felt the cold, it did not rip through him the way it did through her. He always had a warm spot at his center, probably some gift of magical confluence. Lucky, fiery bird.

She loved feeling close to the spirits of the winter, and by luxuriating in the warm airs of Loki's temporary reprieve, she felt she'd grown soft. There was a distance between her and the winter, which was a state unbecoming the Winter Witch.

She let go of her envy of Redcrow. She stopped shivering against the wind. She gripped the shaft of her broom, threatened it with a severe whittling, and leaned in toward the shadow of Yggdrasil on the horizon. The full gale force of winter's power embraced her.

By the time she touched down outside the golden doors of Asgard, she was chilled to the bone. Her teeth chattered uncontrollably. She felt half-dead but thoroughly satisfied.

"Oh," said the guard, "it's you."

"Hello again," said Volgha. "I need to speak with Odin."

"Is he expecting you?"

"No, but it's an urgent matter."

"Urgent enough to threaten me with boils?"

Oh good, cawed Redcrow. *He remembers.*

"That was just business," said Volgha, "but this is urgent. Loki has made a mess of things—"

"Ha! Loki. He won't like the sound of that."

"You have no idea."

"I don't, do I? Is that because I'm just a lowly guard, meant only to stand outside and be threatened with boils by people who are far more important?"

Here it comes.

"Look, I know that I was—"

"Rude? Demeaning? Yeah, I remember. I was there. I was the guy being threatened for no reason other than I had a job to do."

"We don't have time for—"

"It's 'we' now, is it? I'm just the guy that watches the door, remember? You made my relative importance abundantly clear the last time you were here."

He's got you there, cawed Redcrow. *I wonder if he's been thinking about this for a while. Maybe since we were last here?*

Volgha shut her eyes tightly, trying to suppress her frustration. It was everything she could do to refrain from unleashing all of her vitriol on this self-righteous twit. She had a world to save, and he'd had his feelings maligned! As ridiculous as it was, she couldn't move forward until she'd soothed this enormous infant of a man.

Just apologize, said Osgrey. *He won't listen to reason while his feelings are hurt. It's human nature.*

"I'm sorry," she said.

"You don't care. You don't even know my name."

Volgha sighed. "You're right. The last time I was here, I'd have melted you into a puddle to get what I wanted. I didn't even bother to ask you your name, and that was rude. I didn't respect that you have a very important job to do, and I didn't care that breaking the rules would spell trouble for you. For all of that, I sincerely apologize."

The guard said nothing. His face had been so thoroughly over-whelmed by the frown that had seized it that Volgha wondered if she'd need a pry bar to unseat it.

"Will you tell me your name?"

Still nothing. She was dealing with a severe case of sore feelings. A fine thing to delay the salvation of the North Pole.

Oh look, he's pouting! cawed Redcrow, not caring to hide his amusement. *Maybe he's just a really big five-year-old. Do you have a sweetie in your basket?*

"I'll tell you what," said Volgha, "out of respect for you and your duty, I will refrain from threatening to use my magic to melt you into a puddle of warm goo, which would be no trouble for me at all. Instead, I will very humbly beseech you to admit me to see Odin. That's your solemn duty, and I know that a man of your caliber takes his work seriously."

The guard fidgeted but said nothing.

"Of course, a lesser man than you might refuse to do his duty out of spite. That sort of man would have no claim to the moral high ground over a petulant and selfish witch, now would he?"

Not bad, cawed Redcrow.

"I know what you're doing!"

"I'm not *doing* anything. I'm just figuring out whether you're the honest sort of fellow who will do his duty despite his feelings, or the unscrupulous sort which requires a good face-melting to teach him a lesson."

A moment later, Volgha was led before Odin by an exasperated guard. In true father-of-the-gods fashion, he was sitting upon a golden throne.

"The mortal witch," greeted Odin. "You are welcome once again in the halls of Asgard! Speak your truth, that I might hear it."

Sounds like he's in a god-almighty sort of mood, said Redcrow. *Wouldn't hurt to flower up your language a bit, I think.*

Volgha nodded.

"Mighty Odin," she said with a curtsey, assuming that asking a god for a favor would be best preceded by some flagrant flattery. "The realm of Midgard is soon to find itself in peril."

"Peril?" questioned Odin. "Go on, and speak true."

"It is the result of a folly gone awry," said Volgha. "In an attempt to play a trick, Loki—"

"Loki!" Odin bellowed. "That foolish sack of villainy and deceit! What's he done now?"

"That which he has both done and undone was to move the sun. Mighty Odin. Sir."

You're nearly close enough to lick his boots, cawed Redcrow. *I said flowery language, not sycophancy! We're still the Wardens, show some dignity.*

"Done and undone? Then all is set to rights?"

"I would that it were so, Allfather. The perilous effect of his foolishness will soon be felt in Niflheim, where the giants are very near to claiming the Horn of Frost!"

"Fool!" shouted Odin. "A curse on his hide!"

"I beseech you, mighty Odin, Allfather and greatest of the gods, to undo what Loki has very nearly done. Keep the Horn of Frost from the hands of the giants! Block them from returning, and let your banishment hold!"

"What? Oh no, I couldn't."

"What?" Volgha was confused. "Why couldn't you? You've banished them before!"

"Oh, I *could*," said Odin. "It's not a question of ability, but … well, you said it yourself. I'm the father to everyone. All of the gods, all of the Vikings, everyone!"

He's hit his limit of flattery, I think.

"I don't see the problem," said Volgha. "Wouldn't a father want to protect his children?"

"Well, yes, of course," he replied. "But there comes a time in a child's life when a father must *not* protect it. From itself."

"What?"

"What sort of father would I be if I shielded my children from every danger and harm that came their way?"

"The good kind," said Volgha. "The caring kind."

"The *soft* kind!" bellowed Odin. He stood up from his throne and pointed down at her. "The kind of father who coddles his children, lets them grow doughy and soft, and keeps them from their potential! Oh no, Volgha the Winter Witch. I will not be the sort of father who cleans up all of his children's messes. This is one for them to work out on their own."

He sat back down upon his golden throne and assumed a commanding pose. Volgha guessed that it was hard for him to appear anything but godlike, especially upon a golden throne.

"Many of them will die," said Volgha.

"The halls of Valhalla await," he replied.

Well, it seems he's thought of everything. Nothing to do but ask for some anchovies and be on our way, right?

Volgha stood there staring for a moment, but could not think of anything else that she could say that might convince him to intervene. What do you say to a father who would prefer that his children meet their ends as brave warriors than live by his good graces?

Nothing. You talk to the children.

YOU WERE VERY DIPLOMATIC WITH ODIN, SAID OSGREY. *YOU'LL MAKE A fine Warden.*

"I'm not so sure," said Volgha.

I'll do all of the bossing around, cawed Redcrow. *You just talk to the spirits. We're a team, right?*

Volgha didn't know what to say to the Vikings, or how they would take it. At least the guards outside the hall of King Harald knew a witch when they saw one, and refrained from giving her any grief. She didn't even have to threaten them with warts and boils. One of them offered to introduce her to the king, after seeing Redcrow on her shoulder.

Ale and mead flowed freely in the king's feast hall. Volgha thought that the Vikings truly must have been made in the image of their gods. While the food and drink could not have compared to the banquet she'd attended in Asgard, the customs were very much the same. The shouting was largely composed of one person toasting something—"glorious battle" was a common refrain—and everyone within earshot responding at the top of their lungs. Every table was a rollicking maelstrom of axes, shields, beards and furs, everyone toasting, fighting, and hailing gods, brave men and brave women alike.

The warmth of the fires drove the chill from Volgha's bones as she walked toward the high table where King Harald sat with his wife and daughters and sons. They were all smiling, laughing and toasting with the rest of the Vikings. She hated to ruin their revelry with bad tidings, but it was the right thing to do.

"Your Majesty!" the guard shouted over the din. "I present Volgha, the Winter Witch, here to bear you some pressing news!"

"Well met, witch," he said. "Sit with me, and sup at my table!"

"I fear that I may not be welcome after I've delivered my news, Your Majesty."

King Harald's smile fell somewhat, and he raised his hands outward with his palms facing down. The guards beside the table thumbed the butts of their spears against the wooden floor, and the roar of the feasting Vikings faded to a rumbling murmur. King Harald stood up.

"Hold your tongues and lend your ears," he said. "We are visited by a witch, whose prognostication may prove dire! Speak, Volgha the Winter Witch! Let us hear the message that you bear."

Listen to King Fancypants, cawed Redcrow. *Better make it good, they're expecting a show.*

All eyes turned to Volgha. She felt herself blush, suddenly wishing that she'd prepared for this.

"The ... winds of ... fate ... blow hard and cold," she said, hoping that sounded sufficiently ominous. "The frost giants, long ago banished from Midgard by Odin, will very soon make their return. This winter will be made even darker than most, for war comes to Midgard!" *There, that should have been sufficiently theatrical,* she thought.

The entire hall was silent. She looked up at King Harald and saw his eyes go wide. Then he turned to look out over his people, and with a smile, shouted a single word.

"War!"

The room erupted in cheering. Flagons raised high, the Vikings shouted, "War!" back at their king. They drank, they cheered, they punched each other. A couple of Vikings rushed toward Volgha and lifted her up onto their shoulders. Redcrow flapped and rose up, finding himself a perch among the rafters.

"This is joyous news!" shouted King Harald. "You really had me going, pretending it was something ominous!"

"What?" shouted Volgha, incredulous. "You do understand what it means, don't you?"

"Of course! We're going to war!"

He's a fan of war then, cawed Redcrow. *All right, why not? Anchovies all around!*

"Yes, war!" shouted Volgha, as she scrambled down from the shoulders of the Vikings. "Against the frost giants! Many of your people will die!"

"Aye," shouted King Harald. "They'll die in the glory of battle, and be carried by Valkyries up to Valhalla!"

"Valhalla!" shouted the entire assembly, as a single voice.

It sounds like they're on the same page as Odin.

Flagons went up, and they drank a toast to war, to King Harald, to Volgha, to Valhalla, and even once to the frost giants.

Are they really so eager to die? asked Osgrey. *I know their gods tell them that they must die in battle to reach Valhalla, but it's not much nicer than Midgard, really.*

"You've been to Valhalla?" Volgha asked.

Just the once, said Osgrey. *A lot like this, really. Mostly Vikings drinking and punching each other.*

A place was made for Volgha beside King Harald, and hot food and warm wine were set down before her. She was hungry, so why not? Let the Vikings take the news as they liked while she tucked in.

Share and share alike, cawed Redcrow. He flapped down to land in front of her and took a bit of mutton from her plate.

"A magnificent raven," said King Harald. "A friend of yours?"

"My familiar," replied Volgha, who'd given up on correcting the raven thing. "He has a penchant for anchovies if you have any handy."

"Some brined sardines," King Harald instructed a servant.

He ran off, returning momentarily with a plate of sardines for Redcrow.

Not bad, he cawed. *Not anchovies, but not bad.*

"A glorious omen," said King Harald. "Odin sing your praises, you bring wondrous news!"

"Most would not think so."

"Most fear death," said King Harald. "Most will not reach Valhalla! I might fear death as well, if old age taking me in my sleep were the same as dying with my sword in my hand."

"Is it not the same?"

"Of course not! Old men who die in their beds don't reach Valhalla! You have to die in battle, everyone knows that!"

"Fair enough," responded Volgha. The food was very good, so she and Redcrow ate their fill.

"Take a bed in my hall," said King Harald after dinner. "This evening, or any evening! A bearer of such excellent tidings always has a place here."

"Thank you," said Volgha. "What happens next?"

"With the war? I will call my banners, rally the great houses. We will assemble on the anointed fields of battle, and await the giants there."

"You already know where they're going to attack?"

"It has long been known. Outside the city, down the road that leads from the great stone gate. We will set up our tents and await our foe."

Volgha nodded. "I have a friend. His name is Santa."

"Santa!" said the king with a smile. "A great and wise man. We have an alliance."

"He is readying his soldiers now."

"The Faesolde," he said. "Marvelous! We will fight beside them against the darkness. He is ever welcome at my table!"

With that, the king and his retinue left the hall. The drinking and revelry carried on into the evening. Volgha sat aside, sipping wine while Redcrow picked at his sardines.

You know, said Osgrey, *you and Santa may be the only ones who don't want this war.*

"Who *wants* war?" she asked. "They're all fools."

Perhaps. But if they're all keen on charging at each other for a spot of bloodshed, you'd be the bigger fool for standing in the way.

Volgha said nothing. She thought Osgrey might be right, and they shared thought space. No need to give him the satisfaction of acknowledging it aloud. She stared into the fire, thinking of her sister and the dark times to come.

SHE SLEPT VERY LITTLE, PARTIALLY DUE TO THE IMPENDING WAR, AND partially due to the profound snoring of the Vikings in King Harald's hall. It was too loud and forceful to have been naturally occurring, it seemed. They must have taken lessons.

She passed through the doors and into the brisk winter night. That was it, then. Not even a sliver of indigo remained on the horizon. The long dark of winter had finally settled over the North Pole, and unless they managed to defeat the frost giants, none of them might ever see the sun rise again.

She mounted her broom and rose up into the air. Bracing herself against the chill, she aimed toward Santa's Village, and prayed that time was still on her side as she rode off into the freezing night.

TWENTY-TWO

AFTER EVERYTHING THAT THEY'D BEEN THROUGH TOGETHER, Volgha was starting to count Santa among her friends. Still, she decided that it was probably best to knock on the gates of Santa's Village rather than simply flying over them and landing in the square. She could plainly see that there were archers patrolling the walls, and something flying over the wall very quickly in the dark could easily be met with a very put-an-arrow-in-it-and-ask-who's-there-please-afterward sort of welcome.

She knocked, then stood in the light of the faerie lamps with Redcrow on her shoulder. The little portal in the gate slid open and shut again without so much as a word. The gate opened, and an elf waved her in.

"Mistress Volgha," he said with a smile, "you're always welcome, no need to knock!"

"Thanks," she replied, sparing him the rationale. "Where's Santa?"

"He's with the captains of the Faesolde in the armory," answered the elf. "They're not to be dist—"

"In the armory," she said, keeping a brisk stride. "Thanks."

"Yes, but they're not to be—"

"You'd be easier to understand if you weren't interrupted so often!" Volgha was practically jogging now, the distance between them growing rapidly.

"But it's you who've been—"

"See what I mean?"

Volgha was sure that if she turned around, he'd have had a very crestfallen expression on his face. By not turning around, she saved him the embarrassment. That was nice of her.

Those two look like they mean business, said Osgrey.

There were two guards standing outside of the armory, all stiff and staring straight ahead, like it must say you're supposed to do in every guarding manual ever written. Volgha decided to try something she'd seen done once and simply kept walking toward the door without slowing down. By walking at the door with enough purpose, she suggested to the guards that her walking through the door was the natural progression of events taking place, and that they'd be doing something very foolish by trying to impede them.

Their spears crossed in front of her at the last second. It happened so quickly that she wasn't sure if they were immune to the power of suggestion, or if she'd somehow hesitated at the last moment and the suggestion just fell apart. *Oh well,* she thought, *on to plan B.*

She turned to peer down at the slightly shorter of the two guards. She was taller than both of them but reasoned that the greater the distance in height, the more likely she'd be able to intimidate him.

She didn't actually say anything, but her look said "did you know that your spear is blocking my way? It shouldn't be."

The look was met by a deep and disciplined silence. It was the sort of silence that meant "you're not fooling anyone, you know."

It's a very intimidating look, cawed Redcrow. *You should try telling him you're the Warden.*

Not yet, she's not! said Osgrey.

It seemed that there was no fast-talking the Faesolde. She pounded on the door with her fist instead.

"Klaus!" she yelled at the door. "This can't wait!"

The door was opened from the inside, and the guards outside

uncrossed their spears. Striding past the armored elf who'd opened it, she saw Santa standing in the center of the room with four elves. He was wearing his great suit of red steel armor, his right hand holding a long-hafted warhammer that rested on the ground. His helmet was under his left arm.

The elves were all wearing their armor as well. The five of them stood there silently in the center of the room, eyes on the floor as though they were praying.

Fat load of good that'll do, cawed Redcrow, *unless they're praying to the frost giants. Do you think they'd listen?*

Volgha stood quietly for a moment, thinking perhaps they'd finish up and acknowledge her. She looked around the room and saw that all of the armor stands were empty. That made sense. They were preparing for war.

The five of them nodded to each other, then the elves turned and started walking toward the door.

"What is it?" asked Santa, looking at Volgha.

"Odin's staying out of it," she replied.

"Why?"

"Not fair to the Vikings, I guess, if they never get a chance to die in battle."

"That makes sense."

"No, it doesn't!"

"From their point of view."

"It's still stupid."

Santa shrugged. "You won't bring progressive ideas to Viking culture fast enough to make a difference before the frost giants arrive."

"Probably not," said Volgha. "You'd think they'd be less interested in dying, though."

"What was it that couldn't wait?"

"Just that, and King Harald says he already knows where the battle will be fought."

"As do we," said Santa. "He's raising his banners then?"

"Yes," said Volgha. "How is it that everyone knows where this battle is going to happen but me?"

"Probably because you're not a Viking."

"And you are?"

Santa paused. He opened his mouth to speak but shut it before any words made it out. Then he opened his mouth again and gave the words a sporting chance.

"In a manner of speaking," he said. "If we live through this, I'll tell you all about it."

"I look forward to it," said Volgha.

"We're marching for Midgard right after breakfast. Will you join us?"

"Gladly," said Volgha. "I'm starving."

"Oh, you're welcome to that of course," said Santa. "But I meant will you join our war march?"

"Oh." Volgha giggled. It felt good to giggle. It had been a long time. Not very witch-like.

"In a manner of speaking," she said.

"What do you have in mind?"

"I'm going to raid your herbs, then make my way for Howling Hill. I think I'll be a lot more helpful from behind the magical amplifiers."

"Take whatever you need."

Santa had very deep feelings about pre-war breakfast. It could be the last feast for some of his troops, so it should be a good one. His chefs had pulled out all of the stops. Honeyed ham, flap-jacks, sausages, fruit, and more made the tables groan under their weight. Exotic delicacies from foreign lands, which Santa must have been saving for a special occasion, were mixed in with the rest. No anchovies, to Redcrow's chagrin.

Volgha was enchanted by the tingling sensation that this "coffee" gave her. She pocketed a fair quantity of the roasted beans for later, having convinced Santa that they'd surely improve the potency of her magic. Yes, that was why.

Afterward, when they were all milling about the village square in their armor and belching their approval to the chefs, Volgha asked Santa about the stirrup affixed to the butt end of his warhammer. He gave her a big smile and motioned for her to follow him. Several rows of ice blocks stood in front of a barn. The ones that hadn't been broken were about ten feet tall and six feet wide and thick.

"I'm not fond of fighting," said Santa, "but I'm proud of this design."

He put his foot in the stirrup and pulled up on the hammer. There was a series of clicks, and when he was finished, the stirrup was hanging from the butt of the hammer by a two-foot-long steel chain. He swung the hammer at one of the ice blocks, and it practically exploded, sending a hail of ice shards raining down around them. The stirrup was flush with the butt of the hammer again.

"Spring-loaded," explained Santa. "So long as I have time to set it, it will incapacitate a frost giant in a single hit."

"Impressive," said Volgha. "Too bad there's only one of you."

"True," said Santa, "but there are lots of them."

Volgha looked at the armored Faesolde troops. They were carrying long spears, and she noticed that they had stirrups built into the bottoms of them.

"The same idea," said Santa.

"I hope it's enough," said Volgha.

"They've got one apiece," said Santa. "That's all we need."

"I meant … never mind."

"We're off then," said Santa. "Is there anything you need from me before we go?"

"Krespo," Volgha replied. "Leave him with me."

"Krespo? He's no warrior."

"It's not a warrior that I need," said Volgha. "It's quick hands."

Santa nodded, and then strode off. He said something quietly to an elf who was passing by. The elf looked at Volgha, then went running off toward the main workshop.

The Faesolde mounted up in two columns of horses, and Santa mounted one at the front. As the gates opened before them, the wolves ran out howling.

"Ya!" Santa shouted, snapping his reins. The columns followed him into a gallop, and they were off into the night.

A couple of minutes later, Volgha stood in the square. She sighed, her coffee-jittered brain running through the lists of things she'd need to prepare for the trials to come.

"Er, hello, Volgha." Krespo had managed to sneak up on her, whether he'd intended to or not. *That's good*, Volgha thought. Speed and dexterity, that's what she'd need from him.

Volgha smiled at him. "Hello, Krespo."

"Santa said you needed me for something. To tell you the truth, I was hoping to stay out of the fighting."

"You won't need a sword or armor," said Volgha. "But you'll do your part to bring the fight to the giants, that's for sure."

TWENTY-THREE

IT WAS BITTER COLD ATOP HOWLING HILL, WHICH IS WHAT ONE should expect after night has fallen—assuming, of course, that the sun was in its proper position, which it was, once again. The frost had already started to reform on the magical amplifiers, but they still howled with the full force of the winter winds.

It was lucky you found these, said Osgrey. *I didn't know there were any left!*

Of course, you'd know what they are, cawed Redcrow. *I imagine they're nearly as old as you.*

Far older, replied Osgrey, either oblivious to the insult or not caring to fight a bird over it. *A rare find, not many left in the world.*

"Who made them?" asked Volgha.

"Beats me," said Krespo, not taking his eyes off his work.

What Krespo lacked in bravery, upper body strength, self-confidence, conversational skills, lower body strength, martial prowess, jawline, and panache, he made up for in accuracy and attention to detail. The spell that Volgha had pieced together from a few pages of the Grimoire required a lot of things to happen at the same time, and she'd never have been able to do it all on her own. She needed either several weeks to prepare, or a trusty extra pair of hands to work out the herbs for her. She'd seen how deftly Krespo had made his way through her sister's closets when they were searching for the pearls, and she knew that he'd be the man—or rather, elf—for the job.

"How's it coming with the powdered moonstalk?" she asked.

"Nearly there." Krespo was working the pestle with his left hand while he tried to shake the feeling back into the right.

"I need more salt," Volgha told him.

"It's in the other bag," Krespo replied. "No, the other one. No, the *other* one. Oh, just let me."

Volgha said a swear word. They were running out of time.

He thrust a small bag of salt into her hands and got back to work on the moonstalk, hardly breaking his pace. As fast as he was, Volgha was worried that the battle would begin before they were ready.

"Tell me the sequence again," she requested as she made the special squiggly in one quadrant of the circle that would keep her from going mad. She never gave herself time to wonder whether she'd know if she'd ever forgotten to draw that squiggly. Some things are best left unconsidered.

"A pinch of gravelmoss," said Krespo, "a handful of iceroot, two sprigs of rockwort, and five earthbloom petals. Grind them together, sprinkle counter-clockwise into the bowl."

"And whatever you do?"

"Don't let the flame go out."

"You've a real talent for magic, Krespo."

"Thanks." Krespo smiled.

Redcrow was arranging a makeshift nest with a blanket in a wooden crate. He'd been so exhausted after the last time they'd done this, he demanded that Volgha's "elf servant" be made to carry him around in it afterward until he'd regained his strength. Krespo was on board with the idea, in no small part because Volgha had left the "elf servant" bit out when she'd asked him.

"It shouldn't be necessary, though," said Volgha. "Part of the mixture was crafted to give us both extra strength."

Better safe than sorry, cawed Redcrow. *And tell the servant not to jostle the box. I'm a light sleeper.*

Volgha finished triple-checking that she'd drawn all of the necessary squigglies on the salt circle, then looked up to the cloudless sky. The moon was nearly full, the stars were bright, and the Aurora Borealis shimmered green, blue, and gold beyond the mountains. The bitter chill cut through her, but she didn't mind the cold—partially because she'd started going numb in her extremities, but also because this was her element. This was her time. Witches spend years and years growing, drying, and grinding herbs, leafing through old books, talking to rabbits, and evaluating their leavings; not only because that's thrilling stuff, but because it's building toward something. They don't often know what it is, and some unfortunate witches live lives so peaceful that a great purpose simply never comes to them, but if and when it does, they get to see the fruits of all of their labors in one fell swoop.

This was that time for Volgha. The years of seclusion, the endless herb work, the bonfire vigils—that had all been great fun, but now it was all *for* something. It was time to use her magic for the benefit of everyone. Everyone but the frost giants, that is.

Good luck, said Osgrey. *I'm not sure how much help I'll be, but I'll do what I can.*

"Thanks," said Volgha. She hadn't found any sort of empowering-the-retired-druid-who-inexplicably-resides-in-your-mind spells in the Grimoire and just hoped that he'd be all right.

Oh, don't worry about me, he said. *As long as you make it through this, I'll be fine.*

Volgha smiled. Osgrey had always been kind to her. She was glad to have him on her side.

"Are you ready?" she asked, looking at Krespo.

"There's still a lot to do," said Krespo, "but I've got it under control."

"Then let's begin. Remember, no matter what happens, don't break the circle."

Krespo nodded. "Good luck."

She didn't need luck, not really. The last time she'd done astral projection from up here, she'd done the bare minimum and ended up a super hybrid version of herself and Redcrow. This time, she had Krespo to help her, a big pile of herbs, and she'd added a fire spell to her retinue that just might turn the tide in their favor.

She started making the oddly stiff motions that contorted her fingers and whispering the incantations under her breath. She quickly and effortlessly found herself merged with Redcrow again, hovering over Midgard.

It was different this time. She felt more focused, more powerful. If she'd had an ounce of this when she'd gone up against Ghasterly, he'd be a pile of ash now.

She looked out onto the field where the Vikings had erected their defenses. It was hard to miss, what with all of the bonfires.

She saw the twin columns of Santa's troops approaching in the distance, the wolves loping ahead of them. They were being hailed by a group of King Harald's officers when the first blast of the horn sounded.

It was impossibly loud. A thunderclap inside of her own head would have been drowned out by the sound from the Horn of Frost. Vikings and elves alike fell to their knees and threw their hands over their ears.

And just like that, there it was. A hole in the fabric of space with glowing blue edges. It was a hundred feet wide, and snow and ice flew from it on gale force winds.

Another blast issued forth from the horn, still impossibly loud but less so than the first one. The lion's share of the noise had apparently come from the portal ripping open, not from the horn itself.

The note was low and undulating. As its echo rattled her teeth, a great bridge of ice issued forth from the portal. Once the edge of the bridge had touched the ground, frost giants began to pour from the portal. They bore great icicle clubs, enormous boulders, and scowls like Volgha had never seen before.

Volgha recognized the first one through as Gorsulak. He held the horn aloft and greeted the Vikings with a terrible roar as his horde marched forth.

Volgha turned to look at Santa. His columns had turned, and were quickly marching toward the Vikings' bonfires. Santa himself had dismounted his horse and was walking toward the middle of the field. With little more than a thought, Volgha rocketed across the distance between them, stopping scarcely a foot from Santa's side.

Surprised by her sudden appearance, Santa said a swear word.

"Volgha! Are you trying to kill me?"

"Of course not," said Volgha.

"Then don't do that! My heart is still strong, but it needn't be tested so vigorously!"

"Sorry," she said. "Where are you going?"

"To the parlay," said Santa. "It's tradition before a big battle."

"Do the frost giants know about the tradition?"

"We're about to find out."

It was then that Volgha noticed that she was significantly taller than Santa for a change. Even allowing for the fact that she was hovering about a foot above the ground, she was half again his height. She reasoned that was a reflection of her amplified power.

The stopped in the middle of the field, just before King Harald got there.

"Volgha?" he said, obviously surprised to see her. "The last time I saw you, you were just an average-sized woman. My, look how you've grown!"

"Thank you, uncle," Volgha said mockingly.

King Harald laughed. "Your magic is powerful. I'm glad I welcomed you into my hall before."

"I'll need every bit of magic I can muster to see us through this," said Volgha.

King Harald's lips and eyes narrowed as he considered her. "Perhaps. In any case, I'm glad you're on our side."

The ground shook under the weight of Gorsulak's final steps. Even in Volgha's magically enlarged state, the frost giant still towered over her.

"Hello, little bird," said Gorsulak. "I didn't expect to see you here."

"Gorsulak," said Volgha. "You should have stayed in Niflheim. Bad move coming here."

"Well that's rude. I came over here for a friendly chat before we commence with the war-waging. Aren't we all friends here?"

"Hardly," said Santa. "You cannot win this. Why not save the lives of your kinsmen, and give up now?"

"That's more like it," said Gorsulak. "If it's terms of surrender, we'll hear yours anytime!"

"Your pride will be your downfall!" King Harald drew his sword and waved it menacingly at Gorsulak. "Better you should tuck tail and run, and nurse your wounded pride until the sun rises again, than be crushed into dust against our shields!"

"These fields will run red with Viking blood before we start to feel weary," said Gorsulak.

"Your kind don't belong here!" said Volgha. "Go back to where you came from, and leave these decent people in peace!"

Gorsulak and King Harald both took a step backward from Volgha and stared at her.

"Really now," said Gorsulak, "that's just an ugly and hateful thing to say!"

"Volgha, please," said King Harald. "I expect better than that from the people I count as my friends!"

"What?" Volgha was perplexed. "How is what I'm saying any different from what you're saying?"

Santa seemed as confused as she was.

"Trash talk before a fight is one thing," began Gorsulak, "but you sound a lot like Odin right now."

She looked at King Harald. He had an eyebrow raised, and seemed to be nodding in agreement with Gorsulak.

"Odin," Volgha repeated. She pointed at King Harald. "Your Allfather. The chieftain of your gods, who drove these evil monsters from—"

"Oh, will you *please stop*?" King Harald's voice had risen a full octave. "Yes, he's right! You sound like Odin! Gods, you seemed so normal, I thought you were better than this!"

"I'm missing something," said Santa. "Harald, aren't you here to drive the frost giants back into Niflheim, whence Odin banished them?"

"Of course not," replied King Harald. "I'm here to have a war with them!"

Gorsulak nodded.

Santa's brow furrowed in confusion. "I'm still missing something."

"What's the matter?" said Gorsulak. "You don't want to have a war with us just because we're frost giants?"

"I don't want to have a war with anybody! I want to go home and invent things!"

"Could have fooled us," said King Harald, "what with the whole marching-your-troops-to-battle thing that just happened, and the pre-war trash talking."

"So you just ... want to fight each other?" Volgha's stare moved back and forth between Gorsulak and King Harald. "You're not trying to wipe each other out?"

"We're playing to win," answered Gorsulak, "but we're not bringing old bigotry into it."

"Well said." King Harald nodded in agreement. "I didn't think anyone had the nerve to talk like that anymore, even if they believed it."

"Believed what?"

"That frost giants are just unintelligent monsters," said Gorsulak. "We have feelings, you know."

"But Odin banished them from here," said Volgha. "A long time ago! Your Allfather!"

King Harald sighed. "That's true, but we don't go around celebrating it. Odin is ..." Harald looked around, then lowered his voice to a whisper. "He's old. He's set in his ways. He belongs to a generation that lived with those segregationist ideas for their entire lives."

"That's right," agreed Gorsulak. "If the likes of you and Odin had your way, we'd be shipped back to Niflheim without a second thought."

Volgha held up her hands. "I'm not saying—"

"They're no different from us!" said King Harald.

"They're made of solid ice!" said Santa.

"It's not what's inside that counts," said Gorsulak. "Literally, I mean. Figuratively, it's what's inside that counts."

"Fine," said Volgha, "you are people! But you're different. You people—"

"Oh, come on!" Gorsulak tossed his hands up in the air. "What do you mean, *you people*?"

There was a long, awkward silence. Gorsulak and King Harald

stood there with their hands on their hips, staring at Volgha. Santa looked confused and uncomfortable. Volgha was at a loss for words.

"I'm sorry," she said, eventually. "I guess I really had the wrong impression of what was going on here."

"It appears that way," said King Harald.

"As did I," said Santa. "I was brought up to believe that the frost giants were savage beasts who threatened our very way of life until Odin came along and banished them to Niflheim."

"We were all taught that," replied King Harald. "Luckily, most of us were able to see the truth and break away from the old, ignorant ways of thinking." He looked at Volgha. "*Most* of us."

"I really am sorry." Volgha looked up at Gorsulak. "You're the first frost giant I've ever met, and I've only been told that you were monsters."

"Well, now you know different," said Gorsulak.

"Yes, I suppose I do," said Volgha.

"Me too," said Santa. "Thanks for setting me straight."

"Don't mention it," said King Harald. "Now, how about that war?"

"Hang on," said Volgha. "If you've got your heart set on war, I've got a proposition for you."

TWENTY–FOUR

VOLGHA HAD GIVEN UP ON TRYING TO STOP KRESPO'S SCREAMing. It wasn't much farther to the castle now, and it was probably helping him keep warm. The fear was encouraging his white-knuckled grip on the broom as well, and that was as good for his safety as anything else she had at her disposal.

The clouds had moved in, blocking the light of the moon and providing some very fortunate cover for their approach. If the sky had been clear, she'd have cast a spell to call the clouds for just such a purpose; and had anyone asked her if she'd had anything to do with the all-too-convenient cloud cover, the Witching Way would have insisted she take credit.

Claiming credit for naturally-occurring phenomena was a cornerstone of Perceptive Witchery: an art that was more marketing than magic, but all witches needed to know a bit of marketing.

"Seriously, you need to stop now." The silhouette of the castle crept darkly onto the horizon ahead.

"Aaaaaaagh!" said Krespo, or rather he ceased to stop saying so.

"You'll get us caught. Please don't make me drop you."

"Aaaaaaagh!"

"We've been up here for hours now, how are you still this afraid?"

"Aaaaaaagh!"

"I thought you'd have acquired some courage by accident, given all you've been through since this started."

"Aaaaaaagh!"

He was a cowardly little screaming machine whose switch had

gotten stuck in the "on" position. Unfortunately for Krespo, Volgha was more curious than vexed at this point and had resolved to take him for another ride when all of this was over. She wasn't sure what practical application she could find for Krespo's indomitable cowardly fury, but the mystical realms beyond the veil often demanded some eccentric tools. It was as likely as not to come in handy someday.

"Aaaaaaagh!"

Unfortunately for Volgha, they were rapidly approaching the castle, and she had to figure out a way to get them in quietly. The belfry was her preferred entrance, but even with the cloud cover, a screaming missile would have attracted unwanted attention.

"Ugh, fine," she said, and started taking the broom down toward a little copse of trees. It was nearly a mile from the castle, and she could see that there were patrols milling about in between. Chamberlain was less trusting than Alexia, which Volgha found offensive. Just one more reason to overthrow him.

Once they were on the ground, she took a minute to assess the contents of her basket while Krespo gathered what few wits he still possessed. He stared wide-eyed and unblinking at nothing, twitching occasionally.

"This is terribly inconvenient," she said to him.

Krespo nodded. "S-s-sorry." He was wrapped up in Volgha's shawl, trying to stop shivering.

That's top notch cowardice, cawed Redcrow. He chuckled. *It takes a brave person to be seen shrieking like that. A real devotion to the cause of milquetoasts the world over!*

"I honestly don't get it," said Volgha. "At no point in the last several hours did you think 'oh, well, I haven't died of this yet, so maybe I'll just knock off the screaming for a while.' It must have occurred to you that I do this all the time."

"F-f-fear," said Krespo, "isn't r-r-rational."

"You've got a point there. Listen, I am sorry for that, but we had to get here quickly."

Krespo nodded.

I can't wait for the trip back!

"Oh knock it off, Redcrow." Volgha turned back to Krespo. "The Vikings, the frost giants, Santa, the Faesolde, even the wolves—they're all on the march, and if we're not ready in time, this could be a very costly battle."

Krespo nodded again.

Following a swear word, Volgha said, "Krespo, snap out of it! I know the flying was scary, but I need you with me on this!"

Krespo nodded. "A-all r-right."

There's a brave little kitten.

"We'll go in through the secret passage near the old Tickler's grave, but we need to move quickly. Can you walk?"

Shutting his eyes tight, Krespo took a deep breath. He held it, let it out slowly, and opened his eyes again. He looked up at Volgha, his brow wrinkled and his eyes watery, a pleading look that plainly stated that every fiber of his being wanted very much to sit there and do nothing of the sort. But then he stood up anyway.

"I'm w-w-with you."

In that fleeting moment, Volgha admired Krespo's courage. He was a coward through and through, there was no doubt about that, but courage came easily to the brave. Cowards like Krespo fought for every ounce. He was the best sort of coward one could hope to know.

Redcrow hopped around in the snow and cawed in a staccato sort of way, laughing at Krespo.

"That's the spirit, Krespo," said Volgha. "Shut it, Redcrow."

You're no fun.

Reaching into her basket, Volgha found a little strip of dried venison. She held her other arm out and made a clicking sound with her tongue. Redcrow perched on her outstretched arm, and she fed it to him. *Delicious,* he cawed, *and only slightly demeaning.*

She shut her eyes, trying to reach out to Osgrey again. She hadn't heard from him since she and Redcrow had merged on Howling Hill. He was still with her, no doubt about it, but he was sleeping, or something very near it. She hoped he'd wake up soon.

"Through the belfry," she said to Redcrow. "You remember it?"

We had our first date there, how could I forget?

"You're hilarious," said Volgha, and gave him another bit of venison. "Through the belfry, find Matilda. Meet us in the pantry. Understand?"

I'm sure I can manage. Redcrow cawed loudly and flapped his way up into the sky.

"We'll need to go Dim," said Volgha. "Are you listening?"

Krespo nodded. She dug a little pouch out of her basket and tugged at the drawstring to open it.

"This won't make you invisible, but as long as you don't make any sudden moves, people will tend not to notice you. Talking to someone or making direct eye contact will break the spell, so just keep your head down and move as quietly as you can, got it?"

Krespo nodded.

"That's the idea," said Volgha. "I'll be Dim as well, so we won't be able to see each other. Don't *look* for me, understand? Just trust that I'm there."

Krespo nodded. Volgha crouched down, put a hand on his chin, and turned his gaze up to meet hers.

"I didn't let you fall off the broom," said Volgha, "and I won't leave you alone, I swear it."

Krespo flashed just a hint of a smile. "Off we g-g-go, then."

"I'll see you once we're in the secret passages."

A sprinkle of powder, a quick gesture, and a bit of mumbling, and they were both alone on the great frozen plain. Volgha set her eyes on the castle and started walking.

"I KNEW YOU'D COME BACK!" MATILDA THREW HER ARMS AROUND Volgha. Volgha tried very hard not to recoil in discomfort. She liked Matilda, but *boundaries*.

They were standing in the pantry, against the back wall between two stacks of barrels. Krespo sat against a wall, still working very hard at regaining his wits.

Ask her if there are any anchovies in here! cawed Redcrow.

"Later," said Volgha.

"Is he all right?" asked Matilda, looking at Krespo with a mixture of concern and confusion.

"He'll be fine," Volgha replied. "He's just afraid of flying. What's happened here, is my sister still alive?"

"She's fine," answered Matilda. "The tower has a passage running behind one of the walls, and I've found a peephole behind a sconce. I've checked on her every evening. She just looks drunk most of the time."

"That's good," Volgha remarked. "Not about the drinking, but Chamberlain's not killed her. That's something."

"He hasn't killed anybody, but he's filled the dungeons to overflowing. He's gotten paranoid since Ghasterly's disappearance. He thinks everyone is a loyalist sympathizer!"

"That's good," said Volgha, then upon seeing Matilda's incredulous look, hastened to add, "because paranoia will unbalance him. Don't worry, we'll get everyone out soon."

"Good," said Matilda. "I promised them you would."

"Promised?"

"I've been down to visit," she said. "The guards don't pay me any mind because I'm not an adult. Anyway, the head butler is down there—his name is Eustace—and he says he's got everybody down there *onionized*."

"Onionized?"

"It's like a special club for people with jobs. He says everyone who works in the castle should join up."

Volgha shrugged. "That's nice, I suppose."

"He says the crown needs the workers to back it, or else the whole enterprise just sort of falls apart."

"It does?"

"That's what Eustace says," said Matilda.

Volgha had never heard that. If her late parents and her deposed sister were to be believed, the royal family was in charge because ... well, *because*. It was the natural order of things, like the sun rising once a year. Servants had always served. It was the root of the word! It had never occurred to her that they'd think to do otherwise, but now that Eustace had given voice to the idea, it made perfect sense to Volgha. If the servants simply stopped serving, running a castle would be more or less impossible.

"Interesting," said Volgha.

"Yeah," said Matilda, "but what do we do now?"

"I've got an army on the way."

"The Vikings?"

Volgha nodded. "And Santa and his elves, and the frost giants. The wolves, too."

"The frost giants?" Matilda's eyes went wide. "I thought they were the enemy!"

"Things are changing," said Volgha. "We'll talk about it later. Where is Chamberlain now?"

TWENTY-FIVE

VOLGHA WAS FAMILIAR WITH HYPERBOLE, EVEN IF SHE DIDN'T approve of it. When Matilda said that the dungeons were full to overflowing, Volgha suspected hyperbole. However, she hadn't exaggerated a bit. The cells were standing room only, and new stakes had been driven into the walls so that people could be shackled in the hallways.

She and Matilda were slowly working their way to the cell where Eustace was being held. Volgha was Dim, but Matilda was able to wander freely about. They'd left Krespo in a secret passage with a peephole into the throne room so he could keep an eye on Chamberlain. Redcrow was perched atop the belfry, watching for the motley horde of invaders to arrive. Osgrey was still asleep.

The lower dungeons smelled awful. Not even Volgha's brief stay in the upper dungeons could have prepared her for the squalor that they found here. Before they went, Matilda had warned her to wear well-stitched boots, hike up her skirts a bit, and avoid looking down. It had all been good advice.

Eventually, they found the right cell. Matilda tugged on a man's shirt and asked for Eustace. After several minutes of grunting and shuffling, everyone in the cell managed to shift themselves around so that Eustace could come close.

"Hello, Matilda," he said with as much diction and grace as he would use to greet a foreign dignitary. "I hope you're not putting yourself in danger by coming down here, I'd hate to see you arrested."

"Thank you, sir. I promise I'm being careful. I have a favor to ask of you."

"Happy to oblige, though I'm not really in a position to be very helpful at the moment."

"It's very important that you keep your eyes on me," she said. "Don't look around, all right? It's very important."

"Okay ..." Eustace locked eyes with her, providing his full attention.

"I need you to tell me about the onion," said Matilda.

"You mean the union?"

"If you say so," said Matilda. "Anyway, tell me all about it, only pretend you've never told me anything before. And tell me what we'd be capable of doing if everyone joined up."

Eustace narrowed his eyes, then shifted them to his right.

"Look at me!" blurted Matilda. "It's really, really important."

"This sounds fishy," said Eustace.

"I know," Matilda replied, "and I'm sorry I can't tell you why, but I'm asking you to trust me."

"Can you tell me why you can't tell me why?"

"Probably not. But I promise it's not a trick or anything! I'm trying to get everyone out, and this is part of it."

Eustace shrugged—as well as he could at least. "All right," said Eustace. "It's not like they can make prison more *prisony* for me."

Without breaking eye contact, Eustace told Matilda (and Volgha) all about the benefits of unionizing the servants. Better wages, more reasonable hours, the occasional holiday—it all sounded very reasonable to Volgha, who suddenly felt rather sheepish for never having noticed that the servants just always seemed to be there. Yuletide, Saturnalia, the Feast of Saint Baffling, even the first evening of Snugglewatch—they were always there, up with the first bell and working until the last. They probably only ever saw their families if they worked together.

"That's amazing," remarked Matilda. "And how many people have signed up already?"

"Are you sure you're not spying for Chamberlain?"

"On my honor." Matilda held up her hand as a sign of honor. "I've joined the onion myself, haven't I?"

"Union," he corrected. "And yes, that's true. Okay, it's just about everybody down here, so ... around eight hundred people?"

"That's a lot," said Matilda. "And what happens in the case of a dispute between the union and the crown?"

"Oh, that's when the striking begins."

"And what's that?"

"Well, we pick up our union clubs, and start striking anything or anyone within reach until the crown says, 'All right, you've made your point, let's discuss some terms, please.'"

"That sounds great," said Matilda. "If I could get everyone out of here, how quickly do you think you could organize the strike?"

"Well we wouldn't have official union clubs straight away," said Eustace. "They'd have to be ordered, produced, and transported. That would probably take until sun-up. We'd have to use a union supplier, you see."

"That's too long," said Matilda. "How fast could we go without the clubs?"

"Well," Eustace was clearly taken aback by the question, "I suppose we could suspend article 4, section 6 of the union bylaws with a simple majority vote. We definitely have a quorum today, so it's a simple matter of four officers agreeing to call an emergency meeting—"

"Assuming all of that goes without a hitch," said Matilda, "how fast?"

"Well, straight away, I'd imagine."

"Good," said Matilda. "Can you call a meeting right now? There's a plan underway, and we don't have a lot of time."

"I can," said Eustace, "but you owe me an explanation as soon as all of this is over and done."

"I promise," said Matilda. Volgha followed as she started to make her way out, and roll call began behind them.

Our friends are on the way, cawed Redcrow. *Are you sure that this is a good idea?*

"This is so exciting!" exclaimed Matilda, once they'd fetched Krespo and returned to the pantry. "Everything is falling into place. This horrible coup will be over and done before you know it!"

"It's not in the bag yet," said Volgha. "As long as Chamberlain holds the throne room, he's still in charge."

"And it's full of guards," said Krespo. "At least two hundred of them! Even if the servants had their clubs, the guards have swords. A lot of good people are going to die!"

"Not if I can help it," said Volgha. "Redcrow's spotted The Really, Really Big Army headed this way. It's only a matter of time before the war is underway."

I still can't believe that's the official name, cawed Redcrow. *Really, that's the best they could do?*

"It was short notice," said Volgha.

"They'll never make it inside the castle," said Krespo. "Santa said that himself, it's too well-defended!"

"They don't have to. We just have to be patient, and strike when the time is right."

"And then what?" asked Matilda.

"What do you mean?"

"Once it's over, assuming we win, what happens then?"

Volgha sighed. "I don't know. We'll have to figure it out then."

She wants you to take the throne, cawed Redcrow.

"I know," snapped Volgha, "but I don't want it!" She looked up at Redcrow and pointed a finger at him very menacingly. "I'll figure it out, all right? But I've got a lot on my mind right now, and this is just going to have to wait!"

Just think about it, cawed Redcrow. *Being the Warden and the White Queen at the same time? Honestly, I don't know which I'm more excited about!*

"Calm yourself," said Volgha. "I'm not keen on either of those, so don't get any ideas!"

You have to take at least one. It's not fair to me otherwise!

"Fair to you? If you think for one second—"

"All right," interrupted Matilda, "we can figure it out later! But it's going to be soon."

"I know, you're right," said Volgha. "We have to find someone who'd be willing take the throne."

That narrows it down to everyone but you, apparently.

"Then it shouldn't be very difficult!"

"This is why you're perfect for it," said Matilda. "You're already a royal, and you don't want the throne for your own glory."

"I'm not perfect for it," said Volgha. "Wouldn't the perfect person *want* the throne?"

Give it to me then, cawed Redcrow. *I want it.*

"That's not the only qualification." Volgha pinched the bridge of her nose in the vain hope it would quell her frustration.

Well, you've got the rest of them, and we're bonded for life!

"Maybe we can choose another person after a while," suggested Matilda, "but we can't change too much too fast. People don't like it. We need to restore order as soon as the war is over, and a real royal person is the best way."

"What about King Harald?" asked Krespo. "He's leading the Vikings here right now, maybe he could do it?"

Matilda shook her head. "That's just being conquered. They'll hate that, too."

They grew silent again. Volgha didn't have any other ideas, and she really didn't want to have to be queen. She'd renounced her claim willingly because all that she wanted to do was live in the forest and meddle with forces beyond mortal comprehension. Was that really too much to ask?

But Matilda might be right. Who else was there? Her sister was a horrible queen. Chamberlain might have done a good job, but between the treachery and the paranoia, he couldn't be trusted. The people deserved a ruler who would serve something other than her or his own vanity. Who better to wear the crown than someone who wanted nothing to do with it?

A faint *thud* broke the silence. Horns sounded in the distance. The Really, Really Big Army had arrived.

TWENTY-SIX

THE WAITING WAS THE HARDEST PART.
There were still hundreds of people languishing in the dungeons.
Redcrow showed Volgha visions of people dying on the battlefield,
huge boulders being lobbed against the mighty walls of the castle,
and smoke. So much smoke. The fires illuminated the atrocities of
war as the fighting raged on.

Little by little, the guards filtered out of the halls, the dungeons,
and even the throne room as reinforcements were required at the
front. Eventually, the dungeons held nothing but prisoners. The iron
doors were barred from the outside, and they were left to their fates
by the guards who'd been promoted to soldiers.

So it was that the emaciated prisoners cheered, weakly, when the
doors flung open and Volgha walked into view. She took keys from
the hook by the door and handed them to Matilda and Krespo.

"Liberation!" shouted Eustace, as shackles and gates were un-
locked. "Now is the time for action, brothers and sisters. The time
has come, for us—to strike!"

A cheer went up with the level of enthusiasm one would expect
from a child receiving socks as a gift.

"Almost," said Volgha. "The halls of the castle are mostly abandoned, it's just us and the guards in the throne room with Chamberlain. Their strength has nearly dwindled enough for us to overpower
them!"

"And you all look like you're starving," remarked Matilda.

"To the dining hall!" shouted Eustace. The suggestion was met with the enthusiasm he'd like to have gotten when he shouted for a strike. Stinking, disheveled, and delirious with hunger, the union shambled up from the dungeons. They left a filthy brown swath in their wake, with no regard given to who'd have to clean it up. That would be a decision for a new order to make, preferably after a committee of union delegates had thoroughly investigated the matter.

Unsurprisingly, nearly all of the servants who had escaped imprisonment had been the kitchen staff. King Chamberlain's paranoia had very sensibly acquiesced to his stomach, and those of his guards. Luckily for Matilda, she was one of said kitchen staff, and had convinced the rest of them that signing up with the union was in their best interest.

As a result, a bounty had been laid out on the tables to greet them. The cooks had spared no extravagance, laying out the best cuts and all the trimmings.

"Stop!" said Mrs. Stodge, the head cook. She held up her hand and said it with such authority that the shambling horde of starving, liberated prisoners froze like school children whose teacher had started counting to three. She pointed to several wash barrels just inside the doors.

"Hands and faces," she said. "Form a line, the sooner you wash, the sooner you eat!"

As if to punctuate her demand, a *boom* echoed through the hall from the bombardment outside. Mrs. Stodge didn't need the help, though. She had the square jaw and fists-on-hips stance of a woman who'd never been disobeyed in her life. The horde became a queue, and within minutes they were all seated and tucking in. The kitchen staff, Matilda, Volgha, and Krespo were all seated among them, eating their fill of the feast. Matilda had even found some anchovies in the extra-fancy-events pantry, and put them on a little plate next to

Volgha's. Redcrow spread his wings to cover the plate, and he cackled as he ate his fill.

"Eat well, brothers and sisters!" Eustace was standing on a table and shouting above the din. "The time is drawing near! One hour from now, we take the throne room!"

"Point of order," shouted someone from within the partially washed masses, "but union rules clearly state that we're allotted fifteen minutes to digest!"

"Yeah," said another, "we'll have cramps otherwise!"

"Duly noted," shouted Eustace. "That being the case, in an hour and fifteen minutes, we take the throne room!"

A cheer went up, only slightly muffled by hundreds of mouthfuls of food.

There was a wood pile just outside of the kitchens, which served as the fuel source for the ovens. Following supper and the fifteen minutes of union-mandated digestion time, all of the members of the servants' union lined up at the wood pile and grabbed a fire log apiece. They were a far cry from official union cudgels, but they'd serve. Minutes later, they'd amassed in front of the throne room doors, and it was time to get on with the striking.

The occasional *boom* sounded through the hall, reminding them all that they were at war.

"Right," said Eustace, whose constant hand-wringing was doing little to inspire confidence. "Things have gotten out of hand, and it's up to us to put them right again. We're kitchen workers, gardeners, butlers, and laundry maids, not soldiers! But it's our own lives that we're fighting for, and that makes each of us worth ten big brutes in metal armor, who are only fighting for a paycheck. It's going to be ugly in there, but once the striking starts, no one quits until we've won!"

Cries went up, saying, "Yeah!" and, "Let's show 'em!" and, "Who has to go in first?"

Eustace pushed against the door. It didn't budge. He gave Volgha a puzzled look.

"Move aside." Volgha held her breath as she moved between the unwashed-except-their-hands-and-faces union members until she reached the door. She knocked on it three times.

"Who is it?" came a voice from the other side.

"It's Volgha, the Winter Witch. Open this door at once!"

There was a pause and some unintelligible muttering from the other side of the door.

"Sorry," said the voice from the other side. "I'm told that the door must remain closed."

"By order of the royal family, I insist that you open this door!"

There was another pause and some more muttering.

"King Chamberlain says he's the only royal family now, and that you should go away, please. What? Oh, sorry. I'm being told to retract the 'please,' so … retracted."

"Is that Reginald?" shouted Eustace.

Another pause.

"Yeah," replied the voice. "It's me. Is that Eustace?"

"None other!"

"How's it going? Haven't seen you in a while."

"I've been in the dungeons," said Eustace.

"What for?"

"Your King Chamberlain seemed to think that I was a loyalist, and had me locked up!"

"You? Come on," said Reg. "I heard a few people got caught up in that, but you? You didn't even like the queen, always said she was a ridiculous drunk!"

Eustace gave Volgha a sheepish grin. Volgha shrugged and nodded.

"More than a few of us," said Eustace. "Chamberlain locked up almost all of the servants!"

"Is that why we've had to do our own laundry?"

"Probably."

"We're terrible at it."

Volgha gave Eustace a pointed look and waved her hand in a "get on with it" circle.

"Listen, Reg," said Eustace, "the servants are all out here. We've unionized, and we want to air our grievances."

"What's 'oniunized' mean?"

"We've formed a club," said Eustace. "All of the servants are throwing in together to demand better working conditions!"

"Well that sounds like a good idea," said Reg. "Are guards allowed in the onion?"

"We could do it that way," Eustace answered, "though it might make sense for you to have your own union. It's mostly a question of the charter paperwork—"

"Could you please just open the door?" asked Volgha. It was good that they were talking, but it was a pungent conversation from her side of the barrier.

"Hello, Volgha! It's me, Reg!"

"Yes," said Volgha, "hello, Reginald. Could you open the door, please?"

Another silence. This one was longer, then more muttering. Angry muttering. Hard to make out, especially over the booming sounds of the bombardment.

"Are you still there, Reginald?"

"Enough talk!" said the unmistakable voice of King Chamberlain from the other side of the door. "You are in defiance of the crown! I will spare your lives, but only if you go back to the dungeons this instant, and wait there until you can stand trial for your crimes!"

"What crimes?" shouted Eustace.

"Treason! Malfeasance! Conspiracy to form a union, forming a union, and jailbreak!"

Someone else was speaking inside the room, but it was too faint to hear.

"No, *union*, not onion," said Chamberlain. "It's like a committee that gets to negotiate with the crown, only the crown does not negotiate! It tells its subjects what it expects, and it expects those wishes to be obeyed!"

"Just like you obeyed Her Majesty?" shouted Eustace.

"That's different!" countered King Chamberlain. "Look, the door stays shut, there shall be no unions, and you lot should head back to the dungeons if you don't want my elite guard to put you down with swords and crossbows! What? I don't care if they're your friends, they're committing treason!"

A silence erupted violently from the other side of the door. It was the sort of silence that was constantly interrupted by swear words and the sounds of a struggle that involved several people, and *that* was constantly interrupted by the sounds of boulders striking the castle walls.

As silences go, it was not a very respectable one, at least until the sounds of the struggle stopped, and then it was (aside from the bombardment, but one can't have everything).

"Er, Reg?" Eustace knocked lightly on the door.

"Just a minute," said a voice on the other side of the door, which belonged neither to Reg nor to Chamberlain. Volgha looked around at everyone on her side of the door. Everyone shifted nervously.

Volgha decided to concentrate on feeling impatient, as that was less nerve-wracking than whatever feeling everyone else was having at the moment.

You should go in without me, cawed Redcrow. *I can't hold a club.*

Eventually, there was a sound from the other side of the door not unlike that of a heavy bar being lifted. Then there was the sound of a knob turning, followed by the opening of the great wooden doors. Everyone in the servants' union reflexively cringed, and subsequently found their spirits running the gamut from mildly relieved to overjoyed at not being mowed down by crossbows.

Slowly, and with no small amount of trepidation, Volgha led the filthy lot of them into the throne room. The guards were all standing with swords sheathed and crossbows slung, smiling. They parted as Volgha made her way up to the dais. There she finally saw Chamberlain, sitting on the throne, bound and gagged, with Reg holding onto his shoulder. Chamberlain was wearing a sneer and a crooked crown. Reg was wearing a big, goofy smile.

"Hello, Volgha," said Reg. "Are you going to be the queen now?"

"Yes she is," said Matilda.

"No I'm not," said Volgha.

"Yes you *are*," Matilda demanded, hands on her hips. "I'm calling in my favor."

"What? What favor?"

"In the dungeons. I agreed to help you fix the whole Loki thing, but I said you'd owe me a favor, and you agreed."

Volgha remembered. How could she have forgotten about the favor?

Oh, she's good, cawed Redcrow.

"She's got you there," said Krespo.

"No, she hasn't! That's not the sort of thing you collect favors for. It's too big!"

"Says who?" asked Matilda. "We didn't agree to limitations on terms."

A pair of booms rocked the throne room. They must have been getting very close.

"If that's true then she's right," said Eustace. "Contracts with union labor must have limitations placed at signing."

"You stay out of this," said Volgha.

"I'm afraid I can't," said Eustace. "She's a union member, and I'm compelled to advocate for her rights."

"I didn't even know about the union at the time!"

"All the same. I thought witches knew that favors are binding contracts?"

And there it was. The logic was indisputable. If Volgha refused to make good on the request, the entire economy of favors could be ruined for all witches everywhere.

Her hands balled into fists, and she shook with rage. The Witching Way frowned upon being too greedy when collecting favors, but then again, Matilda wasn't a witch. It wasn't fair!

Ooh, cawed Redcrow, in a very gloating way. *Who's concerned about what's fair now?*

"Quiet, you," Volgha snapped. "Look, it was a favor, not indentured servitude. Doesn't it matter that I don't want to be in charge of everything?"

I'm afraid it's your destiny, said Osgrey.

"Oh good," shouted Volgha. "Look who's awake!"

"Who?" asked Krespo.

"Osgrey," replied Volgha. "You don't know him."

Confused glances circulated among all in attendance.

You've done during the course of the sunset what no one in your family has done for hundreds of years, said Osgrey. *You've cared. You're on the cusp of restoring balance to the land! You've proven that you're fit to rule.*

"I was just trying to get everyone to leave me alone," said Volgha. "I don't want to be Queen Volgha, or Warden Volgha, or anything else but the Winter Witch! You can even have *that* title back, I don't need it! I just want to go home!"

That's why it must be you, said Osgrey. *You have the ability to rule and the humility to do what's best for the kingdom, not for yourself.*

"But what about the Witching Way?"

Oh, you'll have plenty of time for that, said Osgrey.

"How? I have a kingdom to rule and a land to quell!"

"You'll have help," said Krespo.

"That's right," said Eustace. "Your popularity with the servants' union is very high right now."

I'll handle all of the high-profile adoration, cawed Redcrow. *For the greater good, so you can keep up the humility.*

"You're a prince," muttered Volgha.

Really?

"No."

Tease.

Everyone was quiet for a moment. Volgha's apparent argument with herself had abated, and the silence was only occasionally broken by the sounds of the bombardment.

A sinking feeling was coming over Volgha. She had to honor the favor, and it didn't seem that anyone else was able to fill the roles. She'd have to take on faith that she'd have help.

Wait. No, she didn't! She'd be the queen, wouldn't she? Her sister hadn't done anything useful in her entire life, which meant that the kingdom must have largely been ruling itself for years.

It seems like you're out of objections, cawed Redcrow.

Volgha sighed.

"All right," she muttered, frowning.

"Really?" said Matilda, smiling brightly.

Volgha shook her head. "It seems I have no choice."

"Well in that case ..." Reg plucked the crown from Chamberlain's head in lieu of finishing his sentence. He held it as Volgha walked up the steps to the dais, pausing with a puzzled expression.

"Do I put it in your head?" Reg asked.

"You can just hand it to me," said Volgha, who was herself unsure of the protocol in this situation. He did so and then lifted Chamberlain out of the throne by his shirt.

Volgha could feel the eyes of the guards and servants alike as she looked at the throne. She hadn't thought that this moment would be so overwhelming, but then, she never thought she'd have to be a queen either. She set the crown on the throne's velvet cushion and turned around, just as the bombardment shook the throne room with another solid hit.

"First things first," she said. "Reg, send a couple of your men to run a white flag up to the battlements."

"You're surrendering?" Reg's triumphant smile turned quickly downward. He appeared to be very hurt.

"No," said Volgha. "The invaders are on our side. I just don't want them to damage the castle any more than they have to."

"Oh." Reg now looked only mildly confused. He pointed to a couple of guards, then jerked his thumb toward the door.

"Now what about him?" asked Reg, giving Chamberlain a good shake.

"Put him in the upper dungeon for now," commanded Volgha.

"The *upper* dungeon?" Eustace seemed unhappy with the decision.

"No one should have to go into the lower dungeons," said Volgha. "You know that better than anybody. Besides, I'll have a use for him shortly."

TWENTY–SEVEN

ALEXIA HAD BEEN BLISSFULLY UNAWARE THAT SHE'D BEEN DEPOSED at all until she was asked to come down from the tower. Then she was furious, especially at learning that Volgha would be the queen in her stead. The sheer petulance of the fit thrown by the ousted lunatic was the stuff of legend, leaving not a single unshattered bit of glass in the throne room. Volgha would have been upset about it, but she knew from her time in Midgard that this sort of thing could be good for the economy.

The former White Queen was entitled Princess Alexia, given an impressive collection of tiaras, and retired to her family's summer villa with a small retinue of union servants and guards. Chamberlain was sent along with her and tasked with reminding Her Highness that she could neither demand anything of her servants that would violate union rules, nor could she execute or imprison them because, among other reasons, the villa had no dungeon.

It's quite possible that the only thing Volgha liked about being a queen was the relative dearth of requirements. If her forebears had done one thing right, it was to ensure that Aurorian monarchs would be free to go as mad as they liked.

I just think you're passing up an opportunity, cawed Redcrow. *Wouldn't you like to wait a few evenings? The courtiers must be foaming at the mouth to lavish affection on their new queen.*

"Absolutely not." Volgha shivered a bit at the thought. She imagined that sort of lavishing would have a very greasy texture. She wanted no part of it.

But think of the economy!

"The economy?"

Yes! All of the investments that they've made in licking your sister's boots have been completely wiped out. The kingdom is in turmoil! Chaos! You have to allow the rebuilding to start, or who knows how long the recession might last?

"An interesting theory," said Volgha, "but my boots won't be the ones worth licking."

She was glad to have found a way around the whole monarchy issue. She was standing in the throne room with Eustace and Reg, awaiting the arrival of Matilda. She'd been summoned from the kitchens and, unsurprisingly, arrived promptly. She shuffled in quickly, her eyes darting warily about the room.

"Yes, Vol—er, Your Majesty?" she said.

"Don't you start," said Volgha.

"Oh," said Matilda, her shoulders relaxing. "I just didn't know, now that you're the queen and all."

"About that," said Volgha. "I'm not sure I appreciate your compelling me onto the throne."

"Beggin' your pardon, Majesty, but you're not sitting on the throne, strictly speaking."

"Nor do I intend to, literally speaking."

Clever girl, that one, said Osgrey. *Cleverness in girls wasn't permitted when I was a boy.*

"Favors are powerful things," said Volgha, "but I'm afraid you've outstretched this one."

"Have I?" Matilda cringed.

"You have. So I've decided to alter our arrangement a bit."

"Have you?" Matilda hunched a bit farther.

You're enjoying this, cawed Redcrow. *You'd be really good at wearing the crown, you know.*

"Wearing a crown is easy," Volgha said to Redcrow, then turned back to Matilda. "Ruling a kingdom is not. You've put me in a difficult situation, so you're going to help me out of it."

"Yes, ma'am," replied Matilda.

"Eustace?"

Eustace cleared his throat and unrolled a scroll. "By order of Her Majesty, Volgha the Witch Queen of Aurora, you are hereby immediately elevated to the rank of duchess, and sworn to the post of Royal Steward. Rise, Duch— Oh bother, you were supposed to be kneeling for that. Oh, well. Duchess Matilda ..."

"Bubble-Spigot."

"Really?" Eustace raised an eyebrow.

"Does 'duchess' outrank 'butler'?"

"Right, sorry. Oh, you may as well kneel and do it properly now. That's it, thank you. Now rise, Duchess Matilda Bubble-Spigot, Royal Steward of Aurora!"

She was officially the filthiest duchess ever to have set foot in the throne room of Castle Borealis, owing to the fact that it was poultry-rending time in the kitchens. She was grinning from ear to gizzard-flecked ear.

"What does this mean exactly?"

"The first step will be ending your membership in the union, I'm afraid." Eustace frowned. "It would be a conflict of interest for you to remain a member."

"Oh," said Matilda, "because I'm a duchess?"

"No," said Volgha, "because you're in charge of running the kingdom."

Matilda's eyes went wide, more with panic than excitement, but there was a bit of the latter. "But what about you? You're the queen!"

"Yes, I am," said Volgha. "That was the deal. I'll be the queen, but I'm appointing you my steward so I don't have to bother with the routine business of running things around here."

"I don't think I'm qualified for this."

"Neither am I," said Volgha, "and that's why we have qualified advisors." She pointed to Eustace and Reg. "They'll help you with the affairs of the castle, and together you'll draw up a list of nobles who can advise you in other areas."

"Shouldn't a royal person be doing this?"

Volgha shrugged. "I don't think so. It's been so long since we've had a ruler who knew what they were doing that you're as qualified as anyone else. And besides ... could we have the room, please?"

Eustace, Reg, and the pair of guards fled the room at alarming speed.

That's the sort of respect you're giving up, cawed Redcrow.

"This is twice you've played the favors game with a witch," said Volgha, crossing her arms. "Getting me to bury an old man is one thing. Trapping me into ruling a sovereign nation is quite another."

"You could have said no," Matilda mumbled.

"And give people the impression that witches don't honor favors? Hardly. Your favor is repaid in full, and this is the one and only command I ever hope to make as monarch. You, Duchess Matilda Bubble-Spigot, will rule my kingdom for me."

Well said, cawed Redcrow. *Perhaps she needs a Minister of Avian Relations? I shall accept generous salary terms, payable in anchovies.*

"What will you do?" asked Matilda.

"Redcrow and I will go back to my cottage," replied Volgha, much to Redcrow's chagrin. "It's witchery that demands my attention. I'll be doing my part for the kingdom, trust me on that."

So you're ready to be the Warden? Osgrey sounded hopeful.

"We'll talk about that later, old man." Volgha was pointing at the ceiling. "First things first."

Fine, fine, said Osgrey. *I'll just sit here in your mind, not retiring to my tree to contemplate the mysteries of nature for an eternity or so. Maybe I'll hum tunelessly until I get there.*

"No humming!"

"Who are you talking to?" asked Matilda. "Or am I not supposed to hum?"

"Never mind. Hum all you like. Not you!"

"Right." Matilda had the look of a girl who'd likely refrain from humming for the foreseeable future, just to be safe.

"I thought you'd be happy about this."

"I am," said Matilda, "mostly. It's just a lot to take in. Do I get to do whatever I want?"

"More or less," said Volgha. "Just keep things running smoothly, and don't be an idiot like my sister."

"All right, then. Will you stay in the castle for the winter, to help me get started?"

"I might as well," said Volgha. "With everything that's happened, I didn't really stock my cottage for the winter. I didn't finish darning my socks, either."

"Great." Matilda grinned widely. "Do you have a way to get in touch with Santa? If I really get to do what I want, I'll need his help with something."

OVER THE COURSE OF THE WINTER, THE CONVERSATIONS BETWEEN Volgha and Matilda were innumerable. The piles of old money were barely diminished in the name of paying the Vikings and the frost giants for their roles in the war. Alexia would have bristled at that, no doubt, but to Volgha—and the piles—it was a small price.

They decided on a number of appointments, none of which went to Redcrow or paid him so much as a herring, but they did manage to settle on a court wizard.

"Are you sure Santa's not going to be upset about it?" asked Krespo.

"I'm sure he'll miss having you around," replied Volgha, "but he knows that this is a great opportunity for you."

"I'm not actually a wizard, though, I've told you before."

I wasn't a wizard either, said Osgrey, *and I managed!*

"Neither was Ghasterly's predecessor," said Volgha. "Technically, neither was Ghasterly. Necromancers don't do half the things that proper wizards do. 'Court wizard' is a traditional title, really."

"Couldn't I be the court ... thinker, or something?"

"We don't want to change too much too quickly," said Matilda. "The average Aurorian citizen can't distinguish one form of magic from another. They just like knowing that the crown has appointed someone to be in charge of wand-waving and such."

"She's right," said Volgha. "Float a spoon past their noses, and they'll start calling you 'Krespo the Magnificent'."

Not in my day, said Osgrey. *You'd at least have had to float a reindeer past them back then. People were impressed with spoons in my granddad's day, though. They'd only just been invented ...*

Volgha tried to tune Osgrey out without letting him know.

Easier said than done, cawed Redcrow. *You're doing well, though. It's almost quiet enough in here for me to have a moment's peace.*

"What must that be like?" asked Volgha, her tone wistful. Her payment for that quip was learning that crows didn't need lips to sneer.

"I don't know anyone else who I can trust with this sort of

thing," said Matilda. "In fact, you and Volgha are the only people I know who can do magic."

"To be honest, I'm a bit terrified to accept."

"I've seen you terrified before," said Volgha. "It's when you do your best work."

"I have two conditions," said Krespo.

"Yes?"

"No flying," said Krespo. "Between Santa's machine and your broom, I've lost enough wits. Never again."

Volgha nodded in acceptance. "Fair enough. What else?"

"I don't want to work in the wizard's tower."

"Why not?" asked Matilda. "It's tradition! Plus, it already has all of the books and everything in it."

"It's creepy," Krespo answered. "I still have nightmares about Ghasterly from that place. And I've seen how high it is from outside. I won't be able to concentrate."

"I'm sure we can work something out," said Volgha, "I just don't know where—"

"How about the dungeon?" asked Matilda.

"The dungeon?"

"Sure," she said. "I can't bear to think of what my union—that is, my *former* union brothers and sisters—went through in there. I'm having the cells removed as we speak, and it'll just be a huge, empty space after that."

"It'll need a good cleaning as well," said Volgha.

"Not to worry," said Matilda with a grin. "We've got bona fide union labor on the job."

"The wizard's cellar," said Krespo. "I like the sound of it."

TWENTY-EIGHT

THE FIRST GOLDEN RAYS OF DAWN DID NOTHING TO ABATE THE chill in the air. It may have been spring, but it still felt like winter to Volgha. Still, she was glad to have nearly frozen to death on the flight to Santa's Village. Warm air currents, in her experience, were more trouble than they were worth.

She touched down right in front of Santa's house, just in time to get doused in snow from a lurch of the jumping holly. She was so numb from the flight that brushing it off was an enormous effort. She did the best she could and knocked twice on the door.

"Your Majesty," said Sergio with a bow. As much as she wanted to chastise him for it, the witch in her simply couldn't protest his overt nervousness. It was just weird not having to do anything to intimidate people. It was almost too easy.

"Hello, Sergio." Volgha pushed past him into the deliciously warm house. Redcrow flew from her shoulder and perched on the back of a chair, while Volgha thrust broom, hat, and layers of black wool into Sergio's waiting hands. On second thought, she took the hat back.

"I'm afraid Santa's not here," said Sergio from beneath the pile of Volgha's flying cloaks.

Typical, cawed Redcrow. *We've flown all this way! He should have more respect for royalty.*

"Do you know where he is?" asked Volgha.

"The armory," answered Sergio. "He never leaves it, not since he came back from the Battle of Castle Borealis."

Oh no, they've named it! Volgha sensed Osgrey slumping and appreciated how hard that was to manage without a body. *That's bad luck. I imagine the bards will write songs about it, too.*

"You disapprove of bards writing songs about battles?" Volgha held a hand up to Sergio and stared off down a hallway.

Not really, said Osgrey, *bards have to work, after all. But a man like Santa's won't like it.*

Volgha nodded. Santa hadn't wanted to march off to war, and people treating it as glorious was sure to weigh on him.

"If it's not too much trouble, Sergio," said Volgha, still shivering uncontrollably, "could I have a cup of tea in the sitting room?"

And some anchovies!

"And something for Redcrow."

"Of course," said Sergio. "No anchovies, I'm afraid, I know he likes them. I'm sure I can dig up something."

VOLGHA SIPPED HER TEA WHILE REDCROW PICKED AT A PLATE OF sardines.

They're just not the same, cawed Redcrow. *Maybe we can go back to Asgard? They've got loads of anchovies there.*

"I'm not sure we're Odin's favorite people just now," said Volgha, who was able to feel her fingers again.

Speak for yourself, said Redcrow. *He said lots of nice things about me.*

"We'll see," said Volgha.

I wouldn't mind seeing Asgard one more time, said Osgrey.

"I thought you couldn't wait to get back to your tree."

Oh, I'd like that, but I'm sure retirement could wait a few evenings. If a trip to Asgard was on the table, I mean.

Sipping her tea, Volgha stared into the fire. She thought about her duties as Warden, and everything waiting for her in her little grove on the valley floor. That was all the adventure she wanted. If she had her way, once she got back home, she'd never leave it again.

Once she was sufficiently thawed, she made her way to the armory. A pair of guards were standing out front as always, and though their steely, straightforward stares never wavered, they somehow seemed relieved that she was there. They made no move to stop her as she opened the door.

The armory was as quiet as it had ever been, though it was more crowded. Santa was there, sitting in front of his armor. As were several dozen Faesolde, likewise sharing the silence.

She crept into the room, doing her best not to disturb the tranquility. Santa didn't look up from his contemplative pose when she approached, so she announced her presence as gently as she could by staring at the back of his neck. After a moment, the hairs started to rise, and Santa turned slowly to look at her. His eyes were red and puffy, and the bags under them suggested that they were there for the long haul.

Santa sighed at Volgha and nodded. Despite his muscular form, he stood at the laborious pace of an old man. It was enough to make Volgha tired just watching. The two of them tiptoed from the armory together and shut the door behind them.

"The sun's coming up," said Santa, his voice far lower and more gravelly than usual.

He's been in there a long time, said Osgrey.

"I wanted to come sooner," said Volgha. "After the war, to see how you were."

"We lost some brave elves," said Santa.

"I didn't know," said Volgha. "We cleaned up the battlefield, and we didn't find any of them."

"They came back here with us," said Santa.

"How many?"

"Too many."

Some of the silence in the armory must have followed them out, and was now taking its turn in the conversation. It was potent, as silences go. It was a long time before Volgha found suitable words to interrupt it.

"I'm so sorry, Santa. It's all my fault. If only I hadn't—"

Santa held up a hand. It stilled the air between them without malice or impatience.

"I've survived more than my fair share of battles," said Santa, "and I can tell you that 'if only I had-or-had-not' is the first step on the path to madness. Whatever you were about to say, you *did*. Yes, a different choice might have ended in a different outcome, but history didn't turn out that way."

"I talked you into this," said Volgha. "You didn't want to go to war against the frost giants, but you did, because we thought that it had to be done. You didn't want to join the Really, Really Big Army and march on Castle Borealis, but I convinced you. You went to war, and people are dead because I convinced you to go."

"I could have said no. The elves could have said no. I'm not their general, they work for me of their own free will."

"Stop talking like that! I'm hardly blameless."

"No, you're not. And neither am I for agreeing to go along with it. And neither are the elves who lost their lives, for they agreed to go along as well."

"So that's it? It's everyone's fault?"

"Yes."

They stood in silence for a while longer. It was a silence particularly well-suited to the dawn, remarkably different from the kind one might not hear at sunset.

"What do we do?" asked Volgha, not meaning to. The words just sort of fell out of her mouth.

"We remember," said Santa. "We accept. We put one foot in front of the other, as hard as it may be, for as long as it takes, until we emerge from our darkness. And then we keep going."

Volgha nodded. This had been her first war, and she never really even saw it. She didn't even see the battlefield afterward—the servants' and guards' unions had made a joint effort to clean it up as quickly as possible so they wouldn't have to wait for the summer thaw.

Santa, on the other hand, had the look of a man who knew war all too well. Sadness and grief were plain on his face, but in a practiced "here we go again" sort of way.

"When was the last time you ate anything?" asked Volgha.

"Well there's no food in the armory, and I've been in there since before the sun started to rise."

"Long enough then," said Volgha.

"Are you ordering me to eat something, Your Majesty?"

"I'll thank you not to call me that."

Santa forced half a smile, but his cheeks appeared to have been caught off-guard in the attempt.

"I'll have Sergio whip us up something," he said. They started walking.

"By the way," said Volgha, "there's one more thing you owe me."

"Is there?"

"You told me that if we survived the war, you'd explain how you're 'sort of a Viking.' The war's over, so spill."

Santa sighed. "That's a really long story. I'll give you some of it over dinner."

THE TALE THAT SANTA WEAVED FOR VOLGHA WAS ONE OF EPIC HIGH AD-
venture, the sort one avoided telling children just before bed. It was beyond
thrilling, just the thing that would guarantee they'd get no sleep at all.

He was from the south, but not by much. He became a man
during a time when kingdoms came and went, crowns barely having
time to muss the hair of one warlord before another came along and
knocked his head off.

One such ephemeral king seized the wares of a merchant ship
and imprisoned her crew, Santa being among them. What followed
was a rollicking tale of jailbreak, mercenary work, and battles before
he went north with as much gold as he could carry. That's when he
met the elves, helped lead them to victory in the goblin wars, and left
the warrior's path a second time to settle here.

"So this makes thrice you've put down the sword," said Volgha.

"Hopefully this time will be the last," said Santa. "So to answer
your question, I've spent a lot of time among the Vikings, but I'm not
one of them."

"Fair enough. One more question, if you'll humor me."

"Yes?"

"When we first met, you were quick to make me your guest.
There was no trust between us then, so why did you?"

Santa smiled. "Trust must be given to be earned. It's something
I've picked up from the Vikings. They don't trust anything that they
can't see clearly."

"So … you were letting me see you?"

"That's the long and short of it."

"You're a wise man, Santa," said Volgha. "I'm glad to call you
my friend. Krespo sends his regards, by the way."

"I'm glad he's doing well. I have a gift for him, would you mind delivering it? The sooner, the better, I think."

"As much as it galls me to do favors, I can't say no to you. What is it?"

"You'll see," said Santa. "Something that everyone will enjoy, I'm sure."

"Speaking of everyone enjoying things, I have a contract for you from my steward."

"Contracts, gifts—are you a monarch or a messenger?"

"I'm a witch," said Volgha. "Vex at your own peril."

"My apologies. What does Matilda have in mind?"

"She says it's a surprise."

TWENTY–NINE

I T'S FOR GHASTERLY," said Volgha.

"Clever," said Krespo with a smile. "Santa always gives the best gifts."

"We'll soon put that to the test, won't we?"

It was a heavy steel box with a padded suede interior. In addition to being a finely crafted work of elfish art, it was the perfect size to hold the bottle in which Ghasterly's spirit was trapped. It could probably keep the bottle safe on a drop from the belfry, though Volgha was not eager to test that theory.

"So he accepted Matilda's contract?" asked Krespo.

"He did." Smiling, Volgha gave a brief nod. "He was enthusiastic about it, actually. I think it will help him keep his mind off the war, and someday put it behind him."

"It's certainly going to be a challenge. A gift for every Aurorian subject, all delivered on the same evening! I'm having trouble wrapping my mind around the logistics."

"He seemed confident that he could manage the production."

"I'm confident as well. Have you ever seen him forge a set of wrenches?" Volgha shook her head. "Well, if you get the chance, don't blink. Anyway, it's the delivery that's going to be problematic."

"Right," said Volgha. "That's where you come in."

"Happy to help, but not if that flying machine is going to be involved. Nothing but trouble, that thing."

The two of them exchanged a stern nod. Their mutual dislike of Santa's flying machine was sufficiently potent to ensure that the infernal contraption would never rise again.

"It's starting to look like a proper wizard's cellar in here," remarked Volgha, who had no idea how a wizard's cellar should look. Wizards worked in towers. That was the proper way of things, wasn't it?

Forests beat towers every time, said Osgrey.

"You would say that," said Volgha, "you're a druid."

I was a druid, now I'm a tree!

"You *were* a tree, now you're freeloading in my thought space, you ephemeral old goat!"

"You have a tree in your brain?"

Krespo needs to learn that court wizards should never appear to be confused, cawed Redcrow, *especially when they are.*

"Agreed," said Volgha. "Anyway, good job on the cellar."

"Right." Krespo still seemed confused, which was fine for the moment. Even among her friends, Volgha needed to maintain mysterious airs.

"Any ideas?"

"Well, it doesn't need window treatments. It hasn't got any windows."

"I mean for Santa's transportation problem."

"Oh, that! Yes, actually. I've had some luck with reindeer."

"Reindeer?"

"He's going to have to fly, you know," said Krespo. "You remember the sleigh ride with Loki? That's not going to cut it. If he's going to make the whole trip in time, he's going to have to fly alarmingly fast. He'll enjoy that, the lunatic."

"You've lost me. What do reindeer have to do with flying?"

"Well, he's going to need something to pull the sleigh, and I don't know of any birds that are big enough. Easier to magic some large animals into the sky than to harness an entire flock of birds."

As if we'd stand for being harnessed! Redcrow bristled.

"Why not horses?"

"I've already done some tests," stated Krespo. "As near as I can tell, they're simply too attuned with the ground. Put a horse a few inches up in the air, and she'll panic. They're no help to Santa on this one."

Volgha's brow furrowed. "And reindeer are different?"

"Strangely enough, yes. It barely even requires any magic to get them flying. Reindeer don't like being told what to do, you see."

"I'm afraid I don't."

"You simply have to suggest to them that they don't belong in the sky, and they bleat out a phrase which I believe in their language means 'oh yeah?' Then it's just a quick flick of the wand, and they're banking and diving like birds."

That's thin ice, cawed Redcrow. *Now it's easy to be a bird, is it?*

"I'm sure that's not how he meant it," said Volgha.

Well, that's how he said it. I doubt he'd appreciate me saying 'cut a Viking off at the knees, and he's an elf but for the pointy ears.'

"Redcrow didn't like the bird comparison?"

"Was it that obvious?"

"He's not that hard to read," said Krespo.

Redcrow squawked.

"Well, you're not!"

Volgha had never heard a crow growl before that. It was amusing, in an unsettling way.

"Let me know if I can help," said Volgha.

"Oh!" Krespo leaped from his chair and ran to a stack of crates. "I almost forgot." He rummaged through one of them and drew out a candle, which he handed to Volgha.

"It's a candle," said Volgha, in lieu of offering thanks.

"It's a teleflame." Krespo smiled broadly. "It's one of a set. When you light it, say the name of another person who has one, and theirs will light as well. You'll be able to talk to each other!"

"Clever," said Volgha, who was leery of being on-call. "Who else has them?"

"Matilda and I each have one, and I'm sending one to Santa as well."

What is the world coming to? Osgrey wailed. *Whatever happened to courtesy? You used to have to call on people in person if you wanted to talk to them. This 'teleflame' is so impersonal!*

Osgrey's resistance to the idea made Volgha like it a little bit more.

It's a step up from the giant green flame that Ghasterly conjured, cawed Redcrow.

"I'd forgotten all about that," said Volgha with a frown.

"What?"

"Ghasterly conjured a portal in my cottage," said Volgha. "A giant green flame. I don't know how to close it."

"Is that what that was? Matilda found its mate a while ago and had me get rid of it. I have Ghasterly's wand, so it's easy for me to cancel anything he's cast previously."

"I hope that's all you're using it for."

"Of course. In any case, it should have canceled both of them. Just teleflame me if it's still there."

"I'll do that," Volgha stated.

THIRTY

THE HUGE GREEN BALL OF FLAME WAS GONE, JUST AS KRESPO predicted. That was good news, though it was discovered alongside a rotting stench that made Volgha gag.

Fine hovel for a queen, cawed Redcrow. *Why do you insist on living here?*

"For the last time, it's not a hovel! It's a cottage, and it's a proper sort of place for a witch and her surly familiar."

I'm not surly, you just rouse the worst of my moods.

"So you're pleasant to everyone else?"

No, I avoid everyone else. I'm stuck with you.

In terms of immediacy, Volgha decided that sorting out the rotting stench was a higher priority than chastising birds. It didn't take long to find the culprit, and would have been even quicker had it not been the one thing she kept avoiding, hoping against hope that it wouldn't be.

It was the stew.

Perhaps the green ball of flame had produced a measure of heat after all, or the warm air had come much, much lower before Loki fixed his folly. The stew usually froze itself solid if there was no fire under it for an evening, but this time, it was a gelatinous glob of blackened putrescence. She poured it into a wooden barrel outside, which she resolved to bury as soon as the sun unfroze the ground a bit. She filled the cauldron with snow, hoping that it could be cleaned out and salvaged.

And she mourned, as much as it was appropriate and not at all insane to mourn the loss of a stew.

It was a proper stew, said Osgrey. *I started it with potatoes and carrots. Years passed, and I became a tree.*

A fitting eulogy, cawed Redcrow.

"Quite," said Volgha.

EVENINGS PASSED, AS THEY ARE WONT TO DO. VOLGHA MANAGED TO quiet her mind enough to return to the Winter Court, where she officially took up the mantle of Warden. Osgrey was glad to get back to being a tree and officially beginning his retirement. Though Volgha spoke with him often, she was glad to have him out of her head. She and Redcrow both very much enjoyed being alone with their thoughts, and having only one other stream of consciousness to ignore was much easier than two. They spent many an evening in the cottage, delving into the mysteries of the Witching Way or ignoring each other altogether.

Volgha managed to clean the old stew's stench from the cauldron, which was a relief. She started a new stew with potatoes and carrots, as a tribute to Osgrey. It didn't yet qualify as a proper stew, though it might eventually. Time would tell.

She occasionally used the teleflame during the course of the year to speak with Santa, Krespo, or Matilda, usually about the gift-giving business. Krespo had worked out the flying reindeer and enchanted the rails of Santa's sleigh so that it would fly as well. Together, they got it so finely tuned that it would move effortlessly through the air at alarming speeds; however, the time trials were never fast enough to get the whole thing accomplished in the space of a single evening.

In the end, they found a very ordinary solution to get it done in time. The castle, the villages, and the outlying homesteads in the kingdom mustered all of the parents together under brightly decorated trees. They drank hot cocoa and sang songs until Santa whizzed by, using the trees as beacons to navigate the dark winter's night. He dropped off presents with the parents, who brought them home and distributed them to all of the children. It was all very hush-hush, as all involved knew the children would expect presents all year round, if they thought their parents had anything to do with it. Better to let Santa take all the credit, and have some peace and quiet on the matter for the rest of the year.

In time, older children began toying with ridiculous conspiracies. They somehow got it into their heads that there *was* no Santa, and that their parents had been doing all of the work themselves. Can you imagine?

AFTERWORD

This was my first novel. Well, it was the first novel that I ever *finished*. My proper first novel was eleven pages long, written in pencil in a composition book, and is probably lost to the world for all time. It was *Ghostbusters 2*. I finished mine before Akroyd and Ramis finished theirs, though mine will likely enjoy less commercial success.

The first version of *The Winter Riddle* was self-published in November 2016. It sold about 40 copies, almost exclusively to people who know me personally. I know a thing or two about marketing, but it turns out that you have to know at least 80 things about marketing to meet with the faintest whiff of success.

I was about a week away from consigning my second novel, *Peril in the Old Country*, to the same fate when I stumbled into a conversation with Lindy Ryan, owner and publisher of Black Spot Books. We talked about my work for a bit, and she encouraged me to submit *Peril* to her for review.

I declined. I had a plan: self-publish three novels, then go out and find a publisher. Who wouldn't want me then, with literally dozens of readers partially interested in what I had to offer next?

My wife, Shelly, talked some sense into me. What could it hurt? At worst, I'd set my scheduled release date back a few weeks. I had no preorders, and in fact, most of my two score readers had no idea that it was coming.

I submitted. Fast-forward a bit, and *Peril in the Old Country* had more fans among the advance readers and reviewers than *The Winter Riddle* had after a year on Amazon. That says a lot about the amazing people at Black Spot Books, and very little about the number of friends that I have.

Fast-forward a bit more, and *The Winter Riddle* comes up in conversation. Lindy thought she saw something special in it, and I saw an opportunity to tidy it up a bit. Melissa Ringsted, my eagle-eyed editor (apologies for the alliteration), tidied it up considerably more. Najla Qamber took the cover treatment to a new level, and I couldn't have been more pleased with the outcome.

For the record, if you read the first version, the story hasn't changed at all; however, this one is at least five thousand times better in every way, and thoroughly worth buying at its full retail price.

ABOUT THE AUTHOR

Sam writes darkly humorous fantasy novels about thing like tyrannical despots and the masked scoundrels who tickle them without mercy. He knows all the best swear words, though he refuses to repeat them because he doesn't want to attract goblins. He lives in California with his wife and son, who renew their tolerance for his absurdity on a per-novel basis.